# MY NAME IS NOELLE

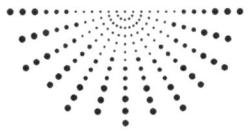

## ANDREA MAXAND

Bell the Cat Books

*For Katy, Kean, & Buster*

# PREFACE

Before you start reading, I want to talk briefly about triggers. Then, just as briefly, I want to discuss what this book is actually about.

This book deals, in flashbacks, with the issue of sexual assault. The main character of the book is wrestling with the fallout from her past experience of being the victim of an attempted sexual assault.

Another primary character has lived through the loss of a family member by suicide, and this is mentioned briefly within the book. If the reader finds either of these issues triggering, it might be best to put down this book and read something else.

That said, at its heart, this is not a book about either sexual assault or suicide. It is a book about persevering through life's obstacles and coming out triumphant on the other side. It's a book about compassion. It's about failing, and trying again. It's about fighting back. It's about music and dancing. It's about discovering places where you belong. It's about the joy of found family, both friends and lovers.

And it's about cats. Because in the end, isn't everything about cats?

# CHAPTER ONE

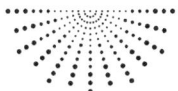

It's Christmas Eve, and I'm kicking ass and taking names.

Well, technically, I'm sparring, and if anyone's ass is getting kicked right now, it's mine.

My taekwondo coach, Conan, is staying late to work out with me because I asked him to. He knows I hate Christmas, so he's doing me a favor. I'm dreading the five block walk back to my apartment, right past all the reminders that it's the festive time of year.

Conan's real name is Walter, but if you saw him, you'd understand why no one calls him Walter. He's six foot two, all muscle, and his head is crowned with a mop of flaming red hair. He looks like a real-life barbarian. Like someone who pillages all the shops around our martial arts school in his spare time. But that would be bad business. Plus, Conan only looks like a barbarian. He's a big fan of peace through strength, with a huge emphasis on peace. I wish I were more like him.

I land a kick on the front of his chest protector.

"Your timing is improving," he says. He sounds impressed.

I swell up a little with pride, as he retreats, then comes back at me with a retaliatory kick that knocks me flat. But that's okay. I don't fight Conan because I can beat him. I fight Conan so I know what it's like to go up against somebody who's better and stronger than I am. He knows I can fight, and win. I just can't best him.

"Need a hand?"

Conan extends one of his ginormous hands to help me up. I let him, then get back in fighting stance. He gives me an amused look. "Let's call it a day, okay, Noelle? If I don't go home soon my girl-friend's gonna kill me."

Conan's girlfriend is a tiny thing, even shorter and smaller than I am. And yet, I know he's right. If he doesn't spend Christmas Eve with her, she will kill him.

"Okay," I concede.

"Got plans?"

He knows a fair bit about my life, but not so much that I can't lie to him when necessary. "Not tonight," I say. "But I'm hanging out with the fam tomorrow on Christmas Day. Hey, do I have time for a shower before you lock up?"

"Make it quick," he says, then goes over to the front desk to signal he wants to wrap things up for the night.

There's only one shower each for male and female students. The fact that I feel safe showering here when I'm alone with Conan is a testament to how much I trust him. But I also just feel good being here at the school. Our school, which is devoted to taekwondo and self-defense classes is technically a dojang, but most of us don't call it that. We all refer to it as "the school" or "our school."

After my shower, I stand in front of the bathroom mirror and release my hair from the elastic band I use to restrain it during taek-wondo class. I clear the steam from the mirror's surface and see my distressed green eyes staring back at me. Green is a holiday color. But I sure haven't got that happy-go-lucky holiday spirit. I look away. It's time to go. As I emerge into the main room wearing street clothes, Conan's ready to lock up.

"Have a good Christmas, Noelle," he says, as I slip out the door. "See you next week."

Outside, it feels like it's going to snow, but Seattle weather is a big tease this time of year. It doesn't snow here often, and especially not on Christmas. As I walk, I pass shop windows decorated in that chintzy style, outlined with garish silver tinsel and strings of lights with red, green, and blue bulbs desperate to throw their puny glow into the street.

I should go right home and see my cat, Milo. He'll be hungry. He's been alone all day, and it's Christmas Eve. But I'm not ready to go home yet. I was hoping the extra sparring session with Conan would wear me out, but it didn't. I'm jumpy, and I don't want to take my supercharged nervous energy home to my super mellow cat. I need more mellowing.

So, I stop at the local Irish bar, O'Shea's, for a quick drink. It's on my way home. It's been there about ten years, but I just started hanging out there in the last several months. They have the best happy hour burgers I've ever tasted, and in the morning they serve Bloody Marys with truly scrumptious breakfast potatoes. You can't ask for more than that.

Inside O'Shea's, it's busier than I expected, but there's one free stool at the bar, and I sink onto it gratefully. As soon as I sit, I notice the strange dude who typically parks himself at the end of the bar is here—on Christmas Eve. I can't hold that against him, though, since I'm also here on Christmas Eve. I've met quite a few of the regulars at O'Shea's, but I haven't met this guy yet. I'm not sure I want to. He emanates an understated but unsettling vibe, like he's about to do something unsavory.

He's got curly dark hair that would be unruly if he let it go, but he keeps it cut short and styled with hair gel. He always wears a long black coat. His name is Vic, which I found out when one of the bartenders yelled for him.

My hunch is that Vic sits at the end of the bar so he can keep an eye on the door. I've often wondered if he works for Kane O'Shea, the bar owner, in a security capacity. Or maybe he's just a weirdo who likes to pretend he's keeping an eye on the action here, because it makes him feel important. Whatever his reason is, his presence always irks me.

Aidan, one of my favorite bartenders is behind the bar. He smiles at me in recognition. "What's your poison?"

"Guinness."

I pull out my wallet to pay for the beer as Aidan starts drawing it from the tap, but the stranger on my left beats me to it.

"I've got it." He nods at Aidan. "Keep the change."

One glance at my beer benefactor tells me two things: he's not my type, and I don't like him. I don't bother to thank him, and sip at the Guinness through the thick foam on top.

"Well, that's rude," the guy drawls. "Buy a girl a drink and she doesn't even say 'thank you.'"

I scan the bar, quickly, to see if there's anywhere else to sit. But all the other barstools are still occupied. I can feel Vic watching from his station at the far end of the bar. Waiting to see if trouble erupts, or just amusing himself? Probably the latter.

I ignore the guy who paid for my beer and say, "Thanks Aidan," as he passes by me on the way to serve another customer.

He smiles warmly. "You're welcome, sweetheart." Aidan calls almost every woman "sweetheart." But whenever he says it, it feels special. Like he meant it just for you. If I were a normal person, I'd probably have a crush on him. But Aidan's already too familiar to me. I'm only into strangers, and only strangers who meet my standards.

Beer guy isn't fazed by the fact that I'm friendly with the bar staff. "Look at you, sitting there drinking that beer like you paid for it yourself. Ungrateful."

I fix him with an unsmiling look and say, "I didn't ask you to pay for my beer."

He's got a squat, squarish neck and small bright eyes that look squished into his face. Short hair. Bad, overpowering cologne, and a button-down shirt that's just a smidge too tight for his torso.

"I didn't ask you to pay for my beer," he mimics, in a high voice. He's pretty drunk, so I don't know if he's always got this shit attitude or if it's his level of intoxication.

I look away from him and take another sip of Guinness.

He holds out his hand, pushing it into my field of vision. "My name's Trevor."

"Not interested."

The guy places his hand near me on the top of the bar and leans in close. Then he says, near my ear, "The only way out is through, honey."

His breath is beery. It also reeks of the garlic mayo they put on the burgers here. I roll my eyes at no one in particular. I'm not going to look at him again. He's not worth it.

But Trevor seems to think he *is* worth it, because he keeps going. "How are you gonna thank me for that beer I bought you?"

I grit my teeth. "Back off."

"I can think of a few things." A drunken laugh. A leer. "How about you get down on your knees and—"

I bring the top of my fist down hard on his hand, then slide off the barstool, away from him. He's shocked for a second. Then he lunges at me.

"Hey! Hey, that's enough man! Let the woman enjoy her drink in peace."

It's Vic. I didn't even see or hear him coming over to us. But now, he's standing between me and the asshole and he's a hundred percent unemotional about it. So, he's security. He must be. It would explain why he's always lurking.

Trevor is having a meltdown. "That bitch just broke my hand!"

Vic gives a dismissive laugh. "A little girl like that? Against you? She didn't even dent your hand."

Trevor lunges at me again, but Vic stops him easily, and Vic is not a huge guy, maybe five foot ten or eleven. People all over the bar are watching us, but I'm watching Vic as he continues to restrain this drunk, belligerent dude with aplomb. A hand to the guy's chest here, a twist of his body there. And Trevor is responding to him like a trained dog. Vic has some serious skills.

Aidan reappears in our section of the bar. "Hey man," he says to Trevor. "Think it's time to settle your tab and hit the road?"

"I paid cash."

Vic gives a feral grin. "Then you can be on your way. Let me escort you to the door."

I slide back onto my bar stool and take a long sip of beer.

"You all right?" Aidan asks.

I nod. "I'm fine."

I watch as everyone in the bar goes back to their own conversations, like the blip in the evening never happened. I decide that's what I'm going to do, too. Pretend like it never happened.

Suddenly, Vic reappears and slips on to the now empty barstool next to me. Before he can speak, Aidan calls out, "Music switch! Kane's on his way in!"

He goes to the sound system and turns off the radio station that's been playing, cutting off Neil Young before he can declare the eternal nature of rock n' roll. A few seconds later, we're awash in traditional Irish reels.

I don't mind the change. O'Shea's isn't like any other Irish bar I've ever been to. When you step inside, it's like you're leaving the city behind and walking into a separate and distinct world.

Kane doesn't like anything but traditional Irish music playing when he's here, and I can kind of see his point. Irish music brings the place alive in a way that other music simply can't. Whenever the traditional music is playing, I'd swear I can spot fairies and leprechauns appearing and disappearing into dark corners.

I'd never say that out loud in front of Kane, however. If I did, he'd laugh at me for ten minutes straight, then make sure I was the butt of every joke told at O'Shea's for the next month. I can just imagine him saying to everyone, "Well, look who's here. It's the woman who sees little green men."

Next to me, Vic clears his throat. "Need something stronger than that?" he asks. He has a distinctly laid back, gravelly tone to his voice that I'm sure most women would think is sexy. Not me though. I'm sure he's fishing for gratitude for "saving" me. It's annoying.

I make eye contact with him. "No, thanks. I'm good."

"That guy didn't spook you too bad, did he?"

I let a half-smile stretch my lips. "I could've handled it on my own, but thanks for doing your job."

His face goes blank. "My job?"

"Aren't you some kind of bouncer or...security here, or something?"

"No. Just a friend of Kane's."

"The owner?"

He looks surprised. "You know him?"

"I've met him. Anyway. Thanks, whatever your reason was." I don't try to hide the cynicism in my tone. He wants something. It might be the obvious thing. Maybe he thinks he'll get lucky. Succeed where the other guy failed. Or maybe he wants something else. But people always want something. I've lived enough life to know that much.

"Do you feel safe getting home?" Vic asks. He looks genuinely concerned. Good actor, then. And now I know his game. He wants to be a hero.

I don't answer his question. Instead, I pick up my pint glass, down the rest of the Guinness, then pull my wallet out of my bag to leave a tip for Aidan. I turn to Vic and give him my full smile. "Thanks for your concern. Have a Merry Christmas."

He's watching me as I walk out the door, I know. I can feel his eyes on my back. But I don't turn around.

# CHAPTER TWO

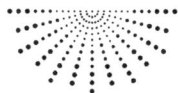

I'm annoyed. All I wanted was to stop at O'Shea's and have one relaxing drink. Instead, I had to fend off one asshole, then, one self-proclaimed knight in shining armor. It's hard to say which is worse. Assholes are assholes. But people who need to be seen as heroes are exhausting.

O'Shea's faces a well-lit street, but the route back to my apartment takes me through several side streets that are much murkier. I keep my gait loud and confident, like I always do.

I'm about halfway home when I hear footsteps behind me. They're thudding, angry footsteps. I turn around slowly.

Somehow, I'm not surprised when I see that it's Trevor, the asshole from the bar. He's still obviously drunk. I can see it in the way he advances toward me on the sidewalk. His eyes are bleary and unfocused. And enraged. He's looking for an encounter. I steel myself mentally.

He moves closer. "Where's all your friends now?" he taunts. "Why'd you come out here by yourself? Looking for me?"

*Hardly.*

"Want to finish what we started, don't ya'?" He tries to advance on me, staggering, but I remain alert. Drunk people are deceptively dangerous. They can have flares of violence that do maximum damage.

"You're drunk," I say, simply. "Why don't you go home."

"I don't feel like it," he mumbles, then moves quickly toward me.

I do a quick block and strike, aiming for his solar plexus, but I miss and hit his upper thigh instead. Even so, he lurches backwards, stunned. "You fucking bitch!"

I'm not expecting a swing at my head. He doesn't aim well because he's drunk, but he's a big guy, and when his fist connects with my skull, it hurts.

There's a split second of blind panic. Then I move without thinking, throwing a sequence of kicks at his chest and face. He stumbles backward, tries to rally himself, and fails. Blood is rushing in my ears. I can't hear anything else.

Until I hear the footsteps. Someone is running toward us. Vic emerges from the darkness, and for the second time tonight, he puts himself between me and Trevor.

"I think that's enough merrymaking for one night, don't you?" His tone is jovial, but there's a dangerous edge to it.

"That cunt tried to kill me! You need to call the cops!"

Vic laughs. "I don't think they'll believe you. She's half your size. Besides, I saw you punch her first, so let's quit the bullshit and go home. Unless you want to hang around so she can press charges?"

"She tried to kill me!" Trevor insists. "I should be pressing the fucking charges!"

Vic gets in his face and speaks calmly. "I've had enough of you for one night. In fact, I've just had enough. Fuck off, and don't come back. If I ever see you at O'Shea's again, I'll throw you out. If I ever see you in this neighborhood again, I'll beat the living shit out of you. Go the fuck home."

Trevor finally seems to understand that he's not going to convince Vic to take his side. He leaves, still muttering, wobbling his way down the street.

Vic comes over to me. In the dim streetlight, he looks gallant and mysterious. Then he grins. That spoils the vibe, because he's got a surprisingly friendly smile.

"Those were some serious moves." He sounds impressed.

"Thanks," I manage. I'm trying to tame the shaking of my limbs. They've been trembling since I landed my last kick on Trevor. But instead, the shaking gets worse.

Vic notices. "Adrenaline." He reaches out his hand and brushes it over my temple. "Gonna have one hell of a shiner."

I flinch away from his hand. "It'll be fine. I'll put ice on it when I get home."

He looks alarmed. "You're not going to drive, are you?"

"Nope. Walk."

"You're kidding, right? Listen, I live right above O'Shea's. I'll get you some ice and a shot of whiskey. For your nerves."

I laugh in his face. "Yeah, sorry. No."

"All right, that's fair. At least come back to O'Shea's. They've got ice. And whiskey."

"I'm not going to go sit in O'Shea's with an ice bag on my head. Thanks for your concern, but I'm fine." I turn to go, start to walk until —fuck it all, I'm dizzy.

"Feeling all right?" Vic calls out.

I turn around. "No."

"Can I walk you home?"

"No."

He starts to speak, then stops. Spreads out his hands in front of him. "Please let me help."

I sigh. "Okay, fine. I could use some ice."

He starts back in the direction of O'Shea's, and I walk with him. Or, not really with him, just next to him. He's got an uncanny ability to match his gait to mine without having it seem like he's making a huge effort. When we get back to the block where O'Shea's is, he starts for the door to the bar.

I stop him. "No. I'm not going in there with a black eye."

He gives me a level look. "I thought you didn't want to come up to my place."

"Lesser of two evils," I mutter.

"All right. C'mon." He backtracks a few steps and moves into a small alcove on the side of the brick building that houses O'Shea's.

There's a door set into the alcove, and when he opens it, we're in a tiny lobby—or more like a large entry space.

To the left, there's a bank of four gold-colored mailboxes. They look like they've been there since the building was built. To the right, there's a carpeted staircase leading to the upper level of the building. The carpet on the stairs is a semi ornate pattern of blue and gold. It also looks like it's been there since the early days of the building.

Vic glances at me. "Can you handle the stairs?"

"I'm walking, right?" I retort.

"Okay, then. Let's get you that ice."

My dizziness makes the stairs more of a struggle than I'd like to admit, but I make it up to the top with him, carefully holding on to the old wooden railing as we ascend.

Once we're in the hall upstairs, I see two wooden doors on each side. He leads me to the door closest to the stairway and opens it. In a corner of my mind, I'm preparing myself to get the lay of the land, then sus out the routes to the door in case I've gone from the frying pan into the fire. But what I see floors me.

There's a kitchen to our left, with an island and barstools. But the rest of the place is an expanse of almost-bare room—and it's enormous. It looks like his "apartment" takes up this entire side of the building.

In the middle of the long, massive space, there's a sparse living room arrangement, with a couch, a couple of chairs, and lamps that sit atop the two end tables. The couch faces a bank of windows that look out over the city, and most of the shades are open, so I can see the night sky through the glass. At the very end of the room, there are a couple of Japanese room dividers that block off the rest of the space.

"Where do the people in the other apartments live?" I ask, bewildered.

He gives a surprised laugh. "What?"

"Aren't there four apartments up here?"

"There used to be. Not anymore."

"So, who lives across the hall?"

He grins. "I do."

"You've got the entire floor?" I was expecting him to have a stereo-

11

typical bachelor's apartment. Something cramped and messy, with grime on the floors and countertops. But not only is this place massive, it's clean.

"Yep," he says. "All mine."

I don't know what to think of his living arrangements. Is he rich? Or is this somebody else's place, and they allow him to live here? He said he was friends with Kane O'Shea. Maybe Kane owns the building, and he lets Vic live upstairs?

"I think...I'm a little loopy," I say.

"Of course. You need ice. C'mon in the kitchen."

I follow him around the kitchen island to his fridge. He opens the freezer and pulls out a bag of frozen vegetables. He walks over to me holding the bag, then he reaches up and once again brushes a finger over the place where Trevor hit me. I don't flinch this time. I'm wary of Vic, but the light touch feels good.

"Hope you don't mind the veggies. That's what I always use when I need to ice something. Hold on, let me get you a towel so you don't get frostbite."

One minute he's there with me in the kitchen, the next he leaves the frozen peas and carrots on the counter and disappears through a doorway that I hadn't yet noticed. He moves like a cat—quick, graceful and powerful.

I look around his kitchen. All the appliances are newish, and there are no dirty dishes in the sink. I wonder if he actually lives here. For a man living alone, the level of cleanliness is unusual. Then it occurs to me that maybe he doesn't live alone.

He re-emerges with a small bath towel draped over one arm and tosses it to me. "There, wrap the ice in that."

I snag the bag of frozen veggies from the counter and wrap the towel around them. Even the towel is clean, I notice, as I press the makeshift ice pack to the place where Trevor hit me. The coolness is a relief. I can feel the bruise emerging, and it hurts.

Vic strips off his coat and drapes it carelessly over one of the barstools. Now, if he were a true neat freak, he would have hung it up in a closet.

"Your wife must spend all her time cleaning," I remark. "This place has that you-could-eat-off-the-floor feeling."

He grins at me. "Wife? I don't have a wife. You want a drink?"

"Uh…no, thanks. I'm all right."

So far, he's been behaving like a harmless person. But anyone can fake harmless. He surveys me, like he's trying to figure me out. I think his eyes are blue, but they have this dark aura that makes it hard to know for sure.

"The cleaning lady comes once a week," he says. "She was here earlier today."

"Cleaning lady?"

"You said you wanted to eat off my floor?"

For some reason, I blush. "Oh right. Cleaning lady. That's why your place is so…clean."

He gestures to the barstools. "Wanna have a seat?"

I sit down. His long black coat is on the barstool next to me. It's got a presence, that coat. Almost like it's another person in the room.

He keeps studying me, and just as I'm starting to think *this is awkward*, he spins around and opens one of his cupboards. I only get a quick glance inside, but it appears to be full of liquor bottles. He sets a bottle of Maker's Mark in front of me. It's a fresh one with what looks like an unbroken seal.

"In case you change your mind," he says. "Still feeling dizzy?'

"A little bit," I admit. "I can sit up. Obviously. But…"

"No rush. Take your time." He grins again. "Where'd you pick up your martial arts skills? You're pretty good."

"Oh. Yeah. I've been doing taekwondo for, you know. A long time, I guess."

"Black belt?"

I wince a little. "No, nothing that cool. Stuck at red belt."

"You'll get there."

"I hope so." I don't tell him that I've been parked at 1st Gup for over a year. That would sound pathetic. "I don't think I could have taken that guy down tonight if he hadn't been drunk." Why did I let that slip? It's bad to show weakness in front of someone you don't know well enough to trust.

"Maybe you wouldn't have," Vic says. "But I saw every move you pulled on the guy after he hit you. You had more than luck working for you."

It sounds good, and I'd like to believe him, but I'm not convinced. "Maybe."

"Was that the first time you've ever had to use it for real?"

"Yeah," I admit.

His eyes gleam. "Different, isn't it?"

I nod, and my memory flashes back to the way he handled Trevor at the bar. Controlling him without seeming to control him.

"What martial arts do you practice?" I ask, because I'm sure he knows at least a couple different styles. Aikido, maybe, because he was able to stop violence without using violence himself. Plus, he gives off an understated vibe of self-mastery.

He shrugs. "I'm a dabbler."

I don't believe him. If he didn't have genuine skills, he wouldn't appreciate mine. I slide my eyes over to the whiskey. I'm still shaky, but I set my ice pack down and reach for the bottle.

"Change your mind?"

Instead of answering him, I start an inspection of the bottle, which reveals that the red wax seal is, indeed, unbroken. I pull the tab to open it.

"You can drink from the bottle if you want," Vic says, casually. "But let me know if you need a glass. I'm gonna find some Christmas music."

After I've removed the wax seal, I screw off the cap, relieved by his offer. I figure that unless he has pre-roofied bottles of whiskey delivered to his home, this is the safest drink I'll ever have in a strange man's apartment.

I tip the Maker's to my lips and take a swig. The relief that floods through my nervous system is immediate. I take one more generous drink, then re-cap the bottle as the sound of holiday music fills the room and gives the place an instant homey vibe. I wonder why Vic's alone tonight. Maybe he's estranged from his family, like me. Or maybe he just hates Christmas. But no, if he did, he wouldn't have turned on the music.

He repositions himself across from me at the kitchen island. "Get enough to drink?"

"Yeah, thanks."

He leans forward, drawing my eyes with the movement. "So why do you think the only reason you leveled that creep tonight is because he was drunk?"

It's too late to be cautious, so I answer truthfully. "Well, like I said, it's the first time it was ever real, you know? No protective gear. No rules. It was adrenaline and luck, and a...hobbled opponent."

"You just need more practice in the real world."

"Maybe. But I mean, what do I do? Go out and provoke fights with people? That's a good way to get arrested."

He smiles, slow. "The secret to not getting caught is being smart enough to avoid it."

"Sure, but even if I could get away with it, I wouldn't pick fights with random strangers anyway. That would be nuts."

Vic has one unruly curl of dark hair that hangs down over his forehead. It's mesmerizing. I want to stop looking at it, but I can't. I can tell he's sizing me up. There's something intense behind his eyes, something he tries to keep out of his speaking voice. But I see it and sense it anyway.

"You should learn to fight dirty," he says. "It's the only way to gain the upper hand in a real fight. I could teach you. If you want."

I'm instantly wary. Why would Vic want to teach me anything? Men don't do nice things for you unless they want something in return. Sure, he went out of his way to show me he wasn't going to spike my drink. He gets points for that. But I'm not buying his "nice guy who just wants to help" act. Because I have no doubt: it's an act.

"You don't even know me," I say. "Why would you want to teach me self defense?"

"You mean why would I want to teach you how to hurt and kill people."

He says it in a matter-of-fact tone. *How to hurt and kill people*. Like he's offering to teach me how to make pizza from scratch. Or how to play a new sport. Or how to paint landscapes.

Should I be running for the door? It was stupid to come here with him, but I was dizzy and injured. It would have been just as stupid to walk home alone or to let Vic walk me home. I should have gone back to O'Shea's. I could have sat there until closing time, then figured out my next move from there. The humiliation wouldn't have killed me, but this situation might.

The radio starts playing a version of "Have Yourself a Merry Little Christmas," and I am *not* feeling it. I want to be home with Milo, feeding him tuna. Listening to him purr.

"Did that freak you out?" Vic asks. "I wasn't trying to scare you. But if you ever get in a real fight, you need to know how to hurt or kill someone. Only if necessary. Like if they're trying to kill *you*."

"Right. That's the same rationale for owning a gun."

"Same principle. Different methods."

"Do you believe it's okay to kill someone who's trying to kill you?" I ask, without thinking.

His voice is calm. "I believe it's a matter of balance."

I feel a tiny shiver move from deep in my gut up through my spine. I try to ignore it. "You don't know me," I repeat. "There's no reason for you to help me." I look him in the eye. "At least, no reason I can think of."

"It was just a suggestion," he says.

Our eyes lock, and I'm not sure what that means or how to feel about it. I break it off and groan. "I fucking hate this fucking Christmas music."

Vic outright laughs. "You do? Why didn't you say something?"

Now I shrug. "Being polite? Anyway, I should get home."

"Of course," he agrees, swiftly. "I'll walk you."

"You don't need to do that. I'm not dizzy anymore." I'm not sure that's true, but I've decided I don't care. I just want to leave.

Vic walks around the kitchen island and snags his long black coat. "I'll walk you."

He won't take no for an answer, apparently. But at least he's not dragging me across the spotless wood floor, behind the Japanese screen, and murdering me in some particularly gruesome fashion—things could be worse.

# CHAPTER THREE

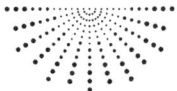

O nce we're out walking on the quiet streets, we don't talk much.
I'm not sure I want Vic to know where I live.I wonder what
his relationship is with Kane O'Shea. For some reason, I always
thought Kane was the one who lived above the bar. I'm not sure why I
thought that. Maybe I heard someone mention it once.

"So—you said you and Kane are friends?"

"What?" Vic's eyes look as if he's been elsewhere in his thoughts.

"You and Kane O'Shea? You're friends?"

"Right. Yeah. We're friends. Been friends for a while."

"Do you rent that apartment from him, then?"

"Which apartment?"

"The apartment over the bar? Do you rent it from Kane?"

He grins. "Something like that."

Something weird is up with Vic and his relationship to O'Shea's.
Though, since he lives above the bar, maybe it makes sense that he
spends so much time there. But it's more than that. I know it is. He's
territorial about O'Shea's.

We walk another block before he speaks again. "Feels like snow."

I instinctively turn my face up to the sky. "Yeah, but it never snows
on Christmas."

"Maybe we'll have a Christmas miracle."

I let out a derisive snort and he chuckles.

"What, don't you believe in Christmas miracles?"

"And you do?" I retort.

"Anything's possible, right?"

I decide to ignore him. We're almost to my apartment, anyway. He seems to sense I'm done talking to him and doesn't push for additional conversation.

When we get there, I say abruptly, "This is me. I'm good. You can go now."

"When are we going to hang out so I can show you some self-defense tactics?"

*Never.*

"I don't think I'm into the maiming and killing thing," I tell him. "I don't practice martial arts to hurt people."

"Why do you practice?"

I hold his gaze. "For self confidence."

"Hey," he says, grinning. "I don't even know your name."

I don't grin back. "That's because I didn't tell you."

"So, what's your name?"

Behind him, there's a row of small shops that face my apartment building. One of them has a banner draped in the window that reads *Joy to the World*. It's hard to see in the dark, but I know it's there because it's been up since the day after Thanksgiving. It's the first thing I see every time I leave my building.

"My name's Noelle."

"Really? Noelle?"

"Yep. That's my name."

"I'm Vic."

"I know."

We look at each other for what feels like a long time, until he points a finger up at the sky. "It's snowing."

I scoff. "It is not."

"Look over there." He gestures down the road to the streetlight, and I see a few white flakes shimmering underneath it, drifting to the ground. For a second, I feel like a kid again, when snow made me giddy and the whole world seemed full of magic.

Then I look back over at Vic and shrug. "It won't stick. It's not cold enough."

"Yeah, but it's pretty."

He's talking about the snow. But he's looking at me.

"I need to get inside. But thanks for the escort." I figure I should at least thank him. I can give him that much.

"No problem. Okay, well…"

"Okay, well…"

"Joyous Noel, Noelle." He turns and starts to walk across the street. Just as I open the building door, he swivels back around and calls out, "Don't forget to keep icing your battle wound."

I stare at him. The snow is starting to come down harder now, though it's melting as it hits the ground.

"Merry Christmas," I say finally, then I go inside.

The moment I open the door to my apartment, Milo is there, winding around my legs, meowing like he has a week's worth of secrets to tell me.

I bend down to pet him. "I'm sorry, buddy. This hasn't been a typical Christmas Eve."

Milo's grey, round face is upturned. His unusually bright green eyes are wide. I love that we both have green eyes. He emits one more sad chirp of a meow.

I bend down and pick him up, and put him over my shoulder, like I'm burping a baby. He immediately starts to purr. I move from the entry way into my tiny galley kitchen.

"I know, I know," I tell him. "I promised to come home right after working out, and I didn't. Can you forgive me?"

He purrs louder, so I know he's not holding a grudge. "Okay, big guy. Can I set you down so I can get you something to eat?"

A few moments later, Milo is happily chowing down on a can of stinky wet food. Tuna flavor. I take a cup of hot chocolate and some ice wrapped in a dishtowel to my window seat. My apartment is a too-small studio, but the window seat makes up for it. At night, I turn out the lights so I can sit in the dark, and the world expands beyond the cramped space, out into the city streets and beyond.

The snow is actually sticking to the street, now. I still don't think it will last, but Vic was right. It is pretty. My semi-sketchy neighbor-hood has assumed a temporary idyllic glow, with the snow coating the sidewalks and drifting past the windows of street-level shops.

Milo approaches the window seat, leaps onto it, and curls up next to me. His tail twitches as he watches the snowflakes drift past the window.

"I got in a fight tonight, Milo."

He turns his enigmatic kitty face toward me. Even in the dark, his eyes seem to glow.

"I won. I mean, the guy was drunk. But I kicked his ass. I actually kicked his ass."

Milo starts to purr again, and I decide I'm going to stay up all night. If the snow's going to be gone by the morning, I want to take it in for as long as it lasts.

# CHAPTER FOUR

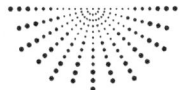

I t's the day after New Year's, and I'm devouring a plate of pancakes, sausages, and eggs in the back booth at a diner where I also work as a waitress. It's dinnertime, but we serve breakfast all day at Jean's Diner & Pancake House.

A hint of cigarette ash wafts up from the amber-colored glass ashtray at my table. We empty the ashtrays frequently during each shift, but they only get washed at night. Even when they're clean, they still reek faintly of cigarettes. I'm slathering my pancakes with maple syrup when one of the other waitresses, Piper, slides into the seat across from me.

"Tell me about the fight," she says, her eyes alight with curiosity. I like Piper. She's always interested in other people, and on the job, at least, she's the kind of person you can count on. She also says what she thinks. Most of the time.

"What fight?"

"You said you got the bruise in a fight," she says, tapping the temple above her own eye. "You did say that, didn't you? I didn't dream it?" She flicks her fingers at the bangs of her jet-black bob, a look that makes her seem one part tough, one part vulnerable.

"No, I got in a fight. You didn't dream it."

She leans forward and lowers her voice. "You didn't get hit by your boyfriend, did you? 'Cause that's different."

I shake my head. "It wasn't my boyfriend. The guy was an asshole, but he definitely left the scene damaged."

Piper points at me. "And *you* damaged him."

"Yeah."

"And you didn't get arrested?"

"Nope." I wonder if I could have. When I went after Trevor, all I was thinking about was getting him to leave me the fuck alone. "He kept saying someone should call the cops, but this other guy showed up. He kind of talked him out of it."

Vic had done more than that, though. He'd also threatened Trevor on my behalf.

"There's another guy?" Piper's eyes go wide. "The plot thickens."

"No plot." I'm adamant. "I'm just lucky Vic was there. I guess."

Piper has a knowing look on her face. Like she thinks something might be going on between Vic and me. Which there isn't. And I know there isn't, because I don't do romantic drama. I don't know Piper well enough to tell her my working theory of human relationships— she's only a work friend. If I did tell her, she might think I'm too strange to hang out with. And I'm realizing I'd kind of like to hang out with her sometime.

As if reading my mind, she says, "Hey, you want to go for a drink later? Or, no, better: buy cheap liquor and chill out?"

We end up back at Piper's place with the cheapest bottle of tequila we could find. She lives in a basement apartment close to the diner. Her apartment is much larger than my studio, with two bedrooms, a real living room, and a more normal-sized kitchen. I'm a bit jealous, but I'd miss my window seat if I lived here.

We sit down on her brown and fraying sofa with the tequila bottle and a couple of glass tumblers that look oddly familiar.

Piper catches me eyeing them and grins. "I swiped them from the Pancake House." She pours each of us a shot. "No salt, no lime, we're slumming it. Sorry about that."

"It's okay," I assure her. "I'm not a purist."

"Skol!" she says, cheerfully, raising her glass.

"'Skol?'"

"It's like the Scandinavian cheers. Not traditionally done with tequila, but we make do with what we have."

"Oh, okay. Then, uh, Skol!" I clink my glass with hers, and we both down our rather generous tequila shots. It burns, but it does the job. I settle back on the sofa and sigh.

"That's a tragic, world-weary sigh if I ever heard one," Piper observes. "Anything you need to talk about?"

"Nah." I try to laugh. I don't want to chase off the first potential not-a-guy friend that I've met in, well, years. I guess that's not strange since I spend most of my free time at the martial arts school, where there's a definite imbalance in the ratio of men to women.

"You sure?" Piper asks. "I'm a good listener. I like to listen to other people talk about their problems. It helps me work through mine. Plus, we're gonna be so plastered I probably won't even remember what you tell me."

Should I trust her? I could use a sounding board. Ever since Vic suggested teaching me how to "fight dirty" I haven't been able to stop thinking about it. Sometimes, when I'm asleep, I have dreams about getting revenge on someone who hurt me a long time ago. I'm always disturbed by the dreams when I wake up, and I can't exactly control them, because they're dreams. When Vic brought up "fighting dirty" he immediately made me think of those dreams.

Piper reaches for the tequila bottle and pours another shot in my glass. "Drink up and tell me all about it."

I down the liquid, wince past the burn, and relax to the next level. Who needs meditation when you have tequila, I think, then remember I'm scheduled to train tomorrow. I probably won't be at my best for my session with Conan. But then the second shot really hits me, and all at once I don't care. It will be fine. Everything will be fine.

"Well," I say, "it's about that guy, Vic?"

"You're into him. I knew it."

"No! Nothing like that. But he said this thing, and it's bothering me."

"Do you think he's into *you*?"

"I think I'm one of the neighborhood chicks he hasn't banged yet."

"Cynical." She laughs. "Okay, what's this thing he said that you can't stop thinking about?"

I hesitate. I don't know any other women who do martial arts. I know they exist, but I've never met any. My sister wouldn't understand it—she was always into fashion, makeup tips, and relationship articles. My high school friends wouldn't have understood, either.

"So I, um, take taekwondo. I mean, I practice it."

"Oh." Piper stares at me. "No wonder you were able to beat up a dude."

"Right. Yes. Maybe. He was also super, super drunk, so I feel like, if he'd been, you know, sober—maybe I couldn't have beat him."

"What does that have to do with this Vic guy?"

"Well, Vic said he wants to teach me how to fight dirty. When you do martial arts as a sport, you have all these rules you have to follow. But when you're being attacked…"

"…there aren't any rules," Piper finishes for me.

I nod. "I guess he wants to teach me how to take down a person who isn't drunk and who doesn't fight…honorably.

Piper is still staring at me. She must think I'm a freak.

"You're so fucking cool!" she gushes. "I knew you were cool, but this is next level. You are so cool."

We are definitely getting buzzed.

She lifts an eyebrow. "So, what's the problem? Don't you want to be, like, an even bigger badass?"

"Well, sure. But the thing he said was, he can teach me how to hurt and *kill* people. That's fucked up, don't you think?"

Piper gives it a moment of drunken consideration. "That's not fucked up. I wish I had some hurt-and-kill-people moves. I'd feel safer walking alone at night. If you're that lethal, they can sense it, right? Then maybe they'll leave you alone. That's a good thing."

She has a point, even if it's being fueled by cheap tequila. And I am intrigued by Vic's offer. I'm a little creeped out by the fact that I'm intrigued, but I can't deny it.

Still, what's his real reason for wanting to "help" me? He's got to have one. I doubt he just floats around the city like a Good Samaritan, offering up his self-defense coaching skills to random women out of the goodness of his heart.

"You sure you don't like this Vic guy?" Piper asks.

"I don't know him well enough to like him or not like him. I just don't trust him." I look around the room, searching for something to help me change the subject. It doesn't take long. There's an acoustic guitar on a stand, right across from us, in the place where most people would keep a TV.

"Who plays the guitar?" I ask. Piper hasn't said anything about roommates, but I figure she must have at least one.

She raises her hand. "That would be me. I play."

"Play me something?"

Piper reaches for the tequila bottle. "If I'm gonna do that, I need another drink." She downs another sizable shot, then gets up and goes over to the guitar.

I wait for her to bring the instrument back to the couch, sit down, and maybe plink out a few sad girlish songs about a bad breakup. But instead, she straps the guitar on, stands up, and starts playing chunky, rhythmic chords. Once she's established a groove, she begins to sing.

She's bewitching. Her voice is rich and syrupy, like molasses. And her song isn't about a bad breakup. It's a seduction. She's not a singer/songwriter—she's a siren, and now it's my turn to be impressed.

When she finishes her song, I stand up and clap and cheer like I'm at a club with a zillion people.

"Oh, for fuck's sake," Piper says, unstrapping the guitar.

"Are you, like, professional? Do you play in a band?"

She rolls her eyes at me. "Hardly."

"But you're so natural."

"I play open mics sometimes," she relents. "But that's just messing around."

"You're really fucking good! Play another song?"

She makes a face at me and sets the guitar back on its stand. Then she whirls around, her usual self, the girl I work with at the diner. "I'm fucking starving. You want to order a pizza?"

By the time we've consumed most of a large pizza, half pepperoni and mushroom for me, half vegetarian for Piper, we've discovered we're both huge fans of MacGyver, and that each of us has a kind of fucked up family situation. Piper tells me about her mom, who threw Piper out of the house for sleeping with her boyfriend when she was seventeen.

"Is that even legal?" I ask.

"No," Piper says with a laugh. "But I was almost eighteen, anyway. I wanted to be gone as much as she wanted me out. I went to live with my boyfriend. She didn't care as long as she didn't have to see it."

"Do you talk to her now?" I ask. I eye the last slice of pepperoni and mushroom and decide to go for it.

She frowns. "Sporadically. How about you and your mom?"

"She and my dad died when I was eleven, but I don't have bad memories of her. Just good ones. My older sister's the one who raised me after that."

"I'm sorry about your mom and dad," Piper says. "What was it like? Growing up with your sister instead of parents?"

"It could be really cool sometimes. And then sometimes it sucked." That's about as much as I'm willing to say. There was a time when my sister was my best friend and my biggest support. But she ruined that years ago. I don't enjoy talking about it.

Piper seems to sense I don't want to be peppered with questions and leaves it alone. She changes the subject, and we talk about the bands we have in common until I decide to go home.

I catch a late bus around one a.m., which lets me off a block from O'Shea's. When I walk by, I see Vic through the window in his usual position at the far end of the bar. He's leaning against the wall, observing. I quicken my pace because I don't want him to see me. I have the illogical feeling he'll come running after me and badger me about learning to maim and kill people. It's a disturbing thought, and I know I need to steer clear of the guy.

But as I walk the last several blocks to my apartment, I'm on edge. The effect of the tequila has mostly faded, but I know I'm not functioning at one hundred percent. If someone were to attack me now, I'd be slower than usual. Then I hear a sound, like someone kicking a rock down the street.

I tense as my heart pounds in my ears. Then I force myself to relax. Ground. Wind up my energy. The air around me is pulsating in time with my heartbeat. Whoever it is, whatever it is, they're going to pay.

I whirl around, ready to fight.

No one's there. The street's completely deserted. I keep scanning the pavement, the spaces between buildings, listening, looking for the danger. But it's quiet. Empty. Devoid of threats.

I stay in a fighting stance for a long time afterward, waiting for the would-be perpetrator to emerge. When nothing happens, I turn back around and start walking, forcing myself to maintain a confident stance, half expecting the enemy to pounce now that I've turned my back. My limbs are shaky,

I have to admit it: what happened with Trevor rattled me. I'm not myself.

Until now, my knowledge of taekwondo has made me confident. I always felt like I was training for the moment I would be forced to defend myself. Now that moment has come and gone, and it worked —my training paid off. I kicked the guy's ass. I know I should feel more confident now, but I don't.

Sometimes I win sparring matches at the school and sometimes I lose them. It's all part of learning and developing your skills. But that night with Trevor, reality sank in. What happens if I get attacked and I lose? What if my skills aren't enough to protect me? It's something I'd never considered until this week, and it's left me anxious and jumpy.

As I walk down the hall to my apartment, I hear Milo meowing. He's a mellow kitty—except when I'm late.

"Hey, sweet kitty boy," I say, shushing him as I walk through the door. "I've got ya. Just hang on."

I don't go to the window seat tonight. Instead, I stay in the kitchen and watch Milo devour his food. I wonder if I could ever tell Piper the real situation with my family. I want to. Maybe I could, if we keep hanging out when we're not at work.

But how do you tell a new friend that your sister's husband tried to rape you when you were eighteen, and that when you told her about it, she didn't believe you? How do you explain that now you and your sister don't get along, even though your sister essentially raised you?

There's never a good time to insert a topic like that into a conversation. At least, not in any normal sort of way. Most days it's something I'd rather stop thinking about altogether. I prefer to focus on things that make me feel good, so I pick Milo up and dance him around the kitchen while he purrs like a tiny furry engine of bliss.

# CHAPTER FIVE

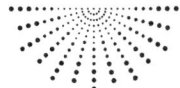

I'm not at my best the next day. I didn't sleep much after I got home from hanging out with Piper. I feel tired in class and have to force myself to stay focused. By the time I get to my one-on-one session with Conan, I'm out of energy for faking it. He keeps dropping me to the mat. I'm used to him besting me, but not so easily every time.

Finally, he stops in the middle of sparring with me and snaps his fingers in front of my face. "Focus, Noelle."

"Sorry."

"Where are you today? You're totally phoning it in."

His bright blue eyes are concerned. Conan's one of the few people in the world who I'm certain actually gives a shit about me, and I have the history of our friendship to prove it. So I don't lie to him. "I got drunk with somebody from work last night."

He raises one of his bushy red eyebrows. "New life habit?"

"No, it was just—it's this girl I work with. She actually wanted to hang out with me. Then she wanted to drink tequila. So, tequila was had. In rather large quantities."

Conan gives me a look. I'm familiar with that look. It means he can see through me. Sometimes I love that about him, and sometimes I really don't.

"I shouldn't have to tell you this," he says, "but you don't need to drink to get people to like you."

"That is actually untrue," I challenge. "People finding other people likable while under the influence of alcohol is a rather common phenomenon."

"You know what I mean. If you have to drink to keep a friend..."

"...then that friend isn't worth keeping," I finish. "Yeah. Yeah, I know. It wasn't like that. It was spontaneous."

"Okay. Just be careful." He starts taking off his protective gear.

I glance at the clock. "We've still got twenty minutes."

"You're out of it. I don't want to accidentally hurt you."

I'm pissed. "Don't treat me like a girl."

Conan grins. "I'm not. If I was treating you like a girl, I'd keep going and make it easy on you. Go home and hydrate and detox. Come back sober next time."

I look up at him. "I need friends who aren't guys, Conan."

"I get it. Hang out with this chick again and try not drinking. If she's cool with it, maybe you've got a friend. Okay?"

I'm not quite pacified, but I know he isn't going to budge. Not every instructor at the school lives an alcohol-free lifestyle, but Conan does. The sessions with him aren't part of my paid membership—he does them as a favor to me, and he probably thinks I've been wasting his time today. I start taking off my own protective gear, feeling the guilt creep in.

On the way home, I walk past O'Shea's and peer inside. Ever since Christmas Eve I've been wary of going there. I'm a bit apprehensive that Trevor will pop up again, but I'm more nervous about running into Vic. He bugs me.

I don't see either of them inside the bar, but that doesn't mean they're not there. You can't see the whole bar from the windows on the street. Then I think, fuck it—I'm hungry and it's happy hour. I go in.

"Hello, sweetheart," Aidan says with a smile as I seat myself at the bar. "Guinness?"

"Actually, just a burger."

"You've got it."

All burgers at O'Shea's come with steak fries. There's never a choice of anything else. Kane believes in keeping things simple.

It's comfortable in here. Everyone's in a good mood, laughing and talking. Eating and drinking. This feeling is why I started hanging out at O'Shea's in the first place. It has all the good vibes and cozy, just intimate enough lighting. It's the kind of place where you can hang out, eat a meal, and mind your own business.

By the time Aidan drops my burger in front of me, my mouth is starting to water. I thank him and take a bite. Bliss. Best burger ever. I'm in happy burger land when I hear a now-familiar voice behind me, ordering a drink.

"Hey, man. Shot of Jamesons and a Guinness."

Aidan nods, casts a quick glance at me, then goes to get the drinks.

"Is this seat taken?" Vic asks.

I turn to face him and gesture to the empty stool. "Does it look taken?"

"Maybe you're here with somebody," he says. "Or waiting for somebody?"

"Just me, myself and I. And my burger." I point to my plate.

"So, you don't mind if I sit down?"

I don't know why he's bothering to ask again, because he's already lowering his ass onto the seat.

I shrug. "It's a free country."

"So they say."

I wonder what he'd do if I told him I do mind. I don't know if I mind. After helping me Christmas Eve, his presence is simultaneously reassuring and disturbing. I'm not sure how to react to him.

Aidan puts Vic's shot and his beer in front of him. He downs the shot, then takes a careful sip from his pint glass. I'm secretly hoping he'll end up with foam on his lip, but he doesn't.

I figure it's best to get to the point. "So, are you gonna try to convince me I should let you teach me how to hurt people?"

"It's not about hurting people," Vic says. "It's about protecting yourself from people who want to hurt you."

"Uh huh. And what do *you* get out of it?"

"What do I get out of it?" he repeats.

"That's what I asked."

Vic raises his eyebrows and gives me a dark, enigmatic grin. "The satisfaction of helping out my fellow man?"

He has extraordinary eyebrows, I notice. They're thick, dark like his hair, and expressive. But however cool I think his eyebrows are, I don't believe him.

"You're a humanitarian," I say, drily.

"Something like that."

"That must be immensely gratifying." I turn back to my burger.

He watches me eat. The motherfucker is actually just watching me eat. That has to be bad manners. I chew, swallow, and look at him. "Do you want a bite or something?"

I meant to put him off guard, but he just grins in the same dark way. This time, the grin is only in his eyes. And for the second time, he's made me blush.

"I ate earlier, thanks," he says. "Listen, do what you want. I get it. Some stranger offering to teach you self-defense skills is outside the norm."

Now, I raise my eyebrows. "You think?"

"Why don't *you* think about it and get back to me if you're into it." He treats me to one more grin. "You know where I live." And with that, he nods, takes his Guinness, and goes to join another table of happy hour drinkers.

He could be a nice guy. But I don't trust nice guys. My sister married a nice guy—he wasn't nice to me. The bottom line is I can't figure Vic out, and I don't like it. Guys like Trevor are scary but they're obvious assholes, and absolutely not heroes.

I'm not sure what Vic is.

I turn my head and watch him listening to someone talking at the table where he's sitting. His mobile eyebrows go way, way up as he's listening, then he bangs the table and roars, "That's unacceptable! Vengeance is ours!"

It sounds ridiculous from where I'm sitting. But everyone at the table bursts into loud, raucous laughter. Inside joke?

I turn back to my burger before Vic can catch me watching him. When I see Aidan, I flag him down.

"Can I get a glass of water please?"

Conan told me to hydrate. Hydration is good for you. For now, I'll focus on hydration.

# CHAPTER SIX

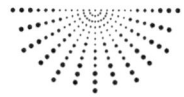

Piper is pumped. She arrives just before her shift and slides into the booth across from me still wearing her black motorcycle jacket.

"You won't believe what I did," she crows.

"What'd you do?"

She's crackling with excitement. "Guess."

"Uh…you robbed a bank and now you're going to run away with a million dollars cash. And you want me to come with you? I'm in!"

"No." She whips a rolled-up newspaper out of her jacket pocket and spreads it out in front of me. It's one of the local papers that writes about arts and culture. It also has horoscopes and classified ads.

Piper opens the paper right to the ads and puts her finger on one of them. It's already been circled multiple times with black ink.

"I answered that."

"To do what?"

She gives me a look.

"What?" I protest. "It's upside down. I can't read it."

She looks back down at the paper. "Oh, right. It is upside down." She flips the paper around, and taps on the ad. "Read that."

*Wanted: replacement singer and rhythm guitarist for four-piece rock band. Original songs a plus. Influences—Joy Division, The Sisters of Mercy, Gene Loves Jezebel.*

"I'm auditioning for their band this weekend. It's all set up. Oh, God. I'm so nervous." She looks at me. "You did say you think I'm good, right?"

"I think you're amazing," I agree, truthfully. "They should totally want you in their band."

"I've never done this before," she confesses. "Answered one of these ads? I always wanted to, but I never had the balls." She gives me an enigmatic look. "Not until I played for you."

"I'm sure you were just finally ready to go for it," I say.

"I'm freaked."

"You'll do great."

Her eyes are imploring. "Will you come with me?"

"To your audition?"

"I know, it's ridiculous. I don't need a chaperone. I'm sure they're not axe murderers or anything."

I'm alarmed. "Do you think they might be axe murderers?"

"Doubt it. But I think I need someone to go with me who actually believes I'm good at this."

"Sure, I'll go. Is it Saturday or Sunday?"

"Saturday. At seven."

"It's a date." I get up from the booth and gather my dishes to take back to the kitchen. "I have to go, but if I don't see you here, I'll see you on Saturday."

Piper nods vigorously. "I'll call you."

After I leave my dishes with the dishwasher, I grab my coat, hat, and mittens from the back room, and go out the employee exit. It's bitter cold, but I feel warmed from all the pancakes, eggs, and sausage I just consumed. Not the healthiest meal, but it had everything I need to help me fight the frigid weather.

It's a deceptively sunny afternoon. The sky is a clear pale blue and everything is lit up with the brilliance of the sun, but I can't feel its warmth.

I'm skipping my taekwondo lesson today. In fact, I've missed a number of them since the beginning of January. Instead I go to the nearest bus stop to wait for a cross-town bus. I'm going to church.

I don't believe in God. That's not why I go. On the other side of the city, there's this church where they put on beautiful choral concerts several times each year. They rehearse on Thursday evenings, and I like to go and listen. It's free, and listening to them sing makes me feel calm inside.

When I get to the church, I dash for the doors to get out of the cold and head straight for the balcony in the sanctuary. The choir is already practicing, their voices wafting into the rafters as I tiptoe down to the first couple of pews in the balcony and slide into one of them. I remove my hat and mittens, unbutton my coat, and settle back to listen.

They're working on something that sounds modern, with clashing, dissonant notes that resolve into pretty chords. Then the whole piece falls into chaos again. It's like an aural mirror of how I usually feel inside. I'm glad I obeyed my inner nudge to come here. I close my eyes and let the sound rush over me.

Time disappears as I listen. I feel as if I'm floating on the music, like it's surrounding me with a protective cloud of sound that nothing else can penetrate. Sometimes they stop and go over difficult sections, but that doesn't disturb me. It reminds me of working on drills and forms at the taekwondo school. But when I'm listening to the choir, I don't have to work. I can just enjoy their process.

When their rehearsal ends, they start chattering to each other, and I'm immediately woken from my trance. Then I hear something clatter to the ground behind me. The floor of the balcony is sloped, and a pencil—the kind they leave in the compartments on the back of the pews—rolls downward and stops near my foot.

I turn around, pissed that someone has invaded my refuge, but freeze when I meet their eyes. It's Vic. He's wearing his signature black coat, and he looks like a messenger of hell trespassing on God's territory.

"What are you doing here?" I whisper. Since choir practice is over, it would probably be okay if I spoke in a normal tone of voice, but it seems disrespectful.

Vic puts a finger to his lips, slides out of his pew, and comes down toward me. He gestures to the pew where I'm sitting. I scoot over to let him in—way over, giving him plenty of room.

He takes the hint and doesn't move too close.

"What are you doing here?" I repeat in a low voice.

"Conan sent me."

I stare at him. "Conan?"

He lifts his eyebrows. "Big guy? Red hair? Seventh degree black belt?"

"*You* know Conan?" I'm flabbergasted.

"Known him a long time."

"I've never seen you training. Never seen you in a class."

"I don't train there."

"So how do you know Conan?"

He hesitates, then half smiles. "Not important. Anyway, he sent me here. He's looking for you. Said you skipped a couple classes."

For a second I can't think how Conan would even know I'm here. Then I remember. Once he asked me if there was anything I did to just chill out, and I'd told him I come here. I figured he'd think I was bullshitting, and I certainly never expected him to remember.

Now I shrug. "Yeah, I skipped a couple classes. It's not a big deal. He knows I'll be back."

"From what he told me, that sounds like the problem. Every time he starts pushing you to go for your black belt, you disappear."

When I don't answer, Vic adds, "He said that's been happening for a long time."

I finally get a handle on my feelings. What I feel is betrayed. "I can't believe Conan told you anything about me."

"Like I said, we go way back."

"Yeah, I don't care. He had no business talking about me to you. Or anybody."

Vic holds his hands up in front of him. "I'm just the messenger."

I slump down in the pew. Out in the sanctuary, there are still a few choir members lingering and talking, but most of them have left. They have a room in the basement where they get coffee and cookies—I snooped on them once. I imagine them all hanging out down there, getting caffeinated and sugar rushed.

"So do you come here a lot?" Vic asks.

I don't answer. I don't want to talk to him. I can't believe he's here. It's as strange as if a talking circus animal had walked up and asked to sit next to me in the pew. Vic doesn't belong in my life, and it feels strange that he's a part of Conan's. I've known Conan for almost five years, and he talks about his girlfriend, his job, and his family all the time, but never Vic. I didn't even know Vic existed until I started hanging out at O'Shea's.

He tries again. "What's the appeal?"

"I like to listen to the music."

"I get that. Kind of helps you untangle your thoughts?"

"Kind of."

"Look, I get it if you don't want any help from me, but I think you should talk to Conan."

"About what?"

"About why you keep avoiding the test for your black belt."

I stand up, frustrated. Coming here was supposed to calm me down, and now I'm agitated again. "I need to get home."

"You want a ride? It's dark. And it's freezing out there."

I laugh derisively to make sure he feels my hostility. "I've been handling the reality of sunsets and winter for two decades. I think I can handle it tonight. Are you going to let me out?

Vic stands up and gets out of the pew. As I pass by him, I say, "Tell Conan if he wants to ask me something in the future, he should ask me himself instead of sending a messenger boy."

He nods gravely. "Noted."

Somehow, I feel like he's laughing at me.

I leave the balcony. I'm still fuming as I exit the church, jam my hat back on my head, and put on my mittens. As I approach the bus stop, my bus roars by. Without stopping.

"Hey!" I run down the street, hoping the driver will see me. They don't. I groan and go over to the printed bus schedule to try to read it. It's behind a plexiglass panel that has been scratched so badly it's hard to make out in the available light. If I'm reading it right, it looks like there won't be another bus for a half hour, assuming the next bus is on time.

I let out a long, frustrated breath, and it hangs in the air like a dense cloud. The frigid wind leaves my cheeks raw, but I can take it. I pull my hat all the way down over my ears, and stuff my hands in my pockets to wait for the next bus, tapping my shoe against the icy spot where a puddle has frozen over.

After several minutes, I have to jump up and down to keep warm. All my extremities are covered, but my face is exposed and the cold seeps in. If I wasn't trying to ditch Vic, I could have gone back inside the church to wait. Damn him.

How did Conan know that Vic knows me? And why would he talk to Vic about my attendance issues? Since the three of us have never been in the same room together, it truly seems like something that should be none of Vic's business.

Out of the corner of my eye, I see a sleek blue El Camino slowly approaching the bus stop. It pulls up to the curb as the passenger side window rolls down. Vic is behind the wheel.

"Cold enough yet?" he calls out.

"Not even close!" I yell back, but my chattering teeth betray me.

"Want a ride anyway?"

Goddamn it. I'm stubborn, but I'm not a masochist.

"Fine." I go to the car and open the passenger side door. The car has leather bucket seats. I settle in and fasten my seatbelt.

Vic pulls the car away from the curb, and we're off. I'm still chilled, but it's warm in his car and I can feel the cold ebbing bit by bit from my body.

"You remember where I live, right?" I ask.

He glances at me. "I know you're somewhere near O'Shea's, so I figure I'll just go there, then you can remind me where you live."

"Sounds good." I still don't want to talk to him. I don't like that he knows more about me than I know about him. I wonder if Conan told him anything else.

"You hungry?" Vic asks. "I could use a burger."

"I just want to go home."

"You got it. Straight home. No burgers."

I sigh. He's giving me a ride. I suppose I could try to be civil. "So, what year's the car?"

"Eighty-seven. Last year they were made."

I shudder involuntarily. Of course he drives a 1987 El Camino. Of all the years I've been alive, 1987 was my least favorite. Vic bugs me, so why would he drive a car manufactured in any other year?

"You into cars?" he asks.

"El Camino, right?"

"That's right." He sounds pleased, like maybe he's found a kindred spirit.

"No," I tell him. It feels sort of good to dash his hopes. "I don't know anything about cars."

He gives a short laugh. "Then why'd you ask about it?"

I look at him, but instead of answering his question, I say, "1987 wasn't my best year."

"How 'bout '88?"

"I'm not an '80s enthusiast in general."

"Well, you're in luck, because the '80s are over. Welcome to 1992." He glances over at me, wearing a shit-eating grin. "Are you always this much fun?"

Something about his smile, aggravating as it is, also makes me feel like I should let him off the hook. "It's not you, okay?" I tell him. "I'm not pissed at you. I'm pissed at Conan. I know you're just the messenger, but he shouldn't have talked to you about me."

"I get that."

"Did he tell you anything else? About me?" As soon as I ask, I wish I hadn't. I don't want to hear what Conan's been saying behind my back.

"Just that you're one of his most talented students, and he's pissed at you for always sabotaging yourself."

"Are you bullshitting me?"

"No bullshit. Would never bullshit about anything when Conan is involved."

"Are you guys, like, good friends?"

"He did me a solid a couple years back," he says, checking his blind spot and switching lanes. "I owe him a lot."

40

"I owe him a lot too," I say softly.

"So, you're gonna go talk to him, right?"

"Yeah," I sigh again. "I'll go talk to him."

"As long as you talk to him, my mission was successful."

He's smiling as he gazes ahead at the road and, maybe it's dumb, but I have to admit I like the way Vic drives. I've always thought you can get a good sense of someone by how they drive a car. Vic is a confident but also careful driver.

Everything outside the car looks frozen, even the buildings. It makes the world seem like it has sharper edges than usual.

When we pass by O'Shea's, Vic asks, "Sure you don't want that burger?"

A burger actually sounds good, but I tell him, "I just want to go home."

"You got it," he repeats and drives me back to my apartment building without any further direction from me. That means he does remember where I live. I'm not sure if that's a bad thing, or a good thing.

"Your destination," Vic says, as he pulls up to the curb outside my building.

"Thanks for the ride." I start to open the door.

"Hey, Noelle."

I look back at him. "Yeah?"

"Promise me you'll talk to Conan."

I'm surprised when I feel my mouth stretch into a grin. "I won't jeopardize your mission. I promise."

"That's all I ask," he calls out as I exit the car. I shut the door without responding.

"He would have a 1987 El Camino," I mutter as I watch him drive away. It's so *him*. A car that can't decide if it's a muscle car or a pickup truck. If it wants to be pretty or ugly. A hero or a villain.

Or, whatever. It's just a car.

# CHAPTER SEVEN

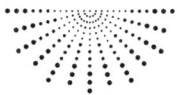

Saturday morning, the day of Piper's band audition, I corner Conan at the school's front desk and plant myself on the floor in front of him. "I'm pissed at you."

He glances up. "She lives. Thought maybe you ran off to join the Peace Corps. Or was it the circus you wanted to join? I always forget which."

I ignore his attempt at humor. "What the hell were you thinking, sending Vic out to find me? How do you even know him, anyway? And how'd you know that *I* know him? It was so messed up when he just...*appeared* in this place I've never seen him before!"

"You make him sound like some kind of supernatural being." Conan shrugs. "I told him you might be hanging out at that church. Sounds like I was right?"

"Yes, but *why* would you tell him that?"

He sighs and leans back in his chair. "Do you know how often you've done that thing where you disappear for a week? It's always when you have almost enough days of perfect attendance to sign up for the black belt test. You always wreck it at the last minute."

"Okay, I know that pisses you off. But what does that have to do with Vic?"

"He came by and while he was here, he mentioned he met this

amazing chick who beat up this dude who was attacking her. I had a hunch. Asked him some questions. Figured out he was talking about you."

"Vic said I was amazing?"

Conan nods. "He did. Gave me a play by play—told me how you took the guy down. That's how I knew for sure it was you."

"Okay, but that still doesn't explain why you sent him to find me at the freaking church. I don't know him very well. Do you trust him?" I'm still in interrogation mode, but I'm also off balance from hearing that Vic thinks I'm "amazing." I might feel a bit…flattered?

This time Conan ignores my question. "How come you didn't tell me you were attacked? Did it slip your mind?"

I shrug. "I kicked the guy's ass. I figured it wasn't important."

"You should have told me."

"Why?"

"We could have analyzed it. Figured out what to do better next time. Worked on some self-defense moves."

That makes me laugh. "Did Vic also tell you he's been breathing down my neck about that? He said he wants to teach me how to 'fight dirty.' Does he just, like, roam around the city, looking for women to 'help?' 'Cause that's kind of…creepy?"

Conan goes quiet for a moment, as if considering his next words carefully. "If you want to learn how to defend yourself—I mean, hard-core defend yourself—Vic's actually a good guy to learn from."

I make a face. "Are you sure? He's like…strange. He's always lurking around like some sleazy-ass ghost. He's a weird guy."

"Vic is…" Conan hesitates. "Vic's a complicated guy. But you don't need to be scared of him." He gives me an earnest look. "I'd leave Annie alone with him. That's how much I trust him."

Annie is Conan's girlfriend, and the only reason they aren't married is because Annie refuses to get married before she's thirty. Conan would marry her in a heartbeat if she'd let him.

"So how'd you meet Vic?" I ask.

Again, Conan looks like he's trying to decide how much to say. "He's kind of a friend of the school."

"I've never seen him here."

"He doesn't come here often."

"He's a friend of the school, but he doesn't come here often? That doesn't make sense." There's definitely something Conan isn't telling me.

"Look, Noelle, don't hang out with him if you don't want to. But if you do want to, he's got my stamp of approval. Okay?"

"Sure."

"So, are you going to start coming back to class?"

"I'll be here next week."

Conan picks up a pen and writes something down on a piece of paper in front of him. Then he looks up. "Are you going to sign up to test for your black belt when your attendance gets back on track?"

I stare at him, then glance at the wall clock and make a horrified face. "Oh crap! I have to go help my friend with this—thing. I promised. I have to go. See you next week!"

He's shaking his head as I rush out of the school. It's hours before Piper's audition tonight. But there was no way I could honestly answer Conan's question. I had to bail.

———

I'M MEETING Piper at her apartment to give her more time to get ready. When she opens her door, I'm immediately jealous of her effortless vibe. She's got black jeans on and an army green sweater that fits her curves like a glove. When she adds her signature black motorcycle jacket to the ensemble, she looks so badass. I'm decidedly less formidable in jeans and a blue sweater. But that's how I usually dress when I'm not training.

We pile into her car, an old Volkswagen Bug that's light blue and loud. As we drive to the audition, she keeps tapping her fingers on the steering wheel in a frantic yet rhythmic way that betrays her nervousness.

She glances at me. "Thanks for doing this. I don't think I could get through it without you."

"Sure, you could," I say. "But thanks for letting me tag along."

I'm excited to meet the band Piper's auditioning for. They're called

Primal Malice. I've seen their name on posters plastered all over the city. They're a band that actually gets gigs—no wonder Piper is nervous. They practice in a detached garage at a house where some of the band members live. As we drive up, they come out to meet us, and the first thing I notice is that they're all tiny people.

I'm average height, and Piper is maybe an inch taller than I am. The band, two guys and a teeny, tiny blond girl all appear to be smaller than us. They're also all wearing black. As we get closer to them, though, I realize the two dudes aren't as small as they seemed—just skinny.

"Hi there!" Piper calls out. "I'm Piper. This is my friend Noelle. She wanted to hang out. Hope that's okay?"

The blond girl shrugs. "More the merrier."

Piper's demeanor is chilled out, but I can tell she's faking it, because she's gripping the handle of the guitar case so tight it looks painful.

We head into the garage, where one of the guys in the band finds me a milk crate to sit on and presents it to me with a flourish and a grin. I'm relieved to see the grin, because I was starting to think none of these people even knew how to smile.

There are shelves on the walls overflowing with different tools and other unknown paraphernalia. It's tight, but somehow they've managed to cram a drum kit, several amplifiers, a mic, and guitar stands in to the limited space.

The other guy is helping Piper set up her guitar. When they test her sound through an amplifier and then a mic, I'm surprised by the volume. I probably won't leave this garage with my hearing intact.

"So, uh," Piper says. "Should I play a song, or should I listen to you all play a song and learn it, or uh, should I juggle, maybe?" Her attempt at a joke doesn't elicit any laughter from the group, and I feel bad for her. She looks my way and I raise my eyebrows.

The smiley guy says, "Why don't you play one of your songs, and we'll try to come up with parts for it?" He goes behind the drum kit and makes a few thump-y, crash-y noises.

"Uh, okay?" Piper looks over at me again, and I give her a smile along with another eyebrow raise. Then a thumbs up. Everyone in the band picks up their instruments. The less smiley guy is on guitar. The tiny blond girl is on bass guitar. Her bass is almost as big as she is.

"Our last singer quit," she says suddenly. "That's why you're here."

Piper speaks into the mic. "Oh. That's a bummer." Her discomfort is amplified for the whole room. "Well. I guess I'll just...."

She starts playing a song. It's the same one she played for me at her apartment. For what feels like too long, the rest of the band is silent. They don't play anything on their instruments. They're still not smiling. They're not talking. If I were Piper, I'd want to melt into the floor.

But then, the drummer starts to play along with her. And then the guitarist. And then the blond girl on the bass. Once they're all playing, they're transformed from slightly odd people dressed in black to almost otherworldly creatures. It's like magic. They've never heard Piper's song before, but they automatically know what to do to make it sound even better.

When she finishes, they all look around at each other, and it's like they're communicating without words. The drummer says, "You got any more?"

"Yeah," adds the bass player. "I want more songs like that."

And that's how I end up spending over an hour in a garage listening to Primal Malice with Piper at the helm. By the time they stop playing, the milk crate is uncomfortable as hell, but I don't mind too much because I feel like I've witnessed something extraordinary. I have no doubt they're going to ask Piper to join their band.

They all tell her their names, which I immediately forget, then say they have a few more auditions to get through, so they'll be in touch with Piper in a week or so.

"How do you feel?" I ask her once we're back inside her car.

"Did that suck?"

"Are you kidding? It was awesome! I was so sure they were going to ask you to join the band tonight."

"I know, me too! It felt so amazing while we were playing. Like we all knew each other already." Piper slumps. "But they didn't, so it must have sucked, right?"

"They said they have more auditions to get through," I remind her.

"But if it was awesome, shouldn't they just know? Shouldn't they be like, 'fuck everyone else, this is our girl!'"

"Maybe they're...methodical?"

"Oh, my God," she groans. "I don't think I can wait for a week. I can't. I want this so bad. I need a drink. Do you want to get a drink with me?"

I think of Conan. Even though I did participate in a night of tequila worship with Piper, I don't usually get drunk, because it does mess with my training.

"I can have one drink?" I venture.

"Sure, drink, don't drink, just come with me. Will you come with me?"

"I'm in."

"Good, I can't stand to think about that audition for another minute."

"You killed it, Piper."

"I hope so. I know, I know, if it doesn't work out, I just keep auditioning for bands, but I really liked them. It felt special. Don't you think it felt special?"

"They're idiots if they don't pick you. Where do you want to go for a drink?"

———

"MORNING MILO!" I call out.

He jumps down from the window seat, meowing frantically, and I feel a pang of guilt. I stayed at Piper's last night. I didn't get trashed, but she did, and I drove her back home in her car. Then we stayed up late talking. Drunk Piper is every bit as mentally sharp as Sober Piper, but with severely depleted motor skills. We both fell asleep on her couch, and I had to rush back home to Milo this morning.

He's standing at my feet now, scolding me. I leave out dry food and water for him all the time, so I know he's not starving to death. Nevertheless, he's not happy with me. When I go to pick him up, he squirms out of my grasp and runs in the kitchen. That means he won't be appeased until I feed him something special.

47

I give him a smidge of real canned tuna with his wet food, and by the time I settle on the window seat with a cup of coffee, all is forgiven. He hops up to join me and lets me pet him as he purrs and observes the street through the window.

The school is closed today. But I know I need to get back to training on Monday. Honestly, Conan should have thrown me out by now. I'm not sure why I have these lapses in commitment. He's right. It does happen a lot. It's never something I plan. I don't mark out the weeks and consciously decide to mess up my attendance record. I don't mean to sabotage my eligibility for belt testing. But lately, I always do.

Sometimes I think it doesn't matter. I started with actual self defense classes at the school, but when I observed a taekwondo class for the first time, I fell in love with it as both a sport and art form. Conan had been teaching that night, and I was impressed by how he used humor and discipline to drive his students to push themselves. I've been working with him ever since, progressing through the belt ranks at a faster-than-average pace. Then, when I reached the last belt level before first degree black belt, I began to struggle.

First, it was a long nasty bout of flu. It took me a month to recover, and another month to get back in condition. Then, I injured my ankle, just a sprain, but it slowed me down. After the injury healed everything should have gone back to normal. But then I started doing the thing where I disappear for a week or two, which obviously bothers Conan, since I used to be such a perfect and eager student. He doesn't understand what changed, and I'm not sure I do, either. I just know that I'm different.

My phone rings, and I immediately feel a sense of dread. Piper and Conan have my number, but hardly anyone else does—except my sister.

I get up as Milo meows in protest and go to the phone.

"Hello?"

"Noelle. It's me."

Yep. It's my sister, Izzy. For a split second I consider pretending I don't know who's calling. "What's up?"

"Well, I haven't talked to you in a while. We didn't see you at Christmas, so I thought I'd call to check in."

There's tension in her voice, but there always is when she calls me. In Izzy's universe, what her husband tried to do to me was a "misunderstanding." I misconstrued his meaning. And in her world, the fact that I don't come home for the holidays means I'm actively trying to hurt her.

I'm not going to take the bait. "How was your Christmas?"

"It was fine. We had dinner with Rob's family on Christmas Eve, and then we went to church. I hope you didn't spend it alone?"

I think about Trevor, and kicking his ass, then the odd visit in Vic's mammoth apartment. "No," I tell her. "I made some new friends, and we hung out. It was fun."

"Well, that's nice, I suppose."

We go quiet.

"Maybe next year you can come to church with us," Izzy ventures. "Or if you don't want to go to church, you could at least meet Rob's family. They're very nice people."

I wonder how many times you have to tell a person that sometimes "very nice people" aren't actually nice. So far, I've tried twice. In person, almost five years ago, the night Rob tried to assault me, and once more over the phone. That phone conversation was two years ago, when I first explained to Izzy why I wouldn't be coming home for Thanksgiving. Both times, it was like talking to a wall.

I don't have the energy to tell her again. "I'm glad you had a good Christmas."

"You're welcome to come home anytime," she adds. She says that almost every time we talk.

"Okay. Have a good rest of your day," I say.

We hang up.

It wasn't a shouty conversation. We didn't fight. On the surface, it was a calm, civil conversation. But my lazy morning with Milo feels ruined. He senses it too and jumps off the window seat, then sits back on his butt and looks up at me. His furry, quizzical grey face makes me laugh, and I kneel down to pet him.

"It's okay, little dude. Everything's fine. I'm fine. You're fine. We're fine."

# CHAPTER EIGHT

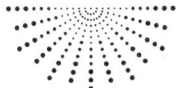

"I got in! I got in, I got in!"

I'm clearing up a table in the back of the Pancake House as Piper rushes at me. I set the ashtray I was about to empty on the table just in time, because she picks me up and spins me around.

Piper is strong. Strong enough to lift me off the floor. Noted.

She sets me back down and grabs my hands. "I got in the band! I got in the fucking freaking band!"

"Primal Malice?"

She nods up and down, vigorously. Her eyes go wide. "Can you believe it? Just like that!"

I catch her infectious happiness and start jumping up and down with her.

"You have to come out with me tonight! I'm meeting them at this club near Denny."

"What time?"

"Nine. I'll come pick you up."

"I'm in."

She hugs me again, then dashes out the door, trailing triumph and exuberance behind her.

---

To GO OUT with Piper that evening, I throw on my favorite pair of jeans and a wine-colored sweater that looks good with it—and by good, I mean the combo makes my ass look fantastic. It's not all black, but it's me.

Piper's car horn honks twice outside.

I make a face at myself in the bathroom mirror. "Good enough."

I give Milo a quick flurry of pets and kisses, then rush down to the street to meet Piper. She's still in ecstatic mode, leaning over to give me a big hug as soon as I'm inside her car.

"We're gonna have a blast!" she enthuses, pulling the car away from the curb. "Or that's what I want. I'm making it awesome for us right now. With my brain."

"Long live your brain," I intone seriously.

"Long live my fucking brain!"

In Piper's presence, I feel like it has to be true: it's going to be an incredible night. I'm still feeling it even as we pull into a dark gravel parking lot behind a run-down building. We get out of Piper's car, and the air is electric with possibility.

"They said the entrance is back here," Piper says as we crunch over the gravel toward the building. It's dark back here, and I'm not seeing anything that looks like a door. We walk along the edge of the building, and just as I'm beginning to wonder if her new bandmates are playing some kind of initiatory joke on her, she yelps in triumph. "Found it!"

I can't see what she's talking about, but she must have discovered some kind of handle, because a door swings open in front of us and we go through.

I'm not prepared for the sight that greets my eyes. We're in a very large room, and the light is somehow both dim and harshly blue at the same time. A couple of enormous, ornate gold chandeliers hang from the ceiling. They look heavy enough to pull the building down with their weight. Or at least crush the sea of people dancing beneath them.

Bodies sway in the eerie light, and every last one of them, as far as I can make out, is clad in black. The music sounds like someone's idea of discordant death throes, and the dancers' limbs jerk in rhythm with the beat as if they're actually enjoying themselves.

This is not a jeans-and-sweaters crowd.

"Do you see your bandmates?" I ask.

Piper is craning her neck, looking around the room. "Not yet."

There are deep booths around the edges of the room, and more black-clad people are sitting in them, looking bored out of their minds as they sip drinks.

Piper glances over at me and grins. "Is this your first goth club?"

"Yes. Apparently yes, it is."

"Oh!" Piper waves her hand at someone across the room. "I see them! Let's go."

We move through the club and as we get closer to her bandmates, I spot the bar in a little corner of the room. By the time we get to Piper's new friends, it's clear they're all following the dress code. As is Piper. I don't know why I didn't notice until now, but she's also dressed in black from head to toe.

"Hey, everyone! You remember Noelle, right?" she says, then turns to reintroduce me. "This is Sven." She points to the tall guitarist guy, who I've yet to see crack a smile. "Mandy," Piper says, gesturing to the bassist, who grants me a nod. "And this is Bill."

Bill grins at me. "How's it going, Noelle?" He's the drummer who seemed friendly before. The guy who found me the milk crate to sit on.

"Pretty good." I shrug, but I smile back at him, because he seems like a nice enough person.

"You want a drink?" Mandy asks us.

Piper glances at me. "Maybe one drink, to get started?"

"You go ahead," I say. I don't care if they drink, but I decide I'm not imbibing. The unfamiliar energy in here makes me want to keep my guard all the way up. We go to the bar, and they order drinks. I ask for soda with lime and no one makes a big deal about it.

Then, without speaking and with drinks in hand, they form a circle near the bar. Piper tries to pull me in, but she's a little late. They all look at each other and down their drinks in one gulp. It's like a toast, only not. I take a cursory sip of my soda.

"Let's go dance!" Bill says. Sven and Mandy follow him as if he's given a command. Piper tugs at my sleeve, so I trail after them out to the dance floor. I figure once we're dancing I'll be more comfortable. I'll lose myself in the music, and I won't mind the vampiric undertones or the awkward sore-thumb feeling—but I'm wrong.

The music is so angular it's hard for me to figure out how to dance to it. They're all on some wavelength that I can't access, heads down, flailing their bodies in patterns that hit me like a foreign language. It's like I'm back at a junior high school dance, still discovering how to move my body to the beat in public.

Piper glances over at me and mouths, "Having fun?"

I mime drinking something and point at the bar. She nods, an almost exact mimicry of the way Mandy nodded at me earlier, then throws herself back into dancing.

I order a second soda with lime, and as I'm paying, someone parks himself next to me. He leans against the bar as I take a sip of the drink. I haven't turned to look at him yet, and he hasn't said a word, but I know it's Vic. Apparently O'Shea's isn't the only place he does his lurking.

I look up at him. "Why are you here? Scouting more students for your elite fighting school?"

He grins. "I don't have an elite fighting school."

"Then I guess you're here for the music?"

"Not your style?" he guesses.

"What gave it away?"

"Your effervescent personality. Completely incongruent with the spirit of this joint."

I give him a withering look.

He gestures to my drink. "What's your poison?"

"Soda and lime."

"You want another one?"

I start to tell him no, but when I try to take a sip from my glass, I realize I've already drained it. I shrug. "Sure."

As he summons the bartender, he remarks, "I don't fit here either."

I give him a once over. Vic is wearing his signature black coat and giving off his usual quasi-foreboding vibe. He absolutely fits here. After he tells the bartender to get another lime and soda, he turns back to me.

"So why *are* you here?" I ask.

He evades the question. "Do you want to see if we can find some-where to sit?"

I don't, really. But then again, I also don't want to go back out on the floor and revisit how I felt at age fourteen. Plus maybe if I talk to him a little, I'll get a better sense of his game.

"Sure, let's go sit down."

He hands me my drink, and we go in search of an empty booth. We finally find one in a back corner of the room. From here the dancers are difficult to distinguish from one another, blending into a sea of black clothing. I've lost track of Piper and her bandmates.

"All these anti-establishment kids sure look alike," I say as we settle into our booth.

Vic gives me a patient look. "If you actually sat down and talked to any of them for an hour, you'd find out they're just people."

"Is that why you come here?" I shoot back at him. "To have conver-sations with the local goth population?"

"I go all kinds of places," Vic replies mildly. "There're lots of inter-esting night spots in the city. Why are *you* here?"

"My friend's here with her band, and she wanted me to tag along with them. But I didn't know she was an actual goth."

Vic laughs. "Does the goth thing bother you that much?"

I sigh. "No. Not really. I just feel out of place. It's like high school. And high school was over a long time ago."

"How long ago?" Vic asks.

"I'm twenty-two," I drawl, in a fake hick accent. "All growed up and everything." I switch back to my regular voice. "How old are you?"

"Thirty. So don't trust me."

I look him in the eye. "Not a problem."

"So what else are you into?" Vic asks.

"What else?"

"I know you're into taekwondo. And I know you've got some issue around getting your black belt. What else is there to know about you?"

I shrug again. "Not much."

"Do you work somewhere?"

"I'm a waitress. Actually, that's a good question for you. Where do you work? Because if you don't work at O'Shea's, but you have that huge apartment over O'Shea's, at this point I've got to assume you're a bored rich guy who's still clubbing at age thirty."

I wait to see if he gets offended.

"I'm not bored." Vic takes a sip of his drink.

I raise my eyebrows at him, and he cracks a smile.

"I'm not rich either. I own the building, that's all. It's less hassle for me to live upstairs than it is to rent out the apartments."

"You own the building? Sounds pretty rich to me."

He shakes his head. "It's not as impressive as it seems. I got it for a steal about seven years ago. The area around O'Shea's was way more sketchy than it is now. I got lucky when I found Kane to be my tenant. He made a ton of improvements to the lower level of the building with his business loan, and the bar makes the street feel like an actual neighborhood. Plus, he always pays his rent."

That might explain why Vic hangs out inside O'Shea's all the time. He wouldn't want anything to mess up Kane's success, because that would hurt him, too.

"Where are you a waitress?" Vic asks.

"Jean's Diner & Pancake House. That's how I met Piper—the friend I'm here with."

"Really?" His face is suddenly animated, like the thought of me working at the Pancake House excites him. "I love that place! I go there for late night pancakes all the time. Never seen you there, though."

I start to tell him I never work late-night shifts, then think better of it. "Maybe you did but you just didn't know it was me."

"I think I'd remember." For an instant, his color-confused eyes flare with what seems like sexual interest. But almost as soon as I see the blaze, it goes out. He leans back a little in the booth and grins amiably. "So, tell me something else."

"About me?"

"Yeah, about you."

"What do you want to know?"

"I don't know. Tell me whatever you want. Whatever you want me to know."

I don't want him to know anything, so I decide to tell him about my working theory of human relationships, guessing he'll either get bored or think I'm kind of strange. Maybe then he'll stop initiating conversations with me when I see him in public.

I take a long sip of my drink, then look at him. "Okay. I have this theory. A working theory of human relationships. You want to hear it?"

"Absolutely."

"It's not super complicated. The premise of it is that every person on Earth is trying to get things. Everybody wants things and everybody tries to get things. That's what drives everyone. Not religion, not curiosity, not science, not altruism. Just wanting things and trying to get them. That's it. All that other stuff is just the reasons we make up to explain why we want whatever we want."

Vic nods. "Everybody wants things. Everyone tries to get things. Got it."

"So," I continue, "the only difference is between, like, *how* people get things. There are three main types of people. Psychopaths and sociopaths—"

Vic holds up a hand. "Are you putting psychopaths and sociopaths in the same category? Because they're not technically the same."

"For the purpose of my theory, it doesn't matter whether they're technically the same. They're *essentially* the same."

He smirks but nods gravely. "Continue."

"So, like I said, there's three main types. Psychopaths and sociopaths are the first type. The second type is assholes. And the third type is people who love you. The first type, psychopaths and sociopaths, they want things, right? But they don't negotiate with you to get things. If you have something they want, they just take it. They don't care if it hurts you. That's how they get things."

"I see." Vic folds his arms over his chest.

Good. Maybe I'm boring him already.

"The second type, the assholes? They know it's wrong to hurt people, to just take things. But they want things anyway, so they find some way to convince themselves that it's actually a good thing to hurt others to get what they want. After a while, they even have fun hurting people to get what they want. That's how *they* get things."

"And what about people who love you?" Vic asks.

"With people who love you, they only love you if you give them what they want. So if you love someone, you have to figure out what that is. And if someone loves you, they have to figure out what you want. It's a negotiation. As long as you're both negotiating, it's still love. But the negotiation usually ends when someone becomes an asshole."

I stop, waiting for him to respond. But he doesn't. He sits there leaning against the back of the booth, like he's mulling it all over. Or maybe like he's bored out of his mind.

"That's it," I finish. "That's my theory."

Still, Vic is silent. I wait for him to say that's the dumbest thing he's ever heard or to jump up, remembering, suddenly, that he's late to meet someone somewhere else—likely across town.

Instead, he looks right at me and asks, "So, what do you want?"

"Me?"

"Yeah. What do you try to get from other people?"

The question shocks me. I didn't expect him to ask me what I want.

The music in the club has shifted to something that's actually danceable. I have an urge to get up, find Piper and her bandmates, and give the goth-y dance moves another go. But Vic is looking at me intently, and I feel like if I don't answer him, I'll be chickening out.

"Honesty," I blurt, before I can think of a good lie. "No bullshit."

"Okay," he says, and leans forward. "Well, no bullshit, I really want to teach you some next level self-defense skills."

"Why?" My voice has suddenly gone hoarse. "What do you get out of it?"

"I want to feel useful."

I believe him. I don't want to believe him. It's my default policy not to believe anyone like him, and by that, I mean any man and most women. But I believe him anyway.

"There you are!" It's Piper, with the rest of her band in tow. Somehow, she already seems like their leader. "We were looking all over for you. We're gonna blow this place and get some pizza. You're coming with us, right?"

I'm not sure why she wants me to go with them, since it looks like she's already one hundred percent in with her brand new bandmates. Mandy is even hanging off her shoulder in this half creepy, half cutesy way.

Then Bill chimes in. "Yeah, c'mon, Noelle. Please come with us. It'll be fun."

I give in. "Okay. Pizza sounds good." I slide out of the booth and turn to Vic. "Thanks for the drink."

"No problem. Let me know if you want to make an old man feel useful."

"Old man" applied to someone like Vic is a joke, but I let it slide. And then, on impulse, I say, "Let's do it. Teach me self-defense."

His eyebrows shoot up. "You serious?"

"No bullshit."

He smiles. He looks genuinely happy. And I'm already wondering what in the hell I just did.

"I'll be in touch," he says.

As I stand up, Piper asks, "Are you still sober?"

"Yeah, I'm not drinking tonight."

"Awesome. Do you want to drive my car to the pizza place? I'm too drunk to drive right now."

"Of course," I say, then turn around and look back at Vic. He meets my eyes and, maybe I'm imagining it, but for a moment I'm sure he's seeing the world my way.

If he is, then he'd know that in this moment, my friends like me because I have something they want: a lack of intoxication. A designated driver. I smirk at him, then break eye contact and follow Piper and her band out to the parking lot.

# CHAPTER NINE

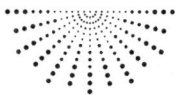

I don't actually get together with Vic until after Valentine's Day, when it finally worked for our schedules.

When we have our first lesson, the weather has changed from icy cold and sunny to standard cold and rainy. I'm soggy and shivering when I meet him in front of his building on a Saturday afternoon. The thought *in front of his building* makes me laugh because it actually is *his* building.

"You look like a drowned rat," he remarks as I walk up to him. "Don't you own a raincoat?"

I shrug. "My hoodie will dry."

"See, if you had a raincoat, your hoodie would be dry already."

"Just let me in before I drown harder."

"Wouldn't want you to drown harder." He pushes the door open, and we head up the stairs to his gigantic apartment.

I'm feeling a smidge nervous about spending time alone with him again, but I remind myself that Conan trusts him.

I notice his kitchen is not quite as spotless as it was the last time I was here. There are dirty dishes in the sink and a crumpled dishtowel on the kitchen island. But other than those two aberrations, it's pretty clean.

As I strip off my sodden hoodie, he says, "Just drape it over one of the stools." He catches my eye. "Do you have time for a quick cup of tea?" When I hesitate, he adds, "It'll warm you up."

"I don't have time for a whole tea ritual," I say.

"I use the microwave method. Three-minute tea bags. No ritual."

"Okay. Yeah, tea sounds good."

I spread my hoodie out on a stool and sit on the one next to it. "So, what are you going to teach me?" I ask.

Vic puts a couple of mugs of water in the microwave, then turns around and leans against the island. "How to kick an attacker in the nuts."

I scoff. "I already know how to do that. That's like Self Defense 101."

"Just trust me."

"Trust you?"

"Trust me for a couple hours. If you think I'm full of shit, you can bail."

"If I think you're full of shit, I will."

The microwave goes off, and he pops a tea bag in each of the mugs. He slides one over the counter to me. "Give it a couple minutes."

"It smells good," I say. And it does. I'm eager for it to be cool enough to drink. I feel chilled to the bone from the rain.

Vic sets a plate in front of me. "For your tea bag when you're ready. It gets strong pretty quick."

We both go quiet as we drink our tea. The rain is still pouring down outside, a hushed roaring sound punctuated by the cry of an occasional seagull. I start to relax.

"I like your kitchen," I blurt, but immediately feel silly. What a random, ridiculous thing to say.

"I like it too." Vic reaches out for my tea mug. "Looks like you're done. Let's get to work."

He takes me over to the other side of his place, the opposite side of the building, then shows me through a small corridor that leads into a full martial arts studio—in his freaking house. Almost the entire floor is covered with thick blue mats framed by gorgeous light wood flooring around the edges.

"Is that bamboo?" I marvel.

"It is."

I become speechless as I absorb what's in front of me.. This—this small *gymnasium*—has been meticulously planned and executed. There are a couple of benches along the side of the room, and storage compartments at the far end that appear to contain protective gear. There's also a large training dummy hanging from the ceiling. It's the nicest gym I've ever been in, if not the largest. But it's plenty large for two people. Or even ten people.

"You okay?" Vic asks.

"It's...overwhelming."

"You ready to get started?"

"Um, sure."

Vic takes off his shoes, and I do the same. Then I follow him over to the training dummy. He whips some kind of marker out of his pocket and starts to draw on the dummy: cartoon eyes, cartoon nose and mouth. A heart where the heart would be. Then lower down, at about groin height, he draws three concentric circles. He stands back and points.

"There's your target. Show me five illegal ways to drop this motherfucker."

He's referring to the fact that within the rules of taekwondo, kicks or punches to the groin are illegal. It feels wrong to aim kicks at the circles on the dummy, but this isn't about art or fair play. This is self-defense.

After I've completed my five strikes, he says, "Good. Now repeat that sequence until I tell you to stop."

I'm used to taking instructions from Conan, and Vic's style is very similar, probably because they're friends. Taking instructions from Vic feels natural, like an extension course from our school.

I'm not even out of breath when he tells me to stop and take a breather. I'm feeling pretty damn proud of myself.

"Need water?" he asks.

"Not yet."

"Okay. Turn your back on the dummy and close your eyes."

I raise my eyebrows at him. This is not standard martial arts or self-defense training.

He repeats, "Close your eyes."

I turn around and close my eyes, and he says, "Now imagine someone's stalking you. It's been going on for a couple of blocks, and you're getting scared. And pissed."

Not exactly a reach of imagination, given my experience.

"When I tell you to open your eyes," Vic continues, "the guy who's been stalking you is gonna be right behind you, and you're gonna get him."

I stand on the mat, remembering the fight on Christmas Eve. The panic when Trevor hit me, that split second before I was able to gain the upper hand. I know I'm safe here, but even so, I feel the hairs raise on the back of my neck. It feels like forever before I hear Vic say, "Open your eyes."

I go at the target on the dummy with more vicious kicks. I'm thinking of Trevor, wishing now that I'd done even more damage. As I channel my anger from that night into a set of balls drawn on a dummy, lashing out over and over again, I start to feel high. Then I realize I'm running out of breath.

"Okay, give him a rest," Vic says eventually, assessing me. "Need some water?"

This time I accept the offer. He goes behind a panel and comes out with a cold bottle of water, which I assume came from a mini fridge hidden behind the screen.

He hands the bottle to me with the top already off, and I drink it down greedily.

"You're doing great," he says.

I shrug and wipe my arm across my mouth. "I'm just doing stuff I already know how to do."

He ignores that. "What were you feeling just now?"

"You mean right now? Or before?"

"When you were hitting the bag."

"I was pissed."

He points at my empty water bottle, indicating I should give it to him. "Ready to go again?"

I hand the bottle over. "Yeah, I'm ready."

He has me close my eyes again, but this time he only says, "Think of someone who makes you want to get revenge."

Immediately, my sister's husband comes to mind. The night he entered my room without knocking. The look on his face right before he came at me.

"Go," Vic says.

I start kicking the target, expecting more anger to come through me. But that isn't what happens. I get sloppy. Half the time, I'm not even hitting the target. More emotion comes up. But it isn't anger. A sob bursts out of me, out of fucking nowhere. I try to squash it down but I can't. I slump forward, hands on my thighs.

Vic's voice sounds like it's coming from far away when he says, "Noelle. Keep going."

"I'm tired."

"Keep going."

I stare at the circles, and they sort of blur together. *Oh God, tears.*

"Noelle..."

Feeling dazed, I wind up my energy. A roundhouse kick outside the circles. A front kick closer to them. Or not. I don't know. I think Vic just said something like, "Push through it." I can't quit. A back kick in the general direction of the circles. Picking up the pace slowly, no longer caring if I hit the target, as long as I keep kicking. And kicking again.

And then something miraculous happens. All at once, I feel nothing. I can focus on the target again, and I'm landing kick after kick in its center. I'm not tired, not hungry, not thirsty. If a machine had feelings, I'm sure this is how it would feel.

"That's enough!" Vic's shout breaks through, and I stop.

It's like coming out of a trance state. I'm breathing hard. I'm also a little shaky, and I can feel sweat dripping down my face. I swipe my hand over it.

"You all right?" Vic asks.

I nod. "That was crazy."

He gives me an appraising look. "I knew you had it in you."

"Had what?"

"The killer instinct."

I don't know what to say to that.

"Don't let it loose at the school," he adds. "You should always respect the rules."

"Of course!" I'm offended. "Conan means a lot to me. I'm devoted to that place." Then I think for a minute and admit, "Except when I blow it off, I guess."

"Well, anyway, good work." He grins at me. "Hungry?"

---

I'M LYING on my bed with Milo beside me. We're listening to a Primal Malice demo tape. Piper gave it to me at the diner earlier this week, and I promised her I'd listen to it.

The recording is rough. They need to get in a real studio with someone who actually knows how to record a band. But even though it's rough, it sounds good. The standout element, though, is Piper's voice. It's like she's channeling someone else when she sings. She's not the exuberant, quirky, mostly self-assured woman I recognize. Singing, she's all confidence.

My emotions are in a snarl. It's been over an hour since I left Vic's place, and I still don't know what to think of training with him.

My preliminary test was whether he'd immediately put his hands on me under the guise of "teaching." When you're sparring with people, eventually there's physical contact. But it's not necessary if you're just showing someone the mechanics of a particular move.

Vic hadn't touched me at all.

The phone rings, yanking me back into the moment. Milo mews at me as I get up to answer it. It's Piper.

"Hey," she says. "I hate to make this call all about me, but did you listen to the tape?"

"I was just listening to it," I confirm.

"What do you think? Is it good, or does it suck?"

I hesitate. It will be easy to tell her that the band sounds good, because they do. But the production quality of the tape itself sucks. I've never been good at lying to people to smooth things over.

Piper reads my hesitation as a bad reaction. "You hate it. You hate it, don't you?"

"No, I don't hate it. You guys sound amazing together. It's like you've always been playing with them."

"Okay, you like the band. What do you hate? Because you hate something."

"I just...think you guys should get someone to record it professionally. Because it sounds like it was recorded in a trash can."

Piper bursts out laughing. "Thank God, I was so afraid you hated my voice. But no, I agree with you. We should find a real producer who can make it sound like we recorded our songs in an actual trash can. On purpose."

I'm bewildered. "What?"

"But you like the band?" Piper presses. "The band sounds good?"

"Well, yeah," I attempt to joke, "for a trash can band." *God. Damn. It.* This is why I never keep women friends. Foot in mouth. Every time.

But Piper just laughs again. "Thanks for listening to it. Hey, are you working tomorrow?"

"Yeah, breakfast shift."

"So am I. See you in the morning!"

"See you."

I hang up the phone, relieved. Being myself hasn't driven Piper away. Yet. I haven't told her about working with Vic and wonder what she'd say about it. Somehow, I have a hunch she'd think it's a good idea.

And I am—officially—working with Vic now. After our session, we had burgers at O'Shea's, then hashed out a schedule for training together. It was surprisingly comfortable spending time with him. As if now that I've given in and agreed to work with him, he can relax.

While we sat at the bar to eat, people would come up to talk with him, and he entertained them with an easy manner that made me feel comfortable, too. I could sit there and listen to the chatter around me, admiring the finely polished wood and brass of the bar, then listen in on a snippet of Vic's conversations and feel like I was a part of it all. Each time Vic ended a chat with someone he'd check in with me, like ask how my burger was or if I needed anything else.

66

"You're so popular," I teased, at the end of one of the mini conversations. "Everybody wants to talk to you."

"It's you," he grinned. "You sitting here makes me look like I'm actually a nice guy."

"So, like, where are you from, anyway?" I asked.

"Kind of all over," he said. "I was a military brat growing up, so we moved around a lot. Landed here about a couple years after high school."

"Which one of your parents was in the service?"

"My dad." Vic glanced at me. "He was a hard ass motherfucker."

I was about to ask him more questions, but then someone else came up to him, so we lost that thread of conversation.

When I decided I was ready go home, he asked if I needed him to walk me back.

"No," I said. "Or do you still need to feel useful?"

A surprised light flickered in his eyes. Then he said, "Only if you've got a use for me."

"Not tonight," I told him.

He let me go without following me out.

Now, I slide onto my bed and settle down with Milo, who jumps on my lap and purrs, rubbing his head against my hand.

"I think I might have some new friends, Milo."

He headbutts my hand a couple of times.

"It looks promising. I mean, I think it does."

More vigorous head butts. A loud purr. Maybe Milo approves of the new people in my life. Then I remember I haven't fed him yet.

"You hungry, little man?"

He gets up and runs into the kitchen, meowing at the top of his lungs. It's a good reminder that Milo has his own priorities, and they aren't always the same as mine.

# CHAPTER TEN

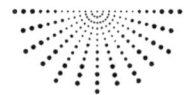

I t's one day before the Ides of March, and Piper's on stage with her band.

She's killing it.

Ever since she took an interest in me, I feel like I've been witness to the moment when a person launches their actual life, the life they've always dreamed of. It's exciting, but also disconcerting, because watching Piper live her dream makes me realize I don't necessarily have any dreams. The closest thing I have to a dream is to get my black belt, but after that, then what? She's approaching the on-ramp to building a legacy, but I feel like I'm just jumping through hoops. And actually, now, since I've stalled on getting my black belt, I'm failing to jump through hoops.

From the stage, she starts stomping her foot in rhythm and pointing at people in the crowd, like she's bestowing her favor on her adoring fans, one by one. So what if the show's in a small shitty club away from the city's main drag? It doesn't matter. Piper is owning that tiny stage so hard it feels like an arena show.

If the rest of the band wasn't so good, or if Piper wasn't equally talented and mesmerizing, I might be laughing into my hands about their goth aesthetic. They're all wearing black, of course, but tonight it's beyond that.

Both Piper and Mandy are made up with white foundation and heavy lipstick, deep red for Mandy, and black for Piper. The guys both have on heavy black eyeliner, and Bill is also wearing black lipstick. Sven, not to be outdone, has teardrops drawn down his cheeks.

They look simultaneously fierce and, to me, ridiculous. But in combination with the music, the look works for them. They're not hiding behind it, so it adds to the performance. They're the opening band on the bill, and the crowd is already pressing against the stage, clamoring for more of them. Piper's reveling in it.

I've been looking forward to her first show with Primal Malice since January. Plus, it was also a relief to come here tonight. It's giving me a focal point outside myself. Something removed from my own problems, and my ongoing and sometimes frustrating association with Vic.

Somebody in the crowd jostles me from behind. I turn around and take in his shaggy hair, baggy jeans, and plaid flannel shirt. Then I give him a death stare.

He backs up. "Hey, sorry!" he yells. "Who is this band? They're like, super weird and kinda cool, right?"

I hate people who try to talk over shows. I point to my ears and make a face, then hold up my hands and shrug to show I can't hear him. Then I move away from him. Dude was about five seconds away from "accidentally" squeezing my ass.

I find a better spot in the crowd. It's closer to the stage, but a bit off to the side, so I can watch the show and still keep an eye out for incoming asshats.

Everyone claps and cheers for a long time after Primal Malice plays their final song. I'm certain if they weren't the opening band, the crowd would call them back for an encore. Maybe I'm biased, but I thought they were phenomenal. Especially since it was their first real show playing Piper's songs.

I go to the bar to wait for her and order a rum and coke. It's the weekend. I can have one drink. Plus, since I started working with Vic almost a month ago, I haven't missed any classes or extra sessions with Conan. Vic's good for me, in a way, even if he sometimes gets on my nerves.

Ever since our second session together, he's been nonstop pressuring me to sign up for my black belt test. Our school does testing for black belts twice per year, in June and December. He wants me to test in June.

After Vic taught me several "maim and kill" techniques—as he gruesomely calls them—I figured he would practice them with me. Do some actual sparring—with protective gear, of course.

But nope. On the day we were set to spar, he invited someone else to join us at his combination apartment/martial arts studio. It was a woman who he said was a good friend and "colleague" of his. He had me spar with her, instead, so I could practice being on the giving and receiving end of all the tactics I'd been learning.

He said it was because he wanted to observe my progress. That he could assess me better if he watched from a bench in the room. Maybe he had a point. But it felt strange to spar with this woman, a person I'd never met, who I'd never even worked out with in a class.

She was tough, though. By the end of our session, I was winded and extremely grateful for protective gear. Without it, I would have been both maimed and killed.

The woman, who Vic had introduced as Sheryl, had just knocked me to the ground when he finally stood up and clapped his hands.

"That's enough for now. That gives me plenty to work with."

Sheryl grinned and offered me a hand, which I accepted. As soon as I was on my feet, she turned to Vic. "She needs a lot of work. But she's good." Then they began chatting without acknowledging me. Their desire for me to leave the room was palpable.

Vic and I had got in the habit of going to O'Shea's for burgers after our sessions, but I sensed he and Sheryl had business to discuss—or maybe he was fucking her and that's why they wanted me out. That wasn't the vibe, though. It felt like two insiders who needed to have a serious conversation, to which outsiders were not invited.

"Well," I said. "Thanks for the workout. Think I'm going to head home."

"See you next week." Vic gave me a brief smile. "And sign up for that test."

"Sure."

He threw me a look, one that said he knew I was full of shit. If Sheryl hadn't been there, he probably would have pressed further. But this time, he let it go.

"Nice meeting you!" I called out to her, even though I wasn't sure I meant it.

"You, too!" she called back. "Good fight, kid."

I didn't get a fake-friendly vibe off her. But, whatever her reason was, she absolutely wanted to be alone with Vic. It didn't seem to have anything to do with me, so I left them to discuss whatever they were going to discuss or do whatever they were going to do.

That was Thursday night. I'm still ruminating about it.

I'd been looking forward to sparring with Vic. Like Conan, I knew he would be a challenge, but a different kind of challenge. Sparring with Sheryl had left me feeling cheated. Not that she hadn't been a challenge—she'd kicked my ass—but I'd been expecting to match my wits with Vic. I'd also missed hanging out with him afterwards. Now that I know him better, I like talking to him.

Now, I drain the last of my rum and coke and scan the tiny club. I don't see Piper or her band members anywhere, so they must still be backstage. The next band is setting up, so I watch them until I see Piper heading in my direction.

She's back in her leather jacket and looking savage in her white foundation and black lipstick. The minute she gets to me, she pulls me into a hug. "I'm so glad you're here."

"You guys were amazing."

"Thanks. The other bands are douchebags. They all think they're the next Alice in Chains, and they are so, very, very wrong. We're leaving. You're coming with us."

That's fine with me. Watching her band play is the only reason I would come out to a place like this, anyway.

"Let's go!" She takes my hand and drags me out the back way. I immediately feel better. Piper seems to actually like me, and I've wanted a friend who isn't a dude for so long. The fact that she's a cool person is just icing on the proverbial cake.

# CHAPTER ELEVEN

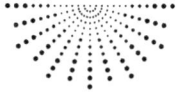

Vic's not home.

We were supposed to meet today. He usually stands out on the street at the entrance to his apartment so he can let me in. It's April now, and tentative flowers are blooming everywhere. At Vic's building, nature is bursting through the concrete via a cluster of flowering weeds growing from the cracks in the sidewalk.

At first, I figure he's late, but as more time passes, I wonder if he forgot about our meeting. If he did, that sucks. He sucks. But maybe something came up. So I head to O'Shea's to see if he's around. It's still a couple hours before happy hour, and there aren't many patrons. I don't recognize the bartender but go up to him anyway.

"Hey. Do you know if, uh, Vic is anywhere around here?'

The guy shrugs. "I don't know anyone named Vic. Sorry. I'm new," he adds, as if he senses someone named Vic might typically be in the bar.

"It's okay," I assure him.

"Can I get you anything?" he asks.

*Why the hell not?* Vic is awol, so I might as well have a drink. "Yeah, I'll have an Irish coffee." O'Shea's has the best Irish coffee. First, they make it with top notch coffee, from beans they grind fresh in house every day. And second, they put a dollop of real whipped cream on top.

I take a seat. Someone slides on to the stool next to me, and I glance over. It's Kane O'Shea.

He smiles at me. "Noelle, isn't it?"

I've met him a couple times before, but it's been a while since I've seen him in the bar. I'm surprised he remembers my name.

"Yeah. Hi...Kane." I feel odd calling him by his first name since I don't know him well. But it would be even stranger to call him Mr. O'Shea.

Kane's a person who's hard to place, age-wise. His hair has gone completely white, and his face is latticed with wrinkles, especially around the eyes. But those eyes glitter with the spark of a much younger man, and when he moves, he's spry.

"Looking for Vic?" he asks.

"Yes." I look up as the bartender places my coffee in front of me and thank him. "Is he around somewhere?"

Kane nods. "On his way. He thought you might come in here, so he wanted me to let you know."

The relief I feel is tangible, though I'm mildly annoyed. I take a large gulp of my Irish coffee. It's delicious. The coffee is strong, and the new bartender was generous with the whiskey.

"Does he expect me to wait for him?"

Kane's eyes dance. "If you want to."

"Did he tell you when he's coming back?"

Now he full-on smiles. "He said he'd be here soon."

I sigh. *Soon* could mean anything. It could mean ten minutes or two hours. I'm not keen on waiting two hours for Vic to show up.

"Thanks for letting me know," I say to Kane, politely. "I think I'll finish my drink first, but then I'm leaving. If he misses me, please let him know I was here."

Kane nods sagely. "That sounds like a reasonable plan."

"I think it is." I take a small sip of my coffee.

"His loss if he doesn't get back to you in time." Kane gets up and slides off the barstool. Then he holds out his hand. "Good to see you again, Noelle."

"Thank you." I shake his hand, which is another confusing mix of old and young. The skin on them already has age spots, but his grip is firm and strong.

He leaves, and I take another tiny sip of coffee. I love being in O'Shea's when it's busy, when every table is full, and it's difficult to find a seat at the bar. But I like it now, too. You can feel the foundational hum of the place, something that's always here, but difficult to discern when there are more people and activity.

The Irish coffee is lovely, but I know I'm savoring the rest of it because I'm hoping Vic will show up. Unfortunately, when the coffee is finally drained, there's still no sign of him.

The new bartender comes over. "You want another?"

I hesitate, then make up my mind. "No, thanks. Just the bill."

I pay my bill and leave a tip, then head for the door. I've waited long enough. I hitch my bag more firmly over my shoulder and turn the doorknob. And there, in the open doorway, is Vic.

He looks surprised but recovers quickly. "You waited."

"You changed our meeting time and didn't tell me."

"I'm sorry," he says. "I understand if you can't do this today."

I roll my eyes at him. "Don't be ridiculous. I live for these sessions with you. If we cancel, how will I even make it through the days and hours until next week?"

"Sarcasm!" Vic says, brightly. "Almost forgot it existed." He steps aside and holds the door open for me. "After you."

I make a face at him, which just makes him laugh. I can still hear him chuckling as he lets the door to O'Shea's fall shut and follows me to his building entrance.

———

TODAY, we're working on blending a few different techniques, including groin strikes and eye gouging. Eye gouging is a self-defense technique that makes me want to vomit when I think about using it on a real, unprotected human being. But that's one of the reasons for practicing these techniques—the repetition trains you to react without thinking when you're in mortal danger.

74

As gruesome as it is, eye gouging isn't easy to execute. When people think of doing it, they imagine their target will be absolutely still and that their own fingers will be like talons of steel. In reality, the average person's fingers aren't strong enough to function as talons of steel, and in a fight, it's almost guaranteed your target will be moving. We've been practicing techniques to get around this reality.

Vic is calling out different scenarios, and the moves to deal with them, which I'm trying to execute on the training dummy. It has value, because it always helps to train your mind to think through different moves and combinations of moves to get them coded in your body and brain.

But the training dummy is a poor substitute for an actual grappling partner.

After Vic calls time, he gets a bottle of water and tosses it to me. I un-cap it and take a long swig.

"Hey, can I ask you something?" I'm wired. It's got to be the Irish coffee. It wasn't a shit ton of caffeine, and I'm not drunk on the whiskey. But I feel both looser and more feisty than usual.

"Ask away," Vic says.

"Don't you think it'd be good if we did some sparring? Like, let me practice all these techniques on you?"

When he doesn't answer, I gesture across the room to the cubbies with the protective gear. "I mean, you have the right equipment, don't you? Protective goggles?"

"Yeah, I have the right equipment."

"So, let's do it!"

He smiles at me, then shakes his head no.

"Why not?"

"I'll have Sheryl back to do some more sparring with you."

"But if I'm going to get a realistic sense of the kind of person who'd attack me, that would probably be someone like you, right? Not someone like Sheryl."

"Sheryl kicked your ass last time she was here," he points out.

"I know, but it's not the same. It's not as...scary."

"Are you scared of me?" he asks.

I drain the rest of my water and walk over to him, then stop just outside the enclosed area where the mini fridge is. I set the empty plastic bottle on the narrow countertop of the enclosure and grin at him. Then I aim a playful side kick at his solar plexus.

Like lightning, his hand shoots out and grabs my foot.

I hop on my other foot, laughing. "C'mon. Let me go and spar with me."

"I don't spar with students."

"But that's crazy. How are we gonna learn how to use what you teach us?" I wriggle out of his grasp, but only because he's loosened it. His hands are like steel. He must be training with people somewhere.

"You'll learn," he says.

I aim another mischievous kick at him, but he quickly moves out of the way, leaving me off balance. His face is expressionless, and I can't read his eyes. I wonder if he's pissed. I try one more time.

"You were late, remember? You owe me."

"I do owe you," he says. "How about a burger? I'll pay for it."

I don't want to let it go, but I'm hungry and I was bummed we didn't have a meal together last time, so I give in.

The only two stools available at O'Shea's are at the very end of the bar, the same place I always used to see Vic sit when I first started coming in here. Aidan is back behind the bar, but Kane has disappeared again.

We each order a Guinness and a burger.

"So, when is Sheryl coming back to spar?" I still think it's stupid that Vic won't spar with me, but I do want the practice. Sheryl is better than nobody, and she's powerful.

"Don't take it personal," he says.

"Take what personal?"

"Me not sparring with you. It's just something I don't do."

"Sure, whatever."

Aidan drops a Guinness in front of each of us, and we both say "thanks" in unison.

The bartender gives a surprised laugh. "You're welcome."

"I get what you're saying," Vic goes on. "About testing your skills. Most real threats *are* men. But most of the game is also in here." He

76

taps his temple. "Fights are won in the mind and your muscle memory."

I was planning to let this go, but he's the one who brought it up. "How can I build muscle memory for fighting someone bigger than me if I don't fight someone bigger than me?"

He grins. "I'm not that much bigger than you."

"You're big enough," I retort. Weirdly, the words sound sexual. I blush.

"Thanks for reaffirming my manliness," he says, drily.

I can't tell if he's being self-deprecating or if he's flirting, and I'm not sure why I'm even thinking this way. Vic now qualifies as someone I know. I'm training with him in an unofficial capacity. We have mutual acquaintances and a mutual friend in Conan. I don't get involved with men I know, and that makes Vic automatically off limits. Strangers are best. Strangers can be dangerous, but strangers won't invade your life and fool you into thinking they're safe—especially if you make sure they remain strangers.

"Okay, fine. You don't spar with students," I say. "I won't bother you about it again."

"I'd appreciate that." He glances at me. "So, when are you going to sign up to test for your black belt?"

I shrug. "I don't know."

"When was your last level up?"

"Over a year ago, I guess."

"Don't you want to advance?"

"Sure. Maybe. I don't know. It doesn't matter. The school is like family. That's what matters."

He gives me an enigmatic look and holds it until I feel squirmy.

"If it's like family," he says, finally, "don't you want to grow up?"

"I don't follow you."

"In a martial arts environment, moving through the belt system is kind of like growing up. A year's a long time to stand still. You should be hungry for it."

"It's a year and counting," I correct him.

"So, you should definitely do it, then."

I give him a quizzical look. "Did Conan tell you to give me a hard time? You don't have to be his messenger guy. I'll tell him to stop it tomorrow when I go in for class—"

Vic puts his hand on my arm. I stare at it, and he removes it immediately. My skin feels warm where his fingers were, like each individual digit was burned into my flesh, only it's not exactly painful. I look up at him.

"I apologize," he says. "But no, Conan didn't tell me to give you a hard time. *I'm* giving you a hard time."

"Why?"

"Because I think you should do it."

"Why?" I repeat.

"It'll make you more confident. And a better fighter."

"No," I meet his eyes. "I mean, why do *you* care if I do it? You're getting what you wanted from me, right? A reason to feel useful? Why do you care if I pass my black belt test?"

I see a flash of annoyance in his eyes. "I'm training you to be a deadly fighter in street situations," he reminds me. "Why wouldn't I want you to be at the top of your game? Do you think it's strange when Conan pushes you to improve?"

"No, but that's his job. What do you do, anyway? What's your job?" I smile when I ask the question so he won't feel like I'm trying to interrogate him, but I want to know. He must do something. At the very least, he goes somewhere to train several times per week. That must cost him money. Where does his money come from? It can't all be from the rent Kane pays him.

He smiles back at me, a disarming smile that leaves me feeling lightheaded. Or maybe that's just imbibing a Guinness on an empty stomach right after a workout.

Aidan swoops in with our plates then. "Sorry it took so long. Kitchen's a bit backed up tonight. One fryer down. Can I get you folks anything else?"

"I'm good," I tell him.

"Not to worry," Vic adds.

I'm not letting this go. "So, what do you do? Where do you work?"

Vic's still smiling the same smile as he says, "I'm the proverbial jack of all trades and master of none."

"So, what, you do odd jobs for Kane and his friends? Teach free-lance martial arts classes?"

He laughs. "Yeah, sometimes!"

He's not going to crack. He's not going to tell me why he gives a shit about my black belt status, and he's not going to tell me what his actual job is. "Must be nice owning a building," I mutter.

"Tell you what," he says. "I'll make you a deal. If you sign up for the test, and if you pass, I'll spar with you—if you still want to by then."

I start to make a crack about how he shouldn't flatter himself—it's not like sparring with him is the one thing I want most in the world—but then stop to consider the offer. Maybe sparring with him isn't the *ultimate* thing I want, but I want it pretty bad. I want to see him in action. I want to know what his fighting style is like. I want to find out just how close I can get to besting him.

"You know," I wheedle, "if you want me to be more confident, I'd definitely feel more confident if you let me fight you."

"I want you to be confident because you're crushing it. Not because of me. Anyway, that's the deal. Black belt, or we don't spar. Take it or leave it."

I'm inclined to keep arguing with him, but I can tell by the look on his face that his mind is made up. I'm getting familiar with that look.

"Fine," I say. "I'll do it. I'll tell Conan."

"Yeah?" He grins. "Just telling Conan about it isn't enough. You have to actually take the test and pass it."

"I'll take the fucking test. And I'll pass it. And then maybe I'll kick your ass, too, since I'll be at the top of my game and so filled with confidence."

"You're on. But what do I get if you bail on the test?"

"License to ridicule me in public every time you see me. But I'm not going to bail."

He holds out a hand. "Let's shake on it."

We shake hands, and then he says, "Can we stop talking about this for a bit? I'm starving."

"Fine by me."

We both attack our burgers, which are delicious, as usual. I feel good, but also strange, like I'm filled with restless energy. When I reach for my beer, I almost knock it over, but Vic stops it from toppling. A bit sloshes on his hand and he wipes it with a cocktail napkin.

"Good save." I nod at the napkin. "Sorry about that."

"No problem." This time his grin is wicked. "But if you're going to kick my ass, better work on those reflexes."

"Shut up and eat your burger."

He chuckles but mercifully goes back to eating. For a split second I wonder if I've made a mistake with this deal. Then I decide: no, I haven't. I'm ready to get my black belt, that's all. Vic just helped me figure it out.

# CHAPTER TWELVE

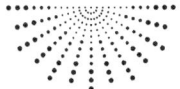

The following week, Piper and I meet at O'Shea's for breakfast. I haven't seen her without her band members for what feels like a long time, even though it's probably only been a month. I wanted to hang without them for once. So now, we're at one of the tables along the windows that face the street.

"This place is adorable," Piper says.

"Adorable?" I echo. O'Shea's has a certain understated charm, but *adorable* is not the way I would describe the ambience.

Now Piper frowns. "No, you're right. That's not the right word. It's…quaint? No, that's not it either. Old fashioned? All that gorgeous wood at the bar."

"Kane's really proud of that," I agree. "They take good care of it."

"I bet. It smells so good in here, too. I can't believe I've never been here before!"

"It's not exactly a goth hang out."

Piper makes a dismissive noise. "I dig the goth aesthetic, and I like goth music and culture. But I like lots of things that aren't goth. Like Van Halen. Sven and Mandy hate them."

"Hate who?" Vic asks. In typical Vic fashion, he's materialized at the edge of our table without announcing himself.

"Van Halen," Piper informs him.

"Who hates Van Halen?"

"I don't hate Van Halen," I say.

"I don't hate them either," Piper explains. "I'm just saying they're not a treasured entity in the goth universe, but I'm still into them."

"Too much spandex for the goths?" Vic guesses.

"Too much fun," she says, laughing. "Hey, speaking of fun, we're having this band dinner thing tonight. It's at this Italian restaurant up on Capitol Hill?" She looks from Vic to me. "You should both come."

"To your band dinner?" I ask, dubious.

Vic just raises his eyebrows and smiles. "Thanks for the invite. Listen, I didn't mean to disturb you ladies. Enjoy your breakfast."

Piper stares at him as he goes out the door. "Who is *that*? He's delicious."

"That's Vic."

"Vic? Oh wait." She stares at me. "Vic? *The* Vic? Your ninja training guy?"

I don't bother to explain to her that ninjas have very little to do with the skills I'm learning from Vic, or that the martial art I practice is Korean in origin, not Japanese. I stand up.

"Actually, I have to ask him something real quick. Can you give me a minute?"

"Sure!" She picks up her menu. "I'll just be here, drooling over this."

"Be right back." I dash out the door.

When I get outside, Vic has already crossed the street, heading away from O'Shea's.

"Vic!" I call out.

He turns around, and when he sees me moving in his direction, he stops and waits for me to catch up with him. When I do he raises his eyebrows again. "What's going on, Noelle?"

"Hey," I say. "I'm sorry that Piper thought you and me were, like, a couple or something. You know, the band dinner invite? I never said anything to her about us being...anything."

He gives me one of his eye smiles. "I didn't think that."

"Oh." I falter. "Well. Okay. Good. Good, I'm glad you didn't think that. That's good."

"So, are you going? To her band dinner?"

"I don't know. Probably. She wants me to, but it will be…awkward. I mean, it's a band dinner. I'm not in the band. Why would you invite somebody who isn't even in your band to a band dinner? And who has a band dinner on a Wednesday?" I feel like I'm babbling. I am. I am babbling. *Why am I babbling, for fuck's sake?*

"When is it?" he asks.

"The band dinner?"

He nods, patiently.

"I'm not sure. I can ask her. They're all nocturnal creatures so uh, probably not before eight?"

"Are you going to feel out of place if you go alone?" he asks.

"It's okay. I'm used to feeling uncomfortable hanging out with Piper and her band. I do it all the time."

Come to think of it, I'm feeling uncomfortable now. I'm not sure what possessed me to run out the door after Vic, but the minute Piper said he was *delicious* I had a strong urge to follow him, so I gave in to it. And now I'm out here, babbling at him.

"She invited both of us," he points out. "Tell you what. If it's later, say after seven, why don't I tag along? What's the name of her band?"

"Primal Malice?"

"Huh. I think I've actually seen that name around. Well, now I *want* to go." He smiles, and I'm pretty sure it's genuine. "Why don't you give me a call around seven and let me know when dinner is?"

"I don't have your number." We've never called each other to set up our sessions. We reconfirm our next meeting each time I work with him.

Vic reaches inside his coat and pulls out a notepad and pen. I wonder what else he has in his pockets. Snacks? Weapons? Pet mice? The possibilities are endless.

He writes on one of the pages, then tears it off and hands it to me. "If I don't pick up right away, just leave a message on the machine. I'll get back to you."

"Are you sure you want to go?" I ask, taking the paper from him and slipping it in my pocket.

"Why not? Figure I should stay in touch with what you kids are up to these days." He winks at me. "Don't want to lose my edge."

"Okay. I'll, uh…call you tonight."

"Talk soon," he agrees, then starts back down the street. I return to O'Shea's and rejoin Piper at our table.

"So, is your sensei coming to dinner?" Piper asks. Her voice is a shade too casual.

"Sensei is Japanese," I correct her. "Taekwondo is Korean. And he's not even teaching me taekwondo, we're working on self-defense."

Piper blinks. "Okay. Is your self-defense instructor coming to dinner?"

"Maybe," I tell her. "If he can make it."

"I think I'm having the French toast with orange marmalade," she says. "Are you ready to order?"

After breakfast, we split up for the day. I head straight to the school to talk to Conan. I still haven't told him about my intention to test for my black belt. I wait until he's done with his class, then corner him at the front desk.

"I want to sign up for the black belt test in June." It's strange to hear the words come out of my mouth. Conan looks shocked, too. For a moment I feel light-headed, and I want to run for the door. But I keep my feet planted on the floor. "Is my attendance record good enough?" I press.

"Let me check." Conan grabs the attendance log from one of the desk drawers and flips through it.

"What does it say?" I hear a loud tapping noise, and turn my head to see who or what is causing it. Then I realize it's my own foot thumping against the floor. Embarrassed, I tuck it behind the opposite leg.

Conan looks up. "You need to keep up attendance for the rest of the week. One more class. Then you can sign up for the test."

"Okay. Then I'll be back to sign up for the test first thing next week."

Conan's tone is level. "You have class Thursday morning. That's tomorrow."

"I'll be here," I promise.

"See you tomorrow," Conan says. It sounds like a challenge—because it is.

I know I've given him plenty of reasons to doubt I'll show up, but I also know I'm going to do it.

"See you tomorrow!" I say cheerfully as I head out the door. I stop by the grocery store to pick up a few things for me and Milo. I have the afternoon free, so I want to chill with him until it's time to get ready for Piper's dinner.

I'm flattered whenever Piper asks me to tag along with her band, but hanging with them never feels natural for me. They're always polite, but I figure that's because they know she's made their band better. They need her, so she's allowed to bring whoever she wants along for the ride. The thing is, around them I'm "Piper's friend." I think that's why I wish we could hang out alone more, like we did the night we drank too much tequila in her apartment.

She calls to tell me she'll pick me up at eight. "I can take both you guys," she says, "if Vic is coming?"

I can hear the barely disguised eagerness in her voice. "He probably is," I confirm. "I'll call him."

"Okay. Either way, see you at eight."

I pull Vic's number out of the pocket of my jeans. His handwriting is spiky and confident. I take it over to the phone and dial his number, and it rings several times before he picks up.

"Vic here."

"Hey, Vic. It's Noelle. So, um, I heard from Piper about dinner. She's picking me up at eight. Or both of us, if you still want to go?"

"She doesn't need to pick us up," Vic says. "I can drive us. Where's dinner at?"

"Oh, um…" I feel dumb because I forgot to ask her. "I'll have to call her back."

"Why don't you do that, and tell me where we're going. Then *I'll* pick you up at eight."

I call Piper back, fill Vic in on the restaurant location, then take a shower and get dressed. On a whim, I curl a few pieces of my hair into ringlets to frame my face, and add a little eyeliner and lipstick as a finishing touch.

Then I drift to the window seat to wait for Vic, wondering if I should wait out on the street instead. I'm not sure I want him to come up here and see my tiny studio apartment. It would suck if he felt sorry for me.

I also wonder why he agreed to go to dinner tonight. He didn't have to. Maybe he's bored? Or maybe he thinks it will be good for a few laughs.

When I hear a knock at the door, I jump. Milo, however, is unfazed. He makes a tiny querying noise, then goes back to surveying the street.

At the door, I stand on tiptoe to see out the peephole. It's Vic.

"Hey," I say as I open the door. "I'm ready to go, so we can—"

"Hey, Noelle." He peers past me into my apartment. "Oh, wow, is that a window seat?"

"Yeah..."

"And you've got a cat!"

"Yes, correct on both counts."

"Do you mind if I take a look real quick? Car's parked right outside."

I hold the door aside. "Sure. Come in."

He walks straight to the window seat. I expect Milo to jump up and run away, but he stays put. He even lets Vic pat him absentmindedly on the head without protest. I shut the apartment door and walk over to them.

"Nice little view you got," Vic says.

"It's nothing like yours."

He doesn't dispute me. "But it's interesting, right? I bet you see crazy shit go down all the time from here."

"Sometimes. Mostly at night, though. It's boring in the daytime."

He looks at me with curiosity in his eyes. "Do you sit here a lot? Contemplate your life?"

Both questions hit me as too intimate. "Yeah, I guess. Listen, we probably better go. I don't want to be late. Piper will be pissed off."

Piper won't actually be pissed if we're late. She'd probably be disappointed if I didn't show up with Vic, but it's hard to make her truly angry.

Vic takes the hint anyway. "Bye, kitty." He gives Milo one last pat on the head, and we go out.

"So, how long have you known Piper?" Vic asks, as he pulls out of his parking spot. He did find a good one, two car lengths down from the front of my building.

"We've been working at the diner together for…I dunno. A couple of years? But we just started hanging out in January, so almost three months, I guess."

"Has she been with this band of hers the whole time?"

Again, I note the combination of carefulness and confidence with which Vic drives. It makes me feel safe. "She wasn't in the band when we first started hanging out. She hadn't even played in a band. I guess I inspired her to audition, or something. Then she did, and everything happened really fast."

"Do you think she's into you?"

I turn my head and stare at him. "Are you saying you think Piper has a crush on me?"

He shrugs and smiles. "Maybe."

I laugh. "Oh, hell no. She's into you. That's why she invited you."

He shares my laugh. "She's not into me. What makes you think that?"

I start to tell him how Piper called him delicious, then decide maybe she wouldn't want me to do that. To be on the safe side, I merely say, "Trust me. She's into you."

"Well, this evening could be more interesting than I thought," Vic muses.

I silently agree.

Vic finds parking just a few yards away from the restaurant, and he grins with satisfaction. "I'm usually lucky with parking," he explains.

"That's a very practical way to be lucky," I observe.

"Isn't it?" He looks over at me. "So do we need a signal?"

"A signal?"

"Yeah. Like, if it gets too awkward or you just want to bail for whatever reason. What's our signal?"

I laugh. "I don't know. I could do a hammer fist on your leg. But I guess that only works if we're sitting next to each other."

"Hard no. I'm not getting anywhere near sparring with you. Not until you get that black belt."

"I talked to Conan about signing up for the test today," I tell him.

"Why'd you just talk about it? Why didn't you sign up?"

"Because I need one more day of perfect attendance before they'll let me."

His tone is almost stern. "You're gonna make it, right?"

"That's the plan," I retort.

He pounds his fist into his other hand. "I thought of a signal. I'll ask how your food is. And if you say it's good, then I know you want to stay. But if you say it's salty, then that's the signal you want to leave."

"I guess that works. Salty means leave?"

"Salty means leave," he nods, then smiles at me. "You ready?"

We get out of the car and he drops a few coins in the grey, double-headed parking meter. As we're walking toward the restaurant he says, casually, "You look nice tonight, by the way."

"Oh." I'm startled. "Uh...thanks."

He opens the door for me. "Let's see what shenanigans we can get into, shall we?"

The restaurant is surprisingly spacious. Piper sees us almost the moment we walk in. She starts waving wildly, so we go over to her.

"We saved you seats!" she exclaims.

She's in all black, and, as usual, so is the rest of the band. Sven and Mandy give us each a cursory nod. Bill is his same friendly self.

The seats they've saved for us are next to each other. Piper ushers me in first, so I'm sitting by Bill on the other side. Vic is right across from Piper.

"We ordered wine," she says, and gestures for Sven to pass a carafe of wine from the end of the table.

"There's, like—bread," Mandy gestures to a basket. I swear, it sounds as if the very existence of the bread makes her sad.

Piper pours wine into a glass for me, and her eyes are sparkling. When she moves to the one in front of Vic's place setting, he puts a hand over the mouth of the glass.

"None for me, thanks."

88

"Oh. Are you training for something? Sometimes Noelle doesn't like to drink because she's got to stay in shape for karate."

"Taekwondo," I mutter, under my breath.

"No," Vic says, smiling at her. "I just prefer not to have any. Is that all right?"

"Of course." Piper sits down.

Bill is fidgeting beside me. "Hey, Piper, why don't you introduce Noelle's friend to us."

I'm impressed. Bill actually knows my name. I'd bet that, ten seconds ago, if you'd asked either Sven or Mandy, they wouldn't have.

Piper smiles at Vic. "We weren't actually formally introduced this morning."

Vic addresses the whole table. "Vic. I'm Noelle's friend."

I feel strangely warm inside when he says that. I don't think it's the wine, because I've only had one sip. But I like being called his friend. I reach for the bread basket and take a slice, then hand it over to Vic.

"And who do I have the pleasure of dining with this evening?" Vic asks as he takes the basket.

His tone is overly formal, and I have a hunch he's doing it on purpose. I have to work hard not to laugh as I butter my bread. Or put spread on the bread. This isn't the kind of restaurant where they leave out pats of cold fresh butter on a plate. This is the kind of place where they put margarine packets wrapped in foil in a mug. But at least they're chilled.

"I'm Bill," Bill calls out from the end of the table. "I'm the drummer."

Everything is silent after that. Vic gestures to Sven. "So, who are you, and what do you play?"

"Sven." He seems irritated by having to say his name aloud. "Guitar," he adds as an afterthought.

Mandy speaks in a monotone without prompting. "I'm Mandy. I play bass."

"And I'm Piper!" she says cheerfully. "So now that we're all introduced..."

"What do you play?" Vic interrupts. He seems focused on her, and suddenly I wonder if he's into her. I can't be certain, because it's a bit too dark in here, but I think maybe her skin is flushed.

"Piper's our leader," Bill breaks in, loudly. "She sings, plays guitar, writes phenomenal songs. We love her. She's fantastic."

My head whips around to stare at Bill. Sure, he's friendly, but spontaneous declarations of affection aren't something I've ever heard him do. Mandy gives him a surreptitious glance from underneath her lashes. She notices it, too. He's completely out of character.

"It must be gratifying to be so admired by your bandmates," Vic says, gravely.

Piper gives Bill a look. "Bill's just flattering me."

"We do love Piper," Mandy says. "She makes the best mixed drinks."

I pick up the bread basket, and pass it to Bill. "Want some bread?"

He takes a slice and begins slapping margarine on it. At the same time, Mandy leans her head against Piper's shoulder. "I love your mixed drinks."

I know I shouldn't care, it's petty, but I feel jealous. Piper's never made me a cocktail, unless pouring cheap tequila into a glass counts as a cocktail. Apparently, we're not on the cocktail-making level of friendship.

"Do you have a specialty?" Vic asks her. "What's your best drink?"

"Kind of whatever's around at my place," Piper says. "I get creative. I make my own variation of Sex on the Beach."

I reach for the bread basket again, and Sven speaks up suddenly. "More bread already? You haven't even finished your first piece."

At first I'm stunned someone is questioning my decision to help myself to more bread. Then I get combative. "I know I'm going to want more when I'm done. What's the problem? Did I take your favorite piece or something?"

I might be imagining it, but I think I hear Vic stifle a laugh next to me.

"Hey, here's our waitress!" Piper calls out. "Is everyone ready to order?"

As it turns out, everyone is not ready to order, so there's a scramble while we all pick up the menus and try to decipher the menu listings in the dim light.

"Is this fettuccine or something else?" Mandy asks, pointing to her menu and looking up. "I can't see all the letters."

"You know," the waitress says, sounding uncertain, "I can just come back? Maybe a little later when all of you are ready..."

Vic folds up his menu and hands it to her. "I'll have lasagna, please."

Following his lead, I also fold up my menu. "I'll have the stuffed manicotti."

Piper takes the hint and places her order immediately after.

"I'll have lasagna, as well," Bill says, standing up to hand his menu to the waitress.

Sven looks up. "Do you serve spaghetti?"

The waitress gives a barely perceptible sigh. "Yes. We serve spaghetti."

Once our meals are ordered, we all fall back to a state of restless silence, that is, all of us except for Piper and Vic.

"I can't believe I haven't met you before now," Piper tells him. "Noelle talks about you all the time."

Vic glances over at me. "She does, huh?"

I shrug and try to catch Mandy's eye, in case she's onto Piper's game. I think she is, but now, she's incredibly absorbed in cutting individual servings of margarine into smaller and smaller pieces on her bread plate. Several of the empty foil packets are stacked next to it.

"Do you think you could teach me self-defense?" Piper asks Vic.

"Do you have any martial arts training?"

"No. But I want to learn some good self-defense moves. That's what you're teaching Noelle, isn't it?"

"Yeah. It is," Vic agrees. "Listen, Piper, I'd love to help you out, but I only work with people who have significant martial arts experience. If you want, I could ask around. I'm sure I could find someone for you."

"Or you could come down to my school and sign up for a class," I offer, helpfully. "They have a self-defense class. No prior martial arts skills required."

"Maybe I'll do that!" Piper says brightly, but I'm not sure if she's pleased. If she was angling for a way to get closer to Vic, taking a self-defense class that doesn't involve him won't cut it.

Sven speaks up from the end of the table. "When's the food coming? Did they say? I'm hungry."

I silently pass him the bread, then turn to Vic. "You should go see their band play sometime. They're pretty great."

Before Vic can respond, Mandy fixes her gaze on me. "Have you seen us play?"

"Um, yeah? Like, quite a few times?"

Piper nudges her. "She was at our first show. And almost every show after that."

"And she's been at a couple rehearsals, too," Bill chimes in.

I turn to him gratefully. "I remember you gave me a milk crate at Piper's audition."

Bill's pleasant expression freezes on his face. "A milk crate?"

"I mean, you know, to sit on? So, I wouldn't have to sit on the floor or stand or, you know... I remember the milk crate," I finish weakly.

Vic's voice cuts through the faltering conversation. "So what kind of music do you all play?"

"Ethereal," Mandy says. "Gothic ethereal."

"I listen to a lot of industrial," Sven adds.

"Bill likes those grunge bands," Mandy says suddenly, but she doesn't sound as if she approves.

"Matt Cameron and Sean Kinney are amazing rock drummers. I'm a rock drummer. Of course I like their bands," Bill explains. "How'd you describe our music, Piper?"

She shrugs. "I'd describe it as good. But that's because of you guys."

"She's a truly amazing singer," Bill goes on, speaking directly to Vic. "She fit in from the first day. She's one of us."

"One of us," Mandy repeats.

"One of us," Sven raises his wine glass. All four of them pick up their wine glasses and clink them across the table, then chant in unison, "One of us!"

My head swivels toward Vic with what feels like a will of its own.

"Guess we're not one of them," he mutters, out of the side of his mouth.

"Thank fuck?" I mutter back.

He stifles a laugh, and I do the same.

Piper catches my eye and raises her glass again. "Here's to all of us!"

We toast. Vic uses his water glass, and I wonder why he's not drinking. I've certainly seen him drink before.

As soon as our food comes and we've settled into eating our meals, Piper turns to Vic again.

"Noelle's right. You should come to one of our shows. We'll put you on the guest list, so you can try before you buy."

"You don't need to do that," Vic says. "I like to support artists, especially local ones. I can pay a cover charge. It won't kill me."

"Okay." Piper smiles at him, her most generous, winning smile. "We can argue about that later."

"Hey, Vic," Bill says from the other end of the table. "How's that lasagna treating you?"

Bill is agitated about something, and I'm not sure what it is. Maybe he doesn't like Vic? Maybe it's me—though he's always been friendly to me. Or maybe it's because Mandy passive-aggressively attacked him for liking grunge bands? All I know is that this dinner is turning out exactly the way I expected it would.

Vic takes Bill's random lasagna question in stride. "It's treating me pretty good. A hell of a lot of cheese, though. How's yours?"

"Oh, you know. It's lasagna." Bill laughs a bit hectically. "It's hard for lasagna to be anything else. It's always going to be lasagna."

"That's...true," Vic agrees.

Piper fixes her eyes on him again, and says, "We have a show in town a month from now. Guest list or not, you should come."

"I'll try to make it," Vic promises.

"I'd love that. We all would." Piper indicates the rest of her band-mates with her eyes.

For a while, our motley posse continues the attempt to make casual conversation while digging into our food, but there's a discernible level of discomfort that makes me feel, well—awkward.

Vic nudges me. "How's the manicotti?"

I look hard at him. Does he want to leave? Maybe he'd rather stay and get to know Piper better. Then again, if he wanted to stay, he could have conveniently "forgot" to ask about my food.

"The manicotti's a bit salty," I say.

He nods. "Maybe there's something we can do about that."

"What's wrong?" Piper asks.

"Oh, nothing," I say. "My meal's just salty."

She makes a face. "Mine too. I think I need more pepper to balance it out. Hey, could we get the pepper down here, guys?"

Bill picks up the pepper shaker from the end of the table and passes it to me. I start to hand it over to Piper, but she says, "You first."

I start shaking the pepper on top of my meal.

Vic clears his throat. "It's been truly wonderful meeting all of you, but Noelle has a test tomorrow, and I promised her I'd get her back home in time to get a good night's sleep."

"Oh, like a martial arts thing?" Piper asks.

"Yeah, it's just a basic skills test," I lie, since Vic has kind of forced my hand.

He nudges my elbow. "Maybe Piper would like the pepper now."

It's fuzzy in the dim light, but it looks like I've deposited a small mountain of pepper on top of my manicotti.

I hand the shaker over to Piper, then try to spread the pepper evenly over the remainder of my food. Honestly, I don't want more of it. It's heavy and cheesy and already sitting in my stomach like a ball of lead.

"Hey, Vic! How soon do you and Noelle need to leave?" Bill asks.

Vic looks at me for confirmation. "Now, I think, if you're all set?"

I can't read Piper. I don't know if she's mad at me, or maybe just disappointed that Vic is leaving. I wish he hadn't made me the reason we need to bail on dinner. But then I realize if he hadn't, he could just go without me.

"Yeah," I confirm. "I guess now would be a good time."

"Well, thanks for coming out tonight," Piper says. "If I'd known it was going to be a bad night for Noelle, I would have scheduled it for a different day."

Vic reaches into his pants pocket for his wallet and pulls out a small wad of bills. I do a double take. While it's not necessarily a ridiculous amount of cash, it's more than I'm used to seeing.

He peels off several bills and places them in front of Piper. "That's to cover me and Noelle. And a big tip."

Piper's eyes go wide, then she glances at me with a "what the fuck?" look on her face. I shrug one shoulder.

"Thanks, Vic," she takes the money. "That should cover it."

He stands up and looks down at me. "Ready to go?"

"Have a great evening, you two," Bill says as I stand up. There's more than the usual friendliness in his voice. He sounds relieved.

"I'll call you later," Piper says to me.

"Sorry about having to bail…"

"Don't worry about it. We'll talk later. Bye, Vic. Thanks for joining our little soiree."

She sounds suddenly cooler toward him, but maybe I'm imagining it.

"It was my pleasure," Vic says.

"Hey," Mandy speaks up. "Noelle, thanks for coming to our shows. Sorry I didn't know you were there. I get really…focused sometimes."

"It's cool." I smile at her. "See you next time."

Vic and I head out.

"So, was that awkward or was that awkward?" I ask.

He laughs. "It was all right. It was just people."

"Thanks for coming and being my buffer. It's super uncomfortable for me, for some reason." Then I admit, "I guess I'm not really Ms. Social myself."

We're at Vic's car, and he opens the passenger door for me. Oddly, the small gesture seems huge, and I'm suddenly shy as I say, "Thanks." Then I feel dumb. It's not like we're on a date.

# CHAPTER THIRTEEN

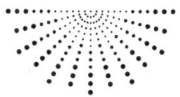

As Vic settles behind the wheel, I say, "I'm sorry if you wanted to spend more time with Piper. I can set you up with her, if you want."

"It's all right," he smiles over at me. "Piper's an interesting person, and I'm sure she's good at what she does. She has that kind of aura. But she's not my type."

He starts up the car as I wonder what his type is. Or, for that matter, what my type is. Since the end of high school, I generally lean toward guys I read as non-dangerous and non-serious. It's not a foolproof system, but so far, it's worked pretty well.

"How was the wine?" Vic asks. "Was it any good?"

"Well, I'm no wine connoisseur. But judging by my non-expert palate, I'd say it was pretty bad."

He laughs. "It even smelled bad. You want a real drink?"

Is he asking me to his place for a drink? Or is he suggesting we go somewhere else?

"What did you have in mind?" I ask.

"We could go to O'Shea's and see what Kane's up to. Or...I just got a brand-new bottle of Scotch. We could break it open. If you want."

"A bottle of Scotch?" I repeat.

"It was a gift. But I'm just as good with a drink at O'Shea's. Up to you."

"Is it expensive Scotch?"

"Not crazy expensive. But it was aged eighteen years. I think it was eighteen. More than ten, for sure."

"Okay." I settle against the seat. "I'm game. I'll try the Scotch, but I can't get drunk. I don't have that bogus test you fabricated. But I do have my class at the school tomorrow. You know, the one I need for my attendance record? So I can test for my black belt."

"Wouldn't dream of being the reason you miss class," he says. "Besides, you don't get drunk on good Scotch. You savor it."

"I'll take your word for it." I look out the car window. A sensation of complete calm steals over me. It's an unfamiliar feeling. I can't remember the last time I was this calm without also being drunk.

I look over at Vic. "How come you didn't have any wine with dinner?"

"Didn't we just discuss this? I could tell it was nasty just by looking at it."

"Was that the only reason you didn't have any?"

He clears his throat. "No."

"So, what's your other reason?"

"I don't drink anything when I drive. I had a DUI when I was nineteen. They threw me in jail for a couple of days, suspended my license for three months. Got slapped with a pretty hefty fine. So obviously I don't want to repeat that, but it was also a wake-up call. I was lucky I didn't hurt anyone other than myself."

I take a moment to digest what he just told me. "What about the night I saw you at the goth club? You were drinking then."

"I was walking that night. I like to walk. But I take cabs a lot, too."

"What's it like?" I ask. "I mean, getting arrested and going to jail."

He laughs. "Seriously?"

"Yeah, seriously."

"It sucks. But it also—well, for me at least—it gets you real clear on what's actually wrong and right."

"Huh," I say.

"Does that freak you out?" he asks.

"No. I've just never known anybody who got arrested. I was curious, that's all."

"Happy to help."

I go silent again until we're back at Vic's building.

"When do you need to be back home?" he asks as he unlocks the door.

"I'm not in a rush. I just need to get, like, five hours of sleep."

He turns to me. "You should get more sleep than that."

I grin. "I'll sleep when I'm dead."

Vic laughs. "You're making me feel old."

The calm sensation that came over me in his car is still with me. In his kitchen, I drape my coat over a barstool and sit on a different one as Vic goes to his liquor cabinet. He brings out the bottle and sets it on the countertop, then turns it so I can read the front label. "It was aged twenty years. Not eighteen."

"Does that mean it's better?"

"Supposed to." He looks at me, but hesitates. "You okay with glasses?"

The bottle is obviously brand new and never opened. And anyway, I trust him now. "Yeah. Glasses are fine."

As he goes to the cupboard, I say, "Hey, isn't this sacrilegious? Drinking Scotch whiskey instead of Irish whiskey, right over Kane O'Shea's Irish bar?"

He places two simple yet expensive-looking glass tumblers on the counter. "They're adjacent cultures, the Irish and the Scots. Distinct, but both Gaelic in origin. I think it's all right." He opens the bottle, carefully pours a portion of amber liquid in each glass, then hands me one. "Remember to sip it," he reminds me, as he picks up his own glass.

"No slamming, just sipping."

"You've got it." He knocks his glass gently against mine. "Cheers."

"Cheers."

The tumbler is fragrant as I lift it to sip.

"What do you think?" Vic asks.

"It's...amazing."

"Give it a minute and let it hit you. This *is* a good one."

"Are some of them bad?"

"Some of them are better than others. But I'd never say no to a bottle of Scotch."

"Oh," I say, "I feel it."

"Hits nice and smooth, doesn't it?"

I nod.

"Take another sip."

Before raising my glass, I glance over at his lonely looking couch. "Do you ever sit over there?"

"Not much," he chuckles. "Although sometimes when it's clear, I sit there so I can look at the stars."

"You can see the stars from here?"

"Yeah a few of them. When it's clear. You know," he says, "I could see the moon tonight when we left your friends. Maybe you can see the stars now."

Vic moves over to the wall and flips a switch. The lights in the kitchen go out, and it's dark in the spacious room except for the glow of street lamps coming through the windows.

He stops and peers through the glass. "There actually are a few stars. You want to see?"

Taking my drink, I walk over to him. The sky isn't pitch black, but it's inky, and I can see the moon plus a smattering of stars.

"City stars are never as impressive," he says, sounding apologetic.

But I can't remember the last time I looked at stars. Maybe when I was a kid? It's been ages. "I think they're beautiful," I say.

"Well, I kind of like them myself." He turns and gestures to the couch. "You wanna sit down? You can still see the stars."

I move to the couch and sit, and Vic takes a seat on the other end.

"Thanks for the real drink," I say. "Totally salvaged the night."

"Your friend's dinner wasn't awful," he says.

"No," I admit. "I know it wasn't awful. The goth thing just bugs me. I don't know why."

"It's just a different kind of armor."

I take another sip of whiskey. "I guess."

"You want to know what I think?" Vic asks.

I look over at him. "I'm not sure. Do I? Or would it maybe be better if you kept it to yourself?"

He laughs, surprised. "I can keep it to myself if you want."

I gaze at the faded stars through the window. I think about all of the stars that we can't see, the ones hidden by the city lights and what they might look like if we were somewhere further away from civilization. "Okay," I say. "Tell me what you think."

"You're sure?"

"Hit me."

"I think Piper's bandmates bug you because you were just starting to get to know her when they showed up. You wanted more time alone with her to build your friendship, but you didn't get it. So now, they irritate you because they're in the way of what you want."

I look at him. In the darkness he seems more like an outline of a person than a solid human being. I'm not sure he's right about me and Piper's bandmates, but he *is* right that I'm irritated—by him. "Are you one of those people who always assumes you know everything about every situation?"

"You said you wanted to know what I think," he reminds me.

"Sure."

"Am I wrong?"

To be fair, he sounds like he's genuinely asking the question, not rhetorically assuming he's right.

"I don't know," I say. "I don't have tons of friends who are women, you know? I don't click with them or something. But Piper actually likes me. I had fun hanging out with her, but she joined the band almost immediately and now we don't really hang out together anymore. I'm always following her and her band around...." I stop, and my words hang in the air. "Yeah. I wanted more time with her. I guess you're right."

"Why don't you just tell her you want to hang out, just the two of you?" Vic asks.

"Well..." I pause. "Because that would be too easy."

He laughs. "Can't have that."

"Absolutely not. Can't you think of some way to make this more complicated?" I look over at him again. He's already looking at me. We share a shadowed grin, then I break eye contact and take another taste of my drink.

"How's it treating you?"

"The, um, the Scotch?"

"Yeah. That."

"Good," I say. "It's good for star watching."

"Can't you see stars from that little window seat in your apartment?"

"The window must not be big enough. I mean, you know, for any of these stars."

"The ones that make it through the city lights," he adds.

"Right."

I hear him shift on the couch. "How'd you end up there? Or have you always lived in that apartment?"

I laugh. "No. I've just lived there a few years."

"So why'd you come here? To Seattle?"

I wonder which version of the story I should tell him. I decide on the honest version, but the one that's light on details. "I wasn't getting along great with my family, and it just seemed like it was time to move out on my own. That way they didn't have to be pissed at me all the time, and I didn't have to be pissed at them."

I'm afraid he's going to want to know why I wasn't getting along with my family, but instead he asks, "So, when did you meet Conan?"

"Like, almost five years ago. I started taking self-defense at the school first, then I moved on to taekwondo."

"Why taekwondo?"

"I mean, at first, I wanted to feel powerful. But it was more than that. I was watching a class one day, and it just seemed kind of beautiful, you know? And I wanted more of it. I guess that's a strange reason to study a martial art."

"I don't think it's strange to see something beautiful and want more of it," Vic says.

As soon as he says it, I feel the Scotch hit me, hard. My cheeks are hot and I'm light-headed. It's like I didn't realize I was actually drinking hard alcohol until now. At least, I think it's the Scotch. But I'm also hyper aware and alert, and I'm pretty sure that's not part of alcohol intoxication, to suddenly feel ten times as alive as you did one minute before.

"How did you get into martial arts?" I ask him, trying to push the feeling away. "And like, how many different styles do you know? Because I have a feeling it's a lot. A lot of different styles. Like at least five."

"I'm only good at two," he says.

"Which two?"

"Taekwondo, like you. And Aikido. Okay, a third one. Fighting dirty." He laughs. "Everything else is dabbling."

"I knew you practiced Aikido!" I exclaim. "The way you handled that guy at O'Shea's the night he was messing with me? You were totally manipulating his energy or something. I've never seen anyone do anything like it. How do you do that? How do you manipulate someone's energy like that?"

I'm pretty sure I'm babbling again. No—I'm positive I am.

"It's not really about manipulation. It's more about *sensing* their energy and using that awareness to put you in a better position to de-escalate the situation."

"Well, it totally looked like you were messing with his energy. I mean, totally."

"Are you okay?" Vic asks. "You seem kind of—freaked out?"

"Do I? You know what— What time is it?"

Vic looks at his watch. "Just after eleven."

"Just after eleven," I repeat. "You know what? Now that I think about it, I should probably get home. I have to feed my cat and take care of a couple other things, and by the time I get to sleep, you know, it's going to be pretty late." I know I'm not making sense. Earlier I told him I wasn't in a hurry. But now all I want is to leave.

"All right," he says. "I can walk you home."

"You don't need to walk me home, I'm fine. I didn't even finish this drink." I hold up the glass with the Scotch in it.

"I don't mind—"

"I don't want you to walk me home!" The words come out more forcefully than I meant them to.

"Are you sure you're okay?"

I stand up. "I'm fine. I just need to go. I'm sorry I didn't finish my drink. It was super nice of you to share that with me." *Super nice? God, I need to get out of here.*

"It's okay. If you need to go home, you should go."

"Yeah. I do." I walk over to the kitchen island and set the glass on the counter. Then I grab my coat and put it on.

Vic walks me to his door.

"You sure you don't want me to come with you?" he asks.

I suddenly feel very tired. "Don't walk me home."

He wants to argue with me, I can tell. But after a moment, he says, "Okay. Stay alert. I'll see you on Thursday. So I guess—tomorrow."

"Right. See you tomorrow."

I walk away from him, then down the stairs and into the street. He's right. I am agitated. I head straight to another bar that's about four blocks away from O'Shea's and only two blocks from my apartment. It's one of the places I go to pick up guys when I'm in the mood for physical distraction.

It doesn't take long to find one. I always choose guys who seem a little bewildered. Never the ones who intrigue me or the guys who are good at witty banter, and definitely not the ones who seem like they might be in search of something beyond a simple hookup. Somebody hot and shy is who I'm after, and I find him in less than fifteen minutes. I don't even finish the drink I ordered—it's just a prop anyway.

I take him back to my place, and once Milo sees me come in, he knows the drill. No food until I'm done with the guy. He goes and sits on the window seat with his back turned to the bed to express his displeasure.

The guy comes fast, and so do I. Once it's over and he falls asleep, I feel better. The strange light-headed, drunk-but-not-drunk sensation I was having at Vic's is gone. I get up and go to the kitchen to quietly feed Milo his pacification snack.

Then I fall back in bed and go to sleep.

I wake up to Milo sitting on top of me and light streaming through the glass over the window seat. It feels like it's later in the morning, maybe nine am.

*Nine am!* I have a class at ten. *Shit.*

The guy from last night is still sleeping in my bed, snoring lightly. I shake his shoulder.

"Hey. Hey…" I don't remember his name. "Hey, uh, big guy. You need to get up. Wake up."

Slowly, he shakes out of his sleep and opens his eyes. He sees me and smiles. "Good morning, beautiful."

"Yeah, good morning. Listen, you have to leave."

"No, I don't. I have the day off. I can stay in bed with you all day." He reaches for me, but I maneuver out of his grasp.

"That's nice, but I don't have the day off, and you need to leave. Now."

When he just stares at me with the same bewildered look that made him so appealing last night, I yell, "You need to leave, okay? You need to leave now!"

"Okay, okay. Jesus." He swings his legs over the side of the bed and scratches his head.

I groan and start gathering his things from the floor, dropping them in his lap. "There's your clothes. Get dressed."

Milo follows me into the kitchen, and I give him a portion of dry food since it's quicker than opening a can. I glance at the clock on the oven—almost nine-thirty. If I take a super-fast shower I can get to my class on time. If I run.

I go back to the main room, and the guy from last night is still sitting on my bed. He's got his jeans on, but nothing else. His shirt is still next to him on top of my comforter.

I march over to him.

"I'm so tired," he complains. "I'm hungover."

"That sucks." I grab his arm and yank him up. "Go home and have some coffee."

It's the shock that makes it work. I pick up his shirt and lead him to the door, pushing him outside. Then I shove the shirt into his hands. "There's a good coffee place two blocks over. Go get some."

I slam the door in his face and rush to the shower. There is no way I'm going to miss class this morning.

No way.

# CHAPTER FOURTEEN

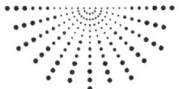

In a reversal of the way things usually work, I approach Piper at the Pancake House while she's on her break.

"Hey," I slide into the booth across from her. She's working on an omelette and reading a book at the same time.

"Oh, hey." She looks up and smiles at me. She doesn't *seem* upset.

"Hey, you're not, uh, pissed about Vic and me leaving early last night, are you?"

"Oh, no, whatever. How'd your testing thing go?"

"It went well." I feel shitty lying to her, but I'm not sure it's worth it to come clean. It sucks though, because I want to talk to her about the mini freak-out I had at Vic's place. But if I tell her about that, she'll know I didn't really go home early to get sleep for my "test."

"Good, I'm glad," she says. "How's Vic?"

"He's okay. Do you want me to set you up with him? I could do that."

Piper sets her book down on the table and leans forward. Then, in a conspiratorial whisper she says, "I hooked up with Bill last night."

"Oh. Oh my god. Seriously?"

She nods, looking gleeful. "He was so jealous of Vic. It was driving him insane."

"Wait, so you aren't into Vic?"

"Nah," she grins. "The most important thing about Vic is that he pushed Bill to make a move. Until last night, I wasn't sure if Bill was into me. Vic being there kind of smoked him out."

"So, was it…good? With Bill, I mean."

Piper stretches her limbs like a cat and winks. "He definitely has potential. Anyway, speaking of Vic—what was up with that big roll of cash he was waving around last night?"

I shrug. "I don't know."

"I mean, have you ever seen anyone carrying that much cash on them? Ever?"

"Never. But, I don't know. Did I tell you he owns the building he lives in? He tries to act like it's nothing, but I think he's probably more rich than he lets on."

"Rich, huh?" She wrinkles her nose. "A rich guy who teaches self-defense. That's— different."

"He's serious about it." It's on the tip of my tongue to tell her about his well-equipped home martial arts studio, but I stop myself. I'm not sure why. She's already acting like there's something suspicious about Vic and his roll of cash. I have a feeling if I tell her anything else about him, she'll just weave it into some developing conspiracy theory.

"Are you into him?" she asks, bluntly.

"No. He's part of the…" I fumble for a word. I was going to say he's part of the scenery, but that isn't right. "He's just one of those people you meet sometimes," I say finally. "Like somebody you have to learn something from."

"Like self-defense?"

"Sure. Like self-defense."

But I know it's more than that. Vic disturbs me. He's disturbed me ever since I first spotted him in O'Shea's. I *have* been feeling more comfortable around him since we started hanging out, but he unsettled me again in his apartment last night. It's why I left so abruptly, I realize.

"You thought it was weird that he wanted to teach you self-defense the first time he brought it up," Piper reminds me.

"Yeah, and back then, you thought it was a good idea, remember? Anyway, I know him now. And I know people who know him. It's okay." I need to put the subject of Vic to bed. I have another mission. "Can I ask you something?"

"Ask me what?"

"Could we, like, hang out sometime? I mean, without your band? They're awesome and everything and I guess now you're dating Bill, but...."

Saying it aloud makes me feel like a kid on the playground asking another kid to play with her. Wanting connection, but afraid of rejection.

Piper's lips stretch into a lopsided smile. "Are you saying you *miss me?*"

"Well, yeah. I do. I miss you."

She reaches her hands across the table and grabs mine. "I miss you, too! I know my life got crazy overnight, but we're gonna do it."

"What about sometime this week?" I venture.

She groans. "We're going out of town this weekend to play a couple shows, and I had to trade shifts with someone else. I'm working like a dog the rest of the week. I'm sorry." She looks anguished. "You just got all vulnerable and now I have to tell you no."

"It's okay," I reassure her. "We'll do it when it works. That's exciting about the shows. Where are you going?"

"Portland and San Francisco!" Then she starts gushing about how the band plans to make it to San Francisco and back in just over forty-eight hours. She's happy and excited so I try to match her level of enthusiasm, because I want to be a good friend.

---

I RUSH HOME to get ready for my meeting with Vic. I wonder if it'll be awkward when I see him. It's not like anything crazy happened. We didn't have sex or make out or even have a fight. But I know I was acting strange when I left his place so abruptly last night, and I'm not sure how he's going to feel about that. Or about me.

Before I can get over there, however, the phone rings. As soon as I answer, I hear, "This is your sister."

Her voice immediately makes me feel tired. "Hi, Izzy."

"Haven't heard from you since New Years."

"Yeah, I know. I've been busy."

"You always are." She sighs. "Well, listen, I don't want to take up too much of your time, but I have an idea I wanted to run by you."

"Um, okay?"

"Me and Rob want to take a weekend off, maybe an extra day, too. Like a Friday or Monday?"

I hate to hear her husband's name spoken aloud. But she never understands that. In her reality, he never tried to hurt me, so why would the mention of his name bother me? To her, such a thought would be absurd.

"Well, great," I say. "Have fun wherever you go."

"I'm sure we will. But, you know, I always worry about the house when we're gone, so I was wondering if maybe you wanted to come here and housesit for us? We'll stock the refrigerator and the pantry. You don't have to buy any groceries. You can just chill out here and watch TV."

My sense of fatigue deepens. Every now and then, she tries something like this. Something—anything—to pull me back in to their orbit. I always turn her down, and she always ends up acting hurt that I'm not willing to behave like a more ideal sister.

"I don't think so," I say. "I usually have to work on either Saturday or Sunday. I can't miss work to housesit for you."

"Can't you find a sub? We can give you some cash if you have to miss a day's pay."

I start to say that it's too hard to predict my schedule. Or point out that I don't have a car to get to them. But of course her solution will be that either she or Rob will pick me up and bring me home.

And that's unacceptable.

"Izzy. I can't do it."

"Why not? You haven't given me a real reason. Just excuses."

"Izzy." I repeat her name. "I can't do it because I don't want to. I don't want to be in your house."

Her voice goes very small and girlish. "Why not?"

"You know why not!"

She makes a noise of disgust. "Are you still clinging to all that stuff from the past? If you would just sit down and talk to him, I know he could explain it to you. But you won't even talk to him. He can't explain anything if you don't talk to him."

"I don't need to talk to him to know what happened." I'm getting a sharp, knifelike pain in my chest. I want to get off the phone, but I feel glued to it.

"You're never going to let this go, are you?" Now she sounds angry. Like she's about to yell. "When are you going to leave the past in the past and be part of our family again?"

"Listen, Izzy, I have to go. I'm late for something."

"Well, I hope you never need help looking after your cat. It helps to have family sometimes, you know."

"Bye, Izzy," I say, and hang up the phone.

Aggravated, I head for the shower, hoping that the stream of hot water will calm me down. It works only moderately well.

———

VIC IS WAITING for me at the entrance to his building when I get there.

"Am I late?" I ask.

"Just about five minutes. No big deal." He unlocks the door and I follow him inside.

As we start up the stairs, I say, "Sorry about bailing on you last night. And wasting your twenty-year-old Scotch. I guess I was in a strange mood."

"I drank yours," he says with a smile, "so it didn't go to waste. Don't worry about it. Everybody has off days, right?"

"Right." I'm relieved he's not upset. But I figure I won't know how he really feels until our lesson is over. If he suggests going to O'Shea's for a burger, we're fine. If he doesn't, we might not be. I hope I can manage to behave normally today. I'm still stressed from Izzy's call.

As soon as we get in Vic's studio, the sight of the training dummy hanging down from the ceiling does something to me. Adrenaline begins to course through my body, and my heart speeds up. I want to get my hands on it. Vic's attending to something in the corner of the room, but when he comes over to me, he stops and stares. I meet his gaze. "What?"

"You look like you want to hit something."

I feel seen. "I guess I do," I admit.

"Why don't you do that? Get it out of your system. I have to make a quick phone call anyway. Then we can get started."

I head over to the training dummy and start punching it. When I want to do something physical to get anger out of my body, it always feels better to punch than kick. Women typically have more power in their lower body than upper body, so most women can deal more lethal kicks than they can punches. But it's still satisfying to do a series of blocks and punches on the bag.

I don't think of hitting my sister or even her husband. I think of the whole fucked up situation. The essence of it. Like it's trapped inside Vic's training dummy, trying to get out, and I'm hitting it to keep it subdued and imprisoned.

When I run out of steam, I sense eyes on me and turn around. Vic's watching me. I'm sweating.

"Doing okay?" he asks.

"I'm fine."

We regard each other for a couple seconds.

"Ready to get started?"

"I'm here, aren't I?"

He hesitates, like maybe he doesn't believe me. But I keep eye contact with him, so he'll know I'm for real.

"Did you sign up for the black belt test yet?" he asks.

"I *just* completed my attendance requirement," I remind him. "Are we going to get started or what? Because if not, I'd rather just keep punching that thing." I gesture at the training dummy.

"Will you tell me when you've signed up?"

"Yeah, I'll tell you, okay? Can you teach me how to hurt people now?"

He finally cracks a smile. "Okay. Let's get started."

We spend the whole time working with a different dummy, one that's supposed to approximate an actual human so I can practice choking an opponent. Even doing it to a dummy makes me feel queasy. I doubt I could hold down a potential attacker long enough to even use the choking move. But Vic's approach is always to give me a full set of tools to use, in case I ever can use them. I power through the session and do my best to ignore the nausea.

When we finish, he asks me again if I'm okay.

"I'm okay. Why do you keep asking me that?"

A lopsided grin appears on his face. "Because I want to know if you're okay."

I stick my tongue out at him. Not the most mature response. But it feels natural.

He just laughs, then raises his eyebrows. "Burgers?"

Down at O'Shea's, it's one of those nights where every other person in the place has something to say to Vic. But it's fine. I'm no longer worried that I freaked him out when I ran out of his apartment. He doesn't care, which means he probably takes it for granted that I'm kind of an odd duck. I can live with that.

When we're almost finished eating, Kane comes over to us.

"Another self-defense lesson?" he asks, his eyes sparking with mirth. I don't think he believes Vic and I are actually working out when I come over here, but since *I* know that's all we're doing, I don't mind.

"Yep," I confirm. "Another lesson."

He thumps Vic on the shoulder. "Well, I hope this one is a good teacher."

"How are you tonight, Kane?" Vic asks. "Keepin' it together?"

"More or less. I just wanted to let you know we're trying something new next Saturday. Not this Saturday, the one after that."

"Something new?" Vic asks.

"A bit of Irish dancing."

I survey the crowded bar. "In here?"

Kane chuckles. "Sounds crazy, doesn't it? We're going to move the tables out of the main room, stack 'em in the closet. I'm daft to let it happen, but it's Mary's birthday, and that was what she wanted."

Mary's a waitress here. You can't see it when she's dressed for work, but she has a huge tattoo on her back that looks like angel wings. The only reason I know is I saw her once changing in the ladies' room when she was getting off her shift. The word is she's been working here since Kane opened the place, and he gives her a lot of credit for its success. She used to wait tables and do the books plus some marketing to drive new clientele to the bar, until Kane got the place on its feet. Then he was able to hire an actual bookkeeper.

"It does sound crazy," Vic agrees. "I can't remember, are your windows shatterproof glass? Because drunk people dancing all night in this room sounds like a window replacement waiting to happen."

Kane brushes off Vic's concern. "It will be fine. We only live once, right?"

I feel Vic bristle, just barely. A couple months ago, I wouldn't have noticed it. But I'm more in tune with his body language, now. He recovers quickly.

"So true. Well, I'll make it if I can."

Kane turns back to me. "And what about you? Are you going to come dance with us?"

"What kind of dancing is it?"

"Just a few reels. It's like square dancing, only much better." Kane withdraws. "I'll leave you two alone. But hope we'll see you both here next Saturday."

He moves on to the next group of people while I turn to Vic.

"Square dancing?"

He laughs. "He'd do anything for that woman."

"Mary?"

Vic nods.

I'm suddenly pierced with jealousy. Not that I'm interested in Kane —I like him, but I don't feel that way about him. I just wish there was somebody in my life who would do anything for me. I wish I could know what that feels like, just once.

"So, are you going to go to this...square dance?" I ask.

He shrugs. "Maybe. Too soon to know what's in the cards for next Saturday."

"Yeah," I agree. I can't imagine showing up for it myself. Besides, Piper will probably have something going on next Saturday, and she'll want me to come with her. Or maybe that will be the weekend we can finally hang out without her band.

I've finished my burger, so I decide to go home to Milo. I hop off my bar stool and fish in my purse for some cash to cover my meal.

"Headin' home?" Vic asks.

"Yeah." I stretch out my hand with the cash.

He pushes it back to me. "Keep it."

"I want to pay for my food."

"And I want to treat you to dinner, so put away your money and go home to your cat."

When I just stare at him, he adds, "That's what you want to do, right?"

"Cats need to eat. You can't let a cat just sit around getting hungry."

"So go feed him, then."

Slowly, I pull back the money and stash it in my purse. "All right. I'm gonna go." I turn on my heel and start for the door.

"Noelle!" he calls after me.

I turn back around.

"Don't forget to tell me when—"

"I'll let you know as soon as I sign up for the test. Promise." I linger long enough to see his face light up with one of the most compelling smiles I've ever witnessed on another human being. It makes me uncomfortable, and at the same time, I want to bask in it. That's confusing. So I turn and head out the door.

# CHAPTER FIFTEEN

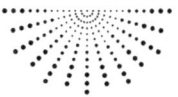

I approach Conan at the school Monday morning. "I'm here to sign up for the black belt test."

Conan looks up from the front desk. "In June?"

"Yep. Do you need to check my attendance record again?"

"Nope." He stands up and snags a clipboard that's hanging on the wall—it's the one we use to sign up for belt testing—and he holds it against his chest as he faces me. "If you do this, you have to follow through, train, and jump through all the hoops. Plus show up for the actual test."

"I always did before," I remind him. "I've tested lots of times."

"I know. But you've been... You haven't been yourself lately."

"I'm going to follow through," I tell him, holding out my hand for the clipboard.

Once I've filled everything out, he finally smiles at me. "Congratulations."

"Thanks."

"Don't fuck it up." His tone is teasing, but I know he's also serious.

At home that evening, once I've fed Milo, I go to the small trinket box on my bookshelf where I keep phone numbers, and pull Vic's number out. It's only the second time I've called him, and I still feel strange doing it. I'm half-hoping he won't pick up the phone. But he does.

"Vic here."

"Are you really here? Or are you there?" I ask.

"Hi, Noelle."

"How'd you know it was me?"

"I can't think of anyone else who would've picked that way to start a phone call. What's up?"

"Oh, nothing. Just called to tell you I signed up for my black belt test today, so you can stop pestering me about it."

"Oh, hey, really? You actually did it?"

"You can ask Conan if you don't believe me."

"I believe you," he says. "I have to get out the door to meet someone, but I'm really proud of you."

I feel a rush of pleasure at his praise. "Thank you. Um, have a good meeting."

He makes a dismissive noise. "Boring business shit. See you Thursday?"

"See you then."

I feel good as I hang up the phone. However, I don't feel as good when I see Piper the next day. I'd been proud of myself for doing as Vic suggested and asking her if we could spend some time alone together. But as soon as I connect with her at the Pancake House, I discover she's acquired a new obsession—Primal Malice is going to do a tour over the summer. One of the bands they met in San Francisco invited Piper and crew to come open for them, so now they're practicing an extra day each week to get ready for it. And then there's Piper's developing relationship with Bill, who is "so much more fascinating and fuckable" than she first thought he was.

When she tells me she and Bill and the rest of the band are going to hang out at this new lounge on Saturday night, I don't know what to say. Do I remind her that we talked about spending time alone together, or would that be pathetic of me? Should I say I have something else to do? I probably need more friends so this kind of thing doesn't derail my emotions.

"You're going to come with us, aren't you?" she implores. She all but bats her eyelashes. "It'll be more fun if you're there."

I cave. "Yeah, sure. Just tell me what time and where."

When we arrive at the club that weekend, I'm relieved to see it's an improvement over the place where we all went dancing in January. It's not as big—more of a lounge than a bar. They serve wine and beer by the glass, and there are little nooks and crannies everywhere with wood-hewn antique upholstered furniture. Some of it is so old I wouldn't be surprised if it were stuffed with horsehair.

While at least half the patrons look goth-y, there are plenty of people here who definitely aren't, which helps me feel less out of place. We all order glasses of wine and settle into one of the nooks with two couches and a couple chairs.

Piper and Bill have claimed an entire couch for themselves. Every time I look at them, their limbs are intertwined in some way, her hand on his knee, his arm snaked around her shoulders. Mandy's sprawled out on the other couch, while Sven and I occupy the chairs. There's an ornate wood coffee table in the center of our little circle to set down our wine glasses, but I keep mine cradled in my hands, sipping at it slowly.

"How'd you find this place?" I ask Piper.

"It's groovy, isn't it? But I didn't find it." She nods at Sven. "He did."

I glance over at Sven, who does not match the eclectic, cozy decor of our surroundings. Tonight, in addition to his typical black attire, he's wearing a cape—also black, of course.

"Way to go Sven," I say, and hold up a hand for him to high five.

He just scrunches up his eyebrows and stares at my hand.

Piper laughs. "I hope this place lasts. I hate it when you find a perfect new place to chill and then they go out of business."

"It's like being socially homeless," Mandy agrees, solemnly.

Bill leans over to Piper and says something in her ear. She screws up her nose in this adorable way, then slaps his knee. "Keep those words out of your mouth."

I feel a disturbance in the air next to my ear, and turn to find Sven leaning in close to me. I reflexively jump, almost spilling my wine.

"How's your beverage this evening?" he asks, gesturing to the glass in my hand.

"It's…it's all right. Uh, how's yours?"

Sven does this odd thing where he shifts his closed lips from one side of his mouth to the other. I'm not sure if it's supposed to be a smile or a grimace.

"It's passable," he says.

"Sven's our wine connoisseur," Piper explains.

"Then the dinner at the Italian restaurant must have been murder for you," I say, without thinking.

"That wine was a perfect match for the food," Piper defends.

But Sven looks at me and nods once. All right. So, we have something in common. We both think the wine at the Italian place was an abomination.

"They should do live music here," Bill says. "Acoustic shows. It would be an awesome space for an acoustic set."

"You mean like, fucking folk music?" Mandy asks.

"Not necessarily. Not all acoustic music is folk music. There's a range of genres that you can cover in an acoustic setting."

I have a sudden epiphany. Bill is not a true goth. He's just a music nerd who's dressing like a goth to fit into the band. He'd grow his hair long and dress like a metal head if he was playing drums for a metal band. I try picturing him in a suit and tie playing for a jazz combo, and it's not hard to do.

"Hey, Noelle," he says. "How's your friend, Vic? Is he coming later tonight?"

"Oh, no. He's fine. But he's not coming." I know Bill is just asking because he doesn't want Vic siphoning away Piper's attention. Now that I'm watching him and Piper together, it's obvious Bill is the person she wanted all along. She knew that hinting at interest in Vic would make Bill jealous enough to finally do something.

Sven turns to me. "If you're not enjoying the wine, I can see if they have something better. We can replace it."

I start to tell him that there's nothing wrong with the wine. Then I realize he's just trying to be nice.

"Sure," I say. "I can try something different."

He takes my glass and swoops away, his cape trailing behind him.

Once he's gone, Piper asks, "How *is* Vic?"

Something about her tone bugs me. Maybe I'm reading her wrong, but she seems to be implying there's something wrong with Vic.

"He's fine."

"Still learning self defense from him?" she asks.

"Yep. Nothing's changed."

"He seems like a unique person," Mandy observes. She's lying on her back on the couch, effectively talking to the ceiling. "Where's he from?"

"I don't know," I admit. "But he said he grew up a military brat, so he's probably from lots of places."

Piper looks like she wants to ask me more questions, but Bill whispers something in her ear again, making her laugh and forget it.

"You should find out where he's from," Mandy says.

I feel kind of dumb that I don't know more about Vic. But we hardly ever talk about anything personal when we hang out. Mostly we talk about martial arts, or the colorful cast of characters that frequents O'Shea's. I still don't have a clear sense of what he does for a living.

Over on the other couch, Piper and Bill are becoming even more entwined. I glance over at the serving area, where Sven is still in line to replace my glass of wine. He's drawing himself up to his full height, exuding a kind of old-fashioned gallantry that I've never noticed before. Maybe he's always had it, but I just couldn't see it.

I've been judging Piper's friends as weird goth mongers, but I don't really know them at all. When did I become like this? Why am I so judgmental? I feel disoriented, and all at once, I don't want to be here. I don't know where I want to be, exactly. But wherever that is, here is not it.

I stand up. "Hey, listen. I'm kind of tired. I think I'm going to head back home."

"Oh," Piper looks startled, but then she recovers. "Do you need a ride home?"

"I'll get a cab." Actually I'm planning to walk. We're not that far away from my apartment, but I'm not going to tell her that or she might feel guilty and try to drive me back.

"Okay, well, thanks for chilling with us for a while."

"Yeah, thanks for the invite. This place is super cool." And it actually is. It's just that there's something I want, or maybe something I'm looking for, and I'm not finding it here.

"Bye, Noelle," Mandy says.

I wiggle my fingers at them. Before I leave, I go down to the serving area to tell Sven he doesn't need to stand in line for me, since I'm leaving.

He seems disappointed. Maybe. Or maybe it's just his face. Then he shrugs and says, "I want to try a different vintage, anyway."

Outside, the streets are wet from a recent April shower, but it's not raining now, and it doesn't feel like it's going to start again soon. I hope I'm right, or I'm going to be looking and feeling pretty soggy by the time I get home.

Now that I'm alone again, I wonder if I'm being immature, wanting time alone with Piper. She seems happy with Bill, and it's not like she doesn't want me around. She's launching her music career and she has a new boyfriend. I might be expecting too much from her, but I don't know for sure, and I hate that.

Even with the rain and even though it's nighttime, the sense of burgeoning spring is all around me. It's like the air has woken up from the dead sleep of winter. I already feel better. In fact, I feel alive—even dangerous. If someone were to attack me right now, I can think of seven different ways I could seriously fuck them up. I wasn't this confident even four months ago, and I'm almost itching to have a reason to use my new skills, to put them into practice in the real world to see if they work against an actual attacker.

At our last session, Vic had Sheryl come to spar with me again, and this time I almost beat her. When we finished, there was that same sense she wanted to talk to Vic alone about something, but I was prepared for it so it didn't bother me as much.

I'm eager to finally spar with Vic after I get my black belt. I can feel the energy building for it. Any time I spar with someone, I glean something essential from them, and I have no doubt I'll learn something amazing from Vic. Even if he kicks my ass—which he probably will.

I'm several blocks away from O'Shea's when I start to hear a hint of Irish music, but as I get closer, I'm certain that's where it's coming from. It has a wild and free energy, and I'm drawn to it. I go up to the front windows of the bar and peer inside.

Up on the small stage is a band of people with acoustic instruments. All the tables in the main room are gone, just like Kane mentioned, and people are dancing in groups in the empty space. It looks chaotic but fun, and there's a lot of laughing.

The music is infectious, so I linger at the window, watching the tumultuous dancing through the glass. *I should leave*, I think. I feel strange, like I'm on the verge of being sucked into a situation I won't be able to control. Yet I keep watching.

And then someone steps in front of the glass, blocking my view. It's Vic. He holds up his hand and crooks his finger forward, beckoning me inside. I shake my head. He makes a larger gesture with his arms, waving me forward and mouthing, "C'mon!" through the glass.

Resistance is futile. The music is too enticing, and now I have a clear invitation.

"Okay!" I mouth back at Vic, then find myself opening the door.

# CHAPTER SIXTEEN

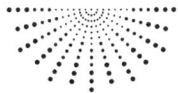

Vic meets me inside the entrance. The music is loud coupled with the sound of feet stomping in rhythm on the floor. It's mayhem in here.

Further back, there are still people sitting at tables and along the bar. But the whole front room, including the part of the bar that spans the front room, has been given over to the dancers. It does kind of look like they're square dancing, only there's something more intricate and lively about it.

"How do they even know what to do?" I ask Vic.

He cups his hand to his ear, and I repeat my question in a louder voice.

"Someone in the band teaches the steps before they start," he explains. "They're gonna teach another one in a bit."

"Did you try it?"

He laughs and shakes his head. "No. Just enjoying the show."

I turn back to the dancers. If you squint your eyes so you can't see the modern clothes everyone's wearing—or, through the window, the cars parked on the street—you could almost imagine we've been transported to a different time.

The music's being made with all acoustic instruments. Nothing is amplified. The stomping has a primal energy that travels through the floorboards to where Vic and I are standing. My own foot starts tapping along with the music, and it's as if the energy of the dancing is swirling all around and above us.

It's affecting Vic too, and I catch his foot tapping near mine. I'm struck by how good it feels to stand next to him.

The music swells to a crescendo then trills to a finish. The dancers stop moving, cheering and clapping for themselves as the band leader moves to the front of the stage and calls out, "Well done! Well done, everyone! Now, who wants to stay and learn the Glencar Reel?"

As some of the dancers leave the floor, I feel a tug on my sleeve.

"You want to give it a try?" Vic asks.

"Oh," I start. "I couldn't...." Then I change my mind. "Sure. Why not?"

He nudges me forward, and we move onto the floor in front of the band.

"We need three groups of six!" the band leader says. "Three groups with three couples!"

Vic tugs at me again and moves us into a group of four already standing near us. "Do you need two more?" he asks.

"Yeah, join us!"

"I'm Vic, and this is Noelle."

The other couples introduce themselves, and the band leader speaks again.

"Okay, looks like we've got our groups! Now I want you to stand in two lines and face each other. We want everyone who's playing the man on one side, and everyone who's playing the woman on the other."

Vic bends down and says in my ear, "You want to play the man?"

I shove him away from me. "You can do it."

He gives a mischievous grin. "If you insist."

We stand facing each other, and Vic seems looser than I've ever seen him. I wonder why. The sensation of him speaking into my ear lingers, and it's disquieting in a not-unpleasant way. But before I have any more time to think about what that could mean, the band leader begins to guide us through the steps.

I try to keep up. A skip and a hop here, move to the side, take your partner's hands. Spin in a circle with everyone. Weave in and out between each other. Make little arches with your hands for other couples to go under. We're going slow, but there's no way I'm going to memorize it all in just a few minutes.

When the band leader calls out, "Now let's try it for real," I give Vic a look of anguish.

"I can't do this!"

"Sure you can!"

We line up to face each other and start to move. Pretty soon we're bumping into the other couples. I'm not used to feeling like I have two left feet.

"Sorry!" I say in horror to a woman as I bash into her.

She just laughs and keeps going.

"Relax," Vic whispers in my ear in an opportune moment that brings his body close to mine. "It's not a test."

We lumber through to the end, making a mockery of all things Irish and dancing.

"Let's take the tempo down," the band leader says, and the musicians start playing more slowly. This time, to my surprise, many of the parts of the dance are still in my memory, and at the slower pace, it's easier to execute them.

Every time Vic gets within range of my ears, he tells me "doing great" or reminds me "this isn't life or death." I appreciate the encouragement, because I haven't felt this physically timid since I was a kid.

We get through the slowed down dance with only a few stumbles, and just as I'm hoping we can continue that way I hear, "Let's pick up the pace!"

And we're off—but it's different this time. I'm starting to get it, and I have a feeling Vic's either done this before or he's a quick study. When I can, I keep my eyes on him, which helps. I'm not getting all the little foot flourishes right, but I'm getting into the movement and rhythm of the group, and it's actually pretty fun.

Sometimes in a martial arts class, you start to feel a collective energy building between everyone in the room. It's like that now, only this energy has a different quality. It's exuberant and buoyant rather than combative and disciplined. Now we're the ones with our feet thumping on the floor to the rhythm of the music, and the weaving in and out with the other couples is starting to make sense.

The band takes us through the dance again and again, and I lose count of how many times we've done it. Vic looks like he's having fun too. I don't think I've ever seen this side of him before. His typically serious eyes are now radiant with joy. Still intense, but a different kind of intensity.

When the band leader calls out that it's the last time through, the dance goes by so fast I'm surprised when it's over, and soon we're all clapping for the band and ourselves. I look up at Vic, knowing I have a giddy smile plastered across my face.

He smiles back. "Want to go again? Or do you want to get a drink?"

"Drink first. I think I'm out of breath!" But I'm not, really. I'm just not used to feeling this carefree. I need a drink to calm down.

"C'mon." Vic puts a light hand on my shoulder, and we push through the crowd on the makeshift dance floor to get to the portion of the bar that's in service.

"That was fun!" I enthuse.

"Ever done that kind of dancing?" Vic asks.

"Never! How about you?"

"A couple of times. Nothing I do regularly though."

"You're a natural."

He grins. "You did all right."

"After I knocked over every person in our circle," I groan.

"But you caught on."

We're up at the bar, and Vic asks what I want to drink.

"Just a Guinness, please."

He orders two pints, plus a shot for himself. There's a new crop of people on the dance floor, and then I see that Kane is dancing with Mary, the waitress.

"Look who it is," I tell Vic, jerking my head in his direction.

"With the birthday girl," he agrees.

"So, are they a couple, or what?"

"Not technically." Then he laughs. "But for all practical purposes: yes." He hands me my beer, then downs his shot before he touches his own pint glass to mine. "Cheers."

"Cheers."

We watch Kane and Mary for a while. They're both easy and nimble on their feet, executing the dance steps together like they've been doing it all their lives.

"So, were you planning on coming by here tonight?" Vic asks.

"No. I was hanging out with Piper and the band, and then when I was walking home I heard the music. I had to investigate."

"You do a lot of walking alone at night?"

Something in his tone makes me spin around sharply to look at him. But his face is neutral.

"I do, yeah," I say. "I refuse to live a life where I'm scared to walk my own ass home when I want to."

He stares at me for a second, then says, "Yeah. Yeah, okay, I get that."

We go to stand at the edge of the crowd gathered around the dancers, and when we've both finished our drinks, he asks me if I want to dance again. I'm game.

Vic is fun. That's something I've never thought about him before. He's always seemed somewhat disturbing and puzzling. Then, after getting to know him better, I considered him good dinner company. But I never would have called him a *fun person* until tonight.

None of the dancing we're doing requires close touching, but every time our hands lock I feel him working his magic on me. It's that thing he does when he handles someone aggressive at the bar. We're dancing, but he's *managing* me. If we were up in his home gym, I'd want to push back and try to make him spar with me.

In this context, though, where we're surrounded by a happy, somewhat-drunk crowd of neophyte Irish dancers, there's no reason to spar. So, instead of trying to take over or push back, I let him manage me. And it's freeing. Like, if I fuck up, just in this one thing—learning a new dance—he'll take responsibility for it. He'll take care of me.

This time when we leave the dance floor, he spies an empty table for two and grabs it, pulling out my chair before I sit down.

"Another drink?"

I shake my head. "Just water."

"Water sounds good, doesn't it? I'll be right back."

While I wait, I take in the gleaming darkly polished wood and brass trim, and the hum of conversations under the music.

I'm happy. In this moment, I know what happy feels like.

From the stage, the band leader calls out that it's going to be the last dance of the night, but I don't feel a need to rush up and join in. I'm sated.

Vic shows up with the water and sits across from me.

"This is the last dance," I tell him.

"Did you want to go again?"

"Nah, I'm good."

"Me, too."

We each sip our water and watch as the last dance plays out, a particularly fast and frenzied reel that makes me feel dizzy from where I'm sitting. When they finish, Vic and I join in the applause, and from the stage, the leader thanks everyone for a wonderful night.

The band starts to put away their instruments, and within seconds, a couple of Kane's bartenders are moving the tables back on to the floor. Vic and I watch them as they reset the tables with bread plates, napkins, and silverware. Then they go back behind the bar and yell, "Full bar! We're back in business!"

"That was impressive," I say. "How long do you think that took them?"

"Less than ten minutes, I think," Vic says. "Kane wouldn't want to lose a minute more of business than he has to." He leans forward. "Do you have somewhere you need to be? I kind of roped you in from the street—I don't want to keep you if you've got other plans."

"No, I'm good." I fed Milo extra before I went out with Piper tonight. And I don't want to leave here yet. O'Shea's, apparently, is a magic place that can make me feel happiness. I don't want to stop feeling happy.

Vic leans back. "I don't need to be anywhere, either."

The part of the bar that spans the front room has filled up again. All the barstools are occupied. Mary is sitting there, leaning across the wooden counter and talking to Kane, who's standing behind the bar. She's wearing a tank top, and a bit of her angel wings tattoo is visible. There's a small clamor around her. People are begging her to sing. It

126

goes on for several minutes until she finally gives in and says, "All right. One song. But only one song. Don't ask for more."

She doesn't go to the stage or anything, but stays right where she is on her stool. I hear her take in a breath, then she begins to sing "Cockles and Mussels." She doesn't turn around and face us. Instead, she sings in the direction of the bottles of liquor and beer taps arrayed in front of her. All we can see is her back with the visible portion of her tattooed wings peeking out from underneath her shirt.

But her voice carries. It carries so well, in fact, that bit by bit, conversations in O'Shea's begin to go silent, until the only sound in the place is Mary singing. Her voice is rich, deep, and perfectly pitched, with a haunting quality that gets in you like a knife. If sirens were real, I figure they'd sound like Mary singing "Cockles and Mussels" with her back to us at the bar.

The emotion that wells up inside me surprises me at first. I try to manage it, the way Vic was managing me on the dance floor, but it's impossible. Tears flow down my cheeks, tears I can't stop and that burn my face as they fall. Listening to her sing is an experience of beauty, but for me, right now, it's also some kind of torture.

When she finishes, the room erupts in raucous applause.

Vic lets out a breath. "Wow. That was amazing. Special." He looks over at me, then notices my face. "Noelle? Are you okay?"

I stand up. "I'm sorry. I'm sorry. I have to go."

"What's wrong?" Vic tugs at my sleeve. "You need to talk about it?"

"I'm sorry," I repeat. "I have to go." I make a beeline for the door, hoping Vic doesn't follow me out.

# CHAPTER SEVENTEEN

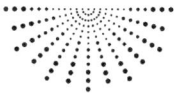

**B**ut of course, he does follow me—all the way around the corner, out of sight of anyone sitting at the window tables in O'Shea's, and near the door of his upstairs apartment.

"What's going on?" he asks as I slump against the brick side of the building.

"Her song. Mary's singing. It got to me. Okay? Just an emotional reaction to music. It happens."

"Sure. Yeah. It happens. And then you order another pint and get on with your evening. How come you had to run out?"

The truth is, I don't know. But for whatever reason, I'm in a state of intense emotion and it's hard to talk to him, to explain anything to him. He looks concerned, but also something else. Something is behind his concern. I'm staring in his eyes, trying to figure out what the thing is, what he's thinking, what he's feeling, when the heavens suddenly dump a torrent of rain on us.

"Shit! C'mon." He takes my arm and pulls me with him to the door, which he opens in record time. Then he ushers me inside.

"I don't want to go upstairs," I say.

"All right," he says after a moment. "We can talk here in the lobby."

"We don't need to talk. I had a reaction to Mary singing a song. That's all."

"That's all, huh?" There's a hint of anger in his tone.

Is that what was behind his concern? Anger? What could he possibly be angry about?

"Yeah," I say. "That's all."

We're standing at the bottom of the wide staircase that leads up to his apartment, and I instinctively feel like we should move to the side, in case someone else comes down the stairs. Then I remember that would never happen, since no one else lives here.

He shakes his head, slowly. "I don't know, Noelle. There's something going on with you."

Now I'm feeling a tinge of my own anger. The new emotion makes my remaining tears dry up fast. "What do you mean?" I ask.

"Oh, I don't know. How about you dragging your feet on your black belt for a year—"

"I just signed up to take the test!" I interrupt. "I told you about that, remember? You said you were proud of me?"

"Or having a meltdown over a song." He looks directly at me. "Or what about prowling around dive bars at night and picking up dangerous strangers?"

I squint at him, wondering what the hell he's talking about. Then I remember. The night of the awkward dinner at the Italian restaurant. How we had drinks at his place and looked at the stars, and then I left without finishing my Scotch.

"You *followed* me?" I bellow. "You followed me home!"

I wait for him to deny it. And if he does, I'll know he's lying.

But he doesn't. "I wanted to make sure you got home safely."

"Oh, bullshit. You were stalking me."

"And you were freaking out that night, remember?" he says. "We were talking, and you got scared about something and just freaked and left. I was worried. So, yeah, I followed you."

"You had no fucking right to do that!" I yell. "What I do with my time is none of your goddamned business."

"I didn't try to stop you, did I? Look, do whatever you want with whoever you want. I don't care. Okay? But you were acting strange then, and you're acting strange now, so forgive me for trying to look out for a friend."

129

"Oh, c'mon," I scoff. "That's what you were doing? Looking out for a friend?"

His eyes flare dangerously. "Believe it or not, yeah. That's exactly what I was doing."

"Okay. Okay, well, you know what? Stop trying to be my friend. Just stop it. You're *not* my *friend*. You've never been my friend. What do you really want from me? Why don't you just tell me the truth?"

That look of mixed emotion is still on his face but intensified. He doesn't answer me.

"C'mon, Vic," I urge. "Tell me what you *really* want. I hate it when people lie. I hate it so fucking much—"

When he takes my arms, his grip is gentle, but then he pulls me against him and kisses me, and there's nothing gentle about it at all. It's one of those kisses that's instantly good. The kind of kiss that can only get better if you keep going. But it's also a shock, and as soon as I realize I'm kissing him back I shove him away from me and slap him, hard, across the face.

"What the hell was that!" I shout. "What the hell *was* that?"

He wipes his hand over his lip and brushes away a tiny trickle of blood. "I'm sorry," he says. "I shouldn't have done it. But you said you wanted me to be honest."

His words hit me like a slap. Then, I'm horrified that I actually hit *him*. It's against the rules in taekwondo to strike someone in the face. The face is off limits. But it's also against my personal ethics. I don't hurt someone unless they're trying to hurt me.

"I shouldn't have... I'm sorry I hit you."

To my surprise, he grins. "I've had worse. Deserved it. Kissed you without asking first. It was an honest impulse. And a reasonable response for you to read it as an attack. Good reflexes, by the way."

A small, incredulous laugh escapes me. "Are you a real person?"

"What the fuck kind of question is that?"

I creep forward and reach my hand up to touch his lip. I can still see the place where I drew blood. It's barely bleeding now. Still, I'm mortified that I did it.

"Don't worry about it," he says. "Hardly a scratch."

I'm so close to him that I can feel his breath against the top of my head. Up close, his body is like a furnace, emanating life-giving heat.

I move my eyes up and meet his. He's usually good at keeping what he's feeling out of his eyes, but tonight's been different. I'm also getting better at reading him. Right now, he's trying to blow this off like it's a joke to give us both an escape hatch—but that's not what he wants. It's not what I want, either.

I stand on tiptoe and kiss him.

We're tentative, at first. Then he slides his hands around my waist and pulls me into him. Darts his tongue in my mouth, quick, like he's daring me to pull away. But I don't. He deepens the kiss, and I let him, opening my mouth so he can explore further. He slides his hand down the length of my spine, stopping and placing it firmly on my ass.

"If we go up those stairs," he says, "I need you to be here with me. For real." He pauses. Looks at me. "So, do you want to come upstairs? Or do you want to go home? Because if you want to go home, you need to tell me now."

"I don't want to go home," I whisper.

"But what do you *want?*"

"Upstairs."

"That's a place, not a desire."

"Jesus, Vic! I want to go upstairs!"

He dips down and puts his arm behind my knees, then lifts me like I weigh nothing. "Then let's go upstairs."

Being carried up the stairs reminds me of dancing with him, how it felt when he was taking charge, guiding me through all the steps. At the door to his apartment, he sets me down gently and unlocks the door.

We go inside, and he takes my hand, tugging me forward past his couch and the big star-watching windows, back behind the Japanese screens at the end of the room. There's more space back here than I first imagined. His bed is large, king sized, I think. It's dark, but there are windows in here, too. They're blacked out from the floor to about four feet up, with just enough light coming in from above that I can see the outline of Vic's face. My heart is pounding hard in my chest.

He kisses me again, sending a jolt of electricity straight to my core.

We move together like we're magnetized. His hands scrape down my back, and I feel each of his fingers through the fabric of my shirt, burning my skin. All the strength in my legs is melting away, and I feel like I'm dissolving into him. He grabs the bottom edges of my shirt and yanks it up and over my head.

I press against him, but he moves back so he can slide his finger under the fabric of my bra. His fingertip grazes my nipple and I shiver. He teases the fabric down to reveal my breast, then bends his head down to suck and kiss it. My nipple goes stiff, and I sigh, loud, loving how it feels.

There's a tiny voice in the back of my mind, an annoying voice telling me I don't *do* this. I don't sleep with people when I know them as well as I know Vic. Maybe he's still a mystery, but he's not a stranger.

I squash the voice down and push it out of range, because I want this. I want him sucking on first one, then my other nipple. I want to feel his free hand sliding below the waistband of my jeans, discovering my bare ass and squeezing my flesh. I've never wanted to have sex with someone as much as I do right now.

I tug at his T-shirt and he helps me to get it off him. His chest is hairless except for a trail from his navel to the waistband of his pants. I swirl my tongue over his smooth, taut skin, then reach down to unbutton the top button of his pants. I plunge my hand inside and wrap it around his erection.

"I can't believe you want me," he kind of breathes, which stops me in my tracks.

My fingers go slack. "What?"

"I'm...that creepy guy your parents tell you to run away from. I've always been that guy."

"Oh, for fuck's sake." I look up at him. "Get over yourself."

He grabs my waist and wrestles me down to the bed. "I'd rather get over you."

"Oh, God," I say on a groan. "Don't ruin it. No puns. I fucking hate—"

He silences me by kissing me, hard, simultaneously sliding his hand below my waistband again, only this time he pushes his fingers inside me, making me cry out.

"How should I ruin it?" he asks, and starts moving his fingers in a slow circle, teasing me.

"Like that is pretty good," I gasp.

He shifts and straddles me with his knees, then yanks down my jeans and underwear in one smooth motion. I help kick them off as he pulls them down my legs. Then he buries his face between my thighs, tasting me with his tongue. He grasps my hips and my whole body quivers as he explores me.

Somewhere in the background, I hear people on the street below spilling out of O'Shea's, talking and laughing, taking the party atmosphere with them as they prepare to wend their separate ways home.

But Vic won't let me focus on the background. His hands and his mouth are bringing me closer to the edge of orgasm, but only to the edge. Maybe not all men his age know what they're doing, but Vic clearly does. No one has ever toyed with me like this, drawing out my pleasure for so long.

When he finally lets me come, it's such a sweet feeling I can barely stand it, like being pushed out of the bounds of euphoria. As I'm recovering, breathing down from the high, he removes the rest of his clothing and slides on a condom that must have been in his pants pocket. Then he takes my hands and pins them above my head.

We look into each others' eyes, and I love how dark his are, like some well where you can never find the bottom. He sinks down between my legs and I open them wider for him, so he can penetrate me. Then he does it.

I lock him close to me with my legs and he begins to thrust inside me. He's powerful, relentless, and my body is hungry for him, meeting his movements with my own, trying to pull him even deeper into me. I've been starving, and he's a feast.

I come again, hard, just as he's finding his own release. We're making noise together—hot, sweaty, embarrassing noise—and I don't care, because I feel free.

"So," I say. "I guess that's the end of the self-defense training, huh?"

He laughs. "Why is it the end?"

"Well, we don't have a professional relationship anymore."

"We never had a professional relationship," he retorts. "Maybe I tried to keep it that way...."

"You tried to keep it that way?" I laugh at him. "Is that what you call it when someone accuses you of lying and your response is to kiss them? That's how you keep it professional?"

"I said I *tried*. But we never had a true professional relationship anyway. We didn't have a contract. You weren't paying me for a service."

I go quiet. "Is that what this was? Payment?"

"Don't be ridiculous." He turns on to his side and props himself up on his arm so he can look at me. "I've been lusting after you ever since you walked into O'Shea's and sat your fine ass down and ordered a burger and a beer. You don't owe me—you did me a favor. I owe you."

I grin and slide all the way below the sheet until my head disappears. Vic claws at it, revealing my face. "Don't vanish on me," he says.

"You did me a favor, too."

He gives me a crooked grin. "I was that good, huh?"

"You were amazing. I feel amazing." I blush, but he's just confessed he's been lusting after me for months, so I can give a little back.

He brushes a strand of hair back from my face. "You *are* amazing."

I feel my blush deepen.

"We can stop working together if you want," he goes on. "But I still want to help you. And I don't have any plans to stop. Just so you know."

"Why do you care?" I ask. "I mean, why do you care if I know how to defend myself?"

His face goes tight and dark. "There's someone I used to know. They could have used some skills when they got in a bad situation. And I...wasn't there for them when they needed me. It doesn't change the past, but I like to help people get those skills. I can't stop every fucked-up thing from happening, but I can stop some of it."

"That…makes sense." I want to know more about the person who got in a bad situation and what happened to her—or him—although I can guess. I wonder if whoever it was is okay and what they're doing now. But Vic seems closed to the topic, and I sense he doesn't want to elaborate.

I decide to let it go. "So, where'd you do Irish dancing? I mean, when you did it before?"

His expression relaxes. "I don't remember. It was easy to pick up."

"For you," I retort.

"You did all right."

"Because I was following you."

"But you had fun, right?"

I grin at him. "Yeah. I had fun."

He reaches under the blanket, and brushes his hand over my bare hip. "Want to have some more?"

"Yeah. You want to spar?"

"Got your black belt yet?"

"Nope."

"Then no sparring. Just fucking." He reaches for me and pulls me on top of him.

I want to spar with him, bad. But I guess fucking is an acceptable alternative.

# CHAPTER EIGHTEEN

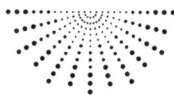

I slip home around eight because I have a late morning shift at the Pancake House. Vic and I didn't sleep much, but I'm running on euphoria and adrenaline.

Milo clamors for food and attention the minute I walk in the door to my apartment, so I give him plenty of both before taking a long, hot shower. Between that and the night of sex with Vic, I feel uncharacteristically languid and stress free.

When I clear the steam off the mirrored medicine cabinet over my bathroom sink, I'm surprised by my reaction. I like the person I'm looking at. I feel good.

At the Pancake House, Piper doesn't come in until I'm taking my meal break. She plops herself down across from me as usual, studying my face.

"What happened to you?" she asks.

"What do you mean?"

"You're kind of like...glowing."

"I am?"

"You are," she confirms. "What did you do last night? After you went home?"

"Not much," I evade.

"Uh huh. Who was he?"

I've never talked to Piper about my unorthodox method for getting laid, so she won't know what a big deal it was for me, sleeping with Vic. What if I tell her and she doesn't understand? Maybe I should just avoid this conversation, but some primal thing in me wants to stake a claim.

"*He* was Vic."

I can't read her expression. "Good old Vic, huh?" she says.

"Yep. It was kind of a crazy night."

"Well, good for you. How is Vic doing by the way? Still flashing around those big rolls of cash?"

There's something unpleasant in her eyes, and I have the distinct sense that she's decided Vic is bad news.

"You know, maybe he just went to the bank or something that day," I point out. "Anyway, I don't think it's as strange as you think it is."

Her face becomes a mask, and the emotion I saw just moments ago seems to evaporate. "I'm glad you had a good night. It was probably a drag hanging around with us, anyway."

"I wasn't planning to see Vic. It just kind of…happened."

Piper gets a knowing look in her eyes. "I doubt many things 'just happen' with that guy."

I'm getting a little tired of her insinuations. "Do you know something I don't? Anyway, I thought you were a fan. I think I remember you saying Vic was 'delicious.'"

"He is delicious. Like I said, I'm glad you had a good time. Just be careful, okay?"

"Um, okay." She's probably warning me because she's trying to be a good friend. But I wish she could just be happy for me instead. Suddenly, I don't like how I feel. I stand up and grab my mostly empty plate. "I should get back on the clock."

"Be there in a few minutes," Piper says. I watch her for a few seconds as she whips a book out of her purse, hoping we're still friends, wishing that it wasn't so hard for me to relate to other women. As she turns to a bookmarked page, she looks up and asks if I want to go out later with her and Bill. I tell her maybe.

At my afternoon taekwondo class, I feel unexpectedly self-conscious around Conan. I don't know how personal Vic gets with his friends or how much he shares with them, and wonder if Conan knows I spent the night with Vic. During class, I veer between trying to avoid eye contact with Conan, and chiding myself about how silly I'm acting.

As I'm leaving, he says, "Hey, Noelle. Can I talk to you for a minute?"

*Oh shit. He knows.*

"Sure," I say, and go over to him as everyone else filters out of the room. "What's up?"

"You've been doing a great job showing up. I just wanted to tell you that, and…." He hesitates.

*Here it comes.* He knows I slept with Vic, and he thinks it's a bad idea. "What's going on?" I prompt.

"If you hit a rough spot going forward, will you tell me? You don't have to tell me what's going on if you don't want to, but will you let me know if you're struggling? Instead of disappearing?"

Slowly it dawns on me that he's not going to give me shit about sleeping with Vic. Either he doesn't know, or he knows and doesn't care. He just wants to make sure I'm okay.

"Yeah," I say, slowly. "I can…tell you. I can do that."

"'Cause I don't want to see you shrink back again, you know? If something comes up, you need to push through it."

"Sure, I get it. I'll tell you if something comes up."

"You promise?"

"I promise."

My answering machine is blinking when I get home, and my stomach jolts as I wonder if the message is from Vic. It isn't.

I didn't expect him to call, and I try to tell myself there's nothing to worry about, since he already said he wants to keep up with the self-defense training. I'll see him again on Thursday. But I wish he'd called.

The message is from Piper. She wants to know if I'll come out with her and Bill. Sven is going, too. I have to admit, I almost want to go just to see what Sven will be wearing. But my curiosity isn't enough to override the bad feelings from my conversation with Piper at the diner today.

Still, I don't want to leave her hanging, so I call her. She picks up after three rings.

"Crazy town!" she crows.

"What?"

I hear laughter in the background. "Hey, Noelle! You coming out with us? I can pick you up in, like, ten or fifteen."

"No, um, actually, I just had a super intense workout. I'm gonna chill at home."

"You sure?" she asks. Based on the noise behind her, I'd guess there are several people over at her apartment. "We're going to go see these obscure UK bands. So obscure I've never even heard of them." She laughs. "Apparently, they don't come here very often."

"Sounds awesome," I say. "But I'm wiped out. I'd probably fall asleep while I'm standing up, and spill my drink, and that would be a mess, so...." My attempt at humor falls flat.

"Okay," Piper says.

I have a feeling it's not okay. I think it's the first time I've turned her down since we started hanging out together, but my mind is made up.

"So have a good time," I tell her. "I'll see you at work."

"Right." Her voice holds an uncertain note. "I'll see you at work."

When I hang up the phone, I feel tense and decide to take another long, hot shower to soothe my nerves. Afterward, I put on sweats and a T-shirt, grab a bag of generic cheese puffs, and sprawl on the bed with Milo. His purrs are so loud they fill up the whole room—until a knock at the door temporarily drowns them out.

Milo stops purring. Taking the cheese puffs with me, I pad up to the door in my bare feet and try to sound confident as I call out, "Who is it?"

There's a pause, then an unmistakable gravelly voice answers. "It's Vic. Can you let me in?"

# CHAPTER NINETEEN

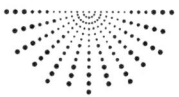

I open the door, and Vic gives me a quick, bright smile. "Is it okay if...?" He gestures inside my apartment.

I stand aside and let him in, pushing the door shut behind him. He smells faintly of cigarette smoke, like he's been chilling in a bar with lots of smokers. He's not drunk. There's some weariness around his eyes, but otherwise he's crackling with energy.

"Did I come at a bad time?" he asks.

"No. I just didn't expect you." I gesture to my grey sweatpants and faded pink T-shirt. Then I hold up the bag of cheese puffs. "Want some?"

"No, thanks."

"Was there something else you wanted?" I look up at him, and his eyes gleam, a corner of his mouth quirks up, and his tongue darts quickly over his upper lip.

All at once I'm weak in the knees, thinking about that tongue and what he was doing to me with it last night.

He moves near and sneaks his hand around my waist to pull me closer. The bag of cheese puffs crunches between us. I fling it down and wrap my arms around him. He lifts me up from the floor, so I wrap my legs around him, too. He carries me to my bed, where he convinces me that when I decided to stay in tonight, I made the right decision.

———

"I'm so glad I came here," Vic sighs.

"I thought you forgot about me," I admit. I hope that doesn't sound insecure, but it's the truth. All day, I've been wondering if our night together was just a fluke, a product of the Irish dancing and the magic atmosphere of O'Shea's.

"I was thinking about you all day," he says.

I feel a small thrill inside. He's not playing it cool; he's telling me how he feels. It's a rare thing, at least in my experience. Then again, I don't usually give boys enough time to have any feelings about me. Vic's not a boy, though.

"Me, too," I say.

"You too what?"

"I was thinking about you, too." It's hard to say the words aloud. It feels risky. But I also want him to know.

Under my blanket, he traces his finger from my knee, over my thigh, and on to my hip. "I'm glad you were thinking about me."

There's a soft thud on the bed, and then the sound of insistent purring.

"Hope you like cats," I say as Milo advances across the blanket. "I let him hang out up here." It's true, though this is unusual—he always stays away when I have guys over. I put out my hand to scratch behind his ears, but he's interested in Vic and stands there staring at him, still purring—but expectant.

Vic reaches out a tentative hand. "Hey, dude."

Milo butts his head into Vic's hand and lets him get in a few more pets. Then he flops down between us, forming a furry barrier.

"I think he likes you," I say.

Vic laughs. "It's a charm offensive."

"So, how come you came by tonight?" I ask. "Just in the neighborhood?"

"Sure. After I went out of my way to get here."

I decide he gets points for that response, but I want more. "Can I, um, ask you a question?"

"Shoot."

"What do you do all day when you're not hanging out at O'Shea's or, like, training people how to defend themselves?" Maybe he'll actually answer the question this time if I don't outright ask him if he has a job.

"I do a bunch of things. I hook Conan up with a lot of the protective gear you guys use at the school, so I get a commission on whatever he buys."

"Oh, so is that how you met him?"

"Yeah, eventually Conan became the go-to guy to purchase equipment for your school. So I started dealing with him directly."

"Okay, well, that's one thing you do. What else?"

"I'm always looking for new business opportunities." He kicks my leg under the blanket. "Now it's your turn to answer a question."

"I guess."

"Why did you put off getting your black belt for a year?"

I go quiet. It's something I've been thinking about, and I don't like the answers I've come up with.

"Is that a bad subject?" he presses.

"No. I mean, it's not my favorite subject. But it's okay, I guess."

He waits.

"I started taekwondo after... Well, after something bad happened. Learning it made me feel powerful. But I've been wondering, you know, what if it's not enough? Anyone could get in a situation where it's not enough—I mean, you saw what happened with that Trevor guy. It could have gone another way. And if I had a black belt and something bad happened to me again, that would just be such a...such a joke."

"Who messed with you?" Vic asks. His voice is calm, but there's a dangerous note just under the surface.

I've never told anyone what happened other than Izzy. It never feels like the right time or place to share. The truth is too raw, too painful, and too awkward. Conan knows I have some issues with my family, but I've never told him what they are. He still thinks I spend

Christmas with my sister and her husband. I've never felt like I could tell him everything. If my own sister didn't believe me, can I really trust Vic?

I look down at Milo, who's curled up like a soft donut between us, still purring. Milo seems to like Vic. Maybe that's enough? More than that, though—I think I want to tell him. This secret has been burning a hole in me for five years. Maybe I even *need* to tell him.

"It was my brother-in-law. My sister's husband? It was just before I graduated high school. I was already eighteen, so. He tried to...." I can't say the word. I keep going, hoping Vic can infer what happened. "He tried, and I fought him off. I stopped him. But I felt like I was lucky it wasn't worse and...that's why I signed up for self-defense classes at the school. I got into taekwondo after that."

Vic lets out a long breath. "I'm glad you fought the bastard off. You want me to hurt him?" His tone is light, but somehow, I don't think he's joking.

"No. It wouldn't help anything. He'd still be in my head."

"What did your sister say?"

"He told her I was lying, and she believed him. She still does."

"I'm sorry. That...sucks."

"I'm sorry to get so heavy."

"I asked." He nudges my foot again. "About the black belt thing... If you got it, and something ever happened to you, there's no shame in that. Knowing how to defend yourself is no absolute guarantee in any situation. It just gives you an edge. Same with the stuff I'm teaching you."

"But you teach people self-defense because of someone you knew, right?" I venture. "Don't you do it to stop bad things from happening?"

"No," he says, surprising me. "I do it because the worst thing in the world is to be in a psychological state where you think you can't fight. If you know how to fight and you lose, at least you know you had a chance. If you know how to fight—you'll try. But if you think you can't fight and someone hardcore messes with you, that fucks up your head for the rest of your life. And then you might just...give up."

"So, it's not about winning, it's about...fighting?"

"For me, yeah. Don't get me wrong, I like to win. But it's always about fighting. 'Cause if you know how to fight, you can keep going. No matter what happens."

"I never thought about it that way," I say. "I always figured martial arts and self-defense were about beating the bullies when they fuck with you."

"They absolutely can be. But you know, if I get jumped by five tough guys with serious skills, the odds are good that I'm gonna lose. Or sometimes, people freeze when they're threatened. They can't control it. The body just shuts down. Or someone pulls a gun, and you don't get it away from them in time. Life's not like the movies."

"No," I agree.

"Listen, Noelle. Don't think of the black belt test as some guarantee of safety. Think of it as an investment in yourself. In your commitment to it and the community you've built there. Conan might want you to teach classes someday. You're valuable. That gives you confidence in all kinds of situations, not just the ones where someone is threatening to physically hurt you."

He's making a lot of sense. It's the kind of thing I wish a parent could have told me.

"Okay. Thanks, Dad," I say, teasing him.

He throws a hungry look in my direction. "Listen, kid. I don't want to be your dad."

"Then don't call me a kid."

"Okay. Listen, *woman...*"

"It's okay." I grin at him. "I don't think of you that way. You were what, eight when I was born? Biologically impossible."

"All right, thanks. Makes me feel a bit less like a cradle robber."

"Oh, you're still a cradle robber. Eight years? That's like, practically an entire generation's difference. You're ancient."

He rolls his eyes. "How'd you fight off your sister's husband?" he asks suddenly. "Or is that a bad thing to talk about?"

"I kneed him in the nuts."

"Before you had any training?"

"Yeah?"

"You are a natural born fighter." He looks at me with a mix of what seems like desire and pride, producing an unfamiliar, pleasant sensation in my chest. "I want to kiss you, but I'm not sure your cat would approve."

"He doesn't need to approve. I'll move him." I reach out to do that, but Milo makes a slightly offended chirp. Then he stands up, stretches, and leaps off the bed, resettling himself on the window seat.

"Is that approval or disapproval?" Vic asks.

"I think that's his way of saying, 'If you humans are going to do that dumb body smashing thing again, I don't want any part of it.'"

"Are we?" Vic asks.

"Are we what?"

"Going to do that dumb body smashing thing again?"

I sit up, then climb over and straddle him. He immediately gets hard.

"Yeah," I say. "But we're doing it this way this time."

"Yes, ma'am," he says, then makes a soft growl as I guide him inside me.

I watch his eyes while I move on top of him, as the pleasure of fucking starts to overtake him. This is my favorite part—right before I come, when I know I'm helping whoever I'm with to get there. In that moment, I feel in control.

It's what I live for.

# CHAPTER TWENTY

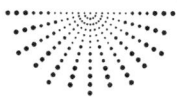

I handle the breakfast rush with Piper from seven until eleven on Tuesday morning, and we work well together, the way we always have. Even if Piper is hungover, she's always on when she's on the job. The customers love her. It makes the shift go super fast.

The night Vic showed up at my place, I told him how I followed his advice about talking to her but that we still haven't hung out alone. He said to ask her about it again. His exact words were, "Don't let it fester. Just call her out. See what she says." While we're cleaning up after the rush, I decide to give it a try.

"Hey," I say to her as we're bundling trays of clean silverware into separate canisters of knives, forks, and spoons. "Remember how we were going to hang out?"

She looks at me, stricken. "Yes. I know. I'm sorry! It's always me and Bill, me and the band, shows out of town. I'm serious, Noelle, my life changed overnight right after I met you. It's never been like this before."

"It's okay. I just miss hanging out with you."

She puts her hand on my arm. "I miss you, too."

"Hey, I had an idea, actually. It's pretty far in advance, so maybe you can make it? I have my black belt test for taekwondo in June, and we can ask friends and family to come watch. Would you want to come?"

Her face goes blank. "When is it?"

"June fourteenth."

Now, her face falls. "Hon, we're going on tour on the tenth. I'll be gone most of the rest of June."

"Oh well. Okay. Then yeah, I guess you can't come."

"I'm really sorry," Piper says. "It's been scheduled for a while now."

"No, it's okay. I get it," I say.

"How about this. We're meeting at that lounge again. The Pink Pauper? Tomorrow night."

"The place with the good wine?"

"Yeah, that place. You know how it's got all those little alcoves? Why don't we find a corner there so we can catch up? I'll just tell Bill to fuck off for a bit. Is that okay?"

She's being reasonable. She's trying. If I don't accept what she's offering, then maybe I'm being unreasonable. And I don't want to be unreasonable. I want to spend time with her.

"Yeah, okay," I say. "We could do that."

"Maybe we could even get there early, before the rest of the gang," she goes on, warming up to the idea. "That way we won't have to deal with them at all."

"Sure, yeah." That already sounds better. "Let's do it."

"It's a date!" She surprises me by giving me a spontaneous squeeze. "I'm glad we're friends. Thanks for putting up with my crazy life."

"It's okay. Everybody's life is crazy."

I guess Vic was right. All I had to do was stop simmering in silence and talk to Piper. Maybe I should keep him around if he's going to be this useful. It's kind of funny, though, that Vic's the one who's helping me stay close to Piper, since she no longer seems to think well of him.

———

WHEN I GET HOME Wednesday evening after class, I have about an hour to get ready before Piper picks me up, but I get distracted when I see my answering machine is blinking.

Thinking maybe Vic called, I stop to listen to the message.

"Hi, Noelle. This is Izzy. Your sister. Rob and I are going to be in Seattle this weekend, and we're coming to see you. We need to work everything out. It's important. We need to be a family again. I know you want your space, but I found your address. I found it months ago, actually, but I was hoping you'd give it to me yourself. We'll be there on Saturday around lunchtime. We can all go to lunch and talk, okay? This has gone on long enough. It's been you and me since Mom and Dad died, and we need to stick together. Okay? We'll see you on Saturday."

*Beep.*

I feel...strange. Almost like I'm no longer here in the room. I'm in some other, undefined dimension, even though I can see that I'm here, in my apartment. Nothing's out of place. But everything has changed.

I lift my hand in the air in front of my face, to reassure myself that I'm not imagining things. I'm surprised to see that my hand is shaking.

I need to snap out of it before Piper gets here. I head for the bathroom, willing the feeling to go away. By the time I've showered, changed my clothes, and put on minimal makeup, it seems to be working. The shaking has stopped, but I'm no longer excited to see Piper. In fact, I don't feel anything. I just know that we made a date to get together, and I know I want us to be friends, which means I need to keep the date.

When she arrives, Piper double parks outside and honks her horn. I peek out the window to be sure it's her car, then I kiss Milo on the head and go downstairs to meet her.

At The Pink Pauper, we grab a table in a tiny nook that's far away from the serving area. Piper goes to get our drinks so I can hold the spot for us. Our table is adorned with a dwarfish antique lamp, and "Man in the Box" is playing at low volume in the background, which cracks me up. Welcome to The Pink Pauper, the home of eclectic decor, fine wine, and understated angst. It's not busy in here yet, but as I wait the place starts to fill up, so I'm glad Piper had the foresight to ask me to guard our table.

She returns with two pint glasses of lager, delivering mine with a flourish, the way she does for customers at work. When she likes them.

"Thank you, ma'am."

"We aim to please." She sits down and treats me to a big smile. "Okay, spill. Tell me all about Vic."

I'm confused. "I thought you decided you don't like him?"

Piper shrugs. "So he carries around big rolls of cash sometimes. I'm sure any of us, given the chance, would do the same. What's he like in the sack?"

"Um…" I laugh, surprised. "He's…really good."

"Well, that's a shocker." She rolls her eyes.

"I definitely didn't like him at first," I admit.

"Oh, yeah? How come?"

"He was always lurking. At the Irish bar, O'Shea's? I thought he was a creepy security guard."

"What *does* he do?" Piper asks, almost murmuring the question before she takes a sip of her beer. "Did you ever find out?"

"Lots of different things, I guess. He helps procure protective gear for the school—the place where I practice taekwondo. But he also owns the building where O'Shea's is. And he teaches self-defense."

"Right. He owns a building and teaches self-defense. Did you ever figure out if he's actually loaded?"

"Still not sure." Vic doesn't act like a guy who's drowning in money. It's not like he drives a super fancy car or throws a ton of money around. But then there's that gorgeous gym he has in his apartment. And what seems to be his lack of an actual job.

"So, he's still a mystery," Piper says. "That's kind of a turn on, right?"

I have a sudden and intense craving to be wherever Vic is, pinned underneath him, with his body heaving over me and inside me. *Turn on* is putting it mildly, I guess.

As far as being in the room with Piper, though, that's fuzzy. I still feel the way I felt after I listened to my sister's voicemail. Disoriented. *She's going to be here on Saturday. With Rob.* Every time I think of them showing up, my brain freezes with panic and it's hard to focus on anything else.

"Noelle?" Piper snaps her fingers in front of my face. "You okay?"

"Oh, yeah, I'm fine." I laugh and take a couple gulps of beer.

"Good. Was worried I lost you there for a second."

"Nope. I'm here. Alive and in color."

Piper leans forward across the table. "Okay, so what about when you're not in bed? Do you guys do, like, karate together?"

The minute the words are out of her mouth, I'm angry. How many times have I told her which martial art I practice? But she never bothers to remember.

"It's taekwondo," I say. It feels like the words are being forced through my lips. "Karate is a Japanese martial art. Taekwondo is a Korean martial art. They aren't the same."

She stares at me for a minute. Then she says, softly, "Okay. My bad. They're not the same. I won't forget."

I know I should stop, but I don't. "Are you sure? Because you've never remembered before."

"Noelle, are you okay?" She sounds concerned, and somehow it's worse.

She shouldn't sound concerned. She should be pissed at me because I'm being an ass. I don't want her to be nice to me. I want her to yell at me.

I stand up. "You know what? I don't think I'm feeling well, actually. Think I'm going to take off."

She stands up, too. "I'll give you a ride back."

"*No.*" I say it with such force that she looks startled. "I need the walk. I just need to walk, okay?"

"Are you sure?"

"Yeah. I'm sure. I'm fine. Self-defense training, remember? Have fun with the band." I turn and leave before she can say anything else. I sense her staring after me, torn between me and her band. But I ignore it and keep going until I'm several blocks away. Until I'm sure that she isn't following me.

# CHAPTER TWENTY-ONE

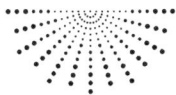

It's raining again, which is typical for late April. It's not raining hard, but it's steady. I'm going to get soaked. As I plough through the drizzle, my mind races with random thoughts. Like how I haven't been to that church on Capitol Hill to listen to the choir in ages. I imagine how they'd sound, singing something antiphonal and somber. I'm also thinking of my sister's message, as her words play on a loop in my head. In the background, car tires *hish* on the wet pavement.

My intention is to go back to my apartment, but somehow I find myself back at O'Shea's. I walk by the bar's windows quickly—I don't want to be seen, but I don't want to go home, either. I lean against the brick near Vic's door. I don't want to buzz his apartment and bother him. It feels good just to be here, where he lives.

The rain is probably making my makeup run, but I don't care. The droplets feel good on my face. A chill is slowly seeping into my bones, matching how I feel inside.

When the door to Vic's building bursts open, I jump. He stops in the dim streetlight and stares at me.

"Noelle?" he says, sounding shocked.

"Hey V-v-v-ic." My voice comes out all chattery and my teeth are knocking together. I guess I'm more cold than I thought.

He reaches out and takes my arm. "Let's get you inside."

He guides me upstairs holding my hand. The minute we're in his place, he says, "You need a shower. You should warm up."

I follow him into his bathroom, dazed. He starts the water while I stand there, waiting to see what he does next.

He comes over to me. "Turn around." I let him spin me so my back is to him, and he peels off my sopping coat. "Can you get in the shower by yourself?"

I nod.

Vic leaves with my coat. For a few seconds, I stare numbly at the water flowing behind the glass doors of the double-sized shower. Eventually, I pull off my clothes, leave them in a heap on the floor, and step under the hot water.

As my skin heats up, I become more aware of my surroundings. Vic's shower, like his in-house gym, seems to have been made to his personal specifications. The tile work is intricate, in different shades of blue, with white interspersed for contrast.

I hear a knock on the bathroom door, and call out, "Come in!"

"I'm leaving you a bathrobe," he says. "I'll hang it on the door. Come out when you're ready."

When I turn off the shower, I squeeze the excess water out of my hair and step out on to the bamboo bath mat. He's left a towel for me, too. I dry off, abandoning my clothes on the floor, and step into the robe he left for me. It looks like something of his. It's navy blue and hits below my knees.

I go to the kitchen first, but he's not there. Instead, I find him sitting on the couch in the semi-dark.

"You get warmed up?" he asks when I join him.

"Yep. All better."

"Good." He turns to me. "So, what the fuck were you doing standing in the rain outside my place?"

I don't have a good answer for him. If I tell him I felt better being near him, even if it was outside, that will sound odd. Maybe creepy. I just shrug, hoping he'll let it go.

"Noelle. There's something going on with you."

He's right. There is. But I don't want to think about it. Not right now. So I crawl on top of him, and kiss him. He starts kissing me

152

back, and I feel him getting hard underneath me. Then he pulls away and holds me at arms' length.

"We should talk," he says, but I can tell it pains him to say it.

"About what?" I press my knees against him and coax his hands down to the belt tie of my borrowed robe.

"About whatever made you stand out there in the rain and risk hypothermia."

"I wouldn't get hypothermia. It's spring." I lean forward and kiss him again, teasing him with my tongue.

Again, he pulls away. "You obviously don't know shit about hypothermia."

"C'mon, Vic." I grind my hips gently on top of him, then bend down and kiss his neck, his jawline, his mouth. "I'm sorry. I'm sorry if I made you worry. Take me to bed? We can talk later."

I feel his resistance breaking down. "Please," I whisper in his ear.

That seems to be the magic word. He grasps my hips and fits his mouth over mine, kissing me hard. Then he stands up, lifting me. I wrap my legs around him and let him carry me to his bed.

We lie awake for a while afterward, listening to the spring rain drip from the eaves and trickle down the gutters. I feel calm again. Like nothing can touch me. Vic's unusual living space seems cut off from the rest of the world, almost like it doesn't belong to it.

Then he destroys my illusion of escape. "So, what was going on with you tonight?"

"Do you actually still want to talk about that?"

"You know how you don't like it when people lie to you?" he asks.

"Yeah...?"

"Well, when you tell someone 'we can talk later,' you should mean it. Otherwise, that's kind of lying, too."

He's right. "I guess I didn't think you'd actually want to talk," I mumble.

"Well, I do. Spill it. What made you so upset tonight?"

"My sister," I manage. "She left me a voicemail. She's coming out here this weekend. With her husband. To visit me."

"Did you ask her to?"

"No!"

"Tell her you don't want to see her."

"You don't understand," I say miserably. "She's in that space where she won't take any crap from me. She's coming here. With him. She won't listen to me if I tell her not to."

Vic sits up in bed and looks down at me. "I'm sorry. I don't understand. What kind of 'space' is it where you just override what someone else wants?"

"She's my sister. She raised me. That gives her, like..." I search for a word. "That gives her certain rights."

"No, it doesn't," Vic says. "You're twenty-two. You're not a minor."

"Well, yeah, but—"

"Is she supporting you financially?" he interrupts.

"No, not since I moved out."

"Then what do you owe her?"

I look up at him, and his eyes are angry, though I know he's not angry with me. I look away. "She's my sister."

"And she's bringing her husband?"

"Right."

"The guy who tried to rape you?"

I flinch at his words, then nod against the pillow.

"What kind of sister does that?"

"I try to stay away," I explain. "I don't go home for holidays anymore. I don't visit them. But sometimes, you know, she comes and visits me."

"Does she always bring her attempted rapist husband with her?"

"No. No, never. That's different this time. She said... She said she wants us to talk it out so we can be a...family again."

His eyes have gone dark. For a second, I think he might lose it. But he doesn't. He gently coaxes me to a sitting position and takes my shoulders so I have to look at him.

"Noelle. Bringing a guy who scares you into your home and forcing you to talk to him is not what someone who loves you would do. I don't want you anywhere near that motherfucker."

I look in his eyes and the concern I see in them is painful. For so long, I've been wishing I could find someone I could open up to. Someone who would see my side of things. But I always thought it

154

would be a relief to find that person. I never expected it to hurt so much.

"I don't know what else to do," I say, finally. "She'll be here. Trust me."

"Look," Vic says, "I found you outside my place on the edge of freezing to death. That's not normal behavior. This is obviously fucking with you."

"I had a fight with Piper, too," I blurt. Then I amend, "Well, not a fight. But I was kind of a jerk to her."

He moves his hand from my shoulder to my face and brushes a piece of my hair back behind my ear. "We'll figure out what to do," he says. "You want a hot toddy?"

"A hot toddy?"

"It'll help you sleep. Plus, it's medicinal, in case you're getting sick."

"What's the medicinal part?"

He grins. "Whiskey, of course."

"Yeah, okay. That sounds good."

"Be right back." He nabs the robe I borrowed from him off the floor and puts it on, but not before I get a glimpse of his truly magnificent ass. I don't deserve this, I think. Despite everything Vic just said to me, I still feel like I'm a bad person because I don't want to see my sister this weekend. I don't believe I deserve a man who seems to actually give a shit about me. Who's hot. And who does a crazy good job of making me come. It's too good to be true.

It's more than I can wrap my mind around.

I listen to him puttering around his kitchen, and the sounds he's making in there blend with the sound of the rain. It's a comforting mix. Even though we were just talking about some real shit, none of this feels real. It's like I'm in a dream.

Presently, Vic returns with two steaming mugs that give off the tang of lemon, the undertone of whiskey, and some other aroma I can't place.

"Careful," he says, handing me a mug. "It's still pretty hot."

I take it from him and inhale the comforting fragrance. "Did I, um… Did I mess up your plans tonight? You were on your way somewhere, right? When you found me outside?

He shrugs. "Nowhere important. Not tonight, anyway. Why didn't you buzz the apartment? I would have come down and let you in."

If I were going to be honest with him, I'd say I felt safe just being outside his door and didn't have the energy to tell him I was here. But I doubt it will make much sense if I say it aloud. Instead, I tell him my other reason, which is also true.

"I wasn't sure you wanted to see me yet. We were meeting tomorrow anyway. You haven't called. I didn't want to crowd you."

"I wanted to call," Vic says, "but I was trying not to crowd *you*."

I stare at him for a second. "Well, that's kind of ridiculous then, isn't it?"

"Ridiculous," he agrees, and we smile at each other.

"Hey," I venture. "Since I've been spilling my guts all week, can I ask you something?"

"Sure." He sounds guarded, but also game, so I forge ahead.

"You said there was someone you used to know—someone you wished you'd helped. Who is that person?"

He goes quiet. I'm waiting for him to say it was his sister or a girl-friend or even his mother. But his answer surprises me.

"It was my brother," he says. "He was younger than me by about ten years. Got bullied a lot. Wasn't athletic, like me. I used to tell him he was cool the way he was, you know. Sensitive, artistic. I told him to be himself."

He stops.

"What happened?" I ask softly.

Vic's eyes are bleak. "He killed himself."

His pain hits me in the chest, as shocking and aggressive as though someone actually punched me. I put out a hand to touch his arm. "Vic...."

"I thought I did the right thing, telling him to be himself. I should have taught him to fight. I should have taught him he wasn't helpless. It's like I said before, even if you lose a fight, if you know how to fight back, at least you know you're in the game. It's not just about kicking some bully's ass. Learning how to fight does good things for your state of mind. But I didn't give that to him."

"Don't blame yourself." I falter in my search for words, not sure of the right ones. I go with what I think is true: "There's no way you can know if that would have stopped him."

"I'll never know either way because I didn't try."

He's haunted. It's plain on his face that he's not over it. I set the empty mug from my drink on the floor, then scoot over to put my arms around him. The amazing thing is that he lets me. The even more amazing thing is that he rests his head on my shoulder and allows me to stroke his hair, to comfort him.

I've never had a moment like this with a guy before. We sit there like that for several minutes, until eventually he slides his arms around me and tightens them so I'm pressed against his chest.

When he starts kissing me, it just feels like an extension of our embrace, like he's trying to get comfort from every inch of me, inside and out. I want the same from him. His whole body is a refuge, and when he enters me again, I have everything I need to feel warm and protected. Vic was the medicine I needed all along. I was just too scared to ask for it.

# CHAPTER TWENTY-TWO

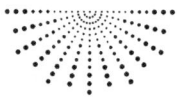

On Thursday, Vic and I do our usual thing. We work on a mix of tactics in his home gym, then get burgers at O'Shea's. He insists on walking me home.

Just before he leaves, he says, abruptly, "I'm going to be here with you on Saturday. I don't want you to be alone when your sister shows up."

"And when she shows up, then what?"

"I'll be here. Or if you don't want to be here, you can come stay with me. But you can't face them alone."

"Those are my only choices?"

"Unless you come up with something better, yeah."

My knee-jerk response is to make up an alternative plan on the spot. I don't have to do what he says just because he says so. But actually, the idea of him being here on Saturday fills me with relief.

"Okay." I reach up and kiss him. "See you Saturday."

Things aren't as easy with Piper. She's her same reliable self on Friday morning at the Pancake House, but she seems uncomfortable around me now. I want to talk to her, but since we're working the same shift, I don't get a chance, and our breaks are staggered.

I try to catch her after we both punch out, but she says she has a rehearsal with the band. I don't know if she's telling me the truth.

When she leaves, I debate whether to chase after her. Tell her I know it was shitty of me to ask her to put aside time for the two of us, then, when she made it happen, for me to bail on her. But the truth is, I'm afraid of how she'll react.

I let her go and take the bus to the church on Capitol Hill. Even though it's not the night for choir practice, I'm in luck. A smaller ensemble of singers is in the sanctuary rehearsing a particularly haunting piece of music. Their voices reverberate back and forth as they sing harmonies punctuated by short sections of what sound like Gregorian chants. I lie on my back on one of the balcony pews and listen.

It's so different from the day when Vic came up here and found me. It's almost May, now, and it's beginning to get warm outside. There's a window open somewhere, and I can feel and smell the spring air wafting into the sanctuary. It's moments like this that make me wish I could stomach religion. It would be so nice to sit here with other people on a Sunday morning sharing an uplifting experience. To believe the words being spoken from the pulpit and take comfort in them. But how can I believe in anything when I know people like Rob could be sitting in the room? People who hurt others and then lie about it? Who then sing hymns of praise to God, signaling to everyone around them that they're just another good person in church on a Sunday?

When I feel I've soaked up enough music, I take the bus home, where I shower and feed Milo. Then I fix some mac & cheese out of a box, adding a can of chicken for extra protein. Once we're both satiated, we drift over to the window seat.

I wonder if Piper's going out tonight. She probably is, but she didn't ask me to go with her. There was no message from her on my machine when I got home.

The intercom for my apartment buzzes. I stare at it. The intercom is kind of a joke, because half the time, the lock on the building's outside door doesn't work. Plus, often people walk in whenever someone else walks out. The intercom buzzes again. It couldn't be Izzy and Rob. They wouldn't drive down early on a Friday night.

Would they? I get up and walk over to the intercom then press the button to answer.

"Hello?" I say.

"Noelle. It's Vic. Is it too late for me to come up?"

Relief floods through me. "Let me buzz you in."

When he knocks on the door, I swing it wide. "Hey," I grin at him. "Come on in."

He holds up a paper bag. "Thought maybe you were hungry. Brought burgers from O'Shea's."

"Oh, that was sweet," I laugh. "I'm stuffed, but you can eat if you want."

"Dammit. I should have called ahead."

"Put the other one in the fridge if you don't want it yourself. I'll eat it later." I go into the kitchen to get him a plate, and he drifts in after me.

"I was thinking—" he starts.

I hold out my hand. "Give me the burger. I'll plate it up for you."

He hands the bag over. "I keep forgetting you work at that diner. I should visit you there one of these days."

Inside the bag, there are two Styrofoam containers with burgers. The lettuce and tomato have been thoughtfully placed on the side of each one. I assemble one of the burgers on a plate and hand it over to Vic, then put the other container in the fridge. "Need condiments?"

He takes the plate from me. "Noelle, I was thinking. I should stay here tonight. I don't know when your sister's coming tomorrow, but if I'm already with you, she can't surprise you in the morning before I get here."

"You don't have to do that," I say. "I'm used to dealing with her on my own."

"Yeah," he agrees. Then he looks earnestly in my eyes. "Are you sure that's a good thing? I keep remembering how you looked when I found you outside. You were almost catatonic. You scared me."

"It's not that big of a deal." As I speak, I'm aware these are words I've told myself many times. "He didn't actually rape me. I stopped him. It turned out okay."

"Yeah," Vic says, slowly. "I know. But *you're* not okay."

"I know," I admit. I feel exposed as he continues to look at me. "So, are you going to eat or what?" Inside, I'm begging him not to push it. Not to ask me what I'm going to do about the fact that I'm not okay. Mercifully, he doesn't.

"Where do you eat in this joint?" he asks. "I don't see a table, no barstools...."

"On the window seat." I lead him over there and we both sit down.

Milo settles on the bed and watches us eat.

"You know," Vic ventures after a few bites. "After my brother— after that all went down, I ended up seeing someone. Just to help me sort things out, you know? Sometimes it helps to talk to someone."

"You mean a shrink?"

"It doesn't have to be that intense. Just a counselor. Just someone to talk to."

"I can't afford it," I say, bluntly. "I don't have health insurance, and I don't think shrinks, or counselors, or whatever they are let you talk to them for free."

He sighs. "No health insurance. There seems to be a lot of that going around."

I pull myself into a cross-legged position on the window seat.

Vic looks over at me. "I'll butt out if you want me to. I just wish you had someone who could help you more—more than I can."

"I started taekwondo because of what happened," I remind him. "It helped me for a long time."

"What changed?" he asks.

"Christmas Eve. When that jerk at O'Shea's attacked me? That's when it changed. Taekwondo was like this mental shield for a few years. It made me feel safe. I'm glad it helped me that night. But it might not always work."

"So, you need a new mental shield?" he guesses.

"Maybe. I don't know what I need. But I'll know when I find it." I meet his eyes. "At least, that's what I think."

"I hope you find it, then," he says.

"Me, too."

———

WE WAKE up in the morning to loud banging on the door. We're both naked under my blankets, and Milo is curled up at the foot of the bed.

At first I think the noise is in my dream. But slowly, as I come back to a conscious state, I realize it's actually happening.

"What the hell is that?" Vic says, quiet.

"Noelle?" a voice calls out from the hall. "Noelle, are you in there?"

"Shit," I say. "It's my sister."

Vic groans. "Of course it is."

I glance over at the clock on my small nightstand. 7:15 a.m. *Jesus, Izzy.*

"Are you going to answer the door or ignore her?" Vic asks.

I should ignore her. Seven in the morning is not a normal time to show up for a visit, especially if you haven't pre-arranged the time. *Especially* if you aren't even invited or welcome. I'm shocked, and yet I'm not. It's something Izzy would do. I slide back under the covers. "Ignore her," I whisper.

We stay quiet, waiting for a moment of prolonged stillness that would indicate my sister has given up. But instead, she pounds on the door again. "Noelle, open up. I'm here with Rob. We'll take you to breakfast."

"She actually brought that motherfucker here?" Vic springs out of bed and starts throwing on his clothes. He finds mine and tosses them to me. "Get dressed."

"What are you going to do?" I ask.

"Ask them nicely to leave, since we haven't had time for breakfast."

"You don't have to do that," I say, pulling on my jeans. "She's my sister. I'll deal with her."

"You shouldn't have to. Not like this."

He's probably right. Izzy's trying to ambush me before I even have a chance to start my day. It was prescient of Vic to offer to stay over last night. If he hadn't, I'd be dealing with this alone.

The knock sounds at the door again. "Noelle!"

"One of us has to go to the door," Vic says. "They're going to piss off your neighbors."

"Okay," I nod. "Go ahead." If I were here alone, I'd risk pissing off the neighbors. But since Vic is willing to act as a buffer for me, I'm inclined to let him.

He goes to the door and partially opens it. "Good morning," he says, pleasantly enough. "Noelle was sleeping. She's not ready to go to breakfast."

"Who are you?" Izzy asks.

"You the boyfriend?" Rob adds.

It's the first time in months that I've actually heard Rob's voice. I hate the sound of it. It makes me want to dive back under the covers again. But I force myself to sit on the edge of the bed, where I can listen to what they're saying.

"I'm Noelle's friend," Vic says. "She's not in the mood for uninvited guests this morning."

"I'm her sister. You can't keep me from her."

"I'm not keeping her from anybody. She doesn't want to see you."

"Noelle!" Izzy calls out, loud. "It's okay, honey. We're here. You're safe."

*Oh for fuck's sake*, I think. She's making it sound like Vic is holding me hostage, and she's making a scene. I need to put a stop to it.

I get up and join Vic at the door. "I'm right here," I tell my sister. "I'm fine."

Rob catches my eye and I look away from him. Everything about him makes me feel repulsed. He's taller than Vic, about six feet, and he's got a larger build. But he's older now, close to forty, and maybe not taking good care of himself. He has a small beer belly.

"Is this your boyfriend?" Izzy asks.

I echo Vic. "He's a friend. And yeah, I'm sorry, I can't come to breakfast. We just woke up and we have plans today."

"But we already had plans," my sister says. "We were going to talk. The three of us."

"I didn't make those plans," I remind her. "*You* made them and left them on my voicemail."

Rob speaks up. "Look, it doesn't matter who made the plans, your sister is right. We need to talk."

*The fucking nerve.* I can't get words out, so I just stare at him, feeling all the unpleasant emotions he evokes pooling behind my eyes.

"Okay," Vic says. "That's enough. You made plans, Noelle didn't agree to them, and now you're harassing her at home early in the morning. I think you should leave."

Rob's getting angry. He draws himself up to his full height and raises his voice. "You don't have a right to tell us to leave. You aren't her family. We are."

Of all the things that make me want to vomit, my sister's husband calling me "family" has got to be near the top. Next to me, Vic is responding to Rob's more aggressive stance by shifting his body between us like a shield.

"I think there's only one family member here," Vic says. "Noelle's sister. Why don't we leave it between the two of them. All right?" He gives Rob a look, and it's not friendly. I've never seen Vic actually fight anyone, but I have a feeling it could happen any moment.

"Noelle, c'mon, get your coat and let's go," Izzy urges.

I feel torn. A part of me still wants to please my sister, my sister who was there for me when our parents died. There are so many good memories between us. Another part of me wants to slam the door in her face. And I'm not proud of this, but a part of me also wants to see Vic kick the shit out of Rob.

In the center of my swirling and confused emotions, I realize I'm the only person who has the power to end this.

"I'm not going to breakfast with you," I say. "Just go home, Izzy."

"We came all this way to talk—"

"I'm not going with you," I repeat. "Please go home."

"You heard her," Vic says. "We've probably woken up the entire floor by now, so I'm going to shut the door."

"Is that what you want, Noelle?" Izzy asks. The look of disbelief on her face is so confusing. If I try to put myself in her shoes, I'd guess the incredulity is because she thinks Rob never tried to hurt me. She can't believe that I don't want to come out to breakfast and let her and Rob convince me of this.

The absurdity of it makes me crazy, and the fact that she can't take me at my word makes my head hurt. "Please go home," I tell her.

It feels like there's an emotional vacuum in the space between all of us. A black hole. I close my eyes, hoping I don't get sucked in.

Then I hear the door shut. Vic's arms go around me, but I don't feel anything. I'm just numb. I'm glad he's holding me and it's better that he's here. But I don't want to cry. I'm not angry. I'm just exhausted.

"That was a trip," he says.

I just nod against his shoulder, wishing I could feel something. It's so quiet in here. The street outside is quiet. My refrigerator isn't humming.

I lift my head off Vic's shoulder. "Where's Milo?"

"Milo?"

"My cat. His name is Milo."

"I'm sure he's around here somewhere," Vic says.

"I have to find him." I go to the windowsill. It's empty, as is the bed. I throw back the covers in case he's hiding in a pile of blankets. Then I go in the kitchen, and look high and low, to see if he's on top of a kitchen cabinet, or on the refrigerator. But the search turns up nothing.

I rush into the bathroom, starting to feel panicked. Every corner of it, including the bathtub, is cat free. I collide with Vic as I come crashing out of the bathroom.

"He's gone!"

"Have you checked under the bed?"

I rush back to the bed and rip off the bedding, throwing it to the floor, then I grab the corner of the mattress. Vic comes over to help me, and we wrest the mattress and then the boxspring off the bed frame. It's dusty under there. But again: no cat.

Vic stands there, looking helpless. Then he says, "Stay here. I'll go look for him."

"I'll go with you."

"You're too upset," he says. "You're going to freak him out. Stay here, and maybe if he found some crazy hiding place, he'll come out for you. If he walked out, he can't be far away. Okay?"

He doesn't give me a chance to agree or disagree and disappears through the door. I hate myself. If I'd gone with my sister right away, maybe this wouldn't have happened. The door was open so long while we were arguing, and none of us were thinking about a curious cat making a break for it.

I sink on to the window seat and start scanning the street outside my apartment, looking for Milo. I imagine him slipping through the door of the building, escaping to the outside, and attempting to cross the street in traffic. Or maybe he's wandering down the hall on a different floor and somebody will steal him. Or hurt him.

It feels like Vic has been gone a long time. I pick my way around the displaced mattress and boxspring so I can check the time on my alarm clock. Now it reads 7:55 am. I can't stay here. I have to look for Milo myself. I find my keys and start for the door.

When I open it, Vic is standing there with Milo in his arms. "Shhh," he says. "Let's get this guy inside before we overwhelm him."

I let Vic in and shut the door. He sets Milo down on the floor, and the little stinker trots right over to the window seat and jumps up on it like nothing happened.

"Where'd you find him?"

"You know how you have that little bench in your lobby? First I went through every floor in the building, knocked on some doors. I was gonna go look for him outside but then I saw him on my way out. He was just chilling on the bench in the lobby like he does it all the time."

I rush at Vic and throw my arms around him. "Thank you."

Then I break from him and go over to the window seat where I kneel next to Milo. "You crazy fucking cat. You scared me." I pet his head, and he purrs and rubs against my hand.

"So…" Vic says from behind me.

I stand up. "You probably have to be somewhere, huh?"

"This afternoon," he agrees. "But, Noelle, you made the right decision."

"What decision?"

"Not going with your sister."

"I hope it was."

"I know it was. They ambushed you."

I sigh. "Yeah. She does that."

He raises his eyebrows. "Does that kind of thing happen all the time?"

"Not all the time. They've actually never been to my apartment before. But Izzy comes down here once a year or so and asks me to have lunch. So, hey, on the upside, I'm good for another year," I try to joke.

Vic doesn't laugh. "That's gotta be stressful."

I shrug. "Dealing with family is always stressful."

"Sure, but this is kind of beyond what's normal. There's got to be a better way."

I take a deep breath and seek out his eyes. "Thanks for getting my cat back. And for standing up for me. And being here. It was...amazing. You're amazing. Can we leave it at that for now?"

He wants to argue with me. I can see it in his face. But he manages to get control of it and says, "All right. For now."

I grin at him. "Good. Want to help me put the bed back together so we can fuck on it?"

He puts his finger to his chin. "Let me think about that. Yeah, okay. I guess that would be all right."

He's adorable. How did I get lucky enough to find someone like him? Someone who's fun and who gives a shit about me? It's like I finally have some life in my life. I point at the boxspring on the floor. "Let's do it!"

He catches me around the waist and plants a kiss on my lips, then releases me.

"What was that for?"

He shrugs. "I just wanted to. I like you."

A shiver goes through me. "I like you, too."

He touches his finger to my nose. "Let's get that boxspring."

# CHAPTER TWENTY-THREE

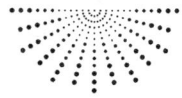

Piper manages to avoid me at the Pancake House for almost two weeks, until a day in early May, when I finally catch her taking a break. I slide into her booth. "Hey. How are you doing?"

She looks up from her plate of food. "I'm good. How're you?"

"I'm okay. Listen, I wanted to tell you I'm sorry I bailed on you the other night. When we tried to hang out at The Pink Pauper? I was having a shitty day, and I took it out on you."

"Sure," she shrugs. "I get it."

But she doesn't sound like she gets it at all.

"Maybe we can try to hang out again?" I say. "I mean, whenever you have time."

"Sure, maybe." Her tone is noncommittal.

"Are you pissed at me?" I ask. I'm afraid to hear her answer, but I need to know.

"I'm not pissed," she says. "I just don't have time to play any weird girl games. Okay?"

"'Weird girl games?' What do you mean?"

She bats her eyelashes. "Oh, I love you so much! Oh, let's hang out. Oh wait, I forgot I had to freak out about something tonight! Or go see my boyfriend, or whatever the hell you did after you left."

I'm stunned. "I wasn't playing a game. I told you, I had a really shitty day."

"Okay. You had a shitty day."

"I did." But I can tell she doesn't believe me, and now I'm a little angry. "But I mean, how would you know when I'm having a shitty day? It's not like we hang out enough for you to notice the difference anyway."

"I want to hang out with you," she says. "Why do you think I invite you everywhere?"

"Right," I retort. "To be a third wheel with you and your boyfriend, and a fifth wheel with you and your band."

"Sorry it's been so awful hanging out with me and my friends."

"It isn't awful, I— Whatever, Piper, I just wanted to hang out with *you!*"

"See," she says. "That's what I mean. Girl games. I'm not playing." She stands up and grabs her plate. "I have to go." She takes herself out of the booth.

I'm stunned she's this pissed at me. She thinks I'm playing games, which isn't true or fair. My family situation was the reason I was so messed up the night we tried to hang out together. I wanted to be honest with her. But we never got a chance to get close enough for me to feel comfortable telling her something so personal, and I'm not about to bring it up now just so she'll feel sorry for me.

At the beginning of the year, I would have thought I'd be closer to Piper by now. That maybe she'd turn out to be the kind of friend I could confide in. I wouldn't have put Vic in the picture at all. But Vic is a bigger part of my life every day, and unless I can figure out how to fix things with Piper, she could be moving out of frame.

For the millionth time, I wonder if my inability to hang on to friendship with another woman is because there's something fundamentally wrong with me, or if it's some kind of damage that was done to me earlier in life.

It's also possible something happened to Piper, and I remind her of someone who played "girl games" with her. If I had to guess what she means by "girl games," it's probably the way girls and women sometimes use modes of belonging and not belonging to hurt each other.

Is she being unreasonable? Or is she right, and I'm the one playing games? Whatever's truly going on, I wish to hell that I could figure it out so I could fix it.

I go through the rest of my shift in a surly mood, barely avoiding snapping at a number of my customers. It's obvious I'm off my game, because my tips are measly. After work, I drag myself to class at the school, since I promised Conan I would be a dedicated student until my belt test.

But I make mistakes. Tons of them. By the time I get home, I feel like I'm failing at everything. Taekwondo. Friendship. Family.

The only thing in my life that doesn't make me feel like a failure right now is Vic, and I decide to find him. I don't care if it's too soon. When I'm with him I feel like I'm breathing fresh air after years of being trapped in a musty room. I need more oxygen.

The air feels soft and warm as I walk to Vic's apartment. I buzz up to his place and decide if he doesn't answer, I'll just go into O'Shea's and get something to eat. Vic's always popping in at the bar, so I'll run into him eventually.

But when someone answers, it's a woman's voice. "Who is it?"

I'm stunned. Why is there a woman in Vic's apartment? Then I think, maybe it's his cleaning lady. Didn't he say he had his place cleaned regularly?

"Is he there? Can you tell him it's Noelle?"

"Oh, hi there, Noelle. This is Sheryl."

Sheryl. Vic's friend. My sometimes sparring partner. My mind flips back to the times we've trained together and how Vic and I never hang out when she's there. I've just accepted it, because why wouldn't I? But now I'm sleeping with him, and that means....

I realize it doesn't mean a goddamn thing. Vic and I haven't had a conversation about being exclusive or anything. In fact, I suddenly remember, when Izzy asked if he was my boyfriend, he specifically insisted that he was my *friend*.

"I'm sorry," I say, as a horrible, yawning pit opens up in my stomach. "I'll come back another time."

"No, Noelle, hold on." I hear her calling out to Vic, telling him it's me.

A couple of seconds later, his voice crackles through the outside intercom. "Noelle, give me a few minutes and I'll be right down. Okay?"

I don't reply, just sink against the wall as I try not to imagine him putting his clothes back on after being in bed with Sheryl. I attempt to reason with myself. Vic truly doesn't owe me shit. Just because he likes being with me doesn't mean he's not involved with anyone else. For that matter, I don't owe him shit, either. I could leave right now and go find someone else to spend the night with.

But I don't want that. I want him. I hate how vulnerable that makes me feel.

Sheryl and Vic come out together.

"I really appreciate your help," he tells her.

"No problem," she says. Then she looks at me. "I hear you're going to get your black belt, huh? When's the test?"

"In June." I try to keep the amplified surliness I'm feeling out of my voice, but it's a struggle. I don't think I'm succeeding.

Sheryl presses my arm briefly. "He's all yours now. I'll see you later." She looks over at Vic. "Stay out of trouble."

He gives her a wan smile. "I'll do my best." Then he beckons to me. "Come on inside."

Once we're in his lobby, I blurt, "I don't care if you and Sheryl are sleeping together. We never talked about other people, but please tell me if you are. Please don't lie to me. Because if you lie to me, I can't..." I trail off, hating how desperate I sound.

Vic was heading for the stairs, but now he stops in his tracks and looks directly at me. "I'm not sleeping with her. Okay? I want you to know that."

"Are you sure? Don't try to make me feel better. I want the truth. Please tell me the truth."

"I think I'd know if I was sleeping with her."

"How do you know her?" I ask.

"We used to teach martial arts together at this community center in town. I don't formally belong to any gym, so sometimes we spar. I gotta stay in shape."

"So, is that why she was here today? To spar?" In my gut, I don't feel like the vibes between Sheryl and Vic were sex vibes. But I do have the sense they were talking about something intense. It was in the tone of his voice when he thanked her for helping him, and even when she teased him about staying out of trouble.

Something is off.

"We can talk about it upstairs," he says.

"Actually, I could use a burger."

He smiles. "Actually, so could I. Let's go eat."

I'm relieved. I am legitimately hungry. But I have this feeling that if we hang out in his apartment, we'll for sure talk about why Sheryl was at his place this evening, and now I don't think I want to know. If I ask him about it while we're in public, he'll likely give me the abridged version. That might be the version I prefer.

I need Vic to be my rock tonight. I need a freaking rock.

Once we're all set with burgers and beer, I say, "Why was Sheryl hanging out at your place?"

"There's some tricky business shit she's handling for me," he says. We're sitting at a table because the bar was completely full, and I swear I see him glance surreptitiously around us before he goes on. "In addition to being a kick-ass martial arts instructor, she's also a financial wizard. I had to get her up to speed on some best and the worst-case scenarios."

"Is that what you guys always talk about after I spar with her? Your, uh, tricky business shit?"

He nods. "Usually, yeah. She's a friend. I've known her for, I don't know, maybe five years or more."

"Are you ever going to tell me what your business actually is? Because, I mean, if you have 'business' you must have some kind of job."

"Actually the stuff I discuss with Sheryl happened a long time ago," he says. "You know how sometimes certain situations in life aren't over until they're over?"

I'm hesitant. "Sure?"

"Sheryl's really good at helping me figure out how to tie up loose ends. She's a very..." he searches for a word. "She's a very pragmatic person."

172

I don't feel like I've learned much more about what Vic does for a living, but I don't have the energy to push further.

"Okay. And you told her I'm taking the black belt test?"

"Yeah. Yeah, I did tell her that. Was that bad?"

"I guess it's okay. It's not like it's a secret or anything."

"I'm just proud of you, that's all."

I can see from his eyes that he means it, and I wonder if he can see the starved look in my own eyes as I say, "I needed to hear that. Tonight especially."

He reaches across the table and takes my hand. His eyes are serious, and something about the way he searches my face shakes me to my core. "If you need to hear it again, I'm incredibly proud of you. You're tackling a physical challenge, but you're also tackling your fear. It's inspiring."

That does something to me, him saying that. I don't go around thinking of myself as inspiring. I don't think of myself as anything at all. Most of the time, I feel like I'm running from something.

"Will you be there for my belt test? I mean, will you come watch?" The words come out in a rush. I'm scared he's going to say no, like Piper did. Even if he has a good reason, I really don't want to hear it.

"Of course," he says without hesitation. "I'd love to be there."

"Thanks." I smile awkwardly and he just smiles back at me. Everything is fine again.

Vic's still holding on to my hand, rubbing his thumb over my skin. It's sexy in this subtle way. I notice no one's coming up to talk to him tonight. Maybe it's because we're sitting at a table instead of at the bar. Maybe it's because even a light touch from him makes me think of more intense, intimate touch. We're probably giving off a vibe.

The light pressure of his thumb on my hand is driving me crazy. I'm afraid I'm going to jump him right here in front of everybody. I catch his eye. "Do you want to go upstairs? And have a...drink?"

His eyes crinkle into a smile. "Thought you'd never ask."

As he signals our server and asks for the bill, I feel like I'm observing events happen in slow motion. Watching him pull money out of his wallet to pay for our meal, waving away my attempt to pay my own share, the way I used to do. Meeting my eyes again with another smile that makes my knees weak.

Later, when I'm naked with him in his bed, I promise myself that whatever happens, I won't forget how good this is right now. Being with someone like Vic. Someone who gets me.

Someone who might actually be on my side.

# CHAPTER TWENTY-FOUR

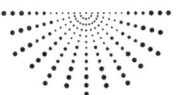

It's several weeks after the aborted family breakfast when Izzy finally leaves me a long voicemail about it. She says it would have been nice if I'd told her about my new boyfriend. She hopes he's treating me well and, if we're happy together, she also hopes that nothing ever comes between us.

She also tells me Rob "is disappointed we didn't get a chance to talk." She suggests a brunch somewhere halfway between Seattle and where she and Rob live. I know, in her mind, that means she's showing me that she'll meet me halfway.

When we were kids and our parents were still alive, Izzy and me fought like normal siblings, and I looked up to her the way little sisters always do. But after our parents died, Izzy became my entire support system. She had to assume full adult responsibilities overnight at age nineteen. I was eleven then and still in awe of her. Until I was sixteen, it was just the two of us making our way through life, going to late night movies, and baking chocolate chip cookies for dinner if we felt like it. Life was fun when it was just the two of us. Or at least, that's how it seemed to me.

But then she met Rob and things changed. She was still Izzy, but now Rob lived with us in our apartment. He filled our space with his hobbies, his political opinions, and his favorite television shows. And maybe I could have got used to all that. But I never felt comfortable around him. I also felt guilty for not loving him because Izzy was happy. I never heard them fight.

Despite how harmonious everything was on the surface, Rob's presence in the apartment made me uneasy. It was hard to be myself. I tried to be more quiet. Less visible. I didn't laugh as often, and I became super conscious of monopolizing Izzy's time. Rob wanted her time now.

I never got used to him. I couldn't relax whenever Rob and I occupied the same room. Until the night he tried to assault me, I didn't understand why he made me feel that way.

I miss how Izzy and I used to be. I miss our childhood selves, and those first five years we had alone together, when we were navigating the aftermath of losing our parents. I'm sure it was harder for her than she let on. I know I probably can't understand just how hard it was.

But every time I think of how she turned me away, how she refused to believe me when I told her what happened with Rob, a wall goes up inside that I can't climb. Since she doesn't believe me, she must think I'm a liar. And how can you have a good or honest relationship with someone who thinks you would lie about something so serious?

Sometimes, I wonder if I should leave it all in the past, reconnect with them and hope that Rob doesn't ever try anything again. But what if he did? What would stop him, since Izzy doesn't believe he did anything wrong in the first place? Either way, knowing my sister thinks I'm a liar hurts. It hurts to hear her voice, to talk to her, to see her.

I don't think I know how to get past it.

———

In mid-May, I take the written portion of my upcoming black belt test. The written test, which is a month before the skills test, is an essay about what becoming a black belt will mean to us, personally. Before we start the test, we listen to a lecture, where the instructors

176

go over all the areas in which we'll have to demonstrate proficiency. They remind us the test is just as much about endurance as it is about demonstrating skill. I'm getting nervous, but in a good way. Ever since Vic said he'd be there to watch me, I've been excited, too.

Until now, moving up the belt ranks is something I've done for myself. For my own sense of confidence. I've never had anyone cheering me on—except for Conan, of course. But he cheers on all of his students. That's his job.

As I'm walking out of the meeting, Conan comes over to me.

"Ready for the skills test?" he asks.

"I will be."

"Good to hear. Hey, I was meaning to ask you. Have you heard anything from Vic lately?"

Something in the tone of his voice makes me nervous. I wonder again if he knows I'm involved with Vic. In fact, it seems silly to keep it a secret. I open my mouth to tell Conan that I'll be seeing Vic tonight.

But before I can get the words out, he says, "If you see him, tell him I hope he's holding up okay. I'm here for him if he needs anything."

"Sure, uh...I'll tell him that." I'm confused. What's going on with Vic?

Conan pats me on the shoulder. "You're doing great work. Keep it up."

"Oh. Thanks." Baffled, I watch him go to the front desk. What does he know that I don't?

Maybe it's a guy thing. If I knew what it was, it would probably bore me. I decide to forget it for now, and rush home to change my clothes and feed Milo. Then I head out to meet Vic at O'Shea's. I arrive first and order a Guinness. People are in good spirits. We've had a stretch of gorgeous weather, and it's not too hot. Every time someone walks in the bar, a rush of fragrant springtime air drifts inside.

I sip my beer slowly, enjoying the opportunity to watch people. The room is a whirl of gaiety and laughter and customers, all happy to be done with their obligations for the day. It's a world of adults who can make their own decisions about their lives. It's glorious, free, and normal. I decide I belong in this world.

I ask Aidan what time it is.

"Six o'clock, sweetheart," he says. "You waiting for Vic?"

I nod. "Yeah."

"I'm sure he'll be here soon."

I don't have any reason to doubt that.

"Want another one?" Aidan asks, gesturing to my almost empty beer glass.

"Not yet," I say. "But if I'm still here in fifteen minutes, ask me again."

Aidan winks at me and moves away to take orders from a group that's just arrived.

Someone taps me on the shoulder. I turn around smiling, thinking it's Vic.

But it's Kane O'Shea.

"Hello, Noelle," he says. His voice is cordial, but the look in his eyes worries me. "Want to come upstairs with me to Vic's for a minute?"

"With you? Is he up there?"

"Not yet."

For the second time today, I'm confused. Something is seriously off, but it doesn't feel like the time to ask questions. "Okay, I need to pay my bill...."

Kane calls out, "Aidan!" His voice cuts over the cacophony of the bar, and Aidan looks up.

"Put this young woman's drink on the house tab, please."

Aidan nods at Kane, who promptly ushers me outside to the entrance of Vic's apartment. To my surprise, he takes out a key and opens the door to the lobby. Or maybe that's not strange, since Kane's business is in the building.

We go up the stairs, and I'm growing uneasy. I'm not afraid of Kane, but his demeanor makes me certain something is wrong. I'm briefly surprised again when Kane also opens Vic's apartment with a key. They must truly be good friends.

Kane flips on the lights in Vic's kitchen, and I sit down on one of the barstools at the kitchen island.

178

"What's going on?" I ask.

Kane hesitates. Then he half smiles, tilts his head just a touch to the left, and says, "Vic's in a spot of trouble."

"Is he hurt? Is he in the hospital?" I'm instantly ready to go wherever he is, but Kane stops me.

"No. He hasn't been hurt."

"So, what's going on?"

"I think it would be best if he told you himself. He'll be back here tonight, if you want to wait for him. But of course, you're not obligated to stay. You can go home if you need to."

"Please tell me what's going on."

Kane's eyes are sympathetic, but I can tell he's not going to budge. "Do you want to wait for him?" he asks.

"Yeah, all right," I give in. "I'll wait."

"I'll give you some privacy," Kane says. "Lock the door after me."

I follow him to the door and lock it behind him, then go back to my barstool to sit and wait. I tap my fingers on top of the kitchen island, expecting Vic to open the door any moment. I'm growing more and more concerned. In less than a year, Vic's gone from a shadowy figure at the end of the bar to someone I count on.

What kind of trouble could he be in?

I sit on the stool for a half-hour before I give up and fix myself a drink. I take it to the couch and sit down to watch the sky grow dark. Vic's couch faces south, and the sun is slipping down toward the horizon off to my right. I sit and sip my drink until the sun disappears. The sky turns a deeper shade of blue, then inky black, and the few visible stars begin to appear.

By the time I hear Vic's key in the lock, my drink is gone and I'm half asleep. I turn around and see him. He looks tired, which is unusual. I start to stand up.

"Stay where you are," he says. "I'll join you."

I hear him pouring himself a drink in the kitchen, then the sound of his footsteps across the wood floor as he comes over.

"Been here long?" he asks.

"Since we were supposed to meet." I try to keep the frustration out of my voice. I still don't know what's going on with him, so I decide I should reserve judgment.

He sits down next to me, then reaches out for my hand. "Thanks for waiting."

"Sure." I look at him. "What's going on?"

"This is going to be hard to explain. Did Kane tell you anything?"

I shake my head. "He said it was better if you tell me."

"Right." He sighs. "Before I explain, I'll just tell you what happened today. There was a trial. It was…my trial. I got convicted of a gross misdemeanor and I'm probably going to have to serve jail time."

There are so many bombshells in what he just said. He's going to jail, so he's not going to be here. He was on trial today because he committed some kind of crime. And whatever this is—he's been keeping it from me.

"If you got convicted why aren't you in jail now?" I ask.

"Because they have the sentencing hearing later. I'm free on bail until then."

"What are you going to jail for? What did you do?"

"Illegal gambling."

"What kind of illegal gambling?"

"Hosting card games. Well, technically, it's called 'professional gambling in the third degree.'" He almost sounds like he's laughing about it.

"You think this is funny?"

The mirth vanishes. "No, it's not. I mean, I suppose I found it a tiny bit hilarious that you can be charged with 'professional' gambling."

"It's not funny." I pull my hand out of his. "Why were you doing illegal professional gambling?"

"This is going to sound like bullshit, okay? But it's also true. I was trying to raise some money for Kane."

"Raise money for Kane? Why?" A sudden thought strikes me. "Is he some kind of criminal, too?"

Vic winces, but says, "No, Kane's not a criminal. Just me."

"If he isn't a criminal, why would he want you to do something illegal to raise money for him?"

"He didn't know."

I fold my arms over my chest.

"I mean," Vic amends, "he knows now. But when I was doing it, he didn't know. He didn't find out until after I was busted."

"What were you raising money for?"

"Medical bills. He's got cancer, and he doesn't have health insurance. It was going to sink him financially. So, I set up the card games and I made sure his bills got paid."

More bombshells. Kane has cancer. I had no idea. I can tell by the expression on Vic's face that he's proud of paying Kane's medical bills. In essence it's an altruistic gesture. But something isn't sitting right with me.

"Why did you have to do something illegal? I mean, did you consider other ways to raise money?"

"I couldn't think of anything else that would raise the amount of money Kane needed in time."

I give him a direct look. "How did you know illegal gambling would work?"

Without flinching, he says, "Because that's how I used to get by."

Everything snaps into place. Vic owning the building. His personal gym. The fact that he doesn't have a regular job.

"Used to get by?" I ask. "When did you stop?"

"'Bout three years ago. I did it for seven years. I was careful. Never got caught. I invested some of it. And when I had enough to live on, I stopped." He seeks out my eyes. "It's not a gambling addiction. I was running the games, not playing them. It wasn't hard for me to quit."

"So why did you?"

He laughs ruefully. "Because I had enough. Seemed pointless to keep going."

I don't know whether to believe him. How much is enough? For that matter, how much does it take to maintain this place? And did he actually need to resort to running illegal card games to pay for Kane's medical bills, or could he have just paid for them?

"You have this ginormous apartment," I gesture to our surroundings. "Didn't you have any other way to get the money?"

"This was the easiest thing to do," he says. "I knew how to set it up. I found the perfect location. But I got sloppy. I let people in on the game I shouldn't have. I was trying to make more money faster, and one of them narced on me."

I want to believe that it was the best solution he could come up with, that he did it for a friend. But I'm having a hard time with that. Vic seems to know everybody, have connections everywhere. It's hard to believe his only choice was to help Kane by doing something illegal.

Maybe he did it because deep down, he wanted to. Maybe he missed being able to get away with something. Maybe he was having fun, until he got caught. Doubts about him are springing up like radioactive weeds. He's watching my face, and I can't read the expression on his.

"Kane doesn't have insurance," Vic repeats. "Do you know how hard that is?"

"I don't have insurance either, remember?" I remind him. "So, yes, I do know. I don't have cancer, but I'd be screwed if I ever got a diagnosis. I get it."

"This fucking system—" Vic starts, but stops when he looks at me.

I'm trying to process how I feel. "What place did you even find that was a perfect location? Or can't you talk about that?"

"I can talk about it. It's all in the court record. I was teaching self-defense classes at the community center, and we did the games there. Not during the daytime—it was at night, after hours. I had access to the building. I knew the police weren't going to check there. But, like I said, one of my players ratted us out."

"You ran an illegal gambling operation at a community center!"

"I know it sounds bad."

"It's insane!"

"Maybe it was," he admits. "But at first, it seemed foolproof. It was foolproof."

Something occurs to me. "Is this the same community center where you met Sheryl?"

"Yes, it is. She was never involved."

I think of the times when Vic and Sheryl wanted to be alone to talk about Vic's "tricky business shit." I have a hunch that even if it's true that Sheryl wasn't involved with his illegal gambling scheme, she knows about it now.

"Do you still teach self-defense at the community center?" I ask.

"No. That ended when I was arrested."

"When was that?"

"Just after Thanksgiving. I've been out on bail ever since then, waiting for today's trial. I'm still free on bail until the sentencing hearing."

"When's the sentencing hearing?"

"Next week."

"And that's when you find out if you're going to jail?"

He nods.

I search his face. "So, when you were teaching self-defense at the community center, did you feel useful?"

He meets my eyes. "Yeah. I felt useful."

"Why would you risk that?"

He puts his elbows on his knees and rubs his hands over his head in a frustrated gesture. "I don't know, okay? It seemed like the best solution at the time. Kane was going to stop getting treatment because he couldn't afford it. He was talking crazy, like he could beat cancer with the power of his mind. He was delusional. I had to help him."

"Couldn't you have sold the building?"

"And leave Kane with a new landlord who might not be a good friend? He would have hated that. He would have hated me if I did that to him."

"You said you have investments. Couldn't you have paid that way?"

"Noelle, I don't know. Maybe? Probably. But that's not what I did."

I have more questions, and they're all piling on top of each other, probably more than an hour's worth of interrogation. But I'm tired. I don't want to ask any besides one.

"How long will you go to jail?"

"I won't know until sentencing, but maximum is a year. I could get a fine with no jail time, but I think this judge is going to do it. Kane found me a good attorney who thinks he can talk the judge down to a lenient sentence. But after today my gut says no."

"Okay."

He reaches out for my hand again. "I know that's a lot to lay on you all at once."

That's an understatement. "Why didn't you tell me about it before?"

"I guess I hoped it would all just disappear. I thought I was going to beat it."

"Why, because you paid off a friend's medical bills?"

"No," Vic says. "That never came up in my conversations with my attorney, because technically, paying medical bills with dirty money could be construed as money laundering."

He's looking into my eyes. Silently asking something of me. And as he continues to look at me, I begin to understand. Kane might have found out what Vic did after the fact, but now he's a part of it. And in a small way, so am I.

"What's the penalty for money laundering?" I ask, my voice barely above a whisper.

"A hell of lot more severe than the penalty for a gross misdemeanor," he says.

Slowly, I move my hand away from his one more time.

He notices, and sighs. "I want to answer all your questions," he says, "but I'm beat. Went straight from court to a long conference with my attorney—that's where I was. I need to sleep."

"Okay. I get it."

He stands up, stretches out his hand, then pulls it back. "Are you coming with me?"

I feel like a broken toy. I want to be happy, to feel like I did when I first showed up at O'Shea's tonight. But I can't. That version of me has vanished.

"I think I'll stay out here," I say, in a small voice.

"All right." He sounds defeated. "We'll talk in the morning. But I need to get some sleep first."

He shuffles away, then comes back and drops a blanket on the couch for me. He hesitates. "You sure you want to sleep here?"

"Yeah. I kind of already was." It's a ridiculous answer but he accepts it.

I want to be mad that he wasn't chivalrous enough to offer me his bed and take the couch himself, but he probably doesn't understand why I don't want to sleep with him.

I take off my shoes, then loosen my clothes and lie down on the couch, pulling the blanket over me. I can see the faint stars shining through the spring evening. They look so cheerful and hopeful.

When I wake up, it feels like the dead of night. It's still completely dark outside, and the streets are quiet. There's no residual noise drifting up from O'Shea's.

I get up to use the bathroom. On the way back, I nab the blanket off the couch and take it behind the Japanese room dividers where Vic's bed is. He's curled up on one side, and there's plenty of room. I lie down beside him, but instead of getting under the covers with him I curl up under the blanket. It's comforting to have him near, but the feeling of comfort is also confusing. I fall asleep again.

———

IN THE MORNING, my confusion is gone.

The day Rob attempted to assault me, he revealed who he was behind his everyday mask. Ever since then, for five years, I've been angry with my sister for refusing to see the truth about him.

What kind of person am I if I refuse to see the truth about Vic? The entire time I've known him, he's been out on bail for committing a crime. And sure, maybe it's a crime that's Robin Hood-like in nature —paying a friend's medical bills—but it's still a crime.

The worst part is that he hid the truth from me. From the very beginning. How do I know he isn't hiding other things from me? How can I trust anything he says? If I ignore all these questions I have and stay with him because I can't bear to lose what we've been building together, how am I any different than my sister?

I start to get out of bed, but his arm goes around me.

"I'm glad you're here," he mumbles, moving his hand down my side and over my hip.

"I can't stay." I roll out of bed. "I need to feed Milo."

He props himself up on one arm. He still looks rough. "Can we talk later today?"

"I don't know." I look at him. "No. I do know. We can't."

"We can't?" He moves in the bed and sits on the edge. "Why can't we talk?"

"Because." My voice shakes. "Because you aren't who you said you are. Because you lied to me. All this time."

"I didn't want to worry you, especially if it turned out all right—"

"You *lied* to me. When you start sleeping with a person, you want to know something like, oh, I don't know, if they're expecting a jail sentence! You kept that information from me."

"Yeah. Okay. I did that."

I'm incredulous. "That's all you have to say?"

"What do you want me to say? I fucked up. Now I have to face it. It's a gross misdemeanor, not a murder charge. Are you going to stand by me?"

My voice raises. "Stand by you?"

"Yeah, you know. Write me letters? Send me care packages? Come by for conjugal visits?" He actually has the audacity to grin fiendishly. My body responds like a traitor. I want him, even now. This sucks.

"I'm not going to visit you," I tell him. "I don't even know who you are."

"Yes, you do," he retorts. All at once, he's serious. "I'm someone who cares about you. I'm not perfect, but I care about you. And you know it." Suddenly, his confidence fades and uncertainty takes over his expression. "You know that, don't you?"

"I don't know what to believe."

"I didn't do this to hurt you," he says. "This all went down before I ever met you. Before I even knew you existed."

"But it is hurting me. Don't you get that?"

"I believe you. I believe that you're hurt. But I'm having a hard time understanding why."

"Because! I thought you were this—person—and you're this whole other thing and you hid that from me. I can't trust someone who does that. I need to be around people I trust. I can't have this conversation anymore. We're talking in circles."

I go out to the couch so I can get my shoes.

Vic follows me. "So, you're leaving? You're scared, and you're going to bail on me. Just like that."

186

Instead of answering him, I slide on my shoes.

He comes over and grips my shoulders. "Don't run away."

We're eye to eye. It makes my stomach hurt to look at him. I'm fighting a combination of desire and revulsion.

"Are you concerned for me or for you?" I ask.

"Both. Do I want your support? Yeah, I do. But it'll be a year, max. It's not a lifetime. I'll make it." He hesitates. "I'm not so sure about you."

"Why wouldn't I make it?"

The look in his eyes is both knowing and sad. "Because you're always running away from some part of yourself. I don't think you'll be okay until you stop."

In that moment, I hate him. "That's bullshit. You don't know me."

"I do know you."

I'm shaking again. "No, you don't." I bust out of his arms and head for the door. He doesn't follow me. When I put my hand on the doorknob, I turn around. Vic is still watching me.

"You lied to me," I tell him.

Then I go out.

# CHAPTER TWENTY-FIVE

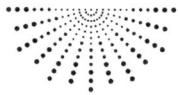

The phone rings. By the fourth ring, I'm pretty sure it's Vic.

He doesn't call me incessantly. More like once a day, and it's been four days since he told me about his conviction. He's left me messages. I haven't listened to them.

But now, because I'm actually in the apartment when he's calling, I'm going to have to hear his message. I consider running to the bathroom and turning on the vent fan, but that's childish. My machine beeps and I brace myself.

"Noelle. It's Vic. Look, I didn't want to tell you this over the phone. If you're there, I wish you'd pick up. I guess I'll just talk. Pick up if you want. If you're there. My sentencing hearing is this coming Friday, and I'd— I'd like you to be there. I'm not asking you to speak on my behalf. I don't want you to. But if you want to go, I'd love that. And I'd love to see you before then. So, if you want that too, then give me a call, I guess."

I can hear the pain in his voice, but I feel dead to it. I'm aware he's far from a hardened criminal. He's someone who lives on the edge of the law, who didn't mind taking a risk to help a friend. Maybe he's foolish, but he's not a menace.

But that's not why I'm hurt. Even more than what he did, I'm hurt because he hid it from me. I hate myself for failing to see through him.

For believing he was somebody different from who he actually is. I'm furious that I let my guard down for him.

On my way back from class on Monday evening, I stop by O'Shea's. I still haven't returned Vic's calls, and I haven't buzzed his place. But I like being at O'Shea's, and the idea that I should stay away from the place just to avoid Vic pisses me off. So I go there deliberately.

I order a shot and a beer. The bartender is unfamiliar, but he's pleasant, and I treat him to a smile when I thank him for the drinks. I down the shot, then chase it with a mouthful of Guinness. There. That feels better. A few minutes later, Kane purposefully takes the stool beside me.

"Good evening, Noelle," he says. "How's life treating you?"

"Oh, you know. All right. How about you?"

"Been better, been worse. I don't want to waste your time, so I'll get to the heart of it. Are you going to the sentencing?"

I stare at him. "Are you?"

Kane holds my eyes. "Of course."

I look back down at my beer glass. "I haven't decided yet."

"What's the reason you wouldn't?"

"I don't know. I'm just not sure if I'm going to go."

"I know it's a shock," he says. "It was a shock when I found out, too. If he'd told me what he was doing, I never would have let him."

I lower my voice. "How did you find out? Because I don't think Vic told his lawyer that he helped you with your bills."

Kane winks at me. "What bills?"

He doesn't seem worried about being implicated in a money laundering scheme. I wonder if he actually *was* aware of Vic's dealings from the beginning. But looking at him, I realize it doesn't matter. All that matters is that he's sick. The thought of it makes me fearful and sad.

"How's your cancer?" I ask, and my voice catches as I realize how strange the question sounds. As if cancer is a relative, or a pet.

But Kane remains calm. "One more appointment, then I find out how my cancer is."

"I'm sorry you have to deal with that. Cancer. It really sucks."

"Sure. It does. But I get by. I'll be all right, one way or the other."

I must look horrified, because Kane pats my hand, briefly. "We all die one day," he says. "You do the best you can until that day comes. Now, will you come to the hearing?"

I know he wants me to say yes. For his understated charm to have worked its magic on me. But I still feel dead inside. I meet his eyes. "I'm sorry. I just can't tell you right now."

"It's all right." Kane stands up. "I hope you'll be there. Have a good night, Noelle."

I wonder if he'll tell Vic that I'm here. I linger a bit over my beer before I leave. I might not be communicating with Vic, but I don't want to scurry around like a frightened mouse in an effort to keep clear of him. Eventually, I pay my tab and go home.

Ever since Vic filled me in on the criminal portion of his life, I've been simmering with suspicion every time I see Conan. How much of this did he know about? He obviously knew something was up based on his comments that day at the school.

I've been training with Conan for several days and I haven't asked him about it, but now I can't hold back. Since I signed up for the black belt test, we haven't had our extra sparring sessions because he doesn't want to be seen as showing me favoritism. I get that, but I miss working out with him one on one. Plus, those sessions were a good way to talk to him about something if I needed to.

I corner him after class instead.

"Conan. I need to talk to you. About Vic."

"Yeah. That's a rough deal."

"How long did you know about him...being out on bail and the card games and...everything," I finish weakly.

"Since he got arrested."

"You knew all this time!"

Conan's eyebrows go up. "Didn't you?"

"No. He didn't tell me until a few days ago."

He shrugs. "Probably didn't want to freak you out."

"Doesn't it freak you out?"

"No? It sucks for him, but he knew the risks he was taking. And it was for his friend's medical bills, so." Conan shrugs again. "I don't blame him."

I'm starting to get a sense that both Conan and Vic operate in a moral universe that's different from my own.

"Isn't he going to have a criminal record now?" I ask.

"For a few years, sure. He didn't commit armed robbery. It'll go away. Anyway, Vic doesn't exactly operate in the standard nine-to-five world. He'll be fine. Eventually."

"You know he could go to jail, don't you?"

"It's a short sentence, right? Vic can handle himself." Conan eyes me curiously. "How come you're so bent out of shape about this?"

I clear my throat. "Vic and I are kind of... We were kind of... I mean, we were starting to..."

A grin spreads slowly over Conan's face. "You and Vic?"

"Well, um. Yeah. Me and Vic."

"Don't worry, Noelle. He'll be fine. Be back before you know it."

"I broke up with him," I admit.

"Because of this? Or something else?"

"He was pretending to be someone he wasn't. He wasn't honest with me."

"Maybe he couldn't talk about his case," Conan points out.

"But *you* knew about it!" I retort. "He told you all about it after he got arrested, right? That's what you said. He's been talking to you!"

Conan sighs. "Look, I'm sorry. I thought the two of you were just friends. And I guess I thought you knew everything."

"It's okay," I falter. "It's not your fault. But everything was going so well, and he just dropped this on me."

"It's a lot if you didn't know about it already," Conan sympathizes. "I know I told you he was a good guy. I still think that."

"He wasn't going to tell me anything," I say. "If he hadn't been convicted? He wasn't even going to tell me. He was going to keep lying to me."

Conan bites his lip. "You'll have to talk to him about it. I'm friends with both of you. I'm not getting in the middle. Go talk to him."

"Sure, yeah. Okay. I'll talk to him."

But I don't. I don't talk to him. And I don't see him before his sentencing.

I do go to the hearing.

Kane gives me directions to the courthouse, and I call in sick for my shift at work so I can be there. I settle in the back of the small courtroom. It reminds me of watching a courtroom scene on television and is simultaneously nothing like that.

For starters, the courthouse is not full of model-thin, perfectly dressed, and unnaturally attractive individuals. In that way, it's not like a TV show at all. And there isn't much courtroom drama. It's procedural and boring.

Both Conan and Kane are there—wearing suits, which is kind of funny. I never could have pictured either of them in a suit. Conan looks uncomfortable in his, like it's a bit too tight and too constraining for him. Kane, on the other hand, looks like a dapper gentleman from another era. They both speak on Vic's behalf, talking about what a responsible member of the community he is, how he's a phenomenal friend, and a fair, conscientious landlord.

The prosecution brings out a family member of one of the people who was busted for gambling along with Vic. They talk about their relative's gambling addiction, and how it's torn apart their family. They obviously believe Vic has made their family member's problem even worse. That moment is a bit dramatic and more TV-like.

But it barely registers. I'm numb during the entire hearing, right up until the judge gives the sentence. A two thousand dollar fine and six months in jail. I won't see Vic for six months. Kane already warned me they would take him away immediately to start serving his sentence, but it's still a shock when the uniformed officers cuff him and escort him out of the room.

He turns and looks at me, and our eyes meet. His are emotional, and I can see myself reflected in them. He's glad I'm here. It was hard to ignore how genuine both Conan and Kane sounded when they stood up for him. I don't blame Vic for anyone's gambling addiction. Plenty of people engage in gambling and don't develop an addiction to it. But I still can't get past the fact that he lied to me. For months.

The moment is over quickly, and Vic is gone. Kane and Conan come over to me.

"It's good you were here," Kane says, showing a rare display of affection by giving me a quick side-hug.

"He'll be out before you know it," Conan adds.

They offer to take me out for a meal, but I tell them I swapped shifts with someone at work and that I have to be there soon. They seem to buy it. Then I take the bus home.

Once I'm there, I kick off my shoes and crawl under the covers, fully clothed. I should snap out of it, I think. Neither Conan nor Kane seem worried about Vic. And they also don't seem to think less of him. They might think what he did was stupid, but how they see Vic as a person hasn't changed in any fundamental way.

I miss him. Or I miss the person I believed he was.

*Liar, liar, liar.*

The word keeps repeating itself in my head like a disembodied nervous tick. I want to sleep. But I can't.

# CHAPTER TWENTY-SIX

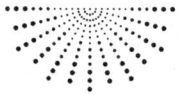

V ic's been in jail two weeks, and I've spent that time trying to forget about him.

It's not easy.

I miss working out with him, sharing meals in O'Shea's, and hearing the raspy rumble of his voice. I miss being with him.

But the thought of seeing him in a prison uniform is depressing. I'm angry at him for being so wonderful and at the same time so messed up. I can't wrap my head around the idea of visiting him in jail, even though Conan and Kane have already done it. It feels like it shouldn't be real.

At the Pancake House, I don't have as many shifts with Piper, and we don't cross paths like we used to. I wonder if she's made an effort to be scheduled when I'm not there. On the rare occasions we do work together, however, we seem to get back in our same old rhythm. She doesn't try to mess me up, and I don't try to mess her up, either. We're still a good team—just without the camaraderie.

We're working together at a dinner shift the first week of June when the rest of Primal Malice comes in to visit her. They all settle at the front counter instead of taking a table, so every time I go to get a coffee or soda refill for someone, I have to walk directly in front of them.

Piper's taking care of them, but I'm uncomfortable having them so near. For all I know, each one of them hates my guts, since I'm not exactly getting along with Piper anymore. I wonder what she's told them.

I'm making a fresh pot of coffee when I hear Bill say, "Hey, Noelle."

I finish filling the machine up with water and push the button to start it. Then I turn around and face Bill and the rest of the band. "Hey. How are you all doing?"

"We miss you," Mandy says.

I blink, wondering if I heard her right.

Sven, who's wearing a tall black stovepipe hat, nods gravely.

"We just wanted you to know," Bill adds. "Hope you guys work it out."

Mandy sees me eyeing Sven's hat and nudges him. "Can't you take that off while you're in here?

Sven glances around the room. "I don't think there's anywhere to put it. I don't want it to get crushed on the floor. Or messy."

"It's all right," I reassure them. "It's not bothering anyone." Actually, I have a feeling Sven's hat is a conversation starter for every other person in the joint.

Piper comes back behind the counter and tells them, "Your meals are up next." Then she looks over at me, as if sensing that I've been making conversation with her friends.

"I'm going to go check in with my tables," I say, and go back out in the main restaurant. I start at the back of the room and work my way toward the door. When I check in with my second table—a group of older women—one of them beckons to me, like she wants to tell me a secret.

I lean closer. "Is there something I can help you with?"

She puts a finger to her lips, then points toward the front counter. "That young man out there, with the hat? Is he dressed for a Civil War reenactment?"

"Um…" I smile. "I don't think so."

"Dressed for the loony bin," scoffs one of her friends.

"I think he just likes unusual clothing," I offer.

"Well," says the first woman, "if he's interested in Civil War reenactment, he'd make a simply stunning Abraham Lincoln. I could connect him to the right people."

"I'll let him know," I promise the lady, as her friend shakes her head in disbelief.

When the members of Primal Malice leave, I catch Bill's eye, and he waves goodbye to me as he and his black-clad companions go out the door. Sven has to take off his hat to fit through.

After the lunch rush passes, Piper and I start cleanup behind the front counter, and I decide to attempt to break the silence between us.

"So, going on your tour soon, probably?"

"Uh, yeah," she says, slowly. "Next week. I just have a few more shifts before we leave."

"Got everything covered for when you're gone?"

"Yep. All covered."

"Well, that's good," I mutter. She doesn't seem to want to talk. It was probably a mistake to attempt to initiate any sort of conversation with her.

Piper lets out a small sigh. "How's Vic?"

I glance quickly around the restaurant. It's mostly empty. There's no one at the counter, and only a few of the booths are occupied. I lower my voice. "He's in jail."

Her eyes go wide. "Oh. Oh wow. Really?"

"Yeah. Illegal gambling."

"How long's he in for?"

"Six months."

"So not felony level."

"Right." I stare at her. How does she know what a felony and non-felony jail sentence would be?

"I've known a few gamblers," she says, as if she anticipated the question.

"I guess you were right about him," I admit. "The big roll of cash?"

She gives a slight shake of her head. "No, it's like you said. He could have just gone to the bank that day. I had a gut reaction when he handed over his cash to pay for dinner. It was a hunch, that's all."

It's awkward between us, then. We haven't truly talked to each other or hung out in so long, it's hard to get back to a feeling of social flow.

"Well, anyway," I say. "Good luck with your tour."

"Thanks. Good luck dealing with the Vic situation."

"Thanks." I don't tell her I'm not seeing him any longer. I don't think we're back at that level of sharing our lives yet. I wonder if we ever will be. I'm glad we talked, but that giddy feeling of meeting someone new and exciting, the way it felt when I started hanging out with her—that's gone. I wonder if it's gone for good.

That night at class, Conan reminds us it's less than two weeks until the black belt test. I decide the best thing I can do is dedicate the remaining time to being as ready for the test as I can. And after that, I'll focus on the next belt up. Maybe taekwondo can still function as a type of mental shield for me—not one that will make me think I'm invincible, but one that will keep me from focusing on the things that make me feel down or weak.

The remaining days before the test, I go to the school more often to work out, so I can get in extra practice for each required element. If I were still with Vic, I know he would let me practice at his place. Kane's been watching over his apartment and his car for him while he's locked up. I'm sure Kane would let me into Vic's place if I asked him to, but I want to leave Vic in the past, and it doesn't seem fair to use his space. I've also stopped going to O'Shea's. I miss it, but I don't want to run into Kane. I'm sure he'll ask if I've visited Vic in jail, and I don't want to have to tell him that I haven't, and that I don't intend to.

For a full week I'm laser-focused on my goal, and I actually start to feel invincible again. I'm getting faster and sharper. Each day, I'm more certain that I'm going to ace the test. I can tell by the way Conan speaks to me in between classes that he's seeing the difference, and he's impressed.

My confidence lasts until precisely June fourteenth, the morning of the test. And then, while I'm brushing my teeth in front of my bathroom mirror, it all dissolves.

Vic was supposed to be here. That's what made this so special: that I would finally have someone besides Conan cheering for me. It was Vic who pushed me to do this in the first place. He was my inspiration, and now my inspiration has abandoned me because he's too stupid or too stubborn to figure out how to help a friend without doing something illegal.

Now I have to do this alone, the way I always have. But it's not enough anymore. Despite how invincible I've been feeling lately, I'd already come to the conclusion that martial arts are not an ultimate weapon to keep me safe. And if they aren't that, why am I still pushing myself to advance?

As I swirl my toothbrush around in circles on my teeth, I realize I don't want to take the test today. It's a bleak feeling that makes me wish I could cry, but I don't. Instead, I feel a resigned resolve solidify within me. I finish brushing my teeth, and then I get dressed for the test. I put on my white dobok and my red belt with the black stripe through it. I will go through with this. I'll let Conan down if I don't.

But I feel so alone.

It's a gorgeous day, not too hot, and not a cloud in a bright blue sky. But none of it touches me as I make my way to the local high school gymnasium where our school's holding the belt test. Friends and family members of the other students line the bleachers in the gym. But there's no one here for me. That's never bothered me before. It bothers me today.

I try to put it out of my mind, but it's hard, especially while we're waiting to get started. It's challenging to focus on being here, in this large space with all the other students and our teachers seated at a long table that's been brought in for the occasion. My mind keeps drifting, and that's not a good mental state for practicing taekwondo, let alone for taking a belt test.

When we start the warmups it's a relief. At least now I'm moving, which helps quiet the anxious thoughts. I've been training hard, and I've built up the physical endurance I need to pass the test. I do well with the demonstrations of our kicking sequences. Some of these things are so second nature to me now that I don't need to be super focused. I could do them in my sleep.

But I'm not plugged in. I'm not here. And when we get to the sparring section of the test, I start to stumble. It's nothing someone who's a stranger to martial arts would notice, maybe, but I'm sloppy. I'm late anticipating the moves coming at me. I'm not at my best, and the more I fuck up, the harder it is for me to concentrate, because I keep worrying about how much I've fucked up.

By the time we get to the board-breaking portion of the test, I'm already well off my game. I can't do it. I know the techniques; I know I've done it before, but I can't focus. I miss the first board completely, which uses up my one free pass right out of the gate. I manage to break the second and third boards, but the fourth one is impossible. I know I could do it under different circumstances, on any other day. But this is a mental block, which makes it even more frustrating.

It's also an emotional nightmare, as I continuously feel overwhelmed by the need to cry. It's not the kind of crying where you can wipe your tears and carry on. This is deep down, from the gut, threatening to bust out of me like a tsunami after an earthquake. I'm not going to be able to hold it back if I stay on the floor and keep trying to break the fourth board. And if I fail to break it, I'll fail the test.

It should be a harder decision, but it's not: I leave.

I run out the door, down the block to a quiet alcove, and force myself to stop crying. I have to, because if I do cry, I'm sure something disastrous is going to happen. Something I can't handle. Something that might break me forever. Forget the black belt test. The most important thing in the world right now is not to cry.

And that battle, I win.

But the test is a dud. I don't bother going back to the gymnasium. I slip into the locker room where we stashed all of our belongings to grab my purse and my keys, then I go home and sleep, because right now, sleep feels like the safest place I could be.

I wake up when I hear my phone ringing and let it go to voicemail.

"Noelle, it's Conan. If you're there, please pick up. If you're not, please call me when you get this."

I rush out of bed to get to the phone. Conan deserves an explanation. I pick up the receiver. "Hey, Conan. It's me. I'm here."

A pause. "You want to tell me what happened?"

"Total breakdown of focus," I say. "I didn't have it. I knew I didn't have it the minute I started."

"That sounds about right," he says. "Any idea why?"

*Vic.* Vic is why. Vic being a liar and a criminal and not being there for me. That's why. It's Vic's fault.

But to Conan, I simply say, "I've had a lot of things on my mind lately."

"All right. I'm proud of you for going through with it, anyway. I guess we know what to focus on for next time."

"No," I tell him. "There's not going to be a next time. I'm not testing for a belt ever again."

"That's a little extreme, don't you think?" he says. "Why don't you sleep on it? Give it a couple of days. See how you feel."

"I don't want to test again." I pause. "I guess that means you don't want me to come back to class, right?"

"That would also be extreme," Conan says. "I won't chase you away. You can stay where you are forever, if you want. But I don't think you'll feel good about yourself if you do."

I'm adamant. "That's how I want it."

"All right," he says, slowly. "Guess I'll see you in class next week."

"See you then. Thanks for checking on me."

"Of course. Take care, okay?"

"Okay." The damn tears threaten again. But I get them under control more quickly this time.

Maybe I can't win every battle, but I'm not going to give in to self pity. If I do that, everything else that's left in my life will fall apart. I'm sure of it.

# CHAPTER TWENTY-SEVEN

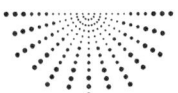

I 've been avoiding O'Shea's because I don't want to talk to Kane, plus I know it would hurt to go there. I'd be aware of Vic's empty apartment upstairs, and hanging out in the bar itself would remind me of getting to know him. I can't imagine the place without Vic.

But one night in late June, on the way back from class, I have an irresistible urge to go back. O'Shea's is the place where I felt happiness for the first time in years. And it's hard to stay away from a place like that. I'll just have to hope that Kane won't be there.

When I walk inside, I immediately spot Aidan behind the bar. His face lights up when he sees me. "Well, hello there, sweetheart! Been a long time!"

"Hi, Aidan." I sit down at the bar and bask in his welcome. I was crazy to stay away.

"Usual?" he asks.

"Yeah. Please," I add.

In mere minutes I'm sipping a foamy pint of Guinness, anticipating a burger. When Aidan drops it in front of me, he says, "Good to see you, Noelle."

I look at him with surprise. I know he recognizes me, but I was never sure he actually knew my name. Apparently, he does.

I'm enjoying my food, happy that I still feel at home here, even though Vic is absent. But then, I didn't know Vic when I was first drawn to this place, so maybe I belonged here all along. My mood picks up. And then, as he is wont to do, Kane O'Shea appears and sits down next to me.

I glance sideways at him. "Hi, Kane. How's it going?"

"I'm doing all right," he says, his tone mild. Then he gets right to the point. "Have you spoken to Vic?"

I turn and face him. "No. I haven't gone to visit him. And I'm not going to."

"Already made up your mind, I see."

Since Kane didn't mince his words, I figure I shouldn't, either. "Don't you think he was wrong? I mean, are you *happy* he broke the law to help you? That he was keeping this massive secret from you the whole time?"

Kane lifts an eyebrow. "No, not happy. I was so angry when he told me what he'd done, he almost gave me heart failure, never mind the cancer."

Immediately, I feel bad. "I didn't mean that the way it sounds. I'm glad you got the treatment you need. How are you doing?"

"Much better," Kane says, "Thanks to Vic."

"Right." I sigh.

"I would never have asked him to do something like this. I hope you know that. But his heart was in the right place. Can you see that much?"

I nod. "I can, but he lied to me. For a really long time. That's why I don't want to see him."

"So that's the sin," Kane says. "Not that he broke the law."

"I can't trust a liar," I tell him.

"No." He nods, surprising me. "I don't suppose you can."

"I don't hate him," I falter. "I just can't—"

"I'm not going to try to convince you to visit him," Kane says. "But I know he'd love to see you."

"You've been to see him, haven't you?"

He nods. "A number of times."

"Is he okay? Is he…doing all right in there?"

Kane gives me a slight smile. "He's fine. Vic can take care of himself." He stands up. "If you change your mind and you want to know anything about getting to the jail, where to park, how it works, just let me know."

"All right."

"Good to see you." He goes behind the bar, vanishing somewhere into the bowels of his own establishment.

Aidan drifts over to me and snatches up my empty pint glass. "Need another?"

"I'm all right." I stand up, then pause. "Hey, Aidan," I say, suddenly.

He stops. "Yes?"

"Thanks for...being here." The words sound silly and inadequate once I've said them aloud.

But he just smiles, then winks. "Thanks for drinking here, sweetheart."

———

PIPER COMES BACK from her tour exhausted, but excited about the future of the band. Bill shows up at the diner to visit her a couple days after she gets back, and I catch them kissing across the front counter. Apparently their relationship survived the rigors of touring, whatever those might be. It's not like I would know.

She's friendly with me, kind of like she was before we started hanging out. All the weird and uncomfortable feelings between us are gone, but the sense that we had a budding friendship has also disappeared. I figure now that's she's had some authentic road experience as a musician, she's decided we're not compatible as friends. Like maybe she's in a different league.

If Vic were still around, I'd ask him for his opinion, but I'm not going to visit him in prison just to talk to him about how to salvage my friendship with Piper.

I throw myself into my classes at the school, and volunteer to help Conan with some of the lower-level classes. Sometimes he needs someone to run them through drills while he handles something else at the front desk. I can't actually teach a full class because I'm not a black belt yet, but it feels good to help out.

He invites me over to his house for the Fourth of July. I don't want to sit around by myself on a holiday, so I go. Everyone else there is part of a couple, and even though they're all friendly to me, I feel a little bit like a charity case.

Conan and his girlfriend Annie rent a house with a decent-sized backyard and a picnic table. We eat a dinner of grilled hamburgers and hot dogs, then hang around sitting in lawn chairs, waiting for it to get dark enough to light fireworks. I listen to everyone talk about shared camping trips and other people they know. Most of the group seem to be Annie's friends, though Conan is at ease with all of them.

As the party winds down, I head over to the picnic table where remnants of our meal still linger—condiment bottles, a plastic bag with extra hot dog and hamburger buns, and a few plates with half eaten food. I start to gather up the bag of buns and the condiments, intending to take them inside when Annie taps me on the shoulder.

A breeze has picked up, and it lifts the dark waves of her hair, tossing them gently. Annie is tiny and beautiful, and it's impossible to be jealous of her because she's such a warm person.

Now, she smiles at me and gestures to the food I'm carrying. "Great minds think alike. I was just coming over here to clean all this up. I'll help you."

We get everything back inside the kitchen, and she starts dumping the unappetizing, uneaten food down the garbage disposal.

I stand uncertainly on the edge of her kitchen. "Anything else I can do to help?"

"Yeah," she turns around and smiles again. "Why don't you hang out and keep me company while I clean up?"

"Sure." I lean against the counter. "Thanks for having me over tonight."

"Thanks for being here." She puts the dirty paper plates in the garbage and takes the ketchup and mustard bottles to the refrigerator. When she emerges, she says, "Conan told me about you and Vic. You want to talk about anything?"

"Oh, uh…" I stammer. I wasn't expecting this.

She holds up a hand. "You don't have to. I was just saying, if you want to. We can talk about it if you want to."

Do I want to? As much as I like Annie, I fear talking about Vic will just make me feel worse.

"No pressure," she says, then adds, "You miss him?"

"Well, yeah," I admit. "Of course I miss him. But it's kind of pointless."

"What's pointless about it?"

"I know who he really is." I shrug. "I can't be with somebody like that."

"I get it," she nods. Then, looking curious, she asks, "What kind of person do you think he is?"

"Just…a criminal. And dishonest. That's the worst part. He didn't tell me anything. I didn't know who he was."

Annie tilts her head to the side a little. "Are you upset with Conan, too?"

"Why would I be mad at Conan?"

"Because he knew what was going on, and you didn't?"

I shake my head. "Conan thought I already knew. Vic probably told him about getting arrested because… I don't know. Because he's another guy, I guess."

"I'm not talking about Vic's arrest. Conan's known Vic for quite a few years." She smiles an inscrutable smile that makes me a touch nervous. "They first met at a card game."

"A card game?"

"When Vic told you about his arrest, did he tell you about his past?"

"Yeah. He said he used to run illegal card games all the time. It's how he made enough money to buy that building…." It suddenly clicks. "Are you saying Conan was one of Vic's players?"

She nods.

"So, were you with him then? What happened? Did he get busted?"

"Conan wasn't always the way he is now," Annie says. "He never got busted at one of Vic's games, but he was always in trouble, you know? He did a lot of dumb shit. He was always trying to be a tough guy, even though he didn't need to. Most people take one look at him and decide he's not worth messing with."

"That's for sure," I agree. Conan intimidates new students at the school without even trying, especially guys, until they figure out he's a truly dedicated teacher.

"I almost left him for good," she confides. "I gave him an ultimatum, but that wasn't what changed him. I needed to draw a line for myself, you know? And he changed because *he* decided to change."

"He must have had a reason," I say. It's hard to imagine Conan being any different than the way I've always known him—a dedicated and passionate teacher of martial arts.

"He had some emotional shit to work through," Annie says. "But the main thing is, I think he woke up one day and decided he wanted to be a constructive force in the world rather than a destructive one."

I narrow my eyes. "Are you saying I should wait for Vic to have an epiphany like that? Because Vic is, like, old. He's already thirty. If he's going to have an epiphany, he should've already had it."

"He did something illegal," Annie agrees. "But he was trying to help a friend. That's constructive, not destructive."

"It was also stupid," I retort. "Vic's smart. He could have found a better way to get the money."

"Maybe," she relents. Then she reaches out and touches my hand. "I understand how you feel, Noelle. He let you down. But I had to speak up for him, because... Well, he's the only other man in the world aside from Conan who I feel completely safe with."

There's something unspoken in her eyes that gets to me. As in, I feel like she gets me. Maybe she gets me a little too much.

"We should probably go back outside," I say. "They're going to think we hate them."

As if he read my mind, Conan pokes his head into the kitchen. "Everything okay in here? We're gonna do the fireworks now."

"Everything's fine," Annie says. "We were just tidying up." She goes over to him, and it strikes me, as it always does, how ridiculously small she looks next to him.

"I understand," she says to me again. "You have to do what feels right."

Conan looks from me to Annie, and even though guys can be clueless, I'm pretty sure he knows we've been talking about Vic.

"No pressure," he says to me, then adds, "whatever the hell you two women are talking about." He scoops Annie off her feet and carries her, shrieking, out to the backyard.

I follow behind them, moving slow. I don't know what to think. I like and respect both Conan and Annie. The fact that she made a point to speak up for Vic is significant. But every time I think of him, this dull hot anger takes me over, and I can't go any further than the feeling that I can't trust him.

The light is fading fast in the backyard, and everyone has already left the lawn chairs to go out to the street for setting off fireworks. I look up at the trees that adorn the yard, wishing I could morph into some kind of airborne creature—a bird or maybe a bat—and fly up into the trees' branches, hidden for the rest of the night.

All around me, throughout the neighborhood, there's the sound of firecrackers going off, the whistling of bottle rockets, and the occasional sonic boom. It feels like a war zone. But it's just a bunch of neighborhood people blowing shit up to celebrate freedom. If I don't join them, my friends might worry that something's wrong. So I follow the path through their tiny vegetable garden and out of the yard, then join Conan, Annie, and the rest of their guests out on the street.

# CHAPTER TWENTY-EIGHT

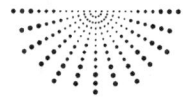

After the Fourth of July, Annie's words kept repeating in my head, that Vic had done something constructive, rather than destructive. I couldn't stop thinking about that. It made me feel like maybe I owed him one visit and a chance to say his piece.

My friends' opinions were also on my mind. At O'Shea's, when I ran into Kane, even though he'd stopped asking me if I planned to visit Vic, I knew he wanted me to do it. Both Conan and Annie thought I should do it, too. Even Piper had tossed off a comment at work, wondering if I'd gone to see Vic in jail yet. Everyone seemed to assume it was something I actually intended and wanted to do.

But it was Milo who tipped the scales. I came home one afternoon and found him curled up on the floor in one of Vic's black T-shirts. I wasn't sure where he'd found it—maybe it had fallen under the bed and Milo had dragged it back out. But it reminded me that of all the men I'd ever brought home, Vic was the only one Milo ever liked. Maybe he was just a cat, but to me, his vote of confidence was significant.

So in late August, I finally caved. Kane was the first person I told about my decision. Since I was already on the approved visitor list, he briefed me on what the procedure would be once I got there. Metal detectors. Pat downs. He told me I'd be talking to Vic at a table in a room with other prisoners. Apparently, the phone booths with transparent glass I'd been picturing were only for high security inmates, not for someone like Vic.

———

ON THE DAY of the visit, as I take the bus downtown to the jail, I wish we *would* have glass between us. I don't want to be close enough for him to touch me. I know it will make me confused.

Getting inside the jail is unpleasant. I understand why they have to search you, but it feels invasive and gross. Kane warned me ahead of time that if Vic already had another visitor during the designated visiting hour, I might not get to see him. It's a first come, first serve situation.

I stand in a waiting area with a group of other people. There's a mother with kids. I figure maybe she's visiting her husband and the kids are visiting their dad. There are also several men, and a few younger women like me. So I guess now I'm a girl who visits her boyfriend in jail. It's surreal.

I shake off the feeling, reminding myself that Vic and I broke up. Plus, I'm not sure if he ever was my boyfriend. We didn't have enough time to establish what we were. I look around the room, trying to be nonchalant, wondering if anyone else is here to visit Vic.

Maybe he has a secret family. Or maybe one of the other young women is also here to visit him, or maybe even one of the other men. A couple of them look tough, and the others just look like professional guys in suits who could maybe be lawyers, but I'm not sure those kinds of meetings happen in a jail cell.

Suddenly, I'm not sure I did the right thing coming here. Did I come here for me, or did I come here because I knew it would make a lot of other people in my life feel better? Kane, Conan, and Annie all approve of this visit. But what's *my* reason? Do I owe Vic a chance? Or do I owe it to myself to get up and get the hell out of here?

The uniformed room attendant interrupts my rumination and starts calling out names of people who will be allowed into the visiting room. I'm glad to see the family is getting in. The kids seem, if not exactly excited, at least less anxious once their mom's name is called.

And then the attendant calls out, monotone: "Noelle Thomas."

So, this is it. I'm going to see Vic.

It's anticlimactic when they let us into the bare visiting room, just a bunch of tables with guys in blue jumpsuits. Nobody looks particularly menacing.

It takes me a couple minutes to spot him, but then I do. I see his eyes first, because he's watching me. I've never been so conscious of someone observing me while I walk. It's a hot day, and I'm wearing a loose sundress I found at a thrift shop. I thought it would be more comfortable for taking the bus downtown, and it was. But if I'm honest, I also wore it to see Vic's eyes pop the way they are now.

I stop at the chair across from him. "Hey."

He gestures to the chair, and with a touch of irony, says, "Welcome. Have a seat."

I sink down on the uncomfortable hard plastic chair and hold his gaze as he continues to look at me. He's a bit thinner than he was, maybe. And his hair is cut super short, like a military haircut. Otherwise, though, he seems like himself. Vital. Not subdued.

I realize I don't know what to say.

Vic takes the lead. "That's some dress. Looks real good on you."

I shrug one shoulder. "Thrift store magic. So, um…" I look around the room, taking in the other conversations happening around us. "How is it…here?"

He mirrors my shrug. "Could be better. Could be worse."

"Does the food suck?"

He gives a quick grin. "I could use a burger from O'Shea's."

In spite of myself, I grin back. "And a shot and a beer?"

"Amen. But it's okay. It's what I signed up for, right?"

"Kane said he's been visiting you a lot."

Vic smiles. "He's been here a few times, yeah. Did he tell you he heard from the doctor? His cancer is in remission. He's going to be okay."

"Oh!" I feel relief wash over me. "No, he didn't tell me. He just said he was doing better, which could have meant anything. I'm glad. That's really good news."

"Best news I've heard in a long time," Vic agrees.

I lean forward and lower my voice. "I haven't told anyone how you helped him."

His eyes are enigmatic. "Don't put that burden on yourself. I don't care who you tell or what happens if you do. And if you ever do tell someone, I'm sure it'll be because you have a good reason."

I study his face more closely. He is definitely thinner. Keeping my voice low, I ask, "Are you sure you're doing okay in here?"

"I'm fine." His smile is reassuring. "There's nothing to worry about. I want to know about you. How are you?"

"Okay. You know. Just working and training. The usual stuff."

"How'd your black belt test go?"

I'm not prepared for the wave of resentment that courses through me when he asks that question. I'm pissed he has the audacity to bring it up. If he could have left it at the small talk level, I could be glad I made the effort to come here, glad I found out Kane is better, and glad I can make everyone in my life happy because I visited Vic like they wanted.

"I blew it," I tell him. "Totally choked when I had to break boards. Actually, it was falling apart before then, but that's the part where I crashed and burned."

He leans forward. "You'll pass next time. Now you know where your weak spots are."

I shake my head. "Not taking it again."

Vic makes a noise of disbelief. "C'mon. Of course you're going to take it again."

"No, I'm not. I'm done with the whole belt rank thing. I know enough to defend myself. That's all I need. It's why I started training in the first place."

"Well, sure," he says. "But don't you want to get better? Wouldn't that *feel* better?"

"I don't think it matters."

Vic leans back in his chair again. "I've never seen this side of you before."

"What side would that be?" I ask, irritably.

"You're acting like a kid. Pretending something doesn't matter to you because you're scared to face it."

Anger rushes through me. "I'm acting like a kid? *I'm* not the person who's rotting in jail for doing something stupid." I see a few heads turn toward us and realize the volume was way up on my voice. I lower it and add, "I'm not the one who went back to doing something illegal that they already quit doing a long time ago."

Vic's eyes flash. "You can take all the cheap shots at me you want. I'm the guy in jail. I'm an easy target. I get it. I can take it. But can you?"

"What do you even mean? Can I take what?"

"Look. Noelle. You got a shit deal, and you've worked really hard to get strong since then. I've already told you I admire that. But you need to pull your head out of your ass."

"Excuse me?"

He starts to reach for my hand, then stops himself. "You've got some kind of block. First it was the way you kept blowing your attendance, so you couldn't sign up for the test. Now you fail the test the first time you take it and say you're going to give up forever? That's not *you*. That's a block."

"How do you know it's not me? We don't even know each other well. We only met, what, six months ago? I hardly know you at all. You hardly know me."

"I know you well enough to know you're full of shit right now."

Why the hell are all the conversations in here so quiet and well mannered? I want to hit him. I want to yell. And if I do those things, I'll be the one making a scene in this room with all the other prisoners and their family members and girlfriends.

"What's the real reason you're quitting?" Vic asks.

"I'm not quitting. I talked to Conan and I'm going to keep training. I'm done advancing, that's all."

He ignores me. "What's the real reason?"

I look at him. Tears threaten to fill my eyes. I choke them back. "You were supposed to be there. You said you'd be there for me."

He looks pained. "I know. I fucked up." Then he straightens up.

"But you can't blame me. That's something separate. It's between us. What's the real reason?"

My voice breaks when I say, "I *do* blame you. You're the real reason. I've always done this by myself. Every belt test. Every single one, I did it by myself. And for once, someone was going to be there for me. You promised. You were supposed to be there. I needed you to be there."

Now he does touch my hand, lightly. "I'm sorry. I really am sorry, hon. I hurt you. That's my fault."

I nod, snuffling back tears. Still, I haven't actually cried, so that's a victory.

He squeezes my hand and then lets go. "But I'm still not your real reason."

God. Damn. Him.

"I can't believe you," I whisper vehemently. "Who gives you the right to act all...morally superior? You're in jail. *Jail.* You're incarcerated."

"You're kidding," he says, drily. "I hadn't noticed. Okay. You're right. I'm in jail. I'm also going to get out. But if you don't figure out the real reason you're scared of that test, you're going to be locked up inside yourself long after I leave this place."

I stare at him. I hate him. I can't believe I ever fucked him.

I stand up. "I have to go."

"Noelle," he says, quietly. "I'm not trying to hurt you, but I can see so clearly what you're doing to yourself...."

"I have to go," I repeat. Then I turn and walk away from the table. My footsteps are deafening on the polished floor as I go straight toward the prison guard who's overseeing the room.

"I'm done with my visit," I tell him. "I would like to go now."

As the guard prepares to let me out of the room, I feel Vic's eyes on my back, but I don't turn around.

# CHAPTER TWENTY-NINE

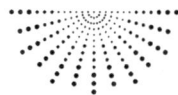

My visit with Vic puts me in a foul mood that I can't seem to shake off. I sleep well that night, but I don't feel better the next morning.

At work, I'm short with the customers. With each interaction, I get snappier. When an older man asks me to send back his plate of biscuits and gravy because he doesn't like the way the gravy's been poured, I lose it.

"I see, sir. You believe the gravy has been poured on these biscuits incorrectly. Did I get that right?"

"Yes." He points to the plate. "They're not completely covered. They should be in the center of the gravy. I can see the biscuits peeking out there. You see that?"

"Oh, I do," I agree. "I see that. Is there a ladling technique you could suggest so our cooks could prevent such a calamity in the future?"

"Beg your pardon?"

"I mean, if it were me," I gesture to myself, "I'd probably take my fork, or maybe my spoon, and cover that little bit of exposed biscuit with some of the extra gravy. You know, do it myself? But if there's a particular technique you could suggest?"

I feel a hand on my shoulder. It's Piper.

"Hi, there," she says, heartily. "What's going on over here?"

"I want a fresh plate of biscuits and gravy," the man says as he glares at me.

Piper swiftly grabs the plate from him. "Coming right up, sir. Hey, Noelle," she nudges me. "Isn't it time for your *break?*"

She bites off the word "break" so hard it sounds over pronounced. But I get her meaning.

"Yeah," I say. "I guess it is."

"I'll take over your tables for you until you're ready," she says. And by that, I know she means *when you're ready to stop being rude to customers.*

The picky gravy guy's a regular, and I've heard Piper complain about him before. His fussiness about his food, coupled with the way he leaves dirty paper napkins all over the table after he leaves, is something she's bitched about—at length—many times. But Piper's better at bullshitting customers than I am. She'll make them think she's their best friend, then trash them mercilessly once they're out of earshot.

I go out back of the diner to take my "break." It's mid-morning and already getting to be hot outside. I'm in the alley with the dumpsters, and it smells a bit ripe. I wish I had a cigarette habit so I'd have something to do with my hands, not to mention a way to mask the dumpster smell.

I've never lost it like that on a customer before. Countless times, I've daydreamed about the things I could say to them when they get rude or belligerent. But I've never actually said those things out loud. Until today.

The back door opens, and Piper comes out. "Hey," she says. "Rachel showed up early for her shift, so she's covering for a few minutes."

"Okay."

"What's going on?" she asks.

The urge to confide in her is strong. I want to tell her everything. About visiting Vic in jail. My family drama. How I failed my black belt test.

I settle for one of those. "I saw Vic in jail yesterday."

Piper pushes her hair back from her face. "Oh yeah? How'd that go?"

215

"Not so great," I sigh. "He just pissed me off. I shouldn't have gone."

"He must mean a lot to you," she says.

I look at her, stunned. "Huh?"

"If he didn't mean anything to you, it wouldn't hurt like this, right? You'd just write him off as a loser and move on."

I slump against the wall of the building. "That's what I've been trying to do."

"But it's not working?"

"Don't we need to get back inside?" I evade.

Piper comes over and stands next to me. "Need help holding this wall up?" she jokes, then adds, "The rush is over. Rachel can handle it."

"How come you're talking to me?" I ask. "You haven't talked to me in forever."

She doesn't answer right away. Then she says, "You want me to leave?"

"No." I sigh. "I'm glad you're here."

She nudges me. "So, what gives? How come you can't move on?"

I draw in a ragged breath. "I thought he had my back. I've never trusted anyone that much. At least, not since..." I stop myself from finishing the sentence. I was going to say, not since I was a kid and my sister started taking care of me. I used to trust Izzy that much. But Piper doesn't know that part of the story.

"So, why can't you trust Vic?" she asks.

"Because he's a criminal. Because he lied to me about it. He hid it from me deliberately."

"No, I get it," she says. "Why was he involved in illegal gambling, anyway? Isn't he loaded?"

"I'm still not sure how loaded he is, but he wasn't suffering." I hesitate, then decide to fill in the rest of the story. Vic did say he didn't care if I told anyone, and it *is* an essential piece of the puzzle. "He did it for a friend who couldn't afford cancer treatment. Said he knew it would be a good way to raise money fast."

"Oh, wow." Piper looks at me. "Don't get mad, but don't you think that's kind of...badass?"

Why does everyone in my life want to romanticize Vic's reason for breaking the law?

"You know, it's possible he did it for the thrill of it," I say. "And maybe he wants to feel like a hero while he's in jail."

"I mean, maybe," Piper says. "But does his friend actually have cancer?"

I nod. "Cancer and no health insurance."

"So, you could be right," she says. "Maybe he did it for a thrill. But also, you know, he *did* something. He actually helped his friend. That's a hell of a lot better than doing nothing." She's quiet for a few moments. "How's the friend doing? The one with cancer?"

I close my eyes. "He's in remission."

"You're really pissed that Vic lied to you, huh?"

I nod again, leaving my eyes closed.

"Well, listen," she says. "I wish we could talk more, but we probably should get inside and help Rachel...."

"Yeah, okay." I push away from the wall.

"No more giving the customers shit about special requests?" she asks, as I open the back door.

"You don't like the gravy guy either," I remind her.

"I don't. But I like tips more than I dislike the gravy guy."

"I'll be on my best behavior," I promise.

I get through the rest of my shift without snarking at any customers, though it isn't easy. I'm glad Piper came to my rescue. But I'm also disturbed, because it seems that Piper, along with everyone else I know, is on Vic's side. They seem to think he should be free to do illegal things because he's an otherwise "good guy." Kane, Conan, Annie, Piper—all of them are willing to cut Vic a lot of slack. Even Vic seems to cut himself a lot of slack. He's accepting his jail sentence without complaint, but he also seems to believe he doesn't deserve it.

Personally, I just wish I could put him in the rearview mirror. The fact that my friends outnumber me doesn't change how I feel. I was wrong about Vic. He's not the medicine I needed or the solution to my problems. He's a convicted criminal and a liar.

After our shift, Piper offers to give me a lift home, and I accept. The minute she puts her key in the ignition and revs up the car, loud vocal harmonies burst through her speakers. She reaches over and turns down the volume.

"Hardcore Fleetwood Mac phase," she explains. "Can't stop listening to them."

"Weird. I wouldn't think of you as a Fleetwood Mac fan."

"Oh, hell yeah. In fact, if my band ever outgrows this goth phase, I'm hoping we can be more like that. All of us can sing. We could totally pull off the harmonies and shit."

"Or you could be a goth band with harmonies," I say, without thinking.

Piper whirls and stares at me. "You know what? That is a fucking great idea. A goth band with harmonies. Holy shit."

She's quiet the rest of the way to my place, and I am too. I'm just glad to be in her car again. To my surprise, instead of just dropping me in front of my building, she finds a parking spot near my place and pulls in.

"Hey," she says. "There's something I need to tell you. It's nothing scary, just something I need you to know."

"Um, okay." I feel nervous again. I'm sure I've offended her in some way. Or maybe she wants to say something about the night I ditched her at The Pink Pauper. Something she needs to get off her chest. I brace myself.

"So..." she says. Hesitates. "Oh fuck, I'll just say it. I'm bi-sexual. Bill knows. The whole band knows. But I never told you, so, y'know. I just thought...you should know too."

"Oh...."

"I always end up with guys," she goes on. "At least so far. Because I always like girls who are straight. It's kind of funny." Then she laughs. But it's a nervous laugh, and she doesn't actually sound like she thinks it's funny.

I turn to her. "Thanks for telling me."

"Sure thing."

"And uh...if I was into girls, like, if I was bi-sexual too? I'd totally be into you. You're pretty awesome."

Her eyes gleam at me, then her face breaks into a wide grin. "Well, maybe someday I'll meet a nice girl like you."

"There's no one like me," I say, deadpan.

"Get the hell out of my car and go feed your damn cat," she laughs.

As I pop the door, she says, "Let me know if you want to come out with us again. Everyone misses you. Especially Sven."

I raise an eyebrow. "Sven?"

"He keeps talking about your good taste in wine."

I laugh. "I can't afford good wine. I just know when it's bad."

"Well, he was impressed. Give me a call if you want to hang."

"I'll do that." I get out of the car. "Thanks for the ride."

"Anytime," she says.

I slam the car door shut and watch her drive away. I was so sure she'd decided I wasn't worth her time. But maybe she simply wanted to tell me her secret and was afraid to do it.

I guess I can relate to that.

# CHAPTER THIRTY

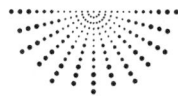

It's hot at the school tonight. The air conditioning in the building has been malfunctioning, so we've been working out in a warm gym. It's muggy and uncomfortable.

Almost everyone in my class is new to me. All but two of my old classmates graduated to black belt, moving on to a different series of classes. I tell myself it doesn't matter. I don't want to stop working out, because if I do, the skills I have will deteriorate. Plus, since I failed my test, Conan hasn't bothered me. He hasn't pushed me to try again or made me feel bad for staying at the same level and I'm grateful for the space.

Right before class, I duck into the small ladies' room where the shower is. As I'm finishing up in one of the stalls, I hear two other students walk in. I'm not paying attention to their conversation until one of them says:

"Hey, is that one girl still in this class?"

"Which girl?"

"The one who had the meltdown during her black belt test?"

"Oh, I heard about that."

"I was there when she flunked it. Couldn't hack it at the end. She ran out and didn't come back. It was intense."

I figure they're probably in here to change for class. Now that I'm paying attention, their voices are painfully easy to hear. *Great.* Just what I need—a reminder of how hard I failed on the day of the black belt test.

"Maybe she was having a bad day," says the second student, with a shrug in her voice.

"Yeah, maybe. But I heard she hasn't moved up for over a year."

"Maybe she had a bad year. You ready?"

"Yeah, okay."

I slump against the stall. I have a vague idea who they are. I recognize their voices, but I don't know their names. I used to know the names of everyone in my class, back when all of us more or less leveled up together.

It is strange not to move up in the belt ranks with your peers. It's the way you play the game. For the first time, I wonder: if I refuse to push myself to the next level, will it become uncomfortable for me to keep training here?

I wait in the bathroom until I'm sure it's been empty for several minutes. That way, when the other two women see me, they won't suspect I overheard them. I join the class as it's about to start. After running through a warmup and drills, Conan sets us up with sparring partners.

Mine is this guy named Ethan. I'm better than him, which I can tell annoys him a little bit. His annoyance annoys me. It also makes me feel self-conscious that I'm in this class, at this level. I'm probably better than everyone here. But it's not because I'm superior. It's because I didn't move up.

I try to re-focus. After all, it's good to learn from people who are more skilled and experienced than yourself. Maybe I'm doing Ethan a favor, being here. Maybe I can help him learn that just because you're fighting a girl, it doesn't mean you'll win. Not if the girl is skilled. Not if she's strong. Not if she's got the kind of stamina you never anticipated. If she's the kind of girl who won't let you mess with her....

"Noelle! Noelle! Stop!"

The voice comes from very far away, and I'm not sure who it is. Then I feel a hand on my arm, pulling me back.

"Noelle." It's Conan. "Back off."

As soon as I recognize him, the room comes into focus. I'm sitting on top of Ethan and I have him pinned to the mat. Like me, he's wearing a chest protector, but his face isn't protected. He looks confused and possibly terrified. I think I can feel him shaking. I'm breathing hard, and all my limbs are tingling with exertion.

"Did I hit your face?" I ask him, horrified.

"Not yet," Conan answers for him, tugging on my arm again. "Why don't you get up and go sit in my office, okay? Just get up off him and go have a seat." He holds out a hand, and I get off Ethan, who looks immediately relieved.

"What happened?" I ask Conan, bewildered.

"Noelle. Please. Go sit in my office. I'll come talk to you in a bit. Okay?"

Finally, he gets through to me, and I go to his office and shut the door. It's a smallish square with a desk, a couple chairs, and a low table with all of Conan's tournament plaques and trophies. There's a poster of Bruce Lee on the wall, right behind where Conan's head would be if he were in here, sitting at his desk.

I feel like Bruce is staring at me, and I drop my eyes.

*Did I hurt Ethan?* I wonder. What happens if he's not okay? And what do I do about the fact that I can't remember what I did or even how or when I pinned Ethan to the mat?

The clock says it's twenty minutes to six. I figure Conan will finish teaching his class before he comes in to talk to me, so I let myself doze off a little. I'm not truly sleeping, though, because I'm aware of the dim noise of different classes going on around me.

When he finally comes back, it's ten minutes after the hour. I jerk awake when he opens the door. He comes around and sits behind his desk, and gives me a look that's full of nothing but concern.

"How are you?"

"I'm okay. How's Ethan?"

"He's fine. You didn't hurt him. You just scared him," Conan says. Then after a moment, he adds, "You scared me too. What the hell happened?"

"I'm not sure." My voice wavers. "I don't remember most of it."

"How much do you remember?"

222

I speak slowly. "We were sparring. I could tell he was pissed that I kept getting the best of him. That pissed *me* off, so then I focused and...then you were pulling me off him."

"All right. I'll tell you what I saw. You were getting the best of him. And then you were taking advantage of that. You stopped backing off him, you kept kicking him, hitting him until he fell. And then you got on top of him and threatened to 'make it worse.'"

"Did I hit him on the chest protector?" I ask, in a small voice. "Or did I hit him somewhere else?"

"You didn't hit him anywhere else," Conan says. "But you were out of control. It was like you couldn't see him anymore."

I think of Vic training me to push through my emotions, drilling me over and over on deadly moves. "I shouldn't've ever worked with Vic," I groan. "It made me too violent."

Conan doesn't respond, so I look up at him. "I mean, don't you think that's it?"

He shakes his head. "It's not Vic."

"But those moves he taught me," I object. "The way he trained me. He trained me not to feel revulsion when I do what I have to do to protect myself. I wasn't like this before."

"But I didn't see you use any dirty moves," Conan says. "Everything you did was legal. The problem was you weren't protecting yourself, and you wouldn't stop. Or maybe you couldn't stop if you don't remember what happened."

"But he taught me to be ruthless—"

"Noelle." The tone of Conan's voice dries up my protest. "You know the difference between an actual threat in the real world and sparring practice in class. Something's not right. You haven't been okay for a long time now. You know that, don't you?"

I can't answer him, so I just fix my eyes on him, fighting tears. They're not spilling. He might not even know I'm on the verge of crying. But it seems like I'm always fighting these fucking tears. I'm so tired of it.

Conan's next words are painful. "I think you need to take a couple weeks off. It'll give you some time to get your shit together, okay?"

"Jesus, Conan, I slipped! It won't happen again. I think I just did it because he had a shitty attitude."

"Take some time, and figure out what happened," he says, firmly. "Then check back in after two weeks. We can decide what to do next from there."

I can tell by his demeanor that he's not going to change his mind. Still, I try one last plea. "How about a day off?"

"Take two weeks," he repeats. "Then check back. And if you need anything, personally, call me and Annie, okay?"

Conan's a good guy. I know that. So he doesn't deserve it when I jump up, saying, "Fine. Fuck it. I'll fucking go."

He tries to say something else, but I'm done talking.

I walk home, agitated and angry, but I don't know if I'm angry at Conan or angry at myself for losing control. I'm still not convinced that my training with Vic doesn't have something to do with that. All that pushing through uncomfortable emotions and learning to function like a machine. Maybe it didn't cause what happened, but it had to have been a part of it.

All at once I'm homesick for my sister and the way it used to be with us. I remember a time when I'd had a fight on the school playground in sixth grade. At that point, our parents hadn't even been gone for a full year, and Izzy was still getting the hang of having to fill the mother role for me.

This kid was taunting me, following me around at recess, saying gross stuff about my developing body. It had been going on for several days, and finally, I'd had enough. I'd pushed the kid so hard he'd lost his balance. The force of the push and my anger had surprised him enough to stop him. He'd left me alone for the rest of recess. I'd been so afraid I would get in trouble for it. Even when I didn't by the end of the school day, I was still scared.

That night, I'd confided in my sister about what had happened and told her I might get in trouble. I remember that she'd hugged me and said I'd done the right thing. That it was good to stand up for yourself. And she'd said that if I did get in trouble, she'd go and talk to the principal for me.

She'd been my champion, then. My protector. I'd thought of her as a sort of comic book warrior, one of a rare class of women fighters who would stand up for what was right. The loss of that relationship with her had cut deep.

As I walk home, I realize that maybe I've wanted to become the warrior I used to believe Izzy was. Maybe taekwondo has been as much about that as it's been about learning to defend myself—a way to see myself as a warrior. But now, I've been banished from the school for two weeks to "get my shit together," which means Conan wants me to learn something.

But other than learning how to not go crazy on other students during class, I have no idea what he has in mind. If I can't figure it out, I'm afraid he'll never let me come back. And if he doesn't: who will I be?

# CHAPTER THIRTY-ONE

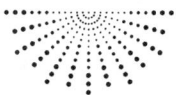

"I'm sorry. I'm so sorry." I say it over and over, like saying it will roll back the last five minutes.

Moments ago, I tripped and dumped a tray of drinks on a table in my section. The couple in the booth is soggy and horrified. Sodas and ice are sopping the table, their clothes, their paper napkins. There's a pool of soda in the ashtray, soaking what was recently a lit cigarette. I'm mortified.

Once again, Piper comes to my rescue. She moves me aside and hands the customers a small pile of bar towels.

"Here," she says. "If you want to clean up in the restroom just head to the back. We'll take care of the table. And if you want to take your meal home, it's on us."

As the customers scoot out of the booth and give me dirty looks, Piper drops some more towels on the table. I start cleaning up the mess, zombie-like. I feel her hand on my shoulder.

"Are you okay?"

I start to say that I'm fine, but then I turn to her and shake my head.

She hesitates, then says, "Come hang out with me tonight?"

I nod vigorously. I don't care if it's with her, or with her and the rest of the band. I just want some place to belong for a few hours.

"You gonna be able to finish your shift?" she asks.

"Yeah. Just let me clean this up first."

"I'll cover for you until it's done."

I make it through the rest of my shift. The couple take Piper up on her offer of free takeout, then leave in this huffy way that I'd usually make fun of, but I'm too rattled. I've always been proud of how light and steady I am on my feet. Underneath my waitress persona is my martial arts knowledge. My strength and balance have always worked for me. I've never tripped or spilled anything before. Not once.

Piper and I finally leave in the early afternoon with our own takeout bag. I'm not sure what's in it, but I think she threw something together in the kitchen before we left. As soon as we're in her car, she turns to me. "Cheap tequila?"

"Oh God, please."

She takes us back to her place, and pours generous shots to go with our takeout, which turns out to be a couple of hastily assembled club sandwiches. She doesn't interrogate me right away, just lets me eat and gives the tequila time to work its magic.

Then she gets right to the point.

"What's going on with you, Noelle? You've been pretty fucked up lately."

I look at her, wondering how to explain. Do I tell her I'm still messed up from visiting Vic in jail? Or about how I lost control in class? Or should I talk about my family?

"Or whatever, don't tell me," Piper says. "If you just want to chill—"

"I think I tried to kill someone in my taekwondo class."

After a long beat, Piper ventures, "Um…all right. You're not locked up, so I'm assuming your intended victim is still among the living?"

"Yeah. Yeah, I didn't kill anybody."

"So, what happened? Was he an asshole to you or something?"

I shake my head. "He was super cocky, but not an asshole. And it wasn't a dangerous situation either way. I shouldn't have had that strong of a reaction."

"It couldn't have been that bad, could it?" Piper points out. "Since the guy's all right?"

"They asked me not to come back for two weeks."

"Oh," she says. "Yeah. I guess that sounds...significant."

I lower my head in my hands. There have been so many times in the past several months where I've had to fight to keep tears down. I wish I could cry now. It would be such a relief. But my eyes are dry.

I feel Piper's hand on mine, tentative. "Hey. So, what else is going on?"

I lift my head. "Can I tell you something that's super messed up?"

"Sure, hon. Tell me whatever you want."

Her eyes are concerned. Compassionate. Can I trust her? Will she believe me?

Here goes nothing. "My sister's husband, my brother in law, he tried to rape me when I was eighteen. I fought him off. But it kind of fucked me up."

"What did your sister say?"

"She doesn't believe me."

"Shit," Piper says.

Before I can stop myself, I tell her everything—the full story about Izzy and Rob, and how he came into our lives. How my sister is pressuring me to forget about what happened so we can all go back to "normal." While I talk, Piper squeezes my hand, and when I've finally taken a breath, she pulls me into a hug. Now would probably be a good time to cry, but I still don't have it in me.

She holds me for several minutes, and I take comfort in the fact that she seems to believe me. Maybe she'll hit me with questions soon, questions like, *"Are you sure that's what happened?"* Or *"Did you misinterpret something?"* But right now she's comforting me. And I need it.

When we pull apart, I know I have to tell her the rest. "It's not just that. I really hated him after that, you know? I didn't like him much before that, but I never hated him."

"It's understandable," she soothes. "I hate him, too, and I've never even met him."

"No," I say. "I keep having these dreams. These dreams where I hurt him, where I really *want* to hurt him."

She squeezes my hand again. "I think that's probably okay, so long as you don't *actually* hurt him. I think it's pretty natural to want revenge."

"You do?"

"Sure. I mean, if someone tries to kill you or if someone breaks into your house, you have a right to defend yourself. Besides, it's instinct. We're still animals."

"But Rob didn't try to kill me."

"The way I see it, he kind of did. Rape is soul murder. Attempted rape is violent. Totally normal to have a defensive reaction to that."

"But these dreams... They're pretty intense."

"Maybe there's something you need to resolve in the real world?" she suggests. "Maybe that's why you keep having the dreams."

"Maybe..."

"Listen," Piper says. "I was raped. About three years ago."

"Oh God, I'm so sorry." I feel dumb for talking about my almost rape.

Like she can read my thoughts, she says, "We're all in the same soup, you know? It's the same violence. There's no need to make comparisons. I think you should talk to someone."

I sigh. "Vic said the same thing."

She half smiles. "Great minds think alike, I guess."

"I can't afford a counselor."

"There are some good free support groups. I can hook you up, if you want."

I'm overwhelmed by what Piper just told me. By the fact that she's being so good to me. Just weeks ago I thought our friendship was over.

"Yeah, maybe," I say. "Maybe I could go to a support group or something. I have to think about it."

"Just let me know. Now, how about another drink?"

At some point in the evening, she calls Bill to let him know she can't hang out with him tonight. I hope he's not angry with me, but I'm grateful.

For the rest of the night, we watch dumb television shows. We don't talk about anything heavy, and sitting on her couch I feel like I've found an oasis. Maybe it's temporary. But it's a place to rest, and it's what I need.

We fall asleep watching TV. In the morning, I wake up before

Piper. She's sound asleep, snoring slightly. I need to get home and feed Milo.

I shake Piper's shoulder. "Hey, I have to go. Piper. Wake up."

She finally opens one eye. "Eh?"

"I have to go, but I don't have a key. I can't lock your door."

She lets out a gargantuan yawn. "I'll lock it." She stands up and follows me to the door.

"Sorry to wake you up," I say, as I open her door.

She reaches out and pulls me into a brief, hard hug.

When she lets me go, I swallow and say, "Thanks."

"Of course," she croaks. "Now fuck off and let me sleep."

I laugh, because I know she's not mad. "Talk to you later." I hear her slide the deadbolt to her door as I go down the hall.

Once I'm out on the street, I decide to walk home. It's a couple miles of city blocks, but I can't bear the thought of waiting for a bus, sitting on it, and watching the buildings rush by outside the windows. I want to be outside with the concrete sidewalk underneath my feet. Listening to the city as it wakes up and hearing the citified birds begin chirping to welcome the morning. Feeling the heat spread through the air as the sun comes up.

When I get back to my apartment, Milo is frantic. I cuddle him and feed him, then make myself coffee and take it to the window seat where he joins me.

Vic was right about one thing. I *am* locked up inside myself. Talking to Piper last night didn't set me free, but sharing my story with her made me understand what Vic meant when he said that. It also made me aware of what he likely sees when he looks at me.

So now, I guess I have to decide if I want to break out of the place where I'm locked up. I hate to admit it, but I'm not sure I do. I have a feeling that, if I do, I'll find that I'm still right back where I was the moment Rob attacked me. Eighteen, not twenty-two. Almost five years behind, terrified, and lost. I can't stand the thought of going back and being that person. It might be easier to keep her locked inside me and pretend that she doesn't exist.

# CHAPTER THIRTY-TWO

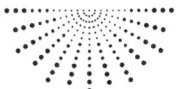

My exile from the school leaves me with an abundance of free time. Part way through the first week of my two-week "break," I have a day off from work and nothing else to do. I feel aimless, so I clean my apartment top to bottom in the morning, which doesn't take long, since it isn't a big place. By the time I'm done, Milo is angry with me. I feed him some treats to placate him, then go out, not sure where I'm headed.

It's Thursday, and that means choir practice at the church. So eventually, I land at the bus stop and catch a bus to Capitol Hill. I don't go to the church right away. It's lunchtime on a weekday, and the choir won't be practicing until the evening.

Instead, I walk around the hill, wandering in and out of shops. This particular neighborhood is super gay-friendly, which means a lot of other counter-cultural types tend to populate the area. I've always loved that this particular church thrives in an urban environment that attracts and embraces so many different types of people.

The cultural ethos makes for an eclectic small-business landscape. I lose track of time as I drift from a shop with incense and metaphysical books, to a thrift store, to a comic book shop. I don't have enough money on me to buy anything. I'm just soaking up the vibes.

Around dinner time I finally wander into the church. It's still too early for choir practice, but I want to be there anyway. I climb the stairs to the balcony. No one else is there, and I sit down in a pew in the first row so I can look out over the sanctuary.

I don't know why I like it here. Part of it's the choir, but that's not all of it. Maybe it's that it feels like a place where you can take a breather and listen. Listen to see if God or the universe or whatever or whoever is in charge has anything to say.

My sister and Rob go to church every Sunday. I wonder if Rob believes in God or if he just plays along for my sister's benefit. I've heard him say he prays, though. I wonder what that's like. Does he avoid talking to God about what he tried to do to me, or does he admit he told me, *"I'm so glad I found you here alone?"* Does he pray about how he grabbed me and pushed me up against the wall, thrusting his hand up my skirt? Does he believe he didn't shove his erection between my legs, even when I told him to stop and get the fuck off me? Does he tell God that he actually said something as dumb and cringey as *"You know you want me, Noelle?"*

On one level the whole thing was so fucking cheesy. Even the way I kneed him in the crotch—a couple times for good measure—and how he fell down clutching his balls. In a movie, it probably would have been good for a laugh. But at home, with my sister's husband, it shattered my world and sense of myself.

Of course, in a movie, my sister would have believed me and dumped his ass. Then we would have gone on to live fabulous lives of our own. We would have found better men, one for her and one for me. Maybe we would have started a business together. Or won the lottery and sailed around the world.

But I'm here in this life the way it actually is, and I have to figure out what I'm going to do with it. I didn't get my happy ending. For a few months I thought Vic might be that for me, but that was just another fantasy. He was good to me, but he pretended to be someone he wasn't. He kept things from me—big things—and in my book, that's the same as lying.

But Vic and Izzy aren't the only disappointments. I'm a trained fighter who apparently can't control herself and who still can't achieve a black belt in her chosen martial art.

Reality sucks.

I don't wait for the choir. I have a hunch listening to them won't help me today. I'm still deeply restless, and I don't know how to calm myself down. On the bus home, I consider stopping at one of the bars where I usually go to pick up a guy for the night. A reliable distraction. I reach up to pull the stop cord as we near one of my usual haunts, but at the last moment, I drop my hand and keep riding.

I don't want a distraction. Not really. I want a cure. I want a key, something that will make me the kind of person who isn't wandering aimlessly in circles, looking for something to save me. Martial arts didn't save me. Vic didn't save me. Piper is amazing and maybe we're truly friends now, but she can't save me either.

I'm tired and hungry when I get home, but I don't feel like eating. I dutifully feed Milo, then notice my machine is blinking with an unread message, so I hit the button to hear it, feeling a gnawing dread in my gut.

"Noelle. It's Izzy. I'm sorry there was a misunderstanding last time. Let's try again. You name the time and place. We'll meet wherever you want. We just want to talk to you. I love you. We're going to make this work."

Another beep, and the message is over.

She's trying to wear me down. It's a tactic she's used successfully in the past. I always cave and meet her somewhere eventually, submitting to a conversation that makes it seem like our relationship is on hold until one day, everything will magically resolve.

*We're going to make this work.*

"No, we're not," I say aloud.

My gut hurts again, but it's different this time. It's that butterfly sensation. The kind you get when you want to do something, but you're afraid to do it. And the reason I feel that way is because now, I know what I need to do.

I pick up the phone and dial Piper's number. It rings four times.

"This is Piper."

"Hey. It's Noelle."

"Hey, Noelle. I know your voice, silly. What's up?"

"You don't have to do this, but I have to ask. Can you cover for me tomorrow morning? And um, can I borrow your car?"

———

PIPER COMES by in the morning, dressed for work at the diner. We had different shifts today so we swapped. I'm going to drop her off at work. Then I'm going to drive up north to visit my sister. I didn't even have to explain the situation to Piper last night. As soon as I told her I needed to go talk to Izzy, she understood.

She doesn't say much as we drive. I know she needs to inhale a half-gallon or so of weak diner coffee before she's fully operational. There's nowhere to park when we get there so I double park right in front.

"Thanks for letting me borrow your car," I say. "I owe you. I'll be back as soon as I can. Definitely in time to cover the dinner shift."

"Are you sure you don't want me to go with you?" she asks. "We could try to find someone to cover for both of us."

"No." I'm decisive. "I need to do this by myself."

"Okay. Well, if you're sure." She sounds dubious.

"I'm sure."

An impatient driver honks their horn behind us.

"Geez. Chill out, motherfucker. God, I need coffee." Piper groans as she gets out of the car. "Good luck."

"Thanks."

Ignoring the person honking behind us, I wait until Piper clears the street before I drive away. Then I head for the interstate to drive north.

When Rob first moved in with us, we all lived in the apartment that Izzy and I had shared since our parents passed. But eventually, they wanted their own house, and that's where we were living the night it happened.

I never liked the place. It wasn't my home. They said it was my home, but it wasn't. It didn't have my memories with Izzy or our parents in it. It had very few things I remembered from our child-hood--old dishes, towels, blankets—Izzy had thrown a lot of those things away in the move to the new house. Things that, while they were "just things," had always reminded me of our family. Since we'd kept them after our parents died, they'd become a part of the life I shared with my sister, too.

For years, I've felt guilty that Izzy had to give up her early twenties to take care of me. I know it's not my fault, but I feel some kind of responsibility, like I owe her something in return. It's made me want to please her and to make things as easy for her as possible.

But today, I'm not going to make things easy for her. I'm going to make things hard on both of us. I'm not looking forward to it. I don't want to do it. I also can't imagine doing anything else.

I push "play" on the tape deck of Piper's car. It's still Fleetwood Mac. She's obsessive, but that's all right. I like Fleetwood Mac. I feel better once I get on the freeway. The higher speeds and the moving cars make me feel like I'm in a cocoon of motion that will keep me safe.

But once I see the exit sign to turn off for my sister's house, the safe feeling fades. My stomach hurts. I remind myself I could turn around and go back. I'm sure Piper would understand. Nobody is making me do this.

But I know I need to do it.

Izzy and Rob live in a pleasant suburban neighborhood that's in a sort of no-man's land near the county line, between Seattle and a few smaller cities that are further north on the map. Most of the homes in their neighborhood are one or two story houses that were built in the sixties or seventies. The neighborhood is row upon row of three-bedroom dwellings surrounded by lush greenery, lawns, trees, rhododendron and hydrangea bushes. A vegetable garden sprouts here and there.

Everything looks a bit dusty as I drive through the neighborhood. August is typically the hottest, driest month in and around Seattle, but the rain will be back soon enough.

I wore jeans and a T-shirt today instead of shorts to keep from sticking to Piper's vinyl seats. But I still feel sticky and hot, as the floral aroma of my own deodorant floods my nostrils. I'm only a few doors away from Izzy and Rob's house.

Just before I get there, I tell myself they may not even be home. If they're not, I'll leave. I won't sit here and lie in wait for them. If they're here, I'll talk to them. If they're not, I'll regroup.

But the moment I edge toward their driveway, I see their car—a nondescript station wagon with wood panel trim. I still remember the day they bought it. How excited they were to have a new car.

I pull in behind the station wagon and turn off Piper's car, stopping Stevie Nicks in the middle of a song. For a few seconds, I just sit there, unmoving. I wonder if they saw me pull up. Or, maybe they haven't bothered to look. Maybe they're in the kitchen. Izzy's cooking something. Rob's talking to her. They didn't hear the car.

I imagine all types of scenarios. They could be in the bedroom, watching TV. Or having sex. Maybe they're fighting. Possibly, they'll come out to the car and ask why I'm here.

But after a while, I realize that's not going to happen. If I want to talk to them, I'm going to have to go knock on the door. So, finally, I get out of the car, lock it carefully, and start the long walk up to Izzy and Rob's front door.

# CHAPTER THIRTY-THREE

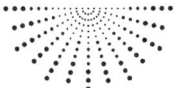

At the door, I stare at the small brass knocker for several seconds. Izzy was so tickled by it when we all moved into the house. She thought it was "fancy." Nobody ever uses it, though. People just knock on the actual door.

I raise my hand, hesitate, then knock. I can feel my heart thudding against my ribcage. I'm starting to regret not bringing Piper with me. I thought this was something I needed to do alone. Now I'm not so sure. Maybe going solo on this one was a bad idea.

I hear footsteps inside the house. They're light, which means it's Izzy coming to the door. Rob has a slightly plodding gait.

When my sister opens the door and stands in the frame, I'm struck by how pretty she is. I've always thought of her as more pretty than me. She got the honey-colored hair, blue eyes, and the hourglass figure. Not only that, but standing in the doorway of her own home, she looks content. Not on edge, which is the way I always feel.

And as I stare, admiring her, that simple realization hits me like I'm a cartoon character who just had an anvil dropped on their head.

*I'm always on edge.* All the time. I can't imagine what it would be like to feel the way Izzy presents. Like she's comfortable in her own life. But I want to feel that way. And that realization is what compels me to push forward.

"Noelle," Izzy says. "We were going to come see you—"

"I decided to come here instead. I have something to tell you. Can I come in?"

She wavers for a moment. I know she senses she's not going to want to hear what I have to say. But in the end, she says, "Sure. Come on in."

Izzy leads me into the living room. It looks almost the same as it did back in high school. Two overstuffed couches, set perpendicular to each other. A coffee table with shelves underneath for magazines. A fireplace, which is the focal point of the room. They keep the television in the dining room so they can watch TV while they're eating, which is a habit I never liked.

Just being in the house brings up strong emotions. It's like a three-dimensional photo album, with visceral sensations to enhance your viewing. Smells. Sounds. Memories. Context.

Instead of asking me to sit down, Izzy says, "Should I get Rob?"

I shrug. "I came here to tell you something. I don't care if he's here or not."

That isn't quite true. I'd prefer it if he wasn't here. But it would be creepier if he's lurking somewhere, listening in on our conversation. Might as well bring him out if he's home.

"I'll go get him," she says, and disappears down the hall to the bedrooms.

I continue to look around the room and assess it in terms of maneuverability. Where it would be to my advantage to fight someone off, if necessary. Where I could make an escape. It's how I survey every room, every bar, every single place I enter. Every time.

What would I do if Rob tried to attack me? I don't think he will. He wouldn't do it in front of Izzy, anyway. Part of his hold on my sister is that she thinks he's a nice guy. A good man. If he attacked me while all three of us are here, that would blow his cover.

Still, what if he did? Could I fight him? Would I use the tactics Vic taught me? How would I feel if I hurt him for real?

I clench and unclench my fists. Even though I didn't come here for a physical fight, I feel like I'm preparing to have one.

Rob follows Izzy to the living room. He looks pissed. As they move into the room, he stands slightly ahead of my sister, like he's trying to protect her. Or maybe like he's trying to intimidate me.

"So, what's going on, Noelle?" he asks.

"I have something to tell Izzy, and I figured you might as well hear it, too."

He folds his arms across his chest and plants his feet further apart. "Then talk."

Yeah. He's trying to intimidate me. It's in his stance and the glowering look in his eyes. Some sick part of me wants him to try something. I want to know if I could take him. What kind of damage I could do.

"Do you want to sit down?" Izzy asks. "Should we all sit down, maybe?"

"I'm fine standing," I say.

Izzy looks flustered. She comes up behind Rob, and gently pushes him aside, so she's near me. Then she sits down on the couch and looks up at me. "What do you want to tell me?"

I wasn't prepared for how something so simple could undo me. It's a visual representation of what I've wanted her to do for so long, to put Rob to the side and listen to me. To truly hear me.

I look at him and sense the anger simmering beneath the surface. But I'm angry too. Being face to face with Rob is like my nightmares come to life. I feel a deep urge to retaliate for what he did to me. For doing it, then lying about it, and painting me as the liar, instead.

But here, outside my dream, I realize something else. Meeting his violence with my own would bind us in some new way. I can feel the potential of it in the room, in the air. And I don't want it to become real. I would go there if I had to, to defend myself. But I don't actually want to go there.

"Noelle," Izzy prompts. "What do you want to tell me?"

"I need you to leave me alone," I say. "I need you to stop calling me. I need you to stop showing up at my place unannounced, and I need you to stop asking me to 'talk.' I don't want to talk. I told you everything I needed to say five years ago."

"I know you've been hurting for a long time," Izzy says. "But you've

239

never let Rob explain things to you. I think if you would just let him—"

"No," I say. "No. That's the problem. He's been explaining it to you. But I was *there*, Izzy. You weren't. Nobody knows what happened better than me. It happened to me. I told you what happened to me. And you either believe me, or you don't."

"Not everything's that simple."

"No. Not everything is. But this is. This *is*. This is simple. This is one of those simple things."

"What's simple?" Izzy asks.

I'm getting tired. It makes me so tired to be here. I can feel the energy draining out of my limbs, slithering to the floor, leaving me abandoned. I shouldn't have to say the same thing over and over.

I'm hurting myself being here. I shouldn't have come.

I hear a snuffling sound from the couch, and I know Izzy is crying.

"Look what you're doing to her," Rob says to me. "You're making her really upset."

"I'm okay." Izzy looks up at me with tears still in her eyes. "I don't know what you want me to do. I've tried to understand, I've tried to invite you back into our family. I don't know what else I can do."

"Believe me," I say. "You could believe me. Believe me when I tell you that your husband tried to rape me. Because he did."

Rob starts to object, and I whirl on him. "You know it's true." I turn back to my sister. "Your husband tried to rape me. That's my reality. In your reality it never happened, but in mine, it happened every fucking day. Every day. We live in two different worlds, and your world is hurting me. Every time you call, every time you show up at my place, every time you invite me over for Christmas, it hurts. I need you to stop. Stop hurting me and just let me live my life. Can you stop? Please?"

Now Izzy is crying hard. But I know, with sudden clarity, that she's not crying for me. She's crying for herself.

"I don't understand," she says. "I don't understand how you can be like this. After all the years I took care of you… Why are you doing this?"

"I think you should go," Rob says.

The look on his face makes my stomach turn. So self-righteous, playing the role of my sister's protector.

And then I realize there's nothing more to say. I can attempt to invent new ways to describe how we live in two different worlds and that coming in contact with their world hurts me. I could ask my sister to do a role play, put herself in my place, ask her to imagine how she'd feel if what I'm saying is true. How would she feel if I had a husband, and my husband had done this to her?

But nothing I say will work. Nothing will get through. I can't make Rob tell the truth, and I can't make Izzy want to believe me. The best thing to do is to leave.

"I don't need you to understand," I say to Izzy. "I just need you to stop asking me to talk about this. I need you to leave me alone. Can you leave me alone?"

"You're so cold," she says, through a haze of tears. "You've changed."

"You're right," I say. "I have changed."

And I have. Because for the first time in five long years, I can see this is a fight I will never win. There's no set of techniques that will work. My sister will never believe me. It's like trying to fight the air with your fists—it's not even a real fight. The only thing to do is walk away.

"Please leave me alone," I repeat. "Please don't make me ask you again."

I turn around and walk the short steps to the front door. It probably takes me seconds, but it feels longer, an undefined stretch of time until I wrench their front door open and shut it behind me. I draw in a deep breath of hot summertime air, then go to Piper's car and get behind the wheel.

# CHAPTER THIRTY-FOUR

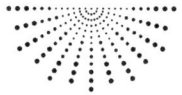

As I drive out of the neighborhood, I feel divorced from my body. It's almost as if I'm watching myself drive the car to the freeway on-ramp and get on the interstate. I'm watching my hands on the steering wheel, observing my own eyes as they navigate the road.

After I've been driving for several minutes, a bank of road signs advertises coffee, food, and gasoline. I decide I could use a cup of coffee and signal to get off the road. But once I pull off at the freeway exit, there isn't much there. Just one fast food place and a convenience store with a couple of gas pumps.

I'm not in the mood for fast food, so I pull into the parking lot of the convenience store. As soon as I turn off Piper's car, the shaking starts.

It begins with my hands, at first just mild trembling, but then they begin to shake more violently. I clamp them on the steering wheel to make them stop, but then the rest of me begins to shiver, deep shivers from my gut, like I've been outside too long on a freezing cold winter day.

But it's hot outside, too hot to sit in a parked car with the windows rolled up. I try to crank my window down, which is difficult, because my hands are shaking again. Finally, I get it down, and put my hands in my lap, between my knees. The shaking and shuddering slowly subsides, and a faint warm breeze moves into the car through the rolled-down window.

Some kind of insect buzzes as it flies by, a hum against the sound of sobs. It takes me a few moments to clue in to the fact that the sobs are coming from me. I can't stuff them down. I have to surrender, or the effort to subdue them will be physically painful. I make deep animalistic sounds as I cry from my gut, as the tears overflow and flood through my heart, then spread out through my chest. I'm snuffling, wiping my eyes, and I don't care if anyone walking by the car can see me. The tears are having their way with me, finally, and I'm ready for them.

Eventually, I'm spent. I take a couple of deep breaths. I can hear the roar of the cars rushing past on the nearby freeway, punctuated by the occasional chirp of birds perched in the sparse trees planted in the parking lot.

I know I look horrible. I try to check myself out in the rearview mirror, and of course my eyes are red and puffy. But I don't look away. How many times have I peered in to a mirror, judging this or that thing about my appearance, never being one hundred percent satisfied with what I see? Too many times to count. But now, as I look at my reflection, I'm all right with it. In fact, I'm more than all right with it. I look like shit, but I feel good.

A few moments later, I plant my feet on the asphalt and walk toward the convenience store. The mid-August sunshine bathes me in burning light as I cross the parking lot. Inside, though, it's like a freezer with the air conditioning blasting. I discover that instead of the usual serve yourself coffee machines, there's an espresso machine behind the front counter. I know that because there's a small line of people at the counter in front of the machine.

I get behind the last person in line, a harried-looking woman with bleached blond hair. She's wearing shorts, a grey T-shirt, and faded blue flip flops. She turns around and does a double take when she sees my face.

"Hard day?" she asks.

"It was," I say.

"Gettin' better?"

"Uh, yeah. Actually, I think it is getting better."

"Sometimes you just need a good cry." She nods. Then she squints at me. "Did you give the man behind the counter your name?"

"My name?"

"Yeah, you gotta go tell him you want coffee, and then he asks for your name and writes it on a cup. Then you get back in line, and when you get up to the front, they have your coffee all ready."

"I didn't give anyone my name," I say.

"Better go do it."

"Right. Thank you." I go up to the counter. There's one guy at the espresso machine making coffees, and another man up by the cash register. The man at the espresso machine looks like he's got too much on his plate already, so I decide to talk to the guy at the register.

"Hi," I say. "How do I pay you for coffee?"

The man smiles. "Let me get you a cup." He turns around and reaches underneath the counter, then pulls out a generic white Styrofoam cup with a plastic lid. Then he turns back to me. "What's your name?"

"It's Noelle."

He takes a marker and writes *"Noelle"* on the cup. He actually spells it right. People usually spell it *"Noel."*

"And do you want straight espresso, a plain latte, or a mocha?"

"A latte, I guess."

He writes a big "L" on the cup just above my name. "That'll be a dollar twenty-five."

I follow him over to the cash register and dig a couple of dollar bills out of my purse.

"Thank you, Noelle," he beams at me. "If you'll just get in line and wait for us to call your name."

As I go back to the line, he sets my cup up on the counter next to the espresso machine. Several new people have filled in behind the lady in the shorts and flip flops, but she catches my eye and gives me a thumbs up.

The line has snaked down an aisle of snacks. I stand there surrounded by brightly colored packages of chips, pretzels, and cookies. It's an extravaganza of sweet and salty processed food.

My eyes are sore from crying, but in my gut I feel only peace. The overhead fluorescent lights, which usually irritate my eyes, aren't bothering me. I'm even all right with standing in line.

I hear the guy making the espresso drinks calling out names. "Katie!" "Benjamin!" "LaShonda!"

My portion of the line moves out of the snack aisle, but other customers have filled in behind me. There's some kind of canned music playing in the store, which is another thing that usually annoys me. But even that sounds good.

"Noelle!"

I'm startled for a split second. "Oh, that's me!" I go up to the counter and the guy working the espresso machine hands over the Styrofoam cup with my name on it.

"Have a nice day."

I take the coffee out to the car, then roll the window down again and drink the whole thing while I sit in the parking lot. I take my time and savor it. It's surprisingly good coffee. Not what I would have expected from a roadside convenience store.

I'm still calm, a deep-down calm that has taken over my chest, my gut, and has spread out to the very tips of all my limbs. The scraggly trees in the parking lot, struggling to stand up to the summer heat, make me proud. Because they're here, they're alive, and they're still trying to stretch their branches all the way to the sky.

When I finish the coffee, I squish the cup a little so it will fit in Piper's cupholder. Then I put the key in the Bug's ignition and point the little car in the direction of home.

———

I SPEND the rest of my two-week exile from the martial arts school working on getting back in shape. Mostly, I do that in my apartment, pushing the bed sideways against the wall so I have a little more space to work out.

It takes Milo a few days to get used to it, but then he makes it into a game by attempting to jump from the window seat to the bed, which is now several feet further away. He falls the first couple times, but then he masters the longer jump, doing it so often and so gracefully that I decide he's part flying squirrel.

The last night of my two-week break, I call Conan.

Annie answers the phone.

"Hey, Annie. It's Noelle. Can I talk to Conan?"

"Of course. I'll go get him." She lowers her voice. "How are you doing?"

"I'm doing okay. I mean, actually, I'm a lot better."

There's a pause on the other end of the line, then Annie says, "You sound better. Is that for real?"

"Yeah," I tell her. "It's for real."

"Hang on. I'll go get Conan."

The moment he's on the phone, I don't mince words.

"I want to come back. I want to take the black belt test again."

"Glad to hear it," Conan says mildly. "You have an attendance requirement to meet."

"I know. So I'll do that, then sign up for the test in two months."

"You sure you're ready?" he asks.

"I'm ready."

"Okay. If you lose control again like you did with Ethan, I'll have to ask you to leave the school permanently. Understand?"

I gulp. "Understood."

"All right. Then I'll see you in class tomorrow."

"See you then."

He hangs up. It was a short conversation. But it didn't need to be a long one. I know that if Conan didn't want me to come back, or if he didn't think I was ready to come back, he would have told me to take more time off. But he didn't.

He's giving me a second chance.

So, all I have to do now is not blow it.

# CHAPTER THIRTY-FIVE

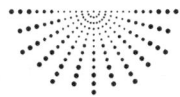

Resuming my training at the school is awkward, mostly because by now, everyone knows me as the girl who had a meltdown during her black belt test and also as the girl who went crazy on another student. Nobody wants to spar with me at first. It's humiliating and awful.

Whenever we don't have an even number of students in class, I have to spar with Conan, which is fine. I like sparring with Conan. But it sucks being the pariah no one wants to deal with.

Ethan especially avoids me. Finally, one day I go to him after class.

"Hey, Ethan."

"Oh…uh. Hey, Noelle."

"Listen, I never apologized for…you know, what happened. What I did. So, I'm sorry. I was out of line."

He looks uncomfortable. "Oh, hey. No problem. You know. It happens."

He's fidgeting, and I can tell he wants to get away from me. "Well, anyway," I say. "Have a good one."

"Yeah, sure."

I leave, unsettled. I don't know what I can do to make things right. Maybe there's nothing I can do. I think I want him to make me feel like myself again, the way I did before I went off on him. But it's not his fault I did that, so it's not really his job to make me feel better.

The next time we're in class together, Conan starts telling different people to pair up. Eventually he points at me. "Noelle. And…Ethan. Go to it."

Ethan looks as panicked as I feel. I wonder what Conan is doing. He makes a space at one end of the mat and tells another student pair to face each other. The rest of us gather around at a good distance to watch.

"We're going to do some mini sparring matches today," Conan says. "We'll have each pair of you go a round or two, then do a quick critique afterward. Then the next pair is up until everyone's had a turn."

The two students bow to each other and begin circling with their hands up to block. I'm having a hard time paying attention to them, because I can't take my mind off the fact that before I leave here today, I'm going to be forced to spar with Ethan again in front of everybody. I look over at him. He doesn't look any happier about the situation than I feel.

"Okay!" Conan calls out. "That's enough. What did they do well?"

Other students call out praise for the pair, and I hope Conan doesn't start calling on specific people to give him analysis, because I don't think I could contribute anything coherent to the discussion. Next, he asks the class to point out what the pair could improve on. Then he lets them go back into the group, and we all clap for them as they rejoin us.

"All right. Next up, Ethan and Noelle."

My heart is pounding hard as Ethan and I go up front and face each other. I'm scared he's going to hurt me. I'm scared I'm going to hurt him. We're both in full protective gear, including headgear, but I'm terrified anyway.

We bow to each other. Then, we begin circling. I'm afraid to kick him, and I keep avoiding it. He does the same. I can feel the other students in the class getting restless, but it doesn't matter. I can't do it.

And then Ethan spins and lands a back kick on the front of my chest protector. It's a shock. I didn't expect it. He lands another one.

He's winding up for a third when I finally snap into motion, do a full pivot, and land a side kick on his chest protector. Points for me.

From that moment on, we're both unfrozen. Ethan's better than I remember. He's less cocky and more focused. I have to work hard to keep him from overwhelming me. But I do. Until the very end, when he aims a well placed kick to my midsection that sets me off balance, and I fall on my butt.

Ethan immediately comes over and offers his hand to pull me to my feet.

"Thanks," I say.

"I think that's enough," Conan says. "Tell me what they did right."

I feel dumb because I fell on my ass, but I'm also flooded with relief. I'm not injured, just embarrassed. And I didn't go nuts on Ethan.

As we rejoin the group of students, he says to me, "Hey, good match."

"Same," I say. I glance over at Conan as he calls up the next pair of students to spar. He doesn't look over at me. But there's an air of satisfaction clinging to him that's as clear as bright red spray paint on a paper-white wall.

He knew what he was doing.

I walk by O'Shea's on my way home. I don't necessarily have to pass by it to get to my apartment, but I'm drawn there. As I walk by the front windows, I see Kane sitting at the bar. He spots me and raises a hand in greeting. I stop for a second and wave back, feeling the pull of the place. The memories. The way, for a short time, that it almost felt like family. But I keep going.

If I were to go in, I'm sure Kane would ask me if I've been visiting Vic, and I haven't. Not since that one time. I don't plan to visit him again.

But I can't forget that Vic was the one who pointed out I've been fighting some kind of block. I'm still fighting it. I'm not sure exactly what it is or even what the shape of it is, but I felt it shift the afternoon I drove up to visit Izzy and Rob, when I told them I can't and won't live in their version of reality.

Standing up to them was huge, but it wasn't everything. There's still something in the way, something I haven't confronted or mastered. Whatever it is, it's just out of the range of my ability to understand it. I've been catching glimpses of it, but I haven't seen it clearly yet. I haven't named it. And without being sure what it is, I don't know how to defeat it.

August slips into September, and on one of the last warm days of the waning summer, Piper suggests a spontaneous drive to a local beach adjacent to wetlands on Puget Sound. The beach is nestled in a little cove fringed with modest sand dunes, and the water is calm. We take our shoes off and sit in the sand, curling our bare toes as we watch a small gaggle of kids shriek and laugh while they run in and out of the water.

When I returned Piper's car after confronting Izzy and Rob, I told her everything that happened. We went out with her band that night, and for the first time, they didn't irritate me. I'm starting to see them for who they are, not just odd and socially awkward people, but people who are important to Piper. Which means they're important to me, too.

"So, how's it going with your martial arts thing?" she asks.

"It's going okay. I'm just glad Conan let me come back."

"Is that dude still pissed at you? The guy you went crazy on?"

"Nah, it's okay. He kicked my ass in a sparring match the other day, so we're kind of even now."

Piper grins at me. "Did you let him win?"

"It kills me to admit it, but no. As it turns out, I'm not invincible."

"Sucks when you find that out, huh? I'm so pissed that I didn't get to be one of the invincible people on this planet."

"I don't think they exist."

"Some people get pretty close." She runs her fingers through the sand and sighs. "What a crazy year. I can't believe how many things have changed."

"Yeah," I agree. "It's one for the record books. Or I mean, it would be if I kept a record book."

"Don't you journal or anything?" Piper asks.

"Negative."

"I do it all the time. Sometimes I go back and read it and think, 'Damn. I am one melodramatic bitch.'"

"People in that...abuse group talk about journaling a lot."

After telling Izzy and Rob to back off, I needed to talk about how it made me feel—almost all the time. Piper was the only person I had to talk to, and I knew it wasn't fair to be constantly unloading on her. So I finally asked her what support groups she recommended, and now I go every week. Everything people say in the group is familiar to me. What happened to them. How they felt when it happened. What's hard for them now. Nobody's experience is exactly like mine, but I recognize my own feelings and struggles when other people talk about theirs. It's not a magic bullet, but it helps.

"Is the group working out?" she asks.

"Yeah, it's pretty good. Thanks for suggesting it."

"I just remembered how much it helped me." Then, with an abrupt change of subject, she asks, "Did you ever go back and visit Vic?"

I shake my head. "Also negative."

"Why not?"

"I don't know what to say. I said everything I had to say the first time I visited him."

Piper looks out to the water, which is lapping the shore in small, polite waves. The water here is so peaceful it feels more like a lake than part of Puget Sound. She turns back to me.

"Do you still think he's a criminal?"

"He is a criminal," I retort. "A court of law said that he committed a crime. That makes him a criminal."

"Okay, scratch that. Do you still think he's a bad person?"

I can't give an automatic answer to that one. The truth is when I think about Vic and what he was to me, all I can think of are good things. Once I got to know him, he was good for me. Or at least, he was until the truth came out.

"He wasn't a bad person to me," I admit.

"Is he a bad person to somebody else?"

"I mean, possibly? I don't know how you can do something illegal and not hurt somebody."

"Sure," Piper says. "But do you think he's a bad person in the same way that you know your brother-in-law is a bad person?"

I sigh. "I know what you're trying to do. No, Vic's not a creep. And he's not violent. But if you asked my sister if Rob's a bad person, she'd say he's a *good* person."

"Well, of course she'd say that."

"But don't you get it? She assumes he's a good person because he's good to her. Just because Vic was good to *me* doesn't mean he's a good person."

"Okay but—do you think it's fair that Vic is in jail for trying to help out a friend, and that Rob's never going to jail for what he did to you?"

The question stops me for a moment. "No," I say finally. "If you look at it in some big picture kind of way, it's not fair. But Vic lied to me, Piper. That's what I can't forget."

"Did he really, though? Did he actually tell you a lie, or did he just keep something from you until he was forced to let you in on a secret?"

I look down toward the water's edge. "Lies of omission are still lies. He should have told me."

Piper's tone is gentle as she says, "Haven't you ever lied to somebody that way? Like, not told them something because you didn't think they could handle it, or because you were afraid it might hurt them?"

Immediately, I think of how I've still never told Conan about my family situation. I suppose I've lied to him every Christmas, when I tell him I'm going to visit my sister. And then, of course, I kept that same information from Piper for a long time, too. But I'm not sure I'm ready to equate that with what Vic did.

"Why are you trying to force Vic on me?" I ask. "I still remember when you were always warning me about him. What happened to that?"

"I'm sorry," Piper says. "I guess I feel bad that I gave you so much crap about him. Once I found out why he was involved in illegal shit, he didn't seem as bad. Like, he didn't fit the stereotype I had of him. But I'll stop. I won't talk about Vic if you don't want me to, okay?"

"Thanks." I don't bother to point out that Vic did illegal shit before he did it on Kane's behalf. He just never got caught the first time.

Still, I haven't told Piper about his earlier illegal gambling activity because I figure it's Vic's business, not hers. Is that also a lie of omission, or is it just leaving a few details out of a story? I also haven't told her how Vic lost his brother. And that has to have shaped how Vic sees the world, as well as how he operates in it. Maybe Annie is on to something when she judges a person's actions by whether they mean to be constructive, or destructive.

"Whatever you decide about Vic, I'm just glad we're hanging out again," Piper says.

I look over at her and smile, relieved. "Me too."

We both go silent and take in the view.

Piper sighs happily. "It's such a gorgeous day."

"The calm before the gloom," I agree.

She groans. "I know. The season of perpetual rain is almost upon us."

"Hey, can I ask you something?"

"Ask me anything," Piper says solemnly.

"When I took my black belt test in June, I failed. I'm going to take it again in December. I know you might have a tour or something else going on, but if you're free, do you want to come watch? Vic was supposed be there last time, but then he had a date to keep with the county jail. So, you know, he didn't make it."

"What's the date?" Piper asks.

"December twelfth. It's a Saturday."

She puts her hand on my arm. "I'll be there."

# CHAPTER THIRTY-SIX

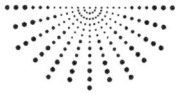

December twelfth arrives quickly.

When I signed up for the test at the end of October, I did it with no fanfare, and I made sure to sign up when Conan wasn't around. This time, I want him to see me master the actual test.

He hasn't mentioned it to me, not once. I haven't talked to him about it either. I'm sure he's afraid I'll ultimately bail or choke on test day. I figure he's trying to protect himself from disappointment. If so, I know how he feels.

My plan, though, is to not let either of us down.

Piper picks me up on the day of the test. It's the first time she's seen me in my dobok, and she does a double take when I get in the car.

"Thank you so much for the ride," I say, as I get in.

"Holy shit, woman, what are you wearing?"

I open my coat so she can see it. "It's called a dobok."

"You look like an extra on the set of some cheesy karate movie." She holds up a hand. "I know, I know, it isn't karate. It's taekwondo."

"Just wait until you see me in protective gear."

"Okay," she says. "Listen, I have to tell you something. Don't get mad."

I give her a look. The last thing I need today is something that might make me mad.

"I invited the rest of the gang to come watch. I told them what I was doing, and they all wanted to cheer you on."

"You mean your band?"

"Yeah, them. Is that okay? I can tell them to fuck off if you want."

"Well, um. What is Sven going to wear?"

She gives a wicked grin. "He did just purchase a new Pope hat. I don't think he'd wear it to this occasion, but with Sven, you never know."

I gape at her in horror as I picture Sven walking into the gymnasium looking like Pope John Paul II, stooping to fit through the door.

She laughs. "Just messing with you. I told him to leave it at home. There is zero chance he will wear it today. But seriously, if you want them gone—"

"No, it's okay," I reassure her. "Actually, it'll be kind of nice to have your band...I mean our friends there. I need the support."

"Yeah, exactly!" she beams. "That's why I asked them. You nervous?"

"Supremely."

"You want me to leave you alone? Do you need to like, meditate or something?"

I look over at her and grin. "Ohm."

"Hey. Don't be making fun of the *ohm*. It's a sacred sound. I use it to meditate."

I'm surprised. "Do you actually meditate?"

"Yeah, I actually do," she says. "It helps me focus. I don't talk about it, but I do it. Every day."

"That explains a lot," I muse.

"Like what?"

"You're so focused when you're onstage. Like you're in a different space in your head. Does meditating help you do that?"

She shrugs. "I mostly do it so I won't do anything stupid, like get actual revenge on my enemies."

"So, it's not a spiritual thing?" I venture.

"It's super spiritual. The practice of non-violence is spiritual as fuck."

The rest of Primal Malice is waiting for us when we get to the high school gymnasium. I'm glad to see them. As usual, they're all wearing black. Sven has his hair slicked back like Eddie Munster. But at least he isn't wearing his Pope hat.

I quickly thank them all for coming, then go back to the student area to meet up with the others. Everyone from my class is testing today, including the two women I once overheard talking about me in the bathroom. And Ethan, of course.

"Hey, Noelle," he says. "You ready?"

"Ready as I'll ever be."

But now that I'm no longer laughing at Piper's reassuring wise-cracks, I'm feeling less sure. The reality is, last time I did this, I lost focus. I didn't make it. And last time, it had nothing to do with not being prepared. It was because I was mentally and emotionally weak. What if I still am?

"Hey," Ethan says. "We got this."

One amazing thing that's happened in the last couple months is that now, Ethan and I get along. I don't want to be a downer for him, so I force myself to smile and say, "Yeah. We totally got this."

When it's time for the test to begin, we go into the main gym to warm up. Conan is sitting behind the judges' table. His face is a stone mask when I glance in his direction. We might as well be strangers.

We start with a run around the room enough times to make a mile. Then we do pushups and sit ups, sixty each. The point of this is to demonstrate that you can execute all the forms, spar, and break boards even when you're physically tired. I've been training for this at home and running a mile several times each week, so I'm prepared.

We demonstrate the kicks and blocks for each belt, from white through red. After we demonstrate the kicks and techniques for each belt, we do another set of pushups or sit ups, though the sets are shorter. It's grueling, but this is the easy part. I'm in good shape, and all of these techniques are a part of me. There's no uncertainty involved.

I do well on the section of the test where we demonstrate self-defense techniques. But then it's time for sparring, and that's when I freak out. We all take a short break to put on protective gear, which gives me too much time to think.

This is the part of the test where I started to struggle last time. I tried to prepare for this part too. The mental part. My mitigation plan is that every time I begin to lose focus, I'll remind myself the problem is in my head by silently repeating the mantra: *In my head*. I've been practicing it as a hidden technique to keep my mind from wandering.

I cling to "in my head" like a lifeline as we all rotate through a series of sparring partners. For me, the whole thing is a blur of bow, fight, strategize, *in my head*, kick, block, *in my head*, kick, punch.

The room disappears, and the world is nothing but the person I'm sparring with, plus everything I've gleaned from over five years of training. Pushing through the exhaustion that's starting to set in, pushing through my own doubt, crowding out the temptation to lose focus. *In my head, in my head, in my head.*

I make it through the sparring section, but I'm not sure how well I've done. When my name is called to advance to the final round, I know I've done well enough to avoid elimination. Next is board breaking.

I know I can do it. I've done it numerous times in class. But of course, this is where I choked last time. It's irrational, but the fear that I won't be able to do it this time either begins to accelerate. I feel it in my gut, in my chest, in my throat. I can't control the feeling.

Instructors hold up the boards for us. Each black belt candidate attempts to break five different boards. They give you three tries for each board. If you don't make it on the third try, you don't get that one.

Every school is different, but our school allows you to lose one of the five. If you lose two, you don't pass. There are different techniques for breaking boards. Some techniques use kicks, and some use punches. I've always been best at breaking boards using kicks. For the test, we have to break at least two boards with kicks, and at least two with punches.

I start with kicks, so I can blow through the first two boards. That strategy works. Then it's board number three, the first one I have to break with my hands.

My focus disappears instantly. I know it's the memory of what happened last time. I should be able to overpower it. I start my silent mantra. *In my head. In my head. In my head.*

But it's not working. My first strike at the board is a dud. I gather myself. *In my head.* Strike again. The board stays intact. A wave of anger and frustration rushes through me, and I go for the third strike.

The board doesn't break. That's my one free pass. If I don't break the next board, I won't get my black belt today.

The instructor holds up a fresh one. I decide to use a different punching technique. Maybe that will do it. But my first strike proves the problem isn't the technique I'm using. It's me. I'm the problem. The board doesn't break.

Like last time, deep tears well up out of nowhere, but I'm no longer mortified by them. I let them come. Strike again.

Fail again.

It's my last chance. If I don't break this board, this time, it's over. I stare at it, overwhelmed with a sensation of looming defeat as tears squeeze out of my eyes. My mantra no longer works. I can't override my self-doubt or my fear. I'm beaten.

Then, out of nowhere, a thought surfaces. *I am the obstacle.* I continue to stare at the board as the thought blooms and takes me over.

*I am the obstacle.*

It's nothing outside myself. It's nothing that has happened to me. It's me.

I focus.

I strike the board one last time.

And it breaks.

When it breaks, something lets loose, and I know I can break the final board. And I do.

Then, like someone flipped a switch, my awareness of the room returns. Friends and family members are clapping and cheering for all of us, and I hear someone give a particularly loud, whooping sort of yell.

It's Piper. She's on her feet as she cups her hand to her mouth and screams, "Way to go, Noelle!" I look up at her, grinning. Whatever happens next, I feel like I've already won.

And then I freeze. The rest of Piper's black-clad crew is seated on the bleachers to her left. All of them are clapping, too, though they aren't standing. But the guy on her right is also standing and clapping steadily.

He looks a hell of lot like Vic. His hair is short, the way Vic's was when I visited him in jail. My eyes are drawn to his face. And then I can't look away.

Because it is Vic. He's here.

I knew his sentence was up at some point this month, but I hadn't heard from him and didn't even realize he'd got out.

Before I can give it more thought, the instructors gather us together in a group to face the judges, so they can read out the names of everyone who will advance to black belt. They go in alphabetical order by last name.

Just because I made it through all the elements doesn't mean I passed. It simply means I made it all the way through the test. The final belt decisions will come from the points we scored during all the elements we tested today. Those points will be combined with the score of the written test we took earlier. If I don't make the top fifty percent, I won't get a black belt.

But it's all right if I don't. I broke through my own mental block. I already feel like a different person.

Ethan's name is called early, since his last name is Cunningham. By the time they get to the last names that start with S, I'm certain I won't make it today. Too many students have already passed for me to pass this time. But they only call out one last name for the Ss before they move on to the Ts.

"Noelle Thomas!"

*Holy shit.* That's me.

From up in the bleachers, I hear Piper let loose with another whooping yell. And it makes me feel good. Super good. Fucking great, in fact.

But I already won today. I won the moment I understood I was my own obstacle. Getting my first-degree black belt is a win, of course. But there will be higher levels and more tests. It never ends.

Today, I got out of my own way. And that was the real victory.

# CHAPTER THIRTY-SEVEN

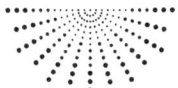

Piper makes her way down to the floor with Bill, Sven, and Mandy trailing behind her. She comes over and gives me a huge hug.

"You were so amazing!" she gushes. "I had no idea."

"That was intense," Mandy agrees, nodding.

"You must be in exquisite physical condition," Sven murmurs. "All those push-ups."

"Don't we get to see you receive your black belt?" Piper asks. "I thought they'd have a big ceremony and give you a trophy."

"No," I laugh. "They'll give them to us in the next few weeks during class."

Piper is pouty. "But I want a ceremony."

"No, it's better this way," Sven says, suddenly. "If they had a ceremony, it would put undue emphasis on the winners. The fundamental thing is the dedication to the art."

We all stare at him.

"Well, thanks, Mr. Miyagi," Piper laughs.

Bill pantomimes the "wax on, wax off" sequence from *The Karate Kid*.

"No, he's right," I say. "That's actually spot on."

Sven ducks his head.

I look at all of them. "Thanks for coming, you guys. It was awesome to have people here. I really appreciate it."

"It was super cool," Bill smiles. "You're a total badass."

"Absolute badass," Mandy agrees. "But can we get out of here now? This gym is giving me high school flashbacks."

"We were going to go get a drink," Piper says. "You want to come with?"

"Sure." Involuntarily, I start searching the gym.

Piper raises an eyebrow at me. "Looking for Vic?"

"Was that actually him?"

She nods. "I told him to sit with us." She lowers her voice. "He was on the edge of his seat the whole time. He was *invested* in you."

I clear my throat. "Where did he go?"

"Not sure." She shrugs. "He split right after they announced your name."

*Of course,* I think. Of course he bailed. I should just put the thought of him out of my mind.

"Listen, can I meet you guys outside?" I ask. "I have to go talk to someone."

"Sure, see you outside."

They head for the exit, with Mandy leading the way. I would have asked them to wait for me, but I could tell she was truly anxious being in here.

I find Conan and wait for him to finish his conversation with another student. Then he turns to me, and his face lights up.

"Hey, you!"

"Hey. I just wanted to say thanks for all your help. Especially over the last year." It's on the tip of my tongue to say I couldn't have done this without him, but he cuts me off before I can.

"It's all you," he says. "You're the one who showed up and got it done. Good job."

"Well, thanks." I bask in his praise for a moment, then decide I might as well ask him. "Did you see? Vic was here."

Conan nods. "I spotted him."

"Did he tell you he was going to be here?"

"Nope. Total surprise. Didn't even know he was out."

"Okay." I feel at a loss for words. Then I say, slowly, "If you see him, will you tell him thanks for coming?"

Another grin breaks across Conan's face. "Sure, I'll tell him. Or you know, you could call him and tell him yourself. But I'll tell him if I see him."

It takes me longer to get out of the gym than I thought it would, because I keep stopping to talk with different groups of students. It would be rude if I didn't, plus I want to talk to them. By the time I make it outside, I'm worried Piper and the band will have already left. But no, they're there in the parking lot, standing next to Piper's car.

Vic is with them.

He's in civilian clothes and looks tough. Flawless. But the leather coat is gone. He's wearing a heavy grey wool overcoat, which somehow makes him seem both older and younger at the same time.

As I approach the group of them, I feel as if my stride is incredibly slow. I'm not sure I'll ever get there.

Bill's the only one who's facing in my direction, and he calls out, "Hey! It's the champion!"

They all turn. But my eyes go right to Vic's.

"So, you're here," I say.

He smiles. "I'm here. You're looking...victorious."

Damn. That smile.

"Hey, guys," Piper says. "Why don't I walk you to your car, then me and Noelle will meet up with you?"

There are murmurs of agreement, and they all walk across the parking lot, leaving me and Vic alone. For a moment, we just take each other in without speaking.

"How do you feel?" he asks, finally. "Do you feel good?"

"Yeah," I say. "Really good. I kind of made a personal breakthrough, you know?"

He nods. "I do know. I know that feeling well."

"So...are you out of jail for good?"

"That's the plan. Got out a week ago. Early release for good behavior. I'm on probation now." He hesitates. "I was going to tell you I was out, but I wasn't sure if you wanted to know. I didn't tell Conan, either."

"Did you tell Kane?"

"Kane knows. I've been in there a lot. Same old gang, you know. It's been good." He gives me a pointed look. "Haven't seen you there, though."

I shrug. "I don't go there much. I mean, I still go there, but I've been busy."

His voice goes lower. "Do you hate it now?"

"No," I look up at him. "I don't hate it. I have good memories of that place. I've been in a few times. Getting ready for the test has taken tons of time, that's all."

"All right," he says. "I don't want to crowd you or make you feel uncomfortable. I just wanted to be here and say congratulations."

"I appreciate that."

"Yeah?"

I see a glimmer of hope in his eyes. But I don't know how I feel. I'm glad he came to watch. Beyond that, though, my emotions are a jumbled mess.

"Are you two ready to go?" Piper asks as she approaches. She leans against her car. "Vic was telling us a story about this weird dude with six toes who he met at the county jail. I have to hear the end."

Vic looks quickly at me. "Only if it's okay with Noelle. I can disappear."

Piper looks at me, too. They're both waiting for my answer.

"No," I say. "Don't disappear. Come with us."

He flashes a quick smile. "I'll meet you there."

"He's driving?" I ask Piper, as Vic walks away.

"He said it's not prohibited. Makes sense to me. He wasn't arrested for drunk or reckless driving."

We get in Piper's car. Before she starts it up, she looks over at me. "How are you doing?"

"Good."

"You kicked ass. Is Vic going to ruin it for you?"

"No, but...did you ask him to come today?"

Piper shakes her head. "It was a total surprise. When I saw him, I did ask him to sit with us. I hope that was okay?"

"It's okay," I reassure her. "I'm glad he was here. I'm just not sure what to say to him."

"Makes sense," she agrees. "I don't think he wants to mess with you. I'm pretty sure he'll split if you want him to go, but if he doesn't, we'll make him leave. Okay?"

"Deal. So where are we going?"

"O'Shea's. Unless you want to go somewhere else? It's your day."

"Let's do it."

The drive to O'Shea's is a clear reminder it's the time of year for chintzy holiday decorations. Red plastic bells; gold, silver, and red tinsel; Christmas greetings spelled out in big letters in store windows. The air outside is crisp and cold, and Piper's little car heater struggles valiantly to keep us warm.

It's the start of happy hour when we get to the bar. After Kane assures us that it's all right, we push a couple empty tables together to accommodate all of us. Vic and Bill end up at one end of our makeshift family-sized table, with me and Sven at the other end, and Piper and Mandy in the middle.

Sven can't stop asking me questions about the test. He wants to know how long I've been studying taekwondo, and how long it took me to learn each element of the art. His questions are super granular, like asking how many degrees I spin for each kick. I have answers for some of his questions, but not all of them.

"How many seconds does it take to execute a roundhouse kick?" he asks, as he spears a deep-fried mozzarella stick on his plate.

"Uhh...I don't know that I've ever timed it out," I say. "Like, probably less than two seconds? But I'm not sure."

"I lost my sense of time while I watched you," he says, earnestly. "I'm hyper aware of time. I *think* in time."

I raise my eyebrows. "No kidding?"

"I've always thought that's what makes me the kind of guitar player I am. Very precise. I'm not a showman. But watching you, I had this sense..." He furrows his brow.

"You had a sense of what?" I prompt.

I'm aware of Bill and Vic speaking quietly at the end of the table. Piper is listening to their conversation, and occasionally she contributes something. Mandy, as usual, is cutting her food into a small army of tiny pieces.

Sven seems to be struggling with his thoughts. "I had a sense, while I was watching you, that it's possible to be precise and a showman at the same time. I suppose that sounds ridiculous."

He looks like he's genuinely wrestling with this concept. On impulse, I say, "You should come check out a beginning taekwondo class at the school. Then you could get a feeling for what it's all about."

"Oh, no," he says. "That would be absurd. I'm not an athletic person."

"Everybody's got to start somewhere, right? And anyway, most people aren't athletic when they start."

"Would I have to wear one of those white outfits?"

"It's customary," I say. "At least until you become more advanced."

Sven frowns. "I'm not typically fond of white."

"Think of it like a costume," I suggest. "Pretend you're a character in a movie or something. You can go back to being your regular self after class."

He blinks a few times. "That might work."

Our drinks arrive then, and Piper immediately holds hers aloft. "To Noelle, for getting her black belt, and for teaching me the difference between karate and taekwondo."

"That's important," Vic chimes in, as everyone else raises their glass.

"Make a speech!" Bill calls out.

"Oh, Jesus," I say. "Thanks for coming out to watch. I love you. Now drink your damn drinks."

"Short and sweet," Sven intones, looking at me.

Piper nudges my arm. "Holding up okay?"

I nod. "I'm fine."

And I am. It's good to be here. I keep sneaking glances at Vic down at the end of the table. He still looks a bit thin, like he did when I went to visit him. But otherwise he's bursting with energy.

He seems to feel me watching and looks up abruptly. My cheeks grow warm, and even though he probably can't see my flush in the lower light, he smiles at me, slow. Like he did see.

And now I'm confused. I look away.

What do I want from him? Do I want anything?

Six months ago, I felt like I needed him to get my black belt. Like I couldn't do it without him. Now, I know that isn't true.

But he's still a part of how I got here. He's still a part of my life. I can't cut him out of the picture. I just don't know where he fits.

Sven commands my attention again by saying, "So if I wanted to explore the world of taekwondo, where would I start?"

"I'll give you the address of the place. You can drop by anytime. One of the owners is this guy named Conan. You can't miss him. He's tall with super bright red hair. Or if that freaks you out, you could tag along with me to a class."

He clears his throat. "I think I'd prefer the latter."

"Sure. Give me your number."

With lightning quickness, Sven summons our waitress and asks for a pen. I'm dimly aware of Vic glancing down the table at us, but I ignore him.

As soon as the waitress drops the pen on our table, I write my name and number on a cocktail napkin and give it to Sven. "So, yeah. Give me a call and we'll work out when you want to come to class with me. I mean, not actually with me, I'm advanced. But I could introduce you to Conan, and maybe you could observe or something."

Sven tents his fingers and gives me an intense look. "Sounds thrilling." Then he frowns. "I'm serious. I don't mean to sound sarcastic."

"No sarcasm detected," I reassure him.

"Are we making plans?" Bill calls out from the other end of the table.

"Sven's interested in taekwondo," I reply. "I'm going to introduce him to my teacher."

Vic's staring at me in this calm, intent way. I meet his eyes and immediately feel a jolt in my gut.

"Did you still want to catch that film on Cap Hill?" Bill asks Sven. "Or do you have other plans, now?"

Sven lets out a beleaguered sigh. "No. I don't have other plans. Is it time to go?"

"If we want good seats, probably, yeah."

"I'm going to hang with Noelle," Piper announces. "I'll catch up with you all later."

Sven, Mandy, and Bill get up and say their goodbyes. But before Sven leaves, he says, "I'll call you. Soon."

I grin at him. "Sounds good."

Again, I'm aware of Vic watching me intently. This time, I'm careful not to lock eyes with him.

Once the rest of the band has left, Piper summons the waitress and orders another round of drinks.

"On me," she says, and tells the waitress to put our drinks on her tab. Then she waves her hand at Vic. "Come down here and sit with us."

Vic scoots down and takes the seat Mandy just vacated. Once he's settled, Piper looks at him, then at me, and declares, "You two need to talk."

Vic looks taken aback, but he chuckles.

"I'm serious," Piper says. She turns to me. "Sven likes you. A lot. He's a good guy, if you're available. But we're going to record an album, and I need him emotionally intact." Then she jerks her thumb in Vic's direction. "So, if you're not done with this one, then you need to be honest with yourself. And maybe him, too, while you're at it, before you break my lead guitarist's heart."

I stare at her, shocked.

Piper sighs. "Yeah, I know, it's your big day, and I'm super fucking proud of you. But I gotta protect my band." She stands up. "I saw someone I know come in here a while ago. I'm gonna go say hello. So..." She waves her hands between the two of us. "Get talking."

She takes her drink with her and leaves. I turn to Vic, and we both burst out laughing.

"I guess we have to talk now," I say. "Piper hath spoken."

"Indeed. But I swear, Noelle, this wasn't my idea. It's all her. I'm not giving you an ultimatum. You can be...confused."

I look at him for a few moments, still not sure what to say. "I am confused," I admit, finally. "I don't know what I want. Do you know what you want?"

He starts to reach his hand across the table then pulls it back. "I thought about you every single day I was locked up. And about how bad I felt for letting you down."

"I survived," I tell him.

"You did more than that. You kicked ass today. I'm proud of you."

It's like a sucker punch to the gut when he says that. Because it still means a lot to me. I still care if he's proud of me. I want him to be.

"Thanks," I say softly.

"Is there anything you want to ask me?" he says.

I study him. He seems sincere, so I decide to ask him a serious question. "Has anything changed? I mean, did going to jail change you?"

He holds my gaze. "I know you hate lies, so I'll tell you the truth. I'm still not sorry I helped Kane. And if the way I did it was the only way to do it, I'd do it again. But next time, I'd be more careful, if I could. Because I know what I did hurt Kane. And it hurt you."

I swallow. "Thanks for being honest."

Vic stands up. "I don't want to keep you. I'm going upstairs." He walks around the edge of the table and comes over to me. "Congratulations. You earned it." Then he drops a quick kiss on the top of my head and goes out the door.

I watch through the front windows as he disappears around the corner. I'm no less confused than I was an hour ago. But in the few moments since he left the table, I already miss him. I know that much for sure.

"So, is that it?" It's Piper. "Are you done with him? Because you and Sven could work, probably. But he's more fragile than he seems, and if you fuck around with him—"

I put a hand on her arm. "I'm not going to get involved with Sven. That would be messy. Okay? If it's easier, I can tell him he needs to go to the school on his own if he wants to start with taekwondo. I'll tell him I don't have time."

She groans and sinks down beside me. "Do whatever you want. It's none of my business. I'm just so afraid we're never actually going to record this album because of something stupid. I want it to happen so bad. The album, I mean."

"It will happen."

"How can you know that?" she asks.

"Because. I know. If you want it to happen, you'll find a way to make it happen."

She casts a sidelong glance at me. "When did you get all wise and shit?"

I shrug. "I'm not. That's the only thing I know. You just tapped the only wise thing I have to say for the next ten years."

"Doubt it. You're a black belt, now. Doesn't that make you instantly wise?"

"More like instantly exploitable," I laugh. "Now I'm eligible to teach classes at the school. I'm sure I'll have a message from Conan on my machine when I get home, asking me to fill in for one of his beginner classes."

Piper glances over at me. "You know what? I like you. Want one more round?"

"Last one," I say. "But yes."

"I'm hungry, too," she says. "Are the burgers here any good?"

We end up staying for dinner. Just before we get our burgers, another group asks if they can take one of our tables, and we help them move it into place.

As I listen to Piper talk about her plans for the first Primal Malice album, I marvel at how much my life has changed in such a short time. And also, how much it hasn't changed at all. At least, not on the surface. I'm still working at the diner. I'm still training with Conan. My past is still my past.

But a lot is different, too. I feel like I belong here. In places like O'Shea's. At the school. In the city itself. And I'm no longer so alone. I have good friends—Conan. Annie. Piper. The rest of her band. And, I suspect, Vic, if I want him to be a part of my life.

I wonder what he's doing upstairs. If he's looking out the window where we did our stargazing. Maybe he went to bed early. Or maybe he's already out for the night. I decide to leave Vic's whereabouts a question mark for now.

Most importantly, though, I'm no longer terrified of my family. I can't be sure Izzy will never show up at my door again without notice, imploring me to accept her version of events. I can't control her. But I've drawn my line, and I feel good about it. I can decide to protect my own life. My own health. The sanctity of my own space. I know I don't have to feel guilty about insisting on these things.

And I don't feel guilty.

I feel lucky.

# CHAPTER THIRTY-EIGHT

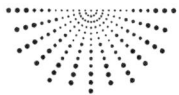

On Christmas Eve, I teach Conan's late-afternoon classes, so he can spend more of the holiday with Annie. We're closing up early tonight—six p.m.

Piper's gone home to visit her family, and Bill went with her. She invited me to join them, but I declined the invitation. It's the first time her family's going to meet Bill, and I thought they should be able to focus on the moment without having to entertain me. Plus, if I'm honest, it would have made me feel like an extra in a sentimental Christmas movie.

Conan and Annie invited me over, too, but I told them no for pretty much the same reason. I have my own plans. I'm going up to the church to listen to the choir sing in the Christmas Eve service. I'm not attending the midnight mass. They have an earlier service at nine, so I'm going to that one.

After I teach my last class, I take a shower and change, close up the school, then get a bus to Capitol Hill. It's different tonight. For one thing, the church is full of people, and most of them are dressed up. I'm wearing jeans and a sweater. A green one, in honor of the holiday, but I'm certainly not dressed up.

When I get to the stairs for the balcony, there's a person at the entrance handing out plain white candles. Each candle is pushed inside some stiff circular paper thing for catching melting wax. I remember candles just like them from when I used to go to church with my sister.

I take a candle and climb the stairs to the balcony. The front rows —where I usually sit when I come here to listen to the choir—are already full. One of the reasons I wanted to be here tonight was to be around people, but now that I am, I'm feeling unexpectedly shy. I go up to the very back row and sit down in solitude. Eventually though, all the rows in the balcony fill up, including mine, and I'm surrounded.

When the service starts, what happens is mostly how I remember it. We stand up and sit back down a lot. When we stand, we sing Christmas hymns. When we sit, someone reads scripture. Sometimes the choir sings without us. That's my favorite part.

At the end, we all light our candles and sing "Silent Night." The sanctuary goes dark, and the ushers light candles for the person on the end of each row. Then we all pass the flame down the line, from individual to individual.

Since I'm sitting in the back of the balcony, I see the entire place go from dark to light as everyone's candles are lit. The darkened edges of the sanctuary become visible again as we continue to sing.

I still don't believe in God. But as I sit there with everyone else in candlelight, I know I believe in something. I can't name it or put a label on it. It's just something I feel, maybe a presence, or maybe it's the collective energy of so many strangers in one space, focused on singing one song on a particular night of the year. If I don't think too hard about who they are or speculate what their individual hurts and harms could be, I can catch a glimpse of something transcendent. I'm not sure what it is, or even if it's something I can put faith in. But I believe it's real.

I'm lucky when I leave the service, catching my bus just as it's pulling up to the stop. It's a clear, cold night, without a cloud in the sky. There won't be any snow this Christmas Eve.

Milo had his Christmas feast earlier today, though I'm sure he'll be glad if I get home before midnight. When the bus lets me off, my intention is to go straight home. But then I find myself wandering past O'Shea's. It's open, of course. I don't see anyone inside I recognize, but it doesn't matter.

I pull open the door and go in, straight up to the bar. The bartender turns around, and I'm pleased to see it's Aidan.

"Hello, Noelle," he says, smiling. "Guinness?"

"Actually, you know what? It's freaking cold outside. Can I have a hot toddy? With Jamesons?"

"Of course, sweetheart. Coming right up."

I sit up and survey the bar, taking in the soft hum of conversations going on around me. The Irish music is already playing, so even though I don't see him around, Kane must be lurking somewhere. Tonight, it's a group singing Irish folk songs and playing traditional instruments.

After Aidan brings my hot toddy, I sip it slowly, lightly tapping my foot to the music. To me, it feels like Christmas here as much as it did back at the church. I yawn and stretch, curling my toes inside my shoes. Then I sense a presence near me and turn my head.

It's Vic of course. I knew I might see him if I came in here, but I wasn't certain of it. I haven't spoken to him or seen him since the day I got my black belt.

"Hey," I say. "How's it going?"

"It's going." He gestures to the empty stool next to me. "Do you mind?"

"Go ahead."

Vic sits down, and I take another sip of my drink. He's still sporting that short haircut from his time in jail. He sees me notice it and shrugs, then runs his hand across his head. "I kind of like it," he says. "It's a lot easier to manage."

"Maybe I should try it," I muse. "I get real tired of messing with my hair all the time."

He surveys me for a few seconds. "Yeah, I could see that. You'd look good as a bald chick."

"How can you tell?"

"Because. Then people would see your whole face, all the time."

It takes me a few moments to realize it's a compliment. As soon as

I register that it is, I'm both pleased and uncomfortable. Am I ready for him to compliment me?

Aidan comes over to us. "Hey, man. What can I get you?"

Vic points to my drink. "Hot toddy?"

"Yeah."

"I'll have one of those," he tells Aidan. Then to me, he says, "I miss you."

I turn my head slowly to look at him. He's calm on the surface, and I know he's not going to do anything explosive or scary. But I can see in his eyes that he wants me.

I want him, too. But I don't know if I can risk it.

"I miss our self defense sessions," I say.

"Is that all you miss?" he asks.

Urgent heat pulses low in my belly.

*Silent Night, Holy Fuck.*

"I'm not gonna push you," he says. "But I saw you here and…I thought it would be stupid not to say something."

"So how come you're alone on Christmas?" I ask. I feel like I'm stalling. "You know why I am."

"You know why I am, too," he replies.

Aidan sets down his drink, and Vic thanks him without taking his eyes off me.

"No, I don't," I say. "You could spend it getting drunk with Kane. Or what about Conan?"

Vic smiles. "He asked me over."

"Yeah. Me, too." I smile back at him, despite myself.

He leans back a bit. "So, then why'd you come here tonight?"

"Because I like how I feel when I'm here."

"Yeah, it's a special place." He takes a taste of his drink. "This is amazing."

"Aidan's a genius."

"That he is."

"Really hits the spot in this cold weather." I flush. I didn't mean it to sound sexual, but something about talking to Vic makes everything sound that way. I could tell him I had toast for breakfast, and it would somehow sound erotic.

"Do you want to talk about the weather?" he asks.

No. No, I don't. I must have come here for a reason. Was it to sleep with Vic? Maybe. But I feel like there's something else. Something unfinished between us.

And then, suddenly, I remember what it is.

I point my finger at him. "You owe me a sparring match."

"A sparring match?"

"You always said you'd do it if I got my black belt."

He lifts an eyebrow. "I remember."

"So. You owe me a sparring match."

He grins. "You want to go right now?"

I pick up my hot toddy glass. There's about a third of it left. I deliberately drain the rest of it while Vic watches me. Then I set it back down on the bar. "Yeah. Let's go right now."

We settle up our tabs. Vic tries to pay mine. But I don't let him.

As we walk out of O'Shea's and around the corner to Vic's place, I'm amped up like a little kid going to Disneyland for the first time. I'm anticipating an experience. I can't wait.

We walk up the stairs, not touching. I know Vic hopes this night will end with us in his bed, and I'm into it. It will probably happen. But sparring with him is what my whole being is keening for.

Inside his place, I'm surprised to see there's a Christmas tree in the corner of his large, spare living room.

"Got in the holiday spirit this year, I see," I remark.

He shrugs. "Why not? You need anything? Water?"

"Not right now. Let's spar."

He laughs. "You're on a mission."

"Yep. I am."

"Well, c'mon then."

He leads the way to his home gym. "We should wear protective gear," he says, as we both remove our shoes. "I don't want you to bash my skull in."

"I'm pretty fond of keeping my own skull intact," I agree.

"You need something to wear?"

I tap my bag. "Got everything I need in here."

276

We go to the cubbies in the back of the room, and he pulls out a helmet, a chest protector, shin guards, and forearm guards.

"I think those should fit you," he says. "But let me know if they don't, we can find you better ones." He points out a changing room through a door just beyond the cubbies. I never noticed it was there before. "You can change in there. I'll meet you on the mat."

Inside the room I shed my jeans and sweater, pulling my dobok pants and black belt out of my gym bag. The jacket is wrinkled, and I would never wear it this way at the school. I always start with a fresh one for class. But I'm not trying to impress Vic. I just want to fight him.

I put on all the protective gear and go out.

Vic is standing in the center of the mat. I do a double take when I see he's wearing a black dobok with his black belt and protective gear. The attire signals that he's advanced. I mean, duh. Of course he is. And at some schools, I could wear a black dobok, since I'm a first degree black belt now. But not at our school.

I walk toward him slowly.

"You okay?" he asks.

"Yeah. I'm okay." I stop in front of him. "You look all official and shit."

"I'm about the same level as Conan," he says.

I have a feeling he's lying. That he's more advanced than Conan. Much more. Although it's possible he isn't. One thing I am sure of, however: He's going to kick my ass.

Still, I'm excited. Whatever he knows, whatever particular magic he has, I'm finally going to get to tangle with it. And after I do, some of it will be mine.

As long as he doesn't kill me.

"Three rounds?" he asks.

"Sounds perfect."

We square up across from each other.

"Standard safety rules?"

"Of course."

"Okay," he says. "After we bow, I'll count three, two, one, and then we start. Okay?"

"Okay."

"You sure you want to do this?" he asks.

"Absolutely."

"Okay. Let's bow."

We bow to each other.

My heart is pounding hard in my chest.

I've never been so excited in my life. This is what I want from him most. To learn. To grow stronger via a clash with someone who possesses superior fighting skills.

"Three, two, one..." Vic counts.

And then I wind up a roundhouse kick and aim straight for his heart.


END

# ACKNOWLEDGMENTS

I would like to thank Matt Cory for the perfect book cover. It captures the essence of the hot fusion of Christmas, Seattle, and 90s angst that I envisioned when I started writing this story. Thank you also to Michelle Meade for her ever insightful editing assistance.

Continuing gratitude to all the friends who support me as I keep pursuing my dream to write.

A special thank you to Joseph F. Murphy, Matt Menovcik, and Beth KS Whiting for your ongoing support.

Thank you also to Amy Crum, Anna Kagley, Kelly Skore, and Dana Whitney. A loud shout out to Bridget, Eymard, Lorenzo, Tiffany, Abbie, Phil, Sherri, and everyone else from the AC crew. You help keep me grounded.

Much gratitude to both Todd Willis and Sheryne Willson for being awesome people who provide kick-ass guidance when I need it. You help me stay focused.

Finally, Dad: even though this time I'm dedicating this book to three very special cats, thanks for leaving me with your belief in my ability to write, and for the ongoing reminders that nothing gets written unless you sit down and write it.

# ABOUT THE AUTHOR

Author Andrea Maxand began her writing career as a songwriter, singer, and performer. She worked with a number of notable musicians from her native Pacific Northwest, including recording an album and EP with indie producer Chris Walla, as well as collaborating with Jason McGerr and Nick Harmer of Death Cab for Cutie on her 2004 album *Where the Words Go*.

These days, however, Andrea exercises her writing talent through the medium of novels and serial fiction. Her "sweet spot" is telling stories about finding happiness on the outskirts of happily ever after in the New Adult genre. The 2019 novella *Boxing Day* was her first published story, and her first novel, *Dreams Fall Like Rain*, was published February 13, 2024. *My Name is Noelle* is her second novel.

Andrea currently lives in the Pacific Northwest with a menagerie of real and robotic cats. When she's not writing or spending time with her fearless felines, she's likely up to something a bit odd and random. But aren't we all?

ALSO BY ANDREA MAXAND

Boxing Day

Dreams Fall Like Rain

My Name is Noelle

www.ingramcontent.com/pod-product-compliance
Lightning Source LLC
Chambersburg PA
CBHW070637260626
47161CB00007B/2741